Food
Person

Also by Adam Roberts

The Amateur Gourmet

Secrets of the Best Chefs

Give My Swiss Chards to Broadway
(with Gideon Glick)

Food
Person

ADAM ROBERTS

HUTCHINSON
HEINEMANN

HUTCHINSON HEINEMANN

UK | USA | Canada | Ireland | Australia
India | New Zealand | South Africa

HUTCHINSON HEINEMANN is part of the Penguin Random House group
of companies whose addresses can be found at global.penguinrandomhouse.com

Penguin Random House UK,
One Embassy Gardens, 8 Viaduct Gardens, London SW11 7BW

penguin.co.uk
global.penguinrandomhouse.com

Penguin
Random House
UK

First published in the US by Knopf 2025
First published in the UK by Hutchinson Heinemann 2025
001

Printed and bound in Great Britain by Clays Ltd, Elcograf S.p.A.

The authorised representative in the EEA is Penguin Random House Ireland,
Morrison Chambers, 32 Nassau Street, Dublin D02 YH68

A CIP catalogue record for this book is available from the British Library

ISBN: 978–1–529–15487–0 (hardback)
ISBN: 978–1–529–15488–7 (trade paperback)

Penguin Random House is committed to a sustainable future
for our business, our readers and our planet. This book is made
from Forest Stewardship Council® certified paper.

For Craig

*"Be careful what you get good at doin'
'cause you'll be doin' it for the rest of your life."*

—Jo Carson to Gabrielle Hamilton,
Blood, Bones, and Butter

Food
Person

SOFT PEAKS

Isabella Pasternak baked treats to bring to work every day: not as a way to endear herself to her co-workers, but as a way to avoid them.

At *Comestibles*, the digital food magazine known for its conversational style, chic design, and hot takes on food ("Are Lima Beans the New Chickpeas?," "The Case for Canned Parmesan Cheese," "Why We're Totally Over Anchovies"), Isabella was more appreciated for her peanut-butter blondies than she was for her personality. That's because, despite years of her late father's regaling her with the same advice—"People skills matter more than book smarts!"—she refused to accept that she needed to network in order to advance. Why go out for work drinks when you can hand out peppermint s'mores, write a cute essay about paninis, and call it a day? For Isabella, forced camaraderie was worse than boneless, skinless chicken breasts.

Which is not to say that she hated people.

On the contrary, Isabella wished that socializing came more naturally to her than baking. If she could communicate as easily with words as she could with butter, flour, and sugar, she would've saved a lot of time (and a lot of calories) spent standing at the tiny kitchen counter in the tiny apartment that she shared with her roommate, Owen, mixing cookie dough by hand because there was no room for a stand mixer, coaxing lemon curd to thicken on the ancient electric-coil stove, and waiting for the chocolate cheesecake to set up in the crowded fridge next to all of Owen's protein shakes.

On a gray and drizzly morning in September, Isabella shuffled into the *Comestibles* building in TriBeCa wearing ratty tan overalls and a tie-dyed Ben & Jerry's T-shirt, fully armed with that day's confection: oatmeal cookies. Not just any oatmeal cookies: Key Largo oatmeal cookies from Maida Heatter's *Brand-New Book of Great Cookies*. A less discerning cookie aficionado might've expected the cookies to taste like citrus because of the "Key Largo" reference, but Isabella could tell you that the reference was due to the fact that Maida Heatter, the legendary cookbook author, lived in Florida, where she died at the healthy old age of 102. The recipe had nothing to do with citrus; with its odd combination of dried cherries, walnuts, and potato chips, it was a Compost Cookie before Compost Cookies were a thing.

Isabella discovered it while thumbing through a torn-up copy of the book, first published in 1995, at Alice's Cookbook Emporium in Greenpoint: her favorite place in the city. Cookbooks—especially used ones—were Isabella's passion, her raison d'être, the thing that delighted her more than anything else in the world, even the food that she produced from their pages. Her dream was to become a cookbook author someday, although that dream was impeded by a slightly inconvenient fact: nobody knew who she was. She took this job at *Comestibles* in order to raise her profile, but the only thing that she'd raised so far was her pant size.

Today's cookie distribution began with the unsmiling security guard at the front desk.

"Cookie?" she asked, holding up the Tupperware and realizing that she didn't know his name, even though she saw him every day.

"What kind?" he asked without turning away from the monitor.

"Oatmeal . . . potato chip," she said, opening the Tupperware, revealing the unusual twist on an American classic.

The guard crinkled up his face.

"Nah," he replied. "I'm not doing carbs this week."

Undeterred, Isabella rode the elevator up, plotting her route, which happened to be the same route that she followed every morning. As the elevator doors opened, septum-ringed Samantha at the front desk sighed with relief to see Isabella showing up with her breakfast.

"Oatmeal cookie?" asked Isabella, opening the Tupperware.

"Can I have two?" she asked, grabbing a couple before Isabella could answer. "My blood sugar is being such a bitch right now."

As Isabella followed her preordained path—from Marketing to Ad Sales to Social Media to Recipe Development—she smiled and nodded at the various co-workers whose names she barely knew, despite having worked there for nearly two years, eavesdropping as they laughed over something that happened on *Love Island*, seeing them all peer over somebody's phone to watch a TikTok of a woman setting her hair on fire while blowing out birthday candles.

"Oatmeal cookie?" she asked, lifting the lid for a gathered cluster, a come-hither look in her eyes.

"Don't mind if I do," said the guy from Marketing who wore a yellow baseball cap every day as if it were a fashion statement when, really, he was going prematurely bald.

"These look so fucking good," said the woman from Ad Sales with a grandmother's face and a teenager's wardrobe.

"Whose recipe is it?" asked the baby-faced brunette from Social who constantly sucked on lollipops, turning her tongue a variety of colors.

"Maida Heatter's," said Isabella, as if everyone would know who that was, though, in fact, half of the people here had received their culinary education from YouTube.

"Salty," said Yellow Baseball Cap.

"Tangy," said Teenage Grandma.

"Are these dried cherries?" asked Lollipop.

"And potato chips," added Isabella, proud of herself for sparking new life into the conversation surrounding the cookies.

As she listened to the group process this bit of cookie news ("Potato chips in a cookie? Who knew!") Isabella pivoted in a direction that she rarely, if ever, endeavored to pivot on her morning circuit.

Comestibles was founded by Dana Scanlan, a no-nonsense former fashion blogger who saw the potential for shifting from fashion into the food space, bringing her hard-won internet wisdom with her. It was Dana who oversaw the site's funky design, its spiky content, its viral videos, and who knew enough financiers to keep the company running even when it wasn't making money (which it frequently wasn't).

Isabella had avoided Dana's office for most of her two years there, partially because Dana terrified her, and partially because she knew what everyone else also knew about their leader: Dana didn't eat. No one had ever seen her consume solid food; she drank green and purple juices throughout the day and complained about how full she was from the extravagant dinner that she'd Instagrammed the night before, at which, people were fairly certain, she'd barely nibbled a breadstick.

On this particular day, Isabella thought it was a good idea to touch base with the person who paid her salary, and who—if inspired—could promote her from staff writer to recipe editor, a natural progression for someone in Isabella's position and a legitimate step forward in her quest to become the next Laurie Colwin or Nigella Lawson. (Another staff writer had been promoted two weeks earlier even though she was hired a month after Isabella.)

Dana's door was always open—she made a point of saying that during monthly meetings ("My door's always open . . . Literally, it's always open . . . Look down the hallway: see my door? It's open")—so Isabella took Dana at her word and walked through the fuchsia-colored doorway into an office so festooned with plants, it felt like a fashionable jungle.

"Hey . . . Dana," said Isabella, interrupting Dana as she punched the keys of her laptop with her index fingers. "Would you like an oatmeal cookie?"

Dana was wearing a light-gray jumper with a chunky pearl necklace that made her look one part Audrey Hepburn, one part Wilma Flintstone. When she looked up from her computer, her face was so red, Isabella thought that the necklace was choking her and that she was gasping for air.

"What did you say?" she asked, eyeing Isabella up and down like an intruder wielding a dangerous weapon.

"I was just . . . I was wondering if you wanted . . ." Isabella opened the Tupperware. ". . . an oatmeal cookie?"

Dana reacted as if the question were so absurd it didn't warrant a response.

"Remind me," said Dana, folding her arms and leaning back in her chair. "Who are you? What do you do here?"

"Isabella," Isabella answered, surprised and slightly wounded that her boss didn't know her identity. She knew that she'd rendered herself invisible, but was she really *that* invisible? "Isabella Pasternak? I'm one of your writers."

"Right, right . . . Isabelle Pasternak."

Dana continued eyeing her up and down, like she was about to push a button on the desk that would either drop Isabella into a swamp or rocket her into space.

"Denise Dashiki is out with Covid," said Dana, after doing some mental gymnastics. "She was supposed to do an Instagram Live today that we've been promoting all week. It's a chocolate-soufflé demo . . . really simple stuff. Do you think you could do it instead? I'm fucked otherwise."

Isabella's face flushed red. What kind of sick, twisted thing was this? Revenge for offering Dana a carb?

"Umm, well . . ." said Isabella, scrambling in her head to come up with any reasonable excuse. "I'm really not that great on camera?"

"Don't sweat it," said Dana, turning back to her computer as if the deal were already done. "It's live, so you won't have a chance to overthink things. Clearly, you love to bake . . . I bet you could make a chocolate soufflé in your sleep."

It was true: chocolate soufflés were one of the first dishes that Isabella had practiced in her parents' kitchen on the Upper West Side; she had read the recipe in *Mastering the Art of French Cooking* with a flashlight under the covers in bed and spent her Bat Mitzvah money on ingredients and soufflé molds because her mother found soufflés "too decadent." At this point, she *could* probably make chocolate soufflés in her sleep (and, given that she was a former sleepwalker, it's possible that she had). The fear wasn't about making a chocolate soufflé; the fear was about making it on camera, specifically what she would say during all of the downtime when she *wasn't* making a chocolate soufflé.

"Are you sure you don't want Arnie or Merrill to do it?" tried Isabella, citing two of the more outgoing *Comestibles* employees whose names she did know. Arnie and Merrill were always talking into their phones as they walked down the hallways, addressing their massive TikTok and Instagram audiences.

"They're overexposed," said Dana, her voice turning cold. "We need new faces, new brands. And I like that you're . . . differently shaped."

Differently shaped?

"I'll see you at eleven o'clock in the studio. Thanks, Isabelle."

Isabella took the finality of the statement as a dismissal, but hovered a second longer—wondering if she should correct Dana's mispronunciation of her name.

"All-righty . . . sounds good," she said, stumbling back into the hallway; mindlessly, she placed the Tupperware on top of a garbage can and walked away, disoriented.

The Key Largo oatmeal cookies may have won the hearts and minds of her co-workers, but Maida Heatter couldn't save her now.

. . . .

The *Comestibles* studio looked like what would happen if a Goop kitchen and a Madewell showroom had a baby. There was the requisite white subway tile behind the all-white stove, pale-pink pots and mint-green pans with wooden handles, a farmhouse basin sink, dried herbs hanging from twine. There was also a lilac teakettle, polished brass knobs on the stove, a jade cake stand next to a stack of mismatched plates. All of it was so exquisite and pleasing to the eye, it was clearly the work of someone who loved the idea of cooking but never actually cooked: in other words, Dana.

As Isabella entered the space, she took a quick inventory of the people in the room. There was Yellow Cap and Lollipop (now with a green one), and, of course, her boss, whose dewy and fresh skin (did she have a midmorning facial?) contrasted with her tense and worried expression as she thumbed her phone like a Juilliard-trained pianist.

"Do you have any other clothes?" asked Dana as Isabella entered the room, wondering how Dana knew that she hadn't changed without looking up.

"Oh, umm . . . sorry," said Isabella, hoping that this was her way out. "I didn't know that I was going to be on camera when I got dressed this morning?"

"I think it works," said Lollipop between sucks. "It's very . . . real."

Yellow Cap walked over with a wireless mic. "Slip this under your shirt," he said. "I'd do it, but I don't want to get into trouble with the whole 'me too' thing."

Lollipop laughed a little too loudly and said, "Oh my God, Todd. That's so fucked up." So that was his name. Todd.

"*You're* fucked up, Liz." Ah: Liz. Liz and Todd. Of course.

To get the microphone under her shirt, Isabella had to unstrap her overalls, which was especially embarrassing with everyone watching . . . including Dana, who, for some reason, chose this moment to look up from her phone. She tried to distract herself by studying the kitchen. All of the ingredients were set out for her: bars of bittersweet chocolate, eggs, flour, salt. There was a circular baking dish for a large soufflé, and the oven was already set for 450.

"The recipe's all printed out for you," said Liz, indicating with her lollipop; her tongue looked like a green oil slick. "It's pretty straightforward. If you screw up, it's totally okay . . . it'll make you more relatable."

"Try not to screw up," said Dana.

Microphone in place, Isabella walked into the kitchen and stood behind the counter. How strange to think that her obsession with cooking began with this recipe written by a woman, famous for her cookbooks, who was also adept at doing what Isabella was about to attempt now herself; only Julia Child was famously extroverted, outgoing, a crusader. Isabella felt more like Julia's soufflé than she did like Julia herself: superficially puffed up, hollow on the inside, capable of deflating with the slightest provocation.

"Going live in one minute," said Todd. "I'll call out questions from people in the chat."

"Try to engage with the questions while you cook," said Liz. "It makes people feel like they're a part of things."

"And be sure to narrate what you're doing while you're doing it," said Todd. "We don't want dead air."

"No dead air," said Liz.

"Dead air is a killer."

"Keep a patter going."

"Tell a personal story."

"Don't overthink it," Dana chimed in, while holding her phone to her ear.

Isabella tried to remember the last time that she'd been in front of an audience. In third grade, her class put on a production of *Charlotte's Web* and she played one of the goats. She wasn't sure if the goats were characters in the book or if her teacher added goats to the story so that everyone would have a part. The goat that she played had no lines but sat onstage during most of the play and occasionally said "bah." At least that was *some* experience, right? Playing a goat in front of an audience? Saying "bah"?

"All-righty, and we're live in five . . . four . . . three," said Todd, holding up the iPad and pressing the button to go live.

Isabella stood there staring at the iPad. Liz urged her on with her lollipop.

"Hi," she began. "My name is Isabella Pasternak."

She paused for a second too long as Todd urged her on with his other hand.

"Today I'm going to show you how to make a chocolate soufflé."

Stiff as a board, she walked over to the ingredients and held up a bar of chocolate, thinking of what to say next.

"If you're making a chocolate soufflé, you're going to need some chocolate," she said. Was this a joke? A segue? An opening sentence? Isabella caught Dana's eye, which reminded her of the eye of Sauron in *The Lord of the Rings*, except less kind.

"This chocolate is . . ." she looked down at the wrapper. ". . . seventy percent bittersweet." She continued studying the label to see if she could get any more material out of this.

"Could you use another kind of a chocolate?" asked Todd, desperate to inject some life into this presentation.

"Maybe," said Isabella, not really taking the cue. "I mean, probably? I wouldn't use milk chocolate. Or white chocolate. I guess it depends on the recipe?"

There was already a bowl of chopped bittersweet chocolate, so she placed it over a pot of boiling water for it to melt and then, in a skillet, started melting butter and stirring in flour to make a paste.

"Can you tell us what you're doing?" suggested Liz.

"Oh, sorry," she said, and walked over to the eggs. "I'm going to separate the yolks from the whites now." Whatever just happened with the chocolate, butter, and flour would remain a mystery to whomever had the misfortune of watching this.

She cracked an egg on the counter a little too aggressively, so the yolk slipped onto the floor like it wanted to get as far away from Isabella as it could. Isabella couldn't blame it.

"We have some egg whites for you over there," called Liz from the sidelines, pointing to a large glass bowl of egg whites.

"Oh, sorry," she said again, reaching for the bowl and a whisk, wondering why she kept apologizing.

She started whisking.

"So, you, ummm . . . you want to . . ." she sputtered as she felt her heart racing faster and faster. "You want to get some air into the whites." She found it hard to breathe; sweat was pooling on the back of her neck and her lower back and places where she'd never felt herself sweat before. "For this . . . you'll want to get to stiff peaks." She forgot to mention that stiff peaks are different from soft peaks in that soft peaks will topple over when you pull the whisk away, whereas stiff peaks will stand up straight.

She kept whisking as Todd watched viewers drop rapidly from a thousand to eight hundred to five hundred and Dana watched over his shoulder.

"How do you know when you're done?" he asked, a hint of panic in his voice.

"You just . . . umm. . . ."

Just then the smell of something acrid hit her nose. She turned and saw that the flour and butter were burning in the skillet, sending up a plume of black smoke, and that the chocolate had seized up in the double boiler.

"Oh fuck!" she said, accidentally dropping the whisk onto the floor. As she swiveled away, she knocked the glass bowl of egg whites to the floor; the Pyrex shattered into a million pieces. She grabbed the bowl of powdery, smoky chocolate and immediately burned her hand, leading her to yell out as she dropped it onto the floor on top of the glass; the charred chocolate bits splattered over the egg whites like an unusually ugly Jackson Pollock.

Dana stepped into the frame.

"Looks like our Isabelle could use a little help," she said, smiling, like she found this whole situation very amusing. "Let's start this over from the top."

And Dana, like a pro athlete entering a Little League game,

stepped into the center of the frame as Isabella backed away and Liz quickly swept away the broken glass and chocolate while another assistant handed over backup ingredients to her boss. Dana, as if it were nothing, as if it were baby stuff, proceeded to demonstrate the entire process of making a chocolate soufflé, from adding a little espresso to the chocolate as it melted in the double boiler, to using a heatproof rubber spatula to keep the egg yolks moving so that they didn't curdle. She did all of this in her designer jumper without getting a splotch of chocolate on her, narrating the whole thing like she was hosting a podcast.

By the time the swap-out soufflé came out of the oven, risen to perfection, Isabella had inched so far away from the kitchen, she was basically in another room.

"All right, time to taste," said Dana, beckoning Liz and Todd into the kitchen, not even bothering to search for Isabella with her predatory eyes.

This was fine with Isabella, who felt just like the egg yolk that had slipped under the counter and was congealing in the shadows—temporarily invisible, but soon to be discovered and discarded. She had no appetite for chocolate soufflé at the moment.

It would be a long time before she had an appetite for chocolate soufflé again.

. . . .

Was I executed in a past life?

This was the question that popped into Isabella's head as she sat across from a smiley, bearded, thirty-something sous-chef with a boyish face whom she was supposed to be interviewing for an article titled "Second Fiddles," about the sous-chefs who prop up famous chefs but get none of the glory.

"So, uh, tell me . . ." she began, fishing for his name.

"Gabe," he reminded her for the second time. His name was Gabe Kohl, and he was a recent graduate of the Culinary Institute of America, just finishing up a stint at Wilderness, a tasting-menu spot in Williamsburg, where he cooked alongside a Noma-pedigreed chef, preparing dishes like fiddlehead-fern lasagna and green strawberry borscht.

Was I pushed off a balcony? Beheaded at the guillotine? Kept in an isolated cell and starved to death? This feeling that she had in the pit of her stomach was eerily familiar: the sense of dread, every footstep portending doom, every face staring at her with a mixture of pity and fear.

"Right," she said. "Gabe. So . . . do you like being a sous-chef?"

Gabe, as perceptive a conversationalist as he was a taster, sensed Isabella's discomfort.

"Are you okay? You seem really frazzled."

Before she could answer, the execution summons arrived. It was four o'clock—five hours had gone by since the video disaster—and she thought that she might actually be in the clear. But then there was Liz, with a purple tongue now, announcing to Isabella in the most casual and lighthearted voice: "Hey, Dana wants to see you in her office."

Dana wants to see you in her office.

Such a benign turn of phrase, yet so deadly. How had this happened? Dana didn't even know that she existed six hours ago, and now Isabella was about to walk the plank, all because she dared to offer this high-achieving woman a Key Largo oatmeal cookie with potato chips.

"Sorry," said Isabella to Gabe as she stood up from her desk chair, perhaps for the last time. "I think we may have to reschedule. It's been a really . . . weird day."

Once again, Isabella walked to Dana's office, this time without her Tupperware to protect her (it had mysteriously vanished off the garbage can; she hoped whoever took it was actually eating the cookies that she'd spent hours making and not dumping them out just for the container).

"Sit," said Dana; she popped two pills and washed them down with a clear green liquid that she slurped loudly through a massive straw.

Beg for mercy, said Isabella's past self. *Fall on your sword. It's your only shot.*

"Dana, I'm so sorry," she began. "I guess I'm really not an 'on-camera personality.'"

"You're not any kind of personality," said Dana, so matter-of-factly it was like she was talking about her dry cleaning. "And I wouldn't really care about the on-camera thing if you had a notable voice on the page, but I've been reading your work for the past twenty minutes and, frankly, I have no idea who you are. Until you came into my office this morning, I didn't even know that you worked here . . . which is messed up, because I'm the one who hired you."

These words were so sharply constructed, so razor-thin in their application, Isabella didn't feel the blade going in . . . She just felt the blood trickling out.

"I guess I don't really like to draw attention to myself in my work?" said Isabella. "I just try to tell the story?"

"And that would be fine if this was *Cook's Illustrated*," Dana continued, throwing the plastic cup into the trash; she started to moisturize her hands with a rare imported moisturizer from Japan. "But *Comestibles* is personality-driven. We want our audience to feel like they're friends with the people writing the articles, cooking on camera, showing up on social. Not like they're watching a sad girl in dirty overalls having a panic attack while whipping egg whites."

Isabella bristled in her seat.

"One of my pieces was submitted for a James Beard award last year?" she proffered, not mentioning that she'd nominated herself in the "emerging voices" category without so much as a response from the foundation.

"If that's true," said Dana, "I wasn't aware of it."

She opened a file on her computer and began tabulating numbers.

"You know that some of our ads get more clicks than your posts?" she said. "I could handle you having zero personality if you were going viral. But you're so far from going viral, it's like you were vaccinated against it."

Isabella felt herself shaking a little and had to push harder into her seat to stop.

"I mean . . . I can try to write more viral articles? Be a little bolder with my 'hot takes'? I've always wanted to examine the chicken-stock industrial complex? Or explore the real differences between imitation and pure vanilla?"

"That'll really blow the lid off the place."

Dana looked squarely at Isabella. "You realize that none of those things would go viral, right? *Comestibles* is sexy, sultry, juicy, gossipy. That's what gets people to click. Do you get what I'm trying to tell you?"

This was the only moment when Dana seemed to have a half-ounce of compassion in her eyes. But Isabella, too earnest for her own good, really didn't understand how to make food writing "gossipy" or "juicy" or "sultry." Her cookbook-writing heroes all wrote elegant prose and thoughtful meditations on the recipes that they made. Would M.F.K. Fisher go viral with *How to Cook a Wolf*? Would Judy Rodgers break the internet with her introduction to *Zuni*?

"I can't say that I do."

The flicker of kindness instantly vanished from Dana's eyes.

"That's what I thought."

Dana swiveled back to her computer and began pounding the keys again.

"Send an email to HR, and they'll sort out your termination. If you need a letter of rec, you can write it yourself and I'll sign it. As long as you don't say that you're good on camera."

So this was it: death by decapitation, with the blade applied verbally. Isabella got up, holding her severed head in her hands, her newly detached forehead sticky with sweat. She didn't bother saying goodbye to this woman, who couldn't even offer a "Good luck" or a "Have a nice day" or a "Sorry to see you go."

And even though she had her jacket, a few framed pictures,

a box of Milk Duds, and three pink furry-topped pens in her cubicle, Isabella marched straight to the elevator.

"These cookies are so good," said Samantha who was, weirdly, eating another one, even though Isabella hadn't given her any more cookies since that morning. *Was Samantha the Tupperware thief?* "What's in here . . . potato chips?"

Ignoring her, Isabella stepped onto the elevator and didn't push a button; she just waited for it to move of its own accord. When she finally reached the lobby, she stepped out and saw the guard who claimed not to be eating carbs cutting into a doughnut with a knife and fork.

Isabella had entered the office that morning shielded by a plastic bin full of cookies; now she was leaving without even a jacket to protect her from the rain. Lowering her head, she stepped directly into it, feeling each drop like a wagging finger from heaven, her father's finger, regaling her with the same advice over and over: "People skills, people skills, people skills."

"Cookie skills, cookie skills, cookie skills," she muttered back, under her breath.

But she knew her argument held no weight. People skills would've gotten her through her day, given her the confidence to talk on camera, helped her navigate the situation with Dana, created a community of supporters who would've marched on Dana's office the second they heard that Isabella was let go.

Instead, she'd used her cookie skills, and her cookie skills had turned her into toast.

2

CHARITY BEGINS ON WEST SEVENTY-SECOND STREET

"I'm not saying I'm happy that you got fired. I'm saying it's *good* that you got fired. That's not the same thing!"

Isabella wasn't sure why she took the 2 train to her mother's apartment on the Upper West Side instead of the G train back to the apartment that she shared with Owen in Greenpoint. It wasn't for succor or moral support, that was for sure. She'd get more solace from a Szechuan peppercorn than she would from her mother, at least when it came to losing her job at *Comestibles*, a job that her mother, Jeannie, had always considered beneath her daughter, a daughter who had so much untapped potential to do good in the world.

"Can we not debate right now?" asked Isabella, hovering in the entryway near a stack of empty birdcages. "You know it's really starting to reek in here, Mom."

Isabella, who hadn't been to her mother's apartment in a week, noted the addition of three moldy aquariums to the mix of discarded pet supplies that were there the last time. In another corner she spotted the ever-growing piles of discarded school supplies and hospital supplies, all of which Jeannie intended to refurbish to bring back to the pet stores, schools, and hospitals that were so eager to get rid of them in the first place.

"I sprayed Febreze Passion Papaya," declared Jeannie, sniffing the air, and moving toward the stove.

"All I smell is rot and decay," said Isabella, only smelling bad things and nothing remotely pleasant or tropical.

"Are you hungry? I made soup."

In a normal home, a mother's offer of soup might be seen as a gesture of goodwill, of healthy parenting, of selfless care and nurture; in Jeannie's home, it felt more like a threat.

"What is it?" asked Isabella, sniffing the air as she cautiously entered the kitchen, unsure if she was still smelling aquarium, school supplies, or dinner.

"Surf and turf," said Jeannie, ladling out a chunky, creamy brown liquid into a thrice-used cardboard bowl from Panera.

Isabella studied the mixture as Jeannie placed it in front of her.

"A can of chili and a can of New England clam chowder," explained Jeannie, grinning, always a bit tickled to see the disgust on her daughter's face.

Canned soup was a staple in the Pasternak home, especially since Jeannie had discovered that she could combine various Campbell's flavors with pantry staples to create all kinds of culinary marvels. There was the time she combined chicken noodle with a jar of salsa to make "Mexican wedding soup." (She sang "Here Comes the Bride" in Spanish as she presented it to her mortified daughter.) And the time she mixed cream of mushroom with leftover white rice from Chinese takeout and called it "mushroom risotto" ("and I didn't even have to stir it!" she cheered as Isabella frowned).

"You know you could just do one soup at a time?" suggested Isabella, lifting the chunky mixture toward her mouth, both repulsed and intrigued, more forgiving than usual because she was ravenously hungry. "There's nothing wrong with just clam chowder."

"Where's the fun in that?"

Jeannie's eccentricities, which predated Isabella, had intensi-

fied after Isabella's father, Oliver, was killed four years earlier
by a Boston Market truck that tipped over on East Forty-sixth
Street, right outside his mid-century-antiques shop. The settlement money—undisclosed in the press and never revealed to
Isabella—made Jeannie a very comfortable woman. She had
enough in the bank to be set for the rest of her life and possibly
half of another life, though Isabella didn't know the sum. Jeannie would now spend her days scavenging the streets, looking
for items to refurbish and redistribute, the way that she used
to hunt for treasures at garage sales and flea markets for her
husband's store (a store that still sat empty, because Jeannie
refused to sell). Though sometimes one man's trash is another
man's treasure, in Jeannie's apartment one man's trash looked a
lot like trash. Her latest kick was taking home expired groceries
and transforming them into meals that were only moderately
edible.

"This is so disgusting it might actually be good?" declared
Isabella, who wondered if her palate was fried from her bad day,
or if her mother might've stumbled onto something notable.

Jeannie hoisted her phone. "Can I get this on video? You
praising my food?"

"I wouldn't call it praise," said Isabella, unable to give her
mother the win. "Let's call it acceptance."

Jeannie, who couldn't sit still before the accident and was
now a million times more fidgety, leapt again to her feet and
started blowing up the balloons that were sitting on the bookshelf, next to a row of bingo-ball machines that she had pro-
cured from a recently bankrupt cruise line.

"What are those for?"

"Sidney Diamondstein, next door, is turning ninety, and
they're throwing him a party in the rec room. I volunteered to
bring party favors."

Jeannie indicated a shelf full of discarded items from Party
City: stained napkins, torn plates, shredded streamers, and
ripped balloons that refused to inflate. As Jeannie huffed and
puffed, making very little progress, Isabella wondered how she

would broach the topic that had really brought her here, even if she wasn't ready to acknowledge the topic herself.

"So, Mom," she began.

"I don't like the sound of that," said Jeannie, panting between puffs.

Jeannie knew her daughter too well and Isabella knew her mother too well for this conversation—clearly about to become a conversation about money—to proceed without any conflict.

When Isabella graduated from Tufts, Oliver—who, unbeknownst to anyone, only had a few months left to live—offered to subsidize his daughter's first year as an intern at *Epicurious*. "She's making good connections there," he declared to a disapproving Jeannie, who was always concerned about their daughter being spoiled, since she herself had grown up spoiled in Westchester. "It's a chance for her to work on her people skills."

After the accident and all the ensuing fanfare—sitting shiva, writing (and rewriting) the obituary, listing the shop and all of its inventory, then unlisting the shop and all of its inventory—Jeannie grew more and more impatient for Isabella to find work. "This is teaching you a very bad lesson," said Jeannie, who had just deposited the seven-figure settlement check into her bank account. "If I keep paying for your life, you'll never be able to stand on your own two feet."

Isabella understood her mother's message. In fact, she agreed with it. But becoming a working food writer took years and years, if not decades, of experience, and even then, accomplished writers like Amanda Hesser cautioned against it. "I can no longer responsibly recommend that you drop everything to try to become a food writer," Amanda wrote on her website, *Food52*, back in April 2012. It was now more than a decade later and things seemed even more bleak.

Which is why, two years ago, when a desperate Isabella got hired for the staff-writer job at *Comestibles*, a job that came with a salary of $35,000 a year, it felt like she'd won the Indianapolis 500, the Boston Marathon, and the Olympic gold medal in pole vaulting all at once.

"See?" gloated Isabella to her mother the day it happened, over butternut-squash-and-Spam soup. "I told you I'd be able to take care of myself eventually!"

It only took three months for Isabella to realize that she would not be able to take care of herself eventually. That glitzy salary of $35,000 a year, after taxes, amounted to $2,300 a month. Despite its tiny kitchen, the apartment that she shared with Owen (whose father, one of the city's top talent managers, was absurdly rich) was $4,000 a month. If they split the bill evenly, that left Isabella only $300 a month for groceries, her cell phone bill, subway fare, clothes, doctors' visits, and other necessities.

Making matters worse was Isabella's passion for cookbooks and cooking her way through them. She'd already spent a small fortune on the baked goods that she brought to work every day, always springing for the fancy "European-style" butter, the twelve-dollar farmers'-market eggs with the bright-orange yolks, the "really good vanilla" that Ina Garten was always yapping about. This alone would've drained her assets, but at night she would cook complicated dishes from the pages of classic culinary texts, often spending more on crafting the dish than it would've cost to order that same dish at a restaurant, even one with a Michelin star.

After a typical visit to Alice's Cookbook Emporium, she would arrive home with some rare tome that she couldn't afford—Paula Wolfert's *Cooking of Southwest France*, Claudia Roden's *Book of Middle Eastern Food*—and the next thing that she knew, she was at Sahadi's, stocking up on saffron (at thirty dollars an ounce) and preserved lemons, and buying an authentic Moroccan tagine to make the authentic Moroccan recipe for lamb with hard-to-find quince and baby okra.

"I may need a teensy little bit of help, financially speaking," Isabella had told her mother the last time that she was brave enough to broach the subject, which was exactly two years ago.

The fight that ensued lasted three days, during which Jeannie told Isabella that her chosen career path was the result of "capitalism run amok" and that there were "eight hundred and twenty-eight million people who go to bed hungry every night." This was Jeannie's favorite statistic, one that she wielded like a weapon in the face of Isabella's "reckless hedonism." The fact that Jeannie lived in a cushy apartment on the Upper West Side was a fact that remained unspoken.

"How can you justify spending that kind of money on something that becomes literal shit when you're done with it?"

"Because," Isabella fought back, quaking in the face of her mother's gale-force winds, "it's what I love."

Owen, who from the very beginning of their friendship found himself taking pity on Isabella, agreed to cut Isabella's rent in half because of all the free meals that he enjoyed as the result of her efforts. The reality that he was now a gym rat, thirty pounds lighter, consuming a diet of protein powders and fibrous vegetables, rarely touching Isabella's creations, was another fact that remained unspoken.

Now Isabella had no income and, more important, no cooking budget.

"The thing is," Isabella tried this time around, "I'm feeling optimistic that I'll find another food-writing job soon."

This was total bullshit, and both Isabella and her mother knew it.

"Let's not fight about this again," said Jeannie, and this gave Isabella a little hope that maybe this time around things wouldn't be so bad. Maybe her mother's new charitable instincts were finally going to be applied to her own daughter? Maybe she felt guilty for refusing to read Isabella's articles because she didn't want to be "an enabler"? Or bailing on Isabella's birthday dinner at Café Boulud because she just couldn't stomach a white tablecloth?

"You know the Gristedes on Eighty-fourth and Columbus?" Jeannie asked.

Isabella nodded as if this were a logical next thing to say in their discussion.

"Uh-huh?"

"I spoke to the manager," Jeannie continued. "They're going to give me all their expired groceries at the end of every week for me to prep and bring to the soup kitchen on Eighty-sixth Street. Obviously, it's way too much for one person to do, and that's where I need your help."

Isabella continued nodding, even though she quickly saw where this was headed.

"So let's make a deal. You help me prep, package, and deliver meals to the soup kitchen every week, and I'll help you out with money until you find your next job. Seems like a no-brainer to me."

This was some dark magic on her mother's part. How could Isabella say no to *charity work* without seeming like an asshole? By no means was she entitled to her mother's money, even if the settlement money from her father's death was probably meant for her, too. And if this were work in any other arena—assembling furniture, mending torn clothing—Isabella could've claimed ignorance. But here she was being asked to do the thing that she loved doing more than anything else in the world in exchange for money that she desperately needed and didn't (necessarily) deserve.

And yet.

The idea of standing in a trash-adjacent kitchen with her mother, rotting fumes filling the air—her mother, who held such contempt for cooking that she'd spent most of Isabella's childhood warping discount lamb chops into leather gloves—was loathsome to Isabella. Not only was her mother not a good cook, she proudly ignored the tenets of good cooking. She didn't understand why anyone would use olive oil or butter when you could spritz cheap nonstick spray into a skillet for half the price and half the calories. She balked at the amount of salt Isabella used, even though Isabella was replicating the techniques of thousands of great chefs and cooks around the world. She bristled at the "unnecessary" ingredients that Isabella "splurged" on at Thanksgiving, these unnecessary ingredients being *cinnamon* for apple pie, or *fresh cranberries* for cranberry sauce when you could buy perfectly good cranberry sauce in a can.

Worse, her mother was lonely and needy and had wanted to spend as much physical time with Isabella as she possibly could since her husband's death. This was nice in theory, but in practice it involved an endless barrage of text messages, boatloads of guilt distributed at inopportune times. "I ate dinner by myself yesterday," her mother would text while Isabella was attempting to fillet a fish for the first time, tackling the sole meunière recipe from Julia Child's *The Way to Cook*, holding the boning knife that she just purchased at Sur La Table at a forty-five-degree angle. Agreeing to her mother's proposal would mean that Jeannie could use Isabella's rent money as leverage to compel her to visit her at all hours of the day and night.

"The thing is . . ." started Isabella.

"Stop saying that."

"Saying what?"

"'The thing is,'" said Jeannie. "Say whatever it is you have to say. Don't start everything with 'the thing is,' it makes you sound wishy-washy."

"Sorry," said Isabella. "The thing is—" She caught herself. "I just need to spend more time on my writing."

Jeannie sighed as if she'd heard this one before, which she had.

"I have a few freelance pieces I want to pitch to *Eater*, and if I can get one of them published, I might be able to submit one for a James Beard award, and if I win one, that'd be really huge for my career."

"Your career as a *food writer*," said Jeannie, putting a spin on the last two words the way Serena Williams might thwack a ball that blasts you directly in the face over the net.

"Yes, my career as a food writer."

Would the old fight start up again? Was there any way to avoid it?

As if the food-writing gods were listening, Isabella's phone started buzzing.

There was only one person who could be calling her at this time of day, and that person was her gay husband.

"Izzy," came the breathless voice on the other end of the phone when Isabella swiped right on the bar under Owen's name. "I've been texting you for an hour! It's an Upper East Side culinary emergency . . . How soon can you get to my dad's apartment?"

Owen had a flair for the dramatic, and there had been countless times in the history of their friendship where he claimed an emergency that turned out to be something as benign as an inverted contact lens (he thought he was going blind) or a pimple that he thought was a rare STD. After the kind of day that Isabella had had, the last thing she wanted to do was take a car through the park to Owen's dad's cold and palatial apartment to deal with whatever crisis Owen had drummed up this time. But, considering the alternative—staying here and arguing with her mother—she opted for the less bad option.

"Twenty minutes, if I take an Uber?"

"You are a goddess, a queen, an angel. I worship you."

"Twenty minutes for what?" asked Jeannie, as Isabella stood up.

"Owen has an emergency," said Isabella, pretending to be put off by the inconvenience of Owen's crisis in the middle of such a gripping discussion.

"So where does that leave us? Are you going to help me with the cooking or what?"

If the word "relentless" hadn't existed before Jeannie Pasternak entered the world it would have to be invented after.

"Let me just think about it, okay?"

"What's there to think about?" said Jeannie, trailing her daughter to the front door. "You need money, I need help. It's a fair trade."

"Love you," said Isabella, kissing her mother on the cheek, using affection as a means of escape.

"I'm getting my first Gristedes handoff tomorrow at one,"

said Jeannie. "If you don't come, don't bother asking me for money. I'm being serious."

"Bye, Mom," said Isabella. She turned away from the door and walked down the long, dusty hallway to the elevator.

"See you tomorrow," said Jeannie, getting in the last word, before closing her door and returning to her various projects.

Once in the elevator, Isabella sniffed her overalls to see if they had the stink of aquarium, birdcage, or Jeannie's "surf and turf." Instead, all she could smell on herself was the one thing that she couldn't smell in the apartment: Passion Papaya Febreze.

3

CAVIAR WISHES
AND CHAMPAGNE DREAMS

"Truffled tater tots with black-garlic aioli."
"Wagyu beef sliders on house-made brioche."
"Tuna tartare with wasabi pearls."

These were the dishes that Isabella heard waiters announcing as she walked into Lionel Schaffer's penthouse apartment on Park Avenue and Seventy-first Street. It always amused Isabella how the rich enjoyed inserting some exclusive-sounding ingredient like "truffle" in front of a dish—truffled fries, truffled mac and cheese—without caring if the truffle flavor came from a real truffle or a bottle of chemicals (aka: truffle oil) that had never met a truffle in its life. As long as it sounded rich—in the moneyed sense, not the culinary sense—it achieved its purpose.

Isabella, still in her overalls, felt comically underdressed for whatever situation this was that Owen had lured her into. When he summoned her, he didn't mention that she'd be walking into a party where the men would be wearing five-thousand-dollar Brioni suits and the women would be outfitted like they were going to an awards ceremony, not to mention the presence of a piano player in a crisp white tux.

"Izzy! Thank God you're here," called the harried and familiar voice pushing through the crowd. Owen always reminded Isabella of a panicked bird: half ostrich, half twink.

"What in Rihanna's name are you wearing?" he asked, eyeing her up and down like a disappointed teacher encountering a favorite student smoking a cigarette behind the gym. He was wearing a plum-colored velvet suit from Moschino that he'd seen in *New York* magazine. "Never mind, it doesn't matter. I need you and your kitchen wizardry. Come!"

He grabbed her by the arm and led her past the power agents, the media moguls, and the well-heeled producers who were sipping champagne in the entryway, not acknowledging her presence—as if admitting that she was also here in the room with them would puncture the illusion that made this gathering feel so exclusive and so grand.

Owen's nerves, which were always in a state of being frazzled, were extra frazzled at the moment, because, after five years of struggling to make it as an actor, he was now working for his father's talent-management company.

Lionel Schaffer's company, Mirror Mirror, was spoken of in the same breath as Anonymous, 3 Arts, and Brillstein. Whereas the other companies were staffed with managers at all levels, Lionel's was famous for being a one-man operation. He made his millions investing his time and energy in the "truly gifted" (his phrase) and being loyal to clients even when they went through public disgraces, ugly divorces, and online cancellations. His ability to revive their careers was nothing short of miraculous, which is how he earned the nickname "the Miracle Worker."

"My dad's going to murder me so hard they're already doing a podcast about it," said Owen, as he led Isabella into the impossibly huge kitchen. At the center was a marble kitchen island the size of their Greenpoint apartment, and above it a crystal chandelier that cost more than Isabella's college education. Surrounding the island were platters of the truffled tater tots and wagyu beef sliders that Isabella had seen earlier, now being reheated by the same waiters who were passing them out. Behind the platters, and illuminated by the crystal light, were eight tins of Ossetra caviar from Petrossian.

"Nice fish eggs," said Isabella, amused at the way caviar,

like truffles, perseveres as both a status symbol and a delicacy. Unlike truffles, however, you can't fake the sensation of authentic beluga caviar. Isabella had only experienced it once before, at her cousin's wedding, and she would forever remember the exciting burst of the black, glistening orbs in her mouth—salty and creamy and so satisfying that she nearly missed the nuptials.

"No, they're not nice fish eggs," said Owen, leaning on the counter. "These fish eggs are going to get me fired!"

Owen quickly related that it was his father's birthday and that he, earlier that day, had been dispatched to hire caterers, waiters, a bartender, and a pianist for this totally last-minute, improvised soirée back at "the old Airbnb" (Lionel's little joke). With zero time, Owen was relieved to get in touch with his father's favorite caterer, The One Percent, who said that they could provide waiters and appetizers but couldn't stay to cook the food à la minute, because of a wedding that they had at the Rainbow Room. Owen gave the go-ahead, then went on to hire the bartender and the pianist.

Only, during all of this, Owen missed a call from Lionel's secretary, Jane, who left an urgent message saying that Lionel also wanted caviar from Petrossian and that she'd put in an order for six tins of Special Reserve Ossetra at four hundred dollars a pop, which arrived at the exact same moment that Owen heard the message, twenty minutes after the caterers left.

"And what's so fucked up is that Petrossian didn't send any blinis, and my dad only eats them on blinis, and now he keeps asking me, 'Where's the caviar?,' and it's not like I can just open a bunch of tins of caviar and hand them out with little spoons or straws or whatever."

Isabella, who was schooled in the art of being a shoulder for Owen to cry on, shook her head. "That really sucks," she said, trying to get down in the well with him instead of trying to pull him out, à la Brené Brown.

"Don't Brené Brown me, you bitch . . . I need your help!" said Owen.

"What do you want me to do? No store sells blinis this late."

"I don't want you to buy blinis, doofus . . . I want you to make them! I know for a fact that you can."

Owen was referring to the time, not too long ago, when Isabella was cooking her way through the *Chez Panisse Menu Cookbook* by Alice Waters, published in 1982. She'd picked up a used copy at Alice's Cookbook Emporium and spent happy nights in bed dreaming of the dishes that she would tackle the next day: Lindsey Shere's almond tart (David Lebovitz called it "the most delicious thing I've probably ever had"), Richard Olney's squid with leeks and red wine (Owen said it looked like octopus intestines), and, most decadent of all, blinis à la russe with clarified butter, crème fraîche, and salmon roe (she couldn't justify buying real caviar, despite her other extravagances).

Owen, who started doing Keto the previous Christmas and hadn't touched a carb in almost a year, happened to be really hungover when Isabella was frying up the blinis à la russe à la Alice Waters. He gobbled up so many, Isabella thought that he might float away, thanks to all of the leavening agents in the batter. Instead, he passed out on the couch and yelled, "No, you sashay away!" in his sleep.

"I can't just whip up blinis," said a put-upon Isabella. She knew that the recipe existed somewhere on her phone, because, as she did with most cookbook recipes, she'd taken a picture of it before she went to the store, but: "The batter has to sit for at least an hour for the yeast to do its thing."

"The yeast will make an exception," said Owen. "C'mon, Izz. I'm begging you. My life is on the line!"

"I don't even know if the ingredients are here," she argued, though as she glanced around the football stadium that was Lionel's kitchen she noted the walk-in pantry that was stocked, floor to ceiling, with flour and sugar and more dried goods than most grocery stores in Manhattan.

"Are you kidding? There's enough food here to survive several famines," said Owen. "The only thing standing in your way is you."

Isabella rolled her eyes at this for several reasons: (a) because it was so cheesy; (b) because it was so manipulative; and (c) because Owen had been saying a variation of this to Isabella from the moment that they met at Tufts seven years earlier and she was too nervous to submit her writing to the school's literary journal.

But arguing with Owen was a lot like arguing with her mother: it took more energy to go to battle than it did to just submit.

"Fine," she relented. "You win."

"I love you," said Owen, giving her a gigantic hug. "I'd get you an apron, but I think your outfit might actually benefit from a little flour on it."

. . . .

When Isabella was in a cooking groove, the world and all of the tricky people inhabiting it fell away. That's how it felt for her as she quietly scoured the pantry for buckwheat flour (next to the teff), yeast (both fresh and dry available), eggs (from a farm upstate), butter (European-style), and milk (full-fat, organic, local). Isabella didn't know who stocked the pantry—did Lionel have a personal chef?—but whoever it was deserved some kind of commendation for thoroughness. How many people on the Upper East Side, besides the Russian oligarchs, keep buckwheat flour?

In the *Chez Panisse Menu Cookbook*—which Isabella cherished as much for its David Goines illustrations as she did for the recipes and the writing—the recipe for blinis à la russe is straightforward. You mix dry yeast with lukewarm milk until it turns foamy, make a well with the dry ingredients (the flours, sugar, salt), then work in three egg yolks along with the milk-and-yeast mixture. At this point, you're supposed to cover it and let it rise for an hour, but as Owen paced the kitchen, watching Isabella's every move, she skipped that pretty necessary step and folded in egg whites that she beat to soft peaks (her second attempt at soft peaks of the day; at least this one was successful).

At last, she was at the stove with Owen at her side, melting butter in a skillet and frying up golf-ball-sized scoops of blini batter.

"Why don't you start opening some caviar tins," suggested

Isabella, not loving having Owen breathing down her neck. "Also, see if you can find some crème fraîche."

"Oui, chef!"

The waiters, who were growing weary of pushing the same appetizers over and over, started gathering around Isabella's blini station as she plated up the first four on a small plate, not as puffy and perfect as she would have liked (the first pancakes are always the worst), but nicely browned and crisp from the butter. Realizing that she would need to start a mini–blini factory here if she was going to make enough for everyone at the party, she set a few more skillets on the stove and started melting butter in them.

Owen, meanwhile, rushed back with the crème fraîche, opened a tin of caviar, and began spooning some of each on the blinis.

"OMG," he said. "These look incredible. If I weren't shitting my pants, I'd eat this whole plate."

"Are there any chives?" asked Isabella, scrutinizing all of the brown and black. "It needs a pop of green."

"I'll go find some," said a cheerful waiter who caught Owen's eye and winked.

"He's cute," said Owen, getting distracted from his work.

"Can you keep it in your pants long enough for us to finish?" Isabella was used to Owen's getting distracted, especially by handsome men.

A few minutes later, Owen lifted a gorgeous plateful of warm blinis, topped with crème fraîche, caviar, and a sprinkling of chives (finely minced by Isabella), and whisked it directly to his father, who was holding court by his enormous staircase. Upon seeing the plate of blinis and caviar, he roared his approval.

"At last!" he said, mid-conversation with a hedge-fund manager who wanted to get into producing. "What's a guy got to do to get some fucking caviar on his goddamned birthday?"

He took the plate from his son, lifted a blini, folded it quickly in half, and shoved the whole thing into his mouth, like he was at Yankee Stadium eating a hot dog. Owen, who was both mesmerized and repulsed by his father, watched as his dad loudly chewed, nodding his head approvingly, mauling another one with his hairy, humongous hand before the hedge-fund manager could even ponder grabbing one of his own.

"Who made these?" asked Lionel. "These are the best blinis I've ever tasted, and I've tasted a lot of blinis."

Owen, delighted and relieved by his dad's reaction, said "Here, I'll introduce you," and led him by the arm to the kitchen, where Isabella was now surrounded by a coterie of waiters ladling fresh blini batter into skillets, flipping blinis with heatproof spatulas, and topping blinis with more crème fraîche, caviar, and minced chives before rushing them out to the guests while they were still warm.

"Dad, you remember Isabella," said Owen, indicating the wild-haired twentysomething in flour-flecked overalls who was concentrating on a sizzling pan, barely aware that anyone else was in the room with her.

"Isabella . . ." said Lionel, as Isabella cooked with deep focus. "Remind me of the connection?"

"She's my best friend and roommate?" said Owen, hurt that his father didn't remember the most important person in his life outside of his immediate family.

"Right, right," said Lionel; as a waiter plated four more blinis, he seized the plate for himself before the waiter had a chance to take it to the other guests.

"It's my party and I'll binge if I want to," declared Lionel as the waiter laughed a subservient laugh.

"Isabella's a food writer," said Owen, trying to talk up his forgettable roommate to his all-powerful dad.

"Is that so?" said Lionel, already three blinis in and eager for more. "Who do you write for?"

Isabella, who usually used cooking as a way to avoid interactions like these, reluctantly looked up from the stove.

"I'm actually in between jobs at the moment," she said, figuring that this was as good a time as any to tell Owen about her recent unemployment.

Owen gave her a "What happened?" look, and Isabella responded with an "I'll tell you later" look of her own.

"So what's the dream?" asked Lionel, enjoying this brief respite from the prosperous crowd.

"The dream?"

"Yeah, the dream," he said, licking crème fraîche from the corner of his mouth. This was his standard question when meeting new artists, whether they were actors, writers, musicians, or, in this case, food writers. As lighthearted and casual as the question seemed, it was a litmus test for Lionel in terms of whom he should take seriously. "Anyone who gets anywhere in this world has a dream, a goal, a destination. What's yours?"

Isabella couldn't remember her dream, even though just an hour earlier she'd been fighting her mother for the right to pursue it.

"Isabella wants to write cookbooks," said Owen, interjecting on Isabella's behalf. "She's obsessed with them."

"Cookbooks, eh?" Lionel puzzled over the idea. "Is there money in that?"

"There is if you're Ina Garten," said Owen.

"It's not so much about the money," said Isabella, so quietly that both Lionel and Owen had to lean in to hear her above the sizzle in the skillet. "I guess it's just something that I love?"

"Well, good for you," said Lionel, having sized Isabella up and now ready to return to his party. "It's good to have something that you love. Thanks for the excellent blinis. Much better than birthday cake, in my humble opinion."

With that, Lionel reentered the living room, Isabella returned to the skillet, and Owen finally returned the glances of the waiter who was still trying to catch his eye.

An hour later, Lionel was passed out on the couch, Isabella was nodding off on the 6 train, and Owen was in the sack with the waiter, celebrating another crisis averted.

4

A SEAT AT THE TABLE

I often ask people what they think of breakfast, and most reply instantly that it is their favorite meal. When pressed to tell what they eat for breakfast, their answers become rather vague. I've decided that they love the idea of breakfast, but they need some good guidance and recipes actually to get them to cook it.

These words, written by Marion Cunningham in *The Breakfast Book* (published in 1987), held extra poignancy for Isabella as she thumbed through its pages the next morning at the tiny kitchen table with room for just one chair in the tiny Greenpoint kitchen that she shared with Owen. She had purchased the book at Alice's Cookbook Emporium just a few days earlier, when she was still employed, and even though she treasured the book immediately—with its soothing pale-green cover and its unpretentious recipes (fresh ginger muffins, yeast-raised waffles)—she treasured it especially for Marion Cunningham's confident, compassionate voice.

They need some good guidance.

Good guidance: that's exactly what she needed. Here she was, twenty-five years old, unemployed, and, worse, unremembered. Nobody at work would miss her or notice that she was gone except for Samantha, who would now have to buy her own breakfast. *Comestibles* readers wouldn't go searching for her byline. Newsletter subscribers wouldn't unsubscribe because she disappeared. Even the guard at the front desk, who saw her every morning and refused her cookies, wouldn't register her absence.

How could she ever expect to pursue a career as a food writer, or any kind of writer, if her presence had zero impact? All of her food-writing heroes had earned their acclaim by making their presence known. Madeleine Kamman. M.F.K. Fisher. Laurie Colwin. Ruth Reichl. Their tenacity and ability to assert themselves gave them endless life experiences to draw from in their writing: travels through the French countryside, disguises for reviewing restaurants incognito, tawdry love affairs, wild escapades, Dionysian feasts with sex and fruit and a pig with an apple in its mouth. When would she get her own pig with an apple in its mouth? Why was the wildest love affair that she'd ever had a twenty-minute in-and-out session with a dental student named Moshe Berkman whom she met on Jdate?

Maybe her mother was right. Maybe this career path was unsatisfying because it was too indulgent, better suited to the selfish types who grab the first dinner roll out of the bread basket, who cut in line at the hostess stand to secure the last table. Maybe the people who were the most successful at food writing were the kinds of people who naturally took up space, who demanded to be heard, who pontificated loudly at dinner parties. Maybe she was struggling because she had the wrong personality for this specific career.

But if she were to give up food writing, what else could she do? She had no talent for fiction, as she'd learned in college. Her imagination was limited to what her characters ate. "Can we go a little deeper here?" her creative-writing teachers would nudge. "What does your main character want besides unpasteurized Brie?"

The place where she felt the most confident—where she knew

who she was, where she felt completely in command and utterly herself—was at the stove. Setting *The Breakfast Book* aside, she stood up to make her signature, nontraditional scrambled eggs. They weren't the custardy kind that Thomas Keller made in his *MasterClass* (which Isabella watched on a plane). They weren't the dried-out kind that you get at a diner (though those were her mother's favorite, especially covered in ketchup). Isabella's were somewhere in between creamy and firm, soft and solid, just the way that she liked them.

She pulled a nonstick skillet out of the overcrowded cabinet. She cut off a tablespoon of Plugrà and started melting it over low heat. In a bowl, she cracked three eggs with bright-orange yolks (she bought them from the Union Square Farmers Market), seasoned them with kosher salt and freshly ground black pepper, and beat them gently with a whisk, trying not to work too much air into them. She just wanted to integrate the white into the yolk so that the finished eggs wouldn't look streaky.

After setting that aside, she placed a slice of sourdough from She Wolf Bakery directly into the toaster, which was crammed in next to the coffeemaker. She pulled some herbs out of the refrigerator (she stored them in a freezer bag with a damp paper towel): a little dill, a little parsley, a little tarragon. She chopped the herbs on her cutting board with her extra-sharp chef's knife, then returned to the fridge for some extra-sharp white cheddar, which she grated on the largest holes of her box grater.

As if in a trance, she poured the eggs into the skillet, coercing them along with a heatproof spatula, cranking up the heat to medium, but keeping them moving, watching as the large curds formed. The toast popped out of the toaster just as she added the cheese and the herbs, folded them in, then guided the just-set eggs onto a plate. She buttered the toast and topped it with some strawberry-rhubarb jam that she'd made last spring.

She brought the plate to the table and placed it next to the Cunningham book, as if planting her own flag in the breakfast firmament. Once she'd eased herself back into her chair, she smiled at her handiwork and lifted a forkful of the still-steaming eggs to her mouth. She might have been a recently fired, directionless twentysomething without any real prospects, but, eating her carefully made scrambled eggs, she knew that, at the very least, she could feed herself and feed herself well. And that counted for something, didn't it?

· · · ·

That's when Owen came bounding in.

She was just finishing her last bite of toast when his bedroom door flung open and he emerged half naked, holding his phone aloft.

"It's my dad!" he said, wearing his designer blue-and-green-striped underwear, a panic-stricken look on his face. Based on the fear in his eyes, it was as if Jesus or Charlie XCX were on the line. "He wants to talk to *you*."

That last word was spoken with such disbelief, such incredulity, and such seriousness, Isabella involuntarily stood up from her seat.

Owen put the phone on Speaker, placed it on the table, and talked loudly into it, as if it were a walkie-talkie: "Hi, Dad, I've got Isabella."

"I have a client named Molly Babcock. You ever hear of her?"

Isabella heard Lionel chomping on something that sounded like a bagel as she contemplated the question.

Hear of Molly Babcock? Was Lionel kidding? Isabella grew up completely obsessed with Molly Babcock. She was the breakout star of *Malicious Angels*, a prime-time soap about the three daughters of a conservative minister who played nice when they went to church, but who became predatory vixens when Daddy was away. The younger sister and the middle sister were PG-13 in their exploits (TP-ing a rival's house, posting a fellow cheerleader's diary online), but the oldest sister, Claire Hatchett—played by Molly—was NC-17 all the way. She was blond and freckle-faced and wholesome-seeming to her father, but everywhere else she was a sinner with a capital "S": slipping Fentanyl-laced coke to a freshman who then ODed at a party, and taking the virginity of her sister's boyfriend, Simon, played by the heart-throb Xavier Mordechai, when the two were supposed to be saving themselves for marriage.

The show was an instant hit, and Molly was the breakout star. She earned a hundred thousand dollars an episode (way more than her colleagues) and appeared on the covers of *People* and *Us Weekly* and showed up on *Jimmy Kimmel* and *Jimmy Fallon* and hosted *Saturday Night Live* (her skit "Emoji Girl"—where she spoke exclusively in emojis—became a meme).

Eventually, as so often happens in these cases, Molly's celebrity led to notoriety: rumors circulated that she was a nightmare on set, that she clashed with the actors who played her sisters, demanding more money, showing up late, not knowing her lines. The gossip was corroborated when the show's creator, Devin Schwartz, killed her off in an episode titled "Come to Jesus," in which Claire and Simon have sex in a church and a crucifix falls from the rafters, impaling her through the chest just as she reveals that she's pregnant.

Despite the huge ratings for Molly's final episode, *Malicious Angels* tanked in its fifth and final season. That's when Molly went into a personal and professional tailspin. No one would hire her because of her bad reputation (she was on every director's "life's too short" list), and Xavier Mordechai, whom she was dating in real life, left her for the actress playing the middle sister, the one that Molly stole him away from in their fictional universe.

During this period, she was caught in viral photos dancing topless at a fund-raiser for cystic fibrosis, peeing in a parking lot next to an unhappy-looking hot-dog vendor in Detroit, making out with a seventeen-year-old fan at a Pink concert (his mother appeared the next day on *Fox News*, denouncing the degradation of Hollywood). And, most notorious of all, flipping off Jennifer Lawrence at the MTV Movie & TV Awards.

After that, she disappeared from the public eye. Isabella knew very little about the fate of Molly Babcock. She supposed Molly might be on social media, but she didn't follow her if she was. In fact, since all the fanfare surrounding her had died down, Molly Babcock's name hadn't entered Isabella's consciousness until this very moment.

"Sure," said Isabella. "I know who she is?"

"Molly's pivoting into the food space," continued Lionel, still chomping loudly. "She wants to be a Reese, a Stanley, a Drew, a Gwyneth. We really like this area for her."

Isabella was doing mental gymnastics as Lionel spoke. *Reese. Gwyneth. Area.*

"She sold a cookbook proposal last year," Lionel continued. "During the pandemic, she did a bunch of cooking on Instagram Live, and it blew up for a while, and the publisher liked the idea of her turning the whole thing into a cookbook. Then the book came due three weeks ago, and when we asked her where it was, she'd barely written down her name."

Because celebrities shouldn't write cookbooks, Isabella wanted to say, but she bit her tongue.

"Now the publisher's asking for the advance back, and Molly says she spent it," said Lionel with a sigh. Isabella got the impression that these sorts of celebrity shenanigans were a common occurrence for Lionel Schaffer.

"So that's where you come in. I read some of your writing this morning, and I like how you don't call attention to yourself in your work. You have a certain absence that makes you perfect for this job."

A certain absence? Was this Dana's *Friars Club Roast* all over again?

"I'll tell you right now, the ghostwriting fee isn't huge. About forty thousand dollars."

Owen gave Isabella an "OMG" look. That was more than she'd made in an entire year at *Comestibles.*

"But it's a way to get your feet wet in the publishing world and make some connections along the way. And since you want to write cookbooks, and since you're in between jobs, I figured it's a no-brainer."

Owen gleefully nodded his head up and down, eyes bright with wonder at this delightful turn of events, marveling at the fortuitous overlap of his father's world and his roommate's.

"So—what do you say? Are you on board?" Lionel asked the question as if the answer were already baked into it, an obvious "yes," like a Hershey's Kiss at the center of a cookie.

Isabella understood her own situation better than anyone. The one paying food job that she'd ever held had been ripped right out from under her just a day ago. The only access that she had to money right now was through her mother, who would use it as leverage to get her to prep questionable food with expired ingredients at all hours of the day and night. She was financially indebted to Owen, who'd already cut her rent in half to support her interest in cooking, even though he never ate the food that she made: a dynamic that was clearly unsustainable.

It really did feel like a gift from the food gods to have this opportunity. Instead of taking a job stocking shelves at Whole Foods, getting yelled at for mixing the green lentils with the brown, she would be cooking and writing and making good money. Her words, credited or not, would be printed in a real cookbook. She would interact with a real cookbook editor and develop a relationship that could potentially lead to books of her own. This was the dream. She was on the cusp of her dream! The very dream that Lionel had asked her about the night before, and now he was making it happen for her. He really was good at his job.

Yet another force was at work inside Isabella; this was the force imagining what it would be like to work with a celebrity as over-the-top and notorious as Molly Babcock. Even though she was a grown adult at twenty-five, Isabella was still a hypersensitive soul. What if Molly was mean to her, like the girls used to be mean to her in middle school, denying her a seat at the table as she stood there with her lunch tray? What if Molly lashed out, said cruel things, talked about Isabella's weight or lack of success or nonexistent sex life? What if Molly offered her drugs and pressured her into doing them, like Claire Hatchett gave drugs to that boy on *Malicious Angels*? What if Molly showed up drunk and accidentally stabbed her with a chef's knife? Or set her on fire? Or Instagrammed an ugly picture of her to her millions of followers?

Isabella hated conflict. What if this whole thing was rife with it? What if she signed the contract and couldn't get out of it? What if she'd be tethered to a psycho celebrity for the rest of her life, never finishing the book, ruining her love for cookbooks and cooking and humanity in general?

And that was the other thing: her love for cookbooks. Did she really want her first foray into cookbook publishing to be some celebrity's throwaway vanity project? Could she, without hating herself, use her hard-won culinary wisdom to help manufacture recipes for kale smoothies and write shallow headnotes about cutting carbs and intermittent fasting? How would she ever be taken seriously by the food world after that? She would always be that food writer who'd sold her soul for forty K.

"So?" pressed Lionel. "I assume it's a yes?"

"Actually . . . I think it's a no," said Isabella, surprising herself as the words left her mouth.

Owen's face fell like a thermometer yanked from a roasted chicken and jabbed into a frozen one.

"It's just . . . it's really not my kind of thing," explained Isabella.

"Making money isn't your kind of thing? Writing a cookbook isn't your kind of thing?" Not much threw Lionel Schaffer, but this rejection came as a shock. Isabella barely had her shit together, and he was offering her a significant opportunity to correct course.

"You're sure, now? I won't call again."

"I'm sure," said Isabella and, almost immediately, the line went dead.

Lionel didn't have time for formalities like "hello"s and

"goodbyes"s, and after her response to his very generous, very thoughtful offer, he especially didn't have time to say "farewell" to Isabella Pasternak.

. . . .

All ships may rise together, but Owen and Isabella were friends because their ships spent so much time sinking in unison.

When they first met, in the basement of their dorm freshman year at Tufts, Isabella was doing a three-thousand-piece jigsaw puzzle with a silent Amish girl from the third floor and humming to herself. Owen, covered in acne and still not out of the closet, recognized a safe harbor, even if the harbor seemed a bit alien. He knew that, in terms of social hierarchy, he was associating himself with bottom-rung freaks and weirdos, but he himself felt like a freak and a weirdo, especially among the loud, fratty straight guys on his floor. Plus, he loved puzzles. So he resisted the voice inside his head that told him to turn away, sat down, and helped complete the Arc de Triomphe, working the border, as he and Isabella traded backstories and the silent Amish girl nodded along.

Fast-forward two years: Owen's acne started clearing up, and he and Isabella became off-campus roommates. As he pursued acting parts that he wasn't suited for ("We just don't see you as Titus Andronicus"), Isabella prepared eclectic snacks for the *RuPaul's Drag Race*–viewing parties that they hosted, which mostly included Owen, Isabella, and whoever happened to be lurking around their hall with nowhere else to go.

It was a natural next step, once they graduated, to become roommates in New York. Owen was there for Isabella after her father's death, a period during which she completely shut down, and Isabella was there for her gay best friend as he faced rejection after rejection attempting to play someone else's gay best friend off-Broadway or in some NYU film student's thesis film. Where they bonded most was in their tiny kitchen, when Isabella would console him with a big pot of Marcella Hazan's Bolognese or a tray of Edna Lewis's biscuits.

Everything shifted the day when Owen stopped eating Isabella's food. This coincided with the moment that he decided to quit the acting biz and "join the dark side" (as he put it), going to work for his intimidating, undermining father. Lionel always told his son that he "lacked the killer instinct," and, as if to prove him wrong, Owen tried to make himself look like a killer. He hired a trainer, joined a gym that he couldn't afford, and bought several suits that did the difficult job of transforming him from adorable imp to high-powered Hollywood type. The only remaining relic of his previous existence was Isabella herself.

"Did that really just happen?" asked Owen, fluttering his eyes in disbelief. "Did you really just say no?"

"I'm sorry," she replied. "It just—it wasn't for me."

"Can you please stop saying that?" said Owen, crossing his arms and leaning against the fridge. "Do you think that every job every person takes is 'for *them*'? Do you think the guy who scrubs shit out of the toilet at Grand Central Station says to his supervisor, 'You know, Frank, this really isn't for me'? Do you think the go-go dancer at the gay bachelor party suddenly stops mid-lap dance and says to the bald gay accountant, 'This really isn't for me'?"

Isabella had never seen Owen angry, especially this angry.

"Why are you so upset?"

"Because! This is your whole future right here—I see it as clear as day—and you can't see it at all."

"What am I supposed to be seeing?"

Owen looked at the floor and shook his head, as if he were burdened with the knowledge of Isabella's entire fate.

"This is as good as it's going to get for you," he said, finally looking her in the eyes. "You're so passive and afraid of everything. You're going to spend your whole life in the shadows if you don't eventually step up. This isn't just a job offer . . . It's a metaphor."

"If you're trying to tell me that not writing Molly Babcock's cookbook is going to ruin my life somehow, I'm sorry, but that's just not true."

"When life gives you a green light, you follow the green light. You don't fiddle with the radio, you don't open the sunroof, you don't text your Pilates instructor. You just step on the gas and you go!"

Isabella understood what Owen was trying to say: that it was ridiculous for her to turn up her nose at an offer like this when she had nothing else going on, when it was so close to her actual dream. But she also had to be true to herself, and this gig didn't feel right. Wasn't that a valid reason? Who was Owen to tell her what was the best thing for her, especially when it came to the thing that she cared most about in the world?

"Maybe I don't want to be a cookbook ghostwriter," said Isabella. "It's all of the work and none of the glory."

"Worry about the glory later," said Owen. "Right now you just need to focus on the work. Focus on making money. Focus on paying me back for all the rent I've been covering for you so you can pay for ingredients that I don't even eat."

These words, more than all the others, stung the most. For Owen to mention the money was to violate one of the unspoken rules of their friendship: that they both knew that he was rich, that he would help her when he could, and that, for the sake of her own dignity, they would pretend that it was in exchange for her passionately rendered gourmet meals.

"I can get another job," said Isabella quietly, trying to calculate the best way to push back without seeming ungrateful.

"What job? You have another job offer better than the one my dad just gave you?"

No, Isabella didn't have another job offer. But there was one place, one establishment that made her happier than anywhere else in New York, and if she could get a job there, she could scrape by, pay Owen, and continue her own writing.

"I can find out if they're hiring," she said.

Owen, still reeling from Isabella's rejection of his father's offer, glanced down at Isabella's plate.

"Were those your famous scrambled eggs? With toast?"

The yellow residue and the brown crumbs gave Isabella's breakfast away. And, knowing her roommate and best friend as well as she did, she knew that she could temporarily make peace by re-creating the breakfast that they'd shared countless times before.

"Two eggs or three?"

"Three," said Owen, stealing Isabella's seat. "And two pieces of toast. I'm too depressed to avoid carbs right now."

Isabella once again began her dance at the stove, conscious of the silence in the kitchen as she cracked three more eggs into a bowl and lowered the bread into the toaster. Owen might have been correct in his assessment of the situation—that she was doomed to spend the rest of her life in the shadows—but here at the stove, she was Leonard Bernstein conducting an edible orchestra. Who needed a seat at the table when the kitchen was her enchanted domain? She cranked the heat to medium and stood guard over the eggs, waiting for them to set the way that she liked them, as she plotted her path to a newer, better job.

5

GO ASK ALICE

The first time Isabella laid eyes on Alice Wheatley, she felt like she was seeing a dream version of her future self.

It was a freezing February afternoon, Dana had canceled work because of a threatening blizzard, and Isabella had just polished off a bowl of shoyu ramen at Ichiddo in Greenpoint when she stumbled into Alice's Cookbook Emporium to get out of the cold. The store, which had no sign, looked at first like any other used-book store, the kind that you see all over New York, the ones with battered-up old copies of *Infinite Jest* and *Confederacy of Dunces* being thumbed through by self-serious, discreetly vaping twentysomething males. But the closer Isabella inspected, the more Isabella realized that she'd entered her own personal cookbook paradise.

On a table in front of her, she saw a handwritten sign that said "Eighties L.A." with hand-drawn sunglasses and palm trees on it, and below on the table were *The Food of Campanile* by Mark Peel and Nancy Silverton (Nancy Silverton was one of Isabella's cooking heroes), *City Cuisine* by Susan Feniger and Mary Sue Milliken (two female food icons who had won the Julia Child Award for Lifetime Achievement), and, of course, Wolfgang Puck's *Recipes from Spago, Chinois, and Points East and West* (Isabella grew up watching Wolfgang hawk his wares on the Home Shopping Network, but also knew, from David Kamp's *The United States of Arugula*, that he was responsible for reinventing California cuisine).

As Isabella wandered deeper into the store, she found shelves organized by cooking tools ("Let's Wok": with books by Grace Young, Fuchsia Dunlop, and Martin Yan), books organized by region ("Be Italian": with books by Waverley Root, Faith Willinger, and Marcella Hazan), and even a table of books by "86ed" chefs: Mario Batali, John Besh, Johnny Iuzzini. (These books were marked with negative price tags; Isabella later learned that Alice would pay customers to take them.)

At some point, Isabella noticed the woman sitting behind the counter, deeply engrossed in a Laurie Colwin novel, who was barely paying any attention to her customers (of whom Isabella was the only one). She wore a red flannel shirt, a canary-yellow cardigan, and pink plastic glasses connected to a chain around her neck. She poured tea from a genuine British teapot into a teacup on a saucer and nibbled on a blueberry scone that she'd probably made herself.

Something about this woman's poise, her self-satisfaction, the ease with which she occupied the space, a space that she had clearly created herself, became an instant inspiration to Isabella. Who needed fame, success, or glory when you could own your own used-cookbook store, where you could hang out all day, chatting with like-minded customers about the early works of Madhur Jaffrey or Richard Olney?

"Excuse me," Isabella finally said, after circumnavigating the store twice. "Do you happen to have *Auberge of the Flowering Hearth*?"

If there was a secret password among cookbook lovers, this may as well have been it. *The Auberge of the Flowering Hearth* was a classic cookbook, published in 1973, by Roy Andries de Groot who lost his vision during the London Blitz. It documented his time traveling the Alpine area of southeastern France, where he stumbled upon an inn run by two women, whose recipes and cooking knowledge filled its pages. Isabella had first heard about it in an interview with Samin Nosrat, who called it "less a cook-book and more a fantastical memoir." She'd made a mental note to look for it from then on.

Alice, whose normal customers were YouTube and TikTok obsessives asking for the latest by Molly Baz, lowered her book and took in the person standing before her, who seemed like a younger version of herself.

"I do have it, but I have to warn you: it's obnoxiously over-priced," said Alice, and she got off her stool and led Isabella to a section labeled "Obnoxiously Overpriced," where—shelved between a first edition of Vincent Price's *A Treasury of Great Recipes* and Ferran Adrià's *A Day at El Bulli*—she pulled out an original copy of *Auberge* with a fifty-dollar price tag.

"Ouch," said Isabella.

"I'll tell you what," said Alice, sussing out this unusually pre-cocious customer. "Tell me how much you want to pay for it, and I'll tell you if that number works for me."

Isabella took the book, thumbed through its pages, and found herself blurting out: "Twenty bucks?"

"Sold," said Alice, and Isabella immediately realized that she could've named any price, because Alice recognized a kindred spirit, and it was a foregone conclusion that the book would be hers.

After that, Alice and Isabella became fast friends. On a typi-cal Saturday afternoon, Isabella would stroll over to Alice's under the pretext of looking for something ("Do you have Clau-dia Roden's *Arabesque*?" "Calvin Trillin's *Tummy Trilogy*?" "*The Artists' and Writers' Cookbook*?") but, really, just to hang out with Alice and gossip about everything going on in the food world.

They both regularly read *Eater* and *Grub Street* and *The Infatuation* and the "Tables for Two" column in *The New Yorker*, even though neither of them had ever had the gumption or the money to go to a buzzy restaurant themselves. When a new *NYT* restaurant review would drop, Alice would rail against Pete Wells and his self-important style, and Isabella would zealously defend him, claiming that she had a crush on him, even though she'd never seen what he looked like in real life.

It reached the point where Alice's Cookbook Emporium felt more like a home to Isabella than her *childhood* home on the Upper West Side, where soup cans and birdcages had more pride of place than she did.

Which is why, after her fight with Owen, it felt so calming and reassuring for Isabella to once again enter the space that made her feel so at peace with herself, so clear about who she was and what she loved. As she entered, Aimee Mann was playing on the Alexa, a table was set up for Halloween ("Blood and Guts," featuring books about offal cookery), and a half-eaten almond croissant was visible on the desk, a clear sign that Alice was there but currently indisposed.

Once again, Isabella perused the familiar shelves, studying the familiar names, these icons of cookbook writing: Dorie Greenspan, Edna Lewis, Yotam Ottolenghi.

Would any of these titans of the food world have submitted themselves to the degradation of ghostwriting a celebrity's cookbook? Would Mimi Sheraton have shepherded Ariana Grande through her trainer's recipe for flaxseed granola? Would Craig Claiborne have given voice to Lil' Kim's love for Rice Krispie treats? Would Joan Nathan have transcribed a hamantaschen recipe for Natalie Portman? (Actually, according to her memoir, Joan Nathan *did* write a vegan matzo ball recipe for Natalie Portman, but that was beside the point.)

The various names taunted Isabella the more that she studied them: these were cookbook authors who mattered, names that would persevere from generation to generation. It had been more than sixty years since *Mastering the Art of French Cooking* was first published, and they were still making TV shows and documentaries about Julia Child. Would Julia have taken this job ghostwriting a cookbook for Molly Babcock? Isabella imagined her reaction:

"Babcock? Poppycock!"

Isabella was tired of being invisible, tired of being passed over, tired of being the person you called in case of an emergency and dismissed as soon as she was no longer useful. She wanted to be a voice, a presence, a name like all these other names. Why couldn't she write a cookbook of her own? A book with her name prominently featured on the cover, ISABELLA PASTERNAK in gold leaf underneath a beautiful platter of Medjool dates and hunks of aged Parmesan cheese? Was that so much to ask for? Was that such a ridiculous path? Why couldn't she be the next Alison Roman? The next Sohla El-Waylly? The next Claire Saffitz?

Because! erupted a voice in Isabella's head. *These people all have YouTube shows! These people put themselves out there on Instagram and TikTok. These people have platforms and audiences and millions of followers. They have brands, pedigrees, reputations, subscribers. You have none of those things.*

She wandered over to the "Blood and Guts" table and thumbed through Chris Cosentino's *Offal Good*. A recipe for milk-braised cow udders caught her eye, and she felt simultaneously repulsed and intrigued. Who in their right mind would ever make milk-braised cow udders? Who in their right mind would ever put a recipe for milk-braised cow udders in a cookbook? Chris Cosentino would. And that's why his name would persevere and her name wouldn't. Pretending otherwise was udder nonsense.

· · · ·

As Isabella continued flipping through the book, examining a recipe for calf's brain and testicles with brown butter, she heard a toilet flush. Alice, wearing high-waisted jeans, a pink-polka-dotted blouse, and tortoiseshell cat-eye frames, emerged from the bathroom and spotted Isabella immediately.

"Is there a holiday I don't know about?" she asked, washing her hands in the bathroom sink that was too large to put in the bathroom itself.

Isabella, per her ritual, placed the book down and walked

over to a stool at the front counter, where Alice, drying her hands on a tea towel, came to meet her.

"If getting fired is a holiday, I don't want to observe it ever again," answered Isabella, eyes darting down to the half-eaten pastry.

"Here, take the rest." Alice could read someone else's hunger instantly. "It's from this new place down the street, and their laminator is on the fritz, so it's more like a dinner roll."

Alice could be a tough cookie when it came to tough cookies, croissants, and other baked goods; Isabella wasn't as discerning.

"So you lost your job," said Alice as Isabella tore in. "It's brutal out there. My sister just got canned from the pharmacy she's been working at for thirty years. Granted, she was stealing Oxy and dealing it from her garage, but still."

Alice always described her family as "Jersey trash," which was hard to believe, given her exquisite taste in cookbooks, eyeglasses, and tea sets.

"You're not hiring right now, by any chance?" asked Isabella, tearing off another piece of almond croissant as shards fluttered in all directions. She figured blurting out the question was the best strategy, considering the nontransactional nature of their friendship.

"Oh, honey, I can barely pay *my own* salary," Alice said, laughing, as she wiped the shards away. "I'm thinking of turning my medieval-cookery section into a pawnshop."

Isabella couldn't tell if Alice was kidding about the pawnshop, but she knew that she was being serious about not having money to hire anyone.

"Don't worry," said Alice, watching Isabella finish the rest of the croissant. "You're young, talented, not fully jaded yet. Something will come along eventually."

"That's the problem: something *did* come along," said Isabella, dusting powdered sugar from her hoodie, and telling Alice about the offer that had come her way that morning, including her many reasons for rejecting it.

Isabella finished with a look of "Can you believe my bad luck?," which Alice returned with a look of total incredulity.

"Let me get this straight. You got offered a gig ghostwriting a cookbook and you said no because . . . you think it'll hurt your chances of becoming a real food writer?"

"Exactly," said Isabella, grateful to have someone in her life who could understand why she would refuse such an opportunity.

"Babe, I've got news for you," said Alice. "Half of the people on these shelves make their livings ghostwriting cookbooks. Otherwise, they wouldn't be able to write cookbooks at all!"

Alice launched off her chair and started grabbing books off the shelves, flitting about the store like a cat who knows where all the treats are hidden.

"I mean, look at Melissa Clark alone," she said, pulling a blue-and-white hardcover book off the shelf. "She ghostwrote Paula Deen's cookbook, if you can believe it." She showed her *Paula Deen's Southern Cooking Bible*, with Melissa Clark's name printed underneath. "And that's just for starters."

She proceeded to show her Melissa Clark's name on cookbooks by four-star chefs like Daniel Boulud and David Bouley. She showed her Melissa's name on the bright-red cover of the White House pastry chef Bill Yosses's book *The Perfect Finish*.

"And that's just Melissa Clark. So many of these books were ghostwritten by names you know. Julia Moskin ghostwrote this for Bobby Flay." She handed her *Bobby Flay Cooks American*.

"Julia Turshen ghostwrote this for someone you might recognize . . ."

She pulled Gwyneth Paltrow's cookbook off the shelf.

"No way!" said Isabella, a huge fan of Julia Turshen's.

"Gwyneth claims she wrote it herself, but she thanks Julia *profusely* in the intro. It was a scandal for a hot minute. The *Times* even wrote about it."

Alice handed the Gwyneth book to Isabella, who flipped to the author's note and saw a picture of Julia Turshen standing next to Gwyneth.

"And don't sleep on J. J. Goode," said Alice, pulling more

books off the shelf. "You'd be lucky to have a career like J. J. Goode!"

She showed Isabella *Turkey and the Wolf* by Mason Hereford with J. J. Goode, *Salt & Straw* by Tyler Malek with J. J. Goode, and *Everyone's Table* by Gregory Gourdet with J. J. Goode.

"That last book won the James Beard award," said Alice, tapping the sticker on the cover.

The speed with which Alice had Isabella racing around the store, and the eagerness with which she spoke, left Isabella reeling.

"The only thing, if you do this," said Alice carrying some of the books back to her chair behind the counter, "is that you must get a 'with.' "

"A what?"

"A 'with,' " repeated Alice. "As in 'A Cookbook by Molly Babcock *with* Isabella Pasternak.' Without a 'with,' you'll really be a ghost, and it won't do anything for your career, because you'll sign an NDA and nobody will know that you worked on it."

Until Alice mentioned getting a "with," Isabella hadn't even considered the possibility that her name might be on the cover of whatever book this was that she'd be helping Molly Babcock write. And wasn't that the dream she was fantasizing about moments ago? Seeing her name on the cover of a book beneath a platter of dates and Parmesan cheese? Swap out the fruit and dairy for a B-list celebrity and Isabella might actually get her wish.

"I don't know," said Isabella, thumbing through some of the books that Alice had pulled. "These are all cookbooks by well-respected food people. Bobby Flay's a famous chef. Gregory Gourdet's a famous chef. Paula Deen's a—"

"Racist," interjected Alice.

"True," said Isabella. "But they're all people who know what they're doing in the kitchen. Molly Babcock spends more time on Page Six than she does at the farmers' market."

"How do you know that?" asked Alice. "You're making a

lot of assumptions here. Molly Babcock might be a better cook than you or me."

Isabella shot Alice a look that said, *Really?*

"Really," said Alice. "I think you're just afraid to do something that takes you outside of your comfort zone. And that's the reason you *should* do it. Comfort zones are overrated. Believe me," she added, indicating the store around her. "I've been trapped in mine for ten years."

Was it her comfort zone that Isabella was afraid of leaving? Or did she just have impossibly high standards when it came to cookbooks?

"I just don't want to write a shitty book," said Isabella.

"Who says it has to be shitty? You know more about cookbooks than I do, and I'm almost twice your age. Bring all of that knowledge and expertise into your work with Molly Babcock and make the book better than it has to be. If the book turns out great, that'll only be good for you and your career."

Isabella needed a pep talk like this, but she really hadn't come here for a pep talk. She'd come here for a job.

"Are you *sure* you don't want to hire me? I can put all of these books back for you right now?"

Alice shook her head.

"The only book that I want you putting back on these shelves," she said, "is the exciting new cookbook by television's Molly Babcock, co-written with the illustrious, fabulous, professional cookbook ghostwriter Isabella Pasternak."

. . . .

Outside Alice's, Isabella felt revivified.

Unlike that freezing February afternoon when she first visited, this was a perfect September day in New York, where the air was crisp enough to be cold except for when the sun shone directly on you, warming you back up the perfect amount. In her puffy brown jacket, she felt like a cozy pancake in an oven being kept warm at two hundred degrees.

As she walked down Greenpoint Ave., she weighed the pros and cons of taking the job.

Pro: her name on a cookbook.

Con: a cookbook by *Molly Babcock*.

Pro: real-world writing experience.

Con: real-world writing experience with *Molly Babcock*.

As she went back and forth in her head, her phone rang. She looked down and saw "Mom" on the screen, and girded herself for what was coming.

"It's all happening," chirped Jeannie, as Isabella lifted the phone to her ear, bristling at the false frivolity in her mother's tone. "Are you close?"

"Close to where?" asked Isabella, not fully remembering where or why she was supposed to be.

"Close to *here*. I just got back from Gristedes, and it's a huge bounty. Expired chicken cutlets, wilted celery, onions caked with dirt. By the time we're done, we'll have six gallons of chicken noodle soup . . . minus the noodles."

Only then did Isabella remember the deal that Jeannie had proposed the night before, and how awkward she felt saying no to her mother's proposal. And now her mother was forcing her hand.

"Mom, I'm in Greenpoint, and I'm actually really busy."

"Busy doing what?"

Isabella pondered the question. She was busy processing Alice's advice? Standing on the precipice of making a major life decision?

The pause hovered long enough for Jeannie to press on without an answer:

"Isabella, I'm not kidding around this time. You're not getting a free handout from me every time you're in a financial crisis. I don't want you to think that, just because there was a settlement check, you don't have to work for the rest of your life, because the fact is, you do."

"I know that."

"Then get on a train and come."

"I can't get on a train and come," said Isabella. "*Because* of work."

"I don't understand. What does that even mean? What work?"

"I got a job offer and I'm taking it."

Jeannie's pause seemed to indicate both delight and disappointment.

"A job doing what?"

Isabella didn't know until that moment that she'd made her decision, but as soon as the words left her mouth, she knew that she'd made it and that the decision was final.

"I'm ghostwriting Molly Babcock's cookbook."

6

ON MOLLY

"Kathy Bates called. She wants her wardrobe back."

It was the next morning, and Owen was scrutinizing every inch of Isabella as she prepared to go meet his first (and only) client as a newly anointed manager. Lionel was so pleased by Isabella's reversal, he gave his son full credit for "turning her" and rewarded him with a promotion, allowing him to bypass all of the hazing and photocopying that the other first-year associates had to endure. (They started calling him "NepOwen" behind his back.) His reward was being assigned exclusively to Mirror Mirror's least relevant and trickiest client: the notorious and unprofitable Molly Babcock. Now Isabella was on her way to meet her in baggy jeans, a fuzzy red sweater covered in cat hair (which was weird, because they didn't have a cat), and black Chuck Taylors.

"I wear this all the time," argued Isabella.

"Which worked when you were sitting in a cubicle all day, writing about potatoes. But now you're meeting a former style icon who was dressed by Mark Jacobs for the 2017 People's Choice Awards."

Sometimes it felt like Owen and Isabella spoke two completely different languages.

"I really don't think she cares what I look like, as long as we get along."

Owen shook his head, trying to be as sympathetic as he could toward this clearly misguided individual.

"Why don't you wear that peach-colored Rachel Comey cardigan that I bought you for your birthday? It's flattering, it's fashionable, and it doesn't make you look like you hand out pigs-in-a-blanket at Costco."

The Rachel Comey cardigan was Owen's olive branch, a way to bridge the gap between his own immaculate presentation—since getting into shape, Owen had more grooming rituals than a horse—and Isabella's default dowdy mode. She hadn't had occasion to wear it yet—it called too much attention to itself for her to wear it to work—but now calling attention to herself didn't seem like such a bad idea, since she was trying to make a good impression.

An hour later, she felt like the peach from *James and the Giant Peach* as she made her way down Canal Street on her way to the place Molly had picked: Corner Bar, a chic celebrity hangout on the Lower East Side. As Isabella passed tourists, construction workers, and a twentysomething filming herself for TikTok with a ring light and a fuzzy microphone, she felt the tiniest twinge of superiority because of whom she was about to meet. On an intellectual level, Isabella knew that being famous wasn't really an accomplishment, per se. In American society, you could marry your brother and have quintuplets and that would make you famous. But on a human level, Isabella was susceptible to the idea that film and TV stars were deities—enchanted, otherworldly creatures—who inhabited a different realm from the rest of us: a realm with its own language, its own signals, its own code of conduct.

When she reached the door of Corner Bar, she looked at her watch.

Eleven fifteen.

The lunch res was for eleven thirty, so she did what she always did in these situations: she walked around the block very slowly, trying not to sweat, until it was eleven twenty-nine, and then she walked through the entryway.

The restaurant itself wasn't crowded. The vibe was exclusive, but not unwelcoming. A casually chic hostess at a podium smiled at Isabella.

"Reservation?" she asked.

That's when it hit Isabella. She'd forgotten a key component of meeting a celebrity for lunch, the essential password that all celebrity lunchmates must be made aware of before the lunch can commence: the pseudonym under which they'd made the reservation.

Isabella panicked.

"Uhm, hi," she murmured. "My friend actually made the reservation? It might be under . . . ?" *Should I say the name? Would that blow Molly's cover? Does Molly still have a cover to blow?* "Molly?" she proffered, leaving out the last name, just to be safe.

The hostess scanned an iPad.

"I don't see anything for a Molly," she said. "But we're not busy right now. Is it just the two of you?"

Isabella nodded, worried now that maybe Molly wanted to sit at a particular table and that her acquiescing to the hostess meant following her to a spot that was entirely wrong for a celebrity lunch. What if the table was too out in the open? Too close to the bathroom? Too near a window where she might be ogled? Did Molly still get ogled? What if not getting ogled triggered her more than getting ogled would?

Before Isabella could verbalize her concerns, the hostess sat her at a perfectly decent table midway through the room. That's when Isabella pondered the question of seating: Did she face the door, so that she could see Molly coming in? Or did she leave that seat for Molly, the seat of power, the one Mafia dons preferred sitting in so that they didn't get shot in the back of the head?

The hostess watched as Isabella vacillated between the two chairs.

"I'll just leave your menus here," she said, placing down two menus; as she walked away, Isabella finally settled on the seat facing the door. She would get up as soon as Molly arrived and ask her where she'd rather sit. Making a bold seat choice and then offering to recant it seemed like the best strategy for meeting a celebrity for lunch, showing that you had a strong sense of self but that you were willing to repress it if necessary.

. . . .

Thirty minutes later, the room was full, glasses were clinking, waiters were scribbling, and Isabella was still alone at the table, a half-consumed glass of ice water in front of her. She hadn't wanted to bother Owen in the thirty minutes that ticked by as she waited. *Celebrities are late,* she reasoned. *It's just a rule. If you text Owen, he'll text back: "She's on her way. Play Wordle."*

But now the waitress was getting impatient—Isabella was too nervous to order anything without consulting Molly first (she'd read the menu sixteen times; the celeriac rémoulade and the poularde rôtie caught her eye)—and by twelve fifteen, Isabella couldn't take the tension anymore. Instead of texting Owen, she called him.

"She's not here," she sputtered as soon as Owen answered. "I thought she might be running late, but it's been forty-five minutes?"

"I'm on it," said Owen, sounding like the professional manager he'd always wanted to be but never had a chance to become. He hung up without saying goodbye, just like his dad, and one minute later he called back.

"She fucked up," he said. "She said Corner Bar but she meant Lodi in Rockefeller Center. She got them confused."

How do you confuse a restaurant in Midtown with a restaurant on the Lower East Side?

"Okay?"

"The good news is that she went too long in the sensory deprivation tank, so you still have time to meet her," said Owen. "How fast can you get there?"

Isabella did the subway math in her head. F train to Forty-ninth Street in . . . "Twenty minutes?"

"Twenty minutes," echoed Owen, hanging up.

Isabella bolted out of her seat. She charged back through the dining room, swept past the hostess without saying anything (she was too embarrassed), and hoofed her way to the F train in record time.

By the time she was on the subway headed north, she was so rattled, so out of breath, she felt like she was at the end of her day's journey, not at the start. And the sweat seeping through her Rachel Comey cardigan made her feel less like a giant peach and more like an overripe peach, the kind that's so bruised and mealy you just have to throw it away.

. . . .

Disheveled, greasy, and completely out of sorts, Isabella arrived at Lodi at twelve forty-five and, once again, didn't see anyone who remotely resembled Molly Babcock waiting for her.

This time, she decided to wait outside the restaurant to intercept Molly on the way in; that way, she wouldn't have to guess Molly's pseudonym or make any difficult decisions about where to sit, table-wise or seat-wise. She wouldn't text Owen about Molly not being there; she would just wait and do as the Owen in her head suggested: play Wordle on her phone.

A few games later (she dipped into the Wordle archives), just as she made her second guess—"ghost" was her first word, and she had two letters right (it was "gassy")—she heard a raspy, familiar voice address her. "Isabella?"

At first, she thought the voice was familiar because it was someone she knew in real life. But then she realized that the voice was familiar because it was a famous one: both threatening and playful, sunny and dangerous. Isabella lowered her phone, and there before her stood the familiar, iconic visage of Molly Babcock.

It's a strange fact of stardom that somehow, through a regular application of serums and visits to renowned facialists (and possibly plastic surgeons), a face that seemed preternaturally young at twenty can seem even more preternaturally young at thirty. Molly's skin was all aglow; her light-brown freckles lit up in the afternoon sun; her crystal-blue eyes sparkled, like they'd been through an eyeball-washing machine. Her full, shoulder-length, golden-colored hair looked healthier than Isabella felt in general. And her makeup was so expensive it made it seem like she wasn't wearing any makeup at all.

"Hey," said Isabella, putting her phone away while gazing at the familiar vision before her.

"I knew you had to be you. You look like an Isabella. Can I give you a hug? Are you a hugger?" Before Isabella could answer, Molly was wrapping her arms around her and squeezing her like they were former best friends reunited after years of estrangement.

"It's so good to meet you," continued Molly, pulling away but still gripping Isabella's sweaty shoulders. "I'm so sorry I'm late; this day is so fucked, and it's not even after one."

Actually, it's one fifteen, Isabella wanted to say, but decided against it.

"Are you hungry?" Molly went on, letting go. "I'm ravenous."

Molly charged toward the hostess stand, and before Isabella could catch up, the hostess was leading Molly to a table that seemed discreet (it was in a corner) but was still part of the main dining area on the patio, so that Molly could be seen or not seen, depending on her mood.

"Do you mind if I put in the order right away?" Molly asked the hostess as Isabella joined her (Molly chose the power seat, facing the room; Isabella's seat faced the clear plastic tarp that acted as an outdoor wall).

Molly turned to Isabella and said, "Do you trust me? I come here all the time."

Isabella nodded, slightly worried that Molly would order them salads without croutons or dressing or anything that wasn't plain lettuce.

"Let's do the house-made ricotta," she began. "The caponata, the white asparagus, and the tuna tartare. Should we share a pasta?"

She asked this of Isabella, who was still processing all of the items that Molly had just rattled off.

"Sure," she said, impressed by both the quality and the quantity of Molly's lunch order.

"Which do you like better?" she asked the hostess, who didn't normally take people's orders but was making an exception for Molly because she recognized her. "The gnocchi estivi with Sungold tomatoes and chanterelles? Or the pici all'Arrabbiata?" (Isabella noted the confident way that Molly pronounced her Italian; giving a real "ch" sound to the "ci" in "pici" and an Isabella Rossellini–like flourish to "all'Arrabbiata.")

"Definitely the pici," said the hostess. "It's my favorite thing on the menu."

Molly paused, processed this factoid, and then considered how much she wanted to defer to this hostess and her tastes. She surprised them both by saying, "You know what? Let's do the risotto. The Salva Cremasco with radicchio sounds *amazing*."

Something about the way Molly referenced the Salva Cremasco—a rare Italian cow's-milk cheese from Lombardy, which Isabella knew about because of an Italian-cheese article that she wrote for *Comestibles*—made Isabella suspicious. Was the ease with which Molly was ordering this meal based on legitimate culinary knowledge? Or was it based on her having rehearsed all of this the night before? Something told her it was the latter.

"Anything to drink?"

"Do you still have the Etna Bianco? The Cottanera?"

"Of course."

"I love a volcanic white," said Molly to Isabella. "Sometimes I *am* one."

Molly looked at Isabella to see if she would laugh. She did, but cautiously.

"I'll have an iced tea," Isabella told the hostess.

"Are you not a drinker?" asked Molly, giving this question some significance.

"I am . . . I just don't normally drink during the day."

"Cancel her iced tea," Molly told the waitress. "Bring her what I'm having."

The waitress nodded and walked away as Molly sat back in her chair with the satisfaction of a performer who'd pulled off a tricky monologue without missing a beat.

"I hope that was okay," she said. "Sometimes you just have to take charge at these small-plate restaurants or you'll be negotiating forever."

Isabella took note of Molly's apologetic way of being domineering: was this a harbinger of things to come?

"So—tell me about yourself," said Molly, looking at Isabella earnestly while also placing her phone face-up on the table. "I want to know *everything*."

"Umm . . . well . . ." stalled Isabella. "I guess there's not a lot to know? I grew up in New York."

"Whereabouts?"

"The Upper West Side."

"I *love* the Upper West Side," said Molly, who saw a text on her phone, quickly pulled it toward her chest, and typed with her thumbs while still making eye contact. "It used to be so uncool, and it's still kind of uncool, but it's *so* uncool that it makes it cool again. Do you know what I mean?"

"Sort of," said Isabella, who didn't think there was anything cool about the Upper West Side and spent as much time as she could avoiding it.

As the conversation continued, the two glasses of volcanic white appeared, and Molly continued texting and sipping while Isabella talked about her time at *Comestibles* (she left out the part about getting fired) and her relationship to Owen, Molly's new manager. By the time she finished, she'd only had one sip of her wine, while Molly polished off her entire first glass.

"Here we have the asparagi bianchi," said a handsome gay waiter, aware of the fallen *Malicious Angels* star at the table but pretending not to be dazzled. "The house-made ricotta. The caponata with pine nuts and fennel. And the tuna tartare with Calabrian chili."

Isabella looked down at the plates—at the perfectly sculpted white mound of cheese, the glistening eggplant, the ruby-like tuna flecked with red chilies—and felt like this was what Cézanne would've posted if he'd had an Instagram.

"I'm so hungry I could eat a miniature pony," said Molly; she stabbed her fork into a white-asparagus spear, lifted it straight to her mouth, and bit off the tip.

It was at this moment that Isabella saw an opportunity. Molly had been grilling her about her life and career and, in a way, deflecting about the real purpose of their get-together: the cookbook that the two of them were apparently going to be writing together.

"So . . ." said Isabella, stabbing a white-asparagus spear of her own. She placed it on her plate and cut it into pieces. "Can you tell me about the cookbook? How far along are you with it?"

"I'm going to need another glass," Molly told the gay waiter as he cleared her first glass away.

"You got it," he said, a small grin on his face (*That Molly Babcock can drink*).

Isabella waited for Molly to answer the question as she lifted the tip of her own asparagus to her mouth. She would normally start from the bottom and work her way up, saving the best asparagus bite for last, but she figured it was good to eat in solidarity.

"TBQH," said Molly, a slight hint of embarrassment appearing on her face, "I haven't thought about the cookbook since I sold it."

This wasn't news to Isabella; Lionel had told her as much when he first called.

"That's okay. But what kind of cookbook do you imagine it to be? Like . . . does it have a premise? A theme? An organizing principle?"

Molly used all her acting skills not to look like a deer in headlights.

"Totally," said Molly, writing a script in her head as she began to speak. "It's sort of like Martha Stewart meets Rachael Ray by way of Alison Roman? Like old-school sophistication meets modern-day aesthetics? Fresh, local, organic ingredients. But not so fresh and organic that average people couldn't get them?"

Molly looked at Isabella intently, judging her reactions to see if she was passing the test. Isabella nodded, even though she had absolutely no idea what Molly was talking about.

"And I definitely don't want anything pretentious in there, like truffle oil. I fucking *hate* truffle oil."

This Isabella could agree with.

"I hate truffle oil, too," she said.

"Good, because truffle oil is disgusting."

Molly stabbed another spear of white asparagus with her fork and bit the tip off. Molly's "just the tip" approach to asparagus felt like something her character would do on *Malicious Angels* to intimidate a horny, religious date.

"I just want the book to be cool, with good recipes and things I'd actually eat. Like there's nothing wrong with nachos. But there has to be a twist. They can't just be nachos. They have to be special nachos. But healthy. Like maybe nachos with sweet potatoes? Cut into little triangles?"

Isabella felt like a first-chair violinist trying to follow a conductor who was having a seizure.

"Here's your glass of white," said the waiter. "I put a little extra in it for you. Our little secret."

"My lips are sealed," said Molly, as she lifted the glass and took another big sip. The waiter beamed as Isabella tried another tactic.

"If you had to reduce the book down to one sentence, it would be . . ."

Molly flashed her first hint of annoyance. Hadn't she given Isabella enough to work with already?

"It's really hard to reduce it down to one sentence," she stated flatly.

"But if you had to," pressed Isabella, eager to find anything to latch on to, anything that would give her a sense of what this cookbook was supposed to be.

Molly took another sip of her wine and put the glass down.

"I guess, if I had to say it all in one sentence, it would be . . ." She searched in her head for the answer. "Comfort food meets healthy food?"

Comfort food meets healthy food. This is something! I could work with this!

"Okay," she said. "I can see that."

Molly smiled like a C-minus student who suddenly got a B.

"Yay," said Molly, glad to be done with the cookbook portion of their conversation.

"The thing is, the kind of cookbooks that I love are autobiographical," continued Isabella, sitting upright in her seat, suddenly feeling activated. "So I'd love to take your concept and weave it through your own personal narrative. Like: What were the recipes you grew up with? Did your mom cook? Your dad? Your grandmother? That kind of stuff. And we could reinterpret those recipes with a healthy spin. And there can be pictures of you as a kid mixed in with pictures of you now and on *Malicious Angels*, and stories about starting your career and staying in shape but also loving food and throwing dinner parties, and all of that stuff."

Molly observed Isabella like she was studying a strange insect that had crawled up the window of her bedroom, drawn in by the light.

"Maybe this is a good time to ask . . . do you think it's possible that I could get a 'with'?" queried Isabella, remembering Alice's words. *Without a "with," you'll really be a ghost, and it won't do anything for your career, because you'll sign an NDA and nobody will know that you worked on it.*

"A what?"

"A 'with,'" said Isabella, realizing too late that she was asking for this too early. "Like 'A Cookbook by Molly Babcock *with* Isabella Pasternak.'"

Isabella hoped that her giddiness and enthusiasm would be

infectious. Instead, Molly reacted like Isabella herself was an infection.

"Isn't the point of having a ghostwriter that nobody knows that somebody helped you write the book?"

It was true, that was the traditional meaning of "ghostwriter." Those "with"s were more like cookbook collaborators rather than traditional ghostwriters.

"I have to go use the little girl's room," said Molly, getting up. "This volcanic white is erupting in my bladder."

"Okay," said Isabella, feeling slightly self-conscious about her big ask so early in their conversation.

Once Molly was gone, Isabella looked down and realized that almost all the food on the table had gone untouched. She wasn't sure whether she'd just royally fucked up the meeting—she was fairly certain that she'd just scared off her future employer—but she *was* sure that it would be a sin to let any of this food go to waste. So she did her good deed for the day and dug in.

. . . .

Isabella left precisely half of the ricotta, half of the caponata, and half of the tuna, on the unlikely chance that Molly would eat her portion when she got back from the bathroom. But as soon as Molly appeared again—fresh and bright and no longer agitated—she walked over to Isabella with an enormous look of apology on her face.

"I hate myself so much right now," she said, putting her hand on Isabella's shoulder. "But I totally fucked up. I have a play reading for a friend that I thought was at three, but it's actually at two."

It was currently two fifteen.

"Oh, that's totally fine," said Isabella, standing up, figuring this was goodbye forever.

"Don't get up," said Molly, pushing her back down. "I gave them my credit card, so you can order anything else you want. You still have that risotto coming."

"Right," said Isabella, who figured that the risotto would be her consolation prize.

"Here, give me your number," said Molly, handing Isabella her phone. "It'll be good to have your contact info."

Does that mean I got the job? Or is she just being polite?

"Sure," said Isabella, who punched in her number.

"Sweet," said Molly, taking the phone back.

The space for the name was still blank, and Isabella watched as Molly began to fill it in. She started putting in the letters for "Isabella," but then stopped herself, a grin on her face. She hit the backspace and erased the letters one by one as Isabella watched. She searched the emojis and found the perfect one.

There, in Molly's phone, she would no longer be known as Isabella Pasternak, aspiring food writer. She would be known as an emoji.

The ghost emoji.

7

A PIECE OF WORK

The text buzzed Isabella awake at three in the morning.

She'd already given up on the idea that Molly was going to hire her by the time she went to bed, four hours earlier. When Owen asked how the meeting went, Isabella said that she honestly didn't know: that at one moment she thought she and Molly were clicking, and then, the next moment, Molly was faking a play reading and leaving early. Owen tried to call and text Molly several times that night to see what was up, but Molly didn't answer. So, after gorging on pad thai and marathoning *Real Housewives*—New Jersey was where their *Housewives* Venn diagram overlapped—they went to their separate bedrooms feeling a potent sense of defeat. Owen blamed himself for not making Isabella wear better shoes. Isabella blamed herself for asking for the "with."

After replaying the lunch over and over again in her head for hours, she fell asleep around three, which is precisely when her phone came alive. Normally, she would've put her phone on sleep mode, but on this night she kept it awake, on the very unlikely, almost nonexistent chance that Molly would ping. And just when she'd drifted off, knowing that the ping would never come, the ping came.

You ever cook an egg in an avocado?

It was such an odd communication to receive in the middle of the night, Isabella had to read it three times before she could process its meaning and its subtext. Was Molly being playful? Mischievous? Friendly? Provocative?

Isabella finally texted, after stopping and starting again three times:

No, but I'm not against it philosophically?

This was Isabella's attempt at a little humor, even if she wasn't sure that it came across like humor. Did it seem like she was being a snob, even though she was making fun of herself for being a snob? Would Molly sense that underneath Isabella's self-parody was a lack of self-awareness about her snoblike tendencies?

Have you ever eaten at an Olive Garden?

Aha! So she was testing her snob quotient. Was that the reason that she didn't respond to Owen's missives? Because she thought Isabella was too full of herself? Too high-and-mighty? Too up her own ass with her speech about weaving the recipes through a personal narrative? Fortunately, Isabella had a surprising answer to this particular question:

All the time with my grandmother. It was her favorite restaurant.

This was completely true. Isabella's grandmother Beatrice (Jeannie's mother) ate almost exclusively at the Olive Garden when she retired to Florida in the early aughts. Isabella, whose own mother's frugality made any kind of restaurant dining—even chain-restaurant dining—seem like an extravagance, looked forward to visiting her grandmother for precisely this reason. Bottomless breadsticks, all-you-can-eat pastas, the Olive Garden may have been where it all began for Isabella: the idea that food could be a pleasure.

55 East 13th Street East Village Apt 5F

That third text from Molly arrived without any instructions or context or indication as to what she meant by it. Was that her address? Was Isabella supposed to go there? Isabella took a leap:

What time?

But Molly didn't respond to Isabella's query.

Instead, she concluded her unexpected string of communication with a benediction.

Goodnight 👻.

. . . .

Roast Chicken and Other Stories by Simon Hopkinson.
Prune by Gabrielle Hamilton.
Cooking by Hand by Paul Bertolli.

These were the cookbooks that Isabella gathered the next morning to bring to Molly's for inspiration. Without enough room for a bookshelf in her tiny room, she kept her most prized cookbooks in stacks under her bed, organized by mood. On the left were the cookbooks that she turned to when she was depressed (*You're All Invited* by Margot Henderson, *Food of Life* by Najmieh Batmanglij); in the middle were the cookbooks that she turned to when she felt bored (*To Asia, with Love,* by Hetty McKinnon, *Eat Me* by Kenny Shopsin); and on the right were the cookbooks that could reinspire her when she felt like quitting (*Zuni,* of course, *The Taste of Country Cooking* by Edna Lewis, and Nancy Silverton's *Sandwich Book*).

When Isabella emerged from her room at eleven and told Owen that she was on her way to Molly's, Owen did a double take.

"Wait—she called you?"

"She texted."

"Thank God!" he said, standing up and processing this new information, partly as Isabella's friend but also in his professional capacity as Molly's manager.

"What's your plan for going over there?"

Owen was nervous that Isabella would come on too intensely, like she probably had the day before. If only Isabella could just quietly execute this cookbook while flattering Molly's ego, he could work on getting Molly back out on auditions, after years of her refusing to take meetings with directors and casting agents. According to his dad, Hollywood had burned her badly, and this cookbook—which she'd endeavored to sell on her own—was her first gesture of wanting to return to the public eye. Owen suspected that the cookbook was a red herring: that underneath her refusal to go out for new parts and shows was a deep desire to do just that, that she just needed to be reactivated, get her confidence bolstered. The cookbook was the magic potion, and Isabella the unwitting wizard.

"I'm bringing some examples of the kind of cookbook we could write," said Isabella, placing the cookbooks in an Alice's Cookbook Emporium tote bag.

"You know you're not writing *The Joy of Cooking*, right? This is more *In the Kitchen with Kris* by Kris Jenner."

"I know that," said Isabella, who, like Owen, had ulterior motives of her own. While Owen was plotting to lure his first and only client back into film and TV, Isabella was plotting to make this book better than it had to be. If she could get Molly to pull from her own life experiences and then finesse that into a powerful collection of stories and recipes, she might have achieved something unexpected. Something notable. And if she did a good job, who knew where it all might lead? Ghostwriting books for Michelin three-starred chefs? Writing cookbooks of her own? Alice was right: this was a huge stepping stone to her dream career.

"Remember: This isn't about winning a James Beard award. It's about keeping the client happy."

"Of course," said Isabella, gathering her tote and heading for the door.

"Why do I get a sense that you're not listening to a single word that I'm saying?"

"Because," said Isabella over her shoulder, "you've always been a very keen observer."

And with that, Isabella headed out the door on her first day of work as a cookbook ghostwriter.

. . . .

Wealth comes in two different flavors in New York: the kind that announces itself and the kind that doesn't want to be seen.

Though Isabella had witnessed the former (diamond collars

on toy poodles, Lionel's unnecessarily huge apartment, Diplo performing at a Bat Mitzvah), she hadn't seen much of the latter. Molly was rich, Isabella was fairly certain, but when she arrived at her apartment on East Thirteenth Street, the building was barely notable. It looked like a college dorm, with antiseptic, institutional vibes. It was brick with metal trim, and the elevator in the lobby, with gray paint peeling off the doors, reminded her of an elevator in a parking garage.

Still, she wasn't here to shop for real estate. She was here to make a good impression. If yesterday she came on too strong, today she would take things a bit easier. She would lie low as she felt Molly out; learn more about her background, her history with food, the dishes that she loved the most, the ones that repulsed her. Riding the elevator up, Isabella knew that these were easy conversations to have if you didn't force them, and that they would be essential to her plan of attack. Molly's biography would form the backbone of their magnum opus, the book that would put Isabella (and Molly?) on the map.

When the elevator doors opened on the fifth floor, which was the top floor, she was surprised to find only one apartment entrance. Usually, an F indicates there are also A through E, but here the only apartment was apparently Molly's. (Had she bought all of the others and consolidated them?)

She rang the doorbell with one hand as she hoisted the heavy cookbook-filled tote with the other. She wouldn't offer up the cookbooks right away; she'd just have them to offer as "homework," though she wouldn't use the word "homework." She'd pretend they were a gift, though a gift that she wanted back. So maybe it wasn't a gift. Whatever! Somehow she would get Molly to read these books.

When the door opened, Isabella was prepared to see Molly out of costume. No makeup, dirty sweatpants, ancient sweatshirt, bags under her eyes from drunk texting about the Olive Garden the night before. Instead, she was greeted by a bug-eyed, brunette replica of Molly, about two inches taller, wearing ripped jeans and a green Jets jersey, and holding a beer.

"So you're the ghost," said the strange vision in the doorway. Her voice was slightly abrasive, slightly manic. If Molly had learned how to dial down her harsher edges, her doppelgänger clearly hadn't.

"Hi. Yes. I'm Isabella?"

The doppelgänger sized Isabella up and down before stepping aside. "She told me you looked like an Isabella."

What did it mean to look like an Isabella? Isabella still wasn't sure.

"I'm Fiona, her sister, in case you didn't figure it out," she said, as she watched Isabella enter.

Isabella took in the surprisingly stylish living room of the apartment. The space was tasteful, slightly retro, but with designery touches: saffron-colored walls, turquoise lacquered furniture, a vintage Danish leather sofa. The problem wasn't the design, it was the maintenance of the area. On every surface were piles of shopping bags, shoe boxes, Amazon boxes, ring lights, hair extensions, laptops, speakers, and random jewelry. There were so many things everywhere, with so many of them still in their packages, the apartment felt less like a living space and more like a very messy store.

"Mol's at the dermatologist," said Fiona, leading Isabella from the living room to the den, which also looked like it had been ransacked. "She says she's getting a mole removed, but we all know that she's getting the 'tox."

It took Isabella a second to realize what "the 'tox" was.

The living room had various awards on a mantel—MTV Award for Best Kiss (the famous death scene from her final episode), a Teen Choice Award for Choice TV Actress, a Satellite Award (whatever that was)—as well as framed pictures from *Malicious Angels*.

"So are you some kind of chef?" asked Fiona, facing Isabella as she led her farther into the apartment. "Because I googled you and I didn't see anything about you working at any restaurants?"

Isabella was all too familiar with this line of questioning.

Normally, when people asked her what she did and she'd respond "Food writer," they'd inevitably reply: "Oh . . . so you're a chef."

"No, not a chef. I write essays and articles about food for various media outlets."

Fiona took a swig from her beer.

"And that's a job?"

"Not according to my mother," said Isabella, attempting levity and instantly regretting it. Not only did Fiona not laugh, her eyes bore into Isabella like two klieg lights announcing the premiere of an extra-violent horror movie.

"You know, I'm the one who helped Molly with the cookbook proposal," said Fiona, once again leading Isabella deeper into the apartment, past framed black-and-white pictures of a younger Molly posing half naked for *Teen Vogue*. "I wrote the introduction, the table of contents, even a few recipes. True, I cribbed most of them from the internet, but the publisher said I could rewrite them later. You'd think she would've given me a shot to do the real thing."

Isabella nodded, trying to project compassion while now comprehending why Fiona was being so hostile.

"I'd love to see the work that you did."

"Why? So you can steal it?"

Fiona's edge was so sharp and sudden, it was like hanging out with a human bear trap.

Isabella followed Fiona as she turned left into a dining room with floor-to-ceiling windows looking north into Manhattan, featuring views of the Empire State Building, the Chrysler Building, and all of the less noteworthy skyscrapers. "She bought this place ten years ago, before interest rates went up the wazoo. Smartest decision she ever made. And, you should know, my sister doesn't make a lot of smart decisions."

As Isabella shifted her attention from the skyline to the dining room table, her gaze arrived at the enormous kitchen, which took up the entire other side of the room. The surfaces were glittery white marble. There was an island in the middle with a farmhouse sink and a pot rack hanging over it filled with vintage copper pots. There were two ovens, a Viking range, and a refrigerator that could've held three replicas of the dinky little refrigerator that she shared with Owen.

"Disgusting, right?" said Fiona, watching Isabella's face. "And guess how much she uses it?"

"It's the nicest kitchen I've ever seen in New York," declared Isabella, completely in awe as she entered the immaculate space. Whereas the living room felt like a flea market inside a swap meet, the kitchen felt like a mausoleum built for a queen. The room was grand and impressive, but also lifeless, as if it were waiting for an Arthur to come remove the chef's knife from the stone—to become its one true heir.

"I hope you're not expecting Molly to help you cook anything," said Fiona as she leaned on the counter. "Because I can guarantee you: she's going to make you do everything on your own."

Isabella, secure in her strategy, shrugged. "That's okay. I mostly just need to ask her about the kind of food she likes."

"Let me answer that. She doesn't like food."

Then why is she writing a cookbook? Isabella wanted to ask for the umpteenth time.

"I'm sure she likes food a *little*. I saw her eat fresh ricotta at lunch yesterday." She left out the fact that it was three dots of ricotta off the tines of a fork.

"Hey, it's your job now, not mine," said Fiona. "Oh, that reminds me."

She reached into her pocket and pulled out a rectangular piece of paper that was slightly crumpled and folded.

"Here's the first half. She'll pay you the second half when you turn in the book."

Fiona handed it over, and Isabella, realizing it was a check, looked down at the number—*$20,000*—and did her best not to express on the outside what she was feeling on the inside.

"Thanks," she said as fireworks exploded, marching bands trumpeted, and Beyoncé sang "Love on Top" all inside her chest.

"And here's some bullshit the lawyers want you to sign." She reached for a folder that was sitting on the kitchen counter. "Standard NDA. You can take it home before you sign it, if you want your lawyer to take a look."

My lawyer? She thinks I have a lawyer?

"Great," said Isabella, slipping the NDA into her tote bag.

"Okay, I've got to peace out. I do social for *The Kitty Lambrusco Show*, so I have to go live-tweet today's episode."

Kitty Lambrusco was a child star who had reemerged in the last decade with her own talk show, a show that quickly sailed up the ratings with its combination of heartfelt interviews, cooking demonstrations, and live musical performances.

"Cool. Thanks for showing me around."

She watched as Fiona entered the living room with her bottle of IPA and turned on the TV. She plopped onto the couch, opened up her laptop, and began live-tweeting to an audience of Kitty Lambrusco obsessives.

Left alone in the kitchen, Isabella struggled to feel a sense of herself in the space.

At first she'd felt like a welcome visitor; now she felt like the hired help. Here she was, in this immaculate kitchen, with no idea of what to do. How was she supposed to get started without anything to start? She hadn't even brought her laptop.

After taking a moment, she decided to orient herself by looking through the drawers and cabinets. If this was where she was going to be working for the next few months (even if Molly wouldn't be there working with her), she ought to familiarize herself with the space.

First she opened the refrigerator and saw something that looked like it was straight out of *2001: A Space Odyssey*. Lining the shelves were packages and packages of prearranged "healthy" meals made by a local company, Eat Petit, with daintily portioned scoops of whole grains (farro, quinoa), roasted vegetables (cauliflower, broccoli), and protein (tofu, chicken), each package carefully labeled with calorie counts and fat content. To Isabella, the whole thing looked like a giant, unpleasant fart.

Things didn't get much better when she opened the cabinets. One shelf held two solid rows of protein powder. Another shelf held two solid rows of soy milk. If AI had a kitchen, it would look something like this.

The more Isabella investigated, the more she realized that this kitchen lacked any kind of personality, any suggestion of a human presence, any hint of soul. If her goal was to extract from Molly a sense of her history and relationship to food, this kitchen was giving her less than nothing. She would've had an easier time analyzing the personality behind an airport vending machine than she would analyzing anything here.

"Hey," said Isabella, walking back toward Fiona, nervous about interrupting her but also loath to waste her time searching through drawers and drawers of nothingness.

"Yeah?" Fiona kept her full attention on Kitty, who was talking about a bad date that she'd had with a Lyft driver.

"The thing is . . . I was going to spend today talking to Molly about the food that she grew up with so I could create a sort of road map for the book. And I figured, since you're her sister, you could give me a little insight into—"

"Let me stop you right there," said Fiona, keeping her face glued to the TV. "I'm her *half*-sister. We didn't grow up in the same house."

"Oh. I didn't realize."

"So I have no idea what she ate growing up. For all I know, it was candy canes and SpaghettiOs."

Candy canes and SpaghettiOs. Sounded like something Jeannie would make.

"Okay. Thanks."

Just as Fiona was starting a new tweet, Isabella interrupted with another question.

"But . . . can I ask . . . what does she eat now? I mean, besides the meals in the fridge?"

Fiona exhaled loudly.

"If it has zero calories and it's devoid of all flavor and texture, she'll eat it. Hope that clears things up."

Fiona turned up the volume on the TV, and Isabella, no better off than she was a moment earlier, wandered back into the kitchen.

No laptop.

No culinary clues.

No Molly.

The only thing that she could think to do was the one thing that she was planning to do in the first place: cook lunch.

So, without saying anything to Fiona, she slid out the front door and rode the elevator down, intent on going to Whole Foods in Union Square to shop for something that Molly might find acceptable for her cookbook. And what did it matter if she didn't? She most likely wasn't going to be there anyway.

. . . .

An hour later, Isabella rang the doorbell again, and Fiona took her time answering it.

"You know, you can't just come and go as you please," said Fiona, on her fourth beer of the morning (Isabella could tell by the empty bottles in front of the TV). "When you're here, you're on the clock."

Fiona watched Isabella's reaction to see if this had any effect.

"I needed to get groceries, since there was nothing to cook," Isabella answered, holding up two full paper bags from Whole Foods.

"Well, I hope you don't think you're getting reimbursed for those. If Molly didn't approve it, it's coming out of your pocket."

Isabella, who actually was hoping to get reimbursed, brushed past Fiona with the bags and entered the kitchen. Owen had told her to take it easy on Molly, but hadn't said anything about being nice to her sister.

Her plan for lunch—and the first possible cookbook recipe—was simple: fish en papillote. It was an elegant technique whereby a fillet of white fish (in this case, cod) is placed inside a square of parchment paper with olive oil, thinly sliced lemons, sliced garlic, and herbs (basil, parsley), plus a splash of white wine, before being folded into a little packet and baked in a 425 oven for fifteen minutes. When it's done, each person gets their own little parcel of gently perfumed fish. The calorie count was low, the gourmet clout was high. Molly, should she ever get back from "the 'tox," would definitely be impressed.

Unsure of where to find a cutting board and knife, Isabella—who didn't want to ask anything more of Fiona for the rest of her employment, if she could help it—searched every cabinet and drawer until she found a still-wrapped-from-the-store plastic cutting board and chef's knife, still in the box, in a broom closet. She unwrapped both and got to work, preheating the oven, thinly slicing the lemon and the garlic, julienning the basil, and passing a knife through the parsley. Knowing that this kitchen wouldn't have any, she had bought a bottle of olive oil. Fairly certain the kitchen *would* have some, she'd skipped buying the white wine. And, sure enough, she found six bottles of Pinot Grigio in a cardboard box underneath the sink.

As the oven heated up, and Isabella prepared her packets, she entered that state of equanimity that frequently comes to those who take solace in everyday kitchen tasks, who find beauty in the smells and the sensations of tearing parchment, drizzling olive oil, arranging citrus and herbs thoughtfully along the surface of the fish. Just as she was about to start folding the packets, in a state of bliss that was surprising considering the inhospitable nature of her environment, she heard keys jangling in the front door, and suddenly an already-too-familiar voice punctured her reverie.

"Fee!" barked Molly, struggling through the doorway. "Can I get a little help? I texted you from the lobby!"

There was a harshness to Molly's tone that completely undercut the sweetness with which she had (mostly) performed at lunch.

"I'm working!" Fiona barked back.

"I'm carrying three bags of skin products and also the dry

cleaning," continued Molly as she bounded into the apartment. "Why does it smell like a warm aquarium in here?"

With that line, Isabella felt her heart leap up into her chest. *The smell*, she suddenly realized. What was the biggest clue of all in this cold, lifeless kitchen? It didn't take a Columbo to realize that Molly didn't like anything that smelled like actual food. Even the actual food looked like it was made of wax.

Before Isabella could make a move to hide the fishy evidence, Molly dropped her bags on the couch and marched straight into the kitchen.

"What are you doing?" she asked, as she entered the space, staring at Isabella like she'd walked in on an unhinged neighbor urinating in the sink.

"I was trying out a recipe for the cookbook," stammered Isabella. "I just thought I'd take a shot."

Molly closed her eyes and took a deep breath. Isabella could almost hear her counting to ten.

"Listen," she said, opening her eyes again to reveal a forced Zen-like countenance. "I realize that you probably had good intentions . . . but I have just one rule when it comes to cooking in my apartment."

"Okay?"

"No. Fucking. Fish."

And with that she went to the sink, opened the cabinet underneath, and pulled out a garbage bag. She went to the counter where Isabella had been working and scooped both parchment squares into it, including the two perfectly translucent, gleaming fillets of fresh cod that Isabella had spent twenty-five dollars on out of her own pocket.

"The smell never comes out," said Molly, as if justifying her actions. "Can you throw this down the garbage chute on your way home? We need to get this out of here right away."

She tied up the garbage bag with the black plastic pulls and handed it to Isabella as if Isabella were already on her way out the door.

"Sure," she responded, dumbstruck by what was happening.

"Sorry if I'm being a bitch right now," said Molly, putting her hand on Isabella's back and ushering her back through the apartment. Isabella grabbed her tote bag on the way, thinking now wouldn't be the time to give Molly homework. "I had a mole removed, and it was really painful."

Before she knew it, Isabella was back in the hallway, holding a garbage bag in one hand and her tote bag full of cookbooks in the other.

"Can you put it down the chute on a different floor? I don't want to take any chances. That smell is already ruining my day," said Molly, before closing the door on her ghostwriter.

Isabella stood there, stunned, feeling more disoriented than the time she confused a Key Food for a Whole Foods and came home with substandard broccolini.

When she came to, she wondered if she could bring the garbage bag full of fish, lemon slices, garlic, and white wine on the subway home to make for dinner. Would she get dirty looks from the other passengers? Would it be worth it? What would Owen say if she came back to the apartment with a leaky garbage bag full of cod?

Ignoring Molly's directive, she opened the chute right across from Molly's apartment and dropped in the bag.

What a waste, Isabella thought to herself as she entered the elevator. *A waste of food, a waste of money, a waste of time.*

Then she remembered the twenty-thousand-dollar check in her pocket, and immediately her spirits lifted.

· · · ·

Even when Isabella did the math in her head—when she took out the inevitable taxes, the cost of living, the ingredients that she wouldn't get reimbursed for (at least for now), the travel to and from Molly's apartment—twenty thousand dollars was an incredible amount of money to deposit into her bank account all at once.

She left Molly's industrial gray building, holding the check like a talisman, a good-luck charm, a piece of evidence that, even if she'd literally just been shown the door, she still had a job. Because, once she deposited that check, that money was hers, and once that money was hers, it didn't matter whether Molly made her throw the fish away or not. Once money exchanged hands, the job had officially started. She was officially a paid ghostwriter.

The depositing wasn't as thrilling as she wanted it to be. She walked into a Chase Manhattan and waited in the little line for a teller, and when it was her turn, she smiled a full smile and flushed a little red, as if the teller would be destabilized by the amount that was on the check.

"Hi," she said, both giddy and embarrassed. "I'd like to make a deposit?"

The blank-faced bank teller barely made eye contact, let alone smiled. Without any fanfare, she deposited the check, and when Isabella left the bank, she held a receipt that confirmed that she was now twenty thousand dollars richer.

Twenty thousand dollars! What to do? How to celebrate?

She was in the East Village, and Isabella, who had a *Terminator*-like ability to scan any neighborhood and know the best places to eat, quickly remembered that a new French bistro had opened near Tompkins Square Park called Snakebite.

According to *Eater NY,* the chef at Snakebite, Casper Dusolier, was a punk-rock import from Paris who took classic dishes and turned them on their heads. His oeufs mayonnaise featured squid ink. His French onion soup was made with kohlrabi. His boeuf bourguignon involved a five-day process so complex it was patented.

Famously, Snakebite offered a sixty-five-dollar prix-fixe lunch menu that was all the rage in the food-writer community.

"Best deal in all of New York," Ruth Reichl wrote on her Instagram after posting a slide show of the dishes that she'd eaten there. Isabella had texted it to herself as a reminder that this lunch existed and that, should circumstances arise in which she might be in the neighborhood with time to kill and money to burn, it would be an excellent option. At the time, the idea that she would have time to kill and money to burn felt impossible. Now it was a reality.

She used her phone to navigate her way there, getting more and more excited by the second. When had she ever treated herself to a fancy solo lunch like this? What would her mother say? "Sixty-five dollars on lunch for yourself? *Are you out of your mind?*"

When she arrived at Avenue A and Sixth Street, she saw the bistro on the corner with a little crowd gathered outside. She walked toward it and saw the word "Snakebite" discreetly printed on the yellow awning. Even the font was stylish.

As she walked closer to the entryway, she felt her eagerness melt into nervousness. She looked through the windows and saw that every table was taken and that there was one seat at the bar, but that the woman sitting next to it, eating by herself, had placed her bag there as a way to shoo other diners away. Would she have the courage to ask the woman to move her bag? Would she have the chutzpah to push through the small crowd to ask for a seat for one? Who did she think she was, anyway?

"Hey!" came a strangely familiar voice.

Isabella turned and saw a smiley, red-cheeked chef hauling out a bag of garbage, just like she'd done moments earlier.

"Isabella, right? I'm Gabe Kohl. You were interviewing me for an article about sous-chefs, and then you ghosted me?"

It all came rushing back to Isabella: the worst day of her life, embodied in a single human face.

"Oh, hey," she said. "Sorry about that. I kind of got fired that day."

Gabe flinched.

"That sucks!"

"Yeah, it really does."

"Are you coming in to eat?" he asked, stepping slightly closer to her, the freckles on his face lighting up in the gray sunlight. "I just started here last week, and the food is seriously bad-ass."

There was no doubting it: Gabe was cute. But Isabella's fantasy of eating lunch here was all about doing it anonymously. She'd imagined herself as a chic literary type, sipping Pinot Gris at the counter while reading a short story in *The New Yorker*. Now that she'd been recognized by Gabe, she'd have to eat lunch as herself by herself, which completely ruined the fantasy.

"No, I can't," she lied, fully capable of eating lunch. "I'm actually really late for a doctor's appointment. But good running into you again."

Isabella skittered away, abandoning Gabe for the second time, as she hurried up to the L train back to Greenpoint.

She might have been twenty thousand dollars richer, but she was still Isabella Pasternak. And Isabella Pasternak didn't treat herself to afternoon flirtations with cute sous-chefs before sixty-five-dollar lunches by notable Parisian chefs.

Isabella Pasternak didn't treat herself, period.

8

BRING TO A RAPID BOIL

"Why don't you just quit? That's what I would do. I would quit."

As was frequently the case, Isabella wasn't sure how she'd wound up at her mother's apartment that afternoon instead of going straight home. Maybe it was because of the way Molly ushered her out the door: like she was less than human, a noxious gas, a mite on a speck of dust that was irritating the fine hairs on the back of her neck. At least her mother lavished her with attention, albeit a toxic sort of attention, the kind of attention that made her feel like a houseplant on the surface of the sun: the rays might occasionally be nourishing, but they mostly set her on fire.

"I can't just quit," she answered, while sniffing a bowl of mysterious solid white matter that her mother placed before her, relieved that it wasn't one of her soups. "I made a commitment."

"A commitment to work for a shallow celebrity who's already treating you like crap?"

"Pretty much. What even is this?"

"Potato Fluff," Jeannie said cheerfully, gobbling up a bite from her own fork. "Gristedes had sixteen jars of Fluff they were throwing away, so I mixed that with sixteen boxes of dried mashed potatoes. I think it's delicious. Will you help me bring it to the shelter later?"

Isabella now understood why her mouth felt more cottony than it did at the dentist's.

"Why do you want to make unhoused people suffer more than they already do?"

Jeannie rolled her eyes. "You're such a snob."

"I know," said Isabella, lowering her head into her hands. "That's the problem. I need to just suck it up and write a shitty cookbook. But I can't bring myself to do it."

"Listen," said Jeannie, attempting to change the subject. "I'm getting fifteen cartons of rejected yellow onions over the next few weeks. Will you promise to help me make a big vat of French onion soup? You can even do a snobby version if you want, just as long as it doesn't cost anything. I want to bring over gallons and gallons of it, so that they have enough for the cold weather."

Isabella was too emotionally drained to fight with her mother.

"Fine, sure, whatever."

"Great," said Jeannie, opening up her purse and pulling out a day planner from 1997 that she'd found at a flea market. "Let's say October twenty-first."

Isabella was still thinking about her cookbook problems as she unconsciously lifted another forkful of potato fluff to her mouth. She immediately spat it out into a napkin.

"Oh, stop being so dramatic," said Jeannie. "You're lucky I didn't add the maraschino cherries."

· · · ·

The next few weeks went something like this.

Isabella would get a text in the middle of the night. One night the text read:

Would Cool Ranch Doritos be good in a salad with ranch dressing??

Another night it read:

Do you know the chef from Torrisi? Can you get me in?

Another night:

Can we make the Alison Roman anchovy pasta without the anchovies?

These would inevitably arrive at the most inopportune hours. Some would come at two, others at four. If Isabella didn't answer, she would wake up the next morning with a string of texts:

Hell.loooo?

Are you there 👻? It's me molly

LOL, now your 👻ing me

seriously, y aren't you replying?

Call me when you get this

The next day, Isabella would arrive at Molly's apartment expecting to be chastised for not texting her back (she'd taken to putting her phone on Do Not Disturb), but, depending on Molly's mood, she would either be lighthearted and carefree, with zero memory of the late-night texts and Isabella's nonresponse, or she would be absent altogether.

The problem was that lighthearted, carefree Molly was way more disturbing to Isabella than dismissive Molly.

"Hiiiii," she'd say, answering the door in yoga pants and a tank top, glowing from a morning workout and a shower. "Can I give you a hug? You look like you could use a hug."

This version of Molly was almost eerily upbeat, as if she'd snorted a line of Zoloft before greeting her ghost. She would be completely passive in the kitchen: deferring to Isabella at every turn.

"Whatever you think."

"Whatever you want."

"I'm not even that hungry."

They'd go together to Whole Foods to get the ingredients for a quinoa salad that Molly saw on Instagram, and Isabella would discreetly try to get any personal information from Molly that she might be able to spin into a recipe headnote (she'd yet to write a solid one).

"Do you remember the first time that you ate quinoa?"

"Maybe in L.A.?" said Molly, scrolling on her phone while Isabella grabbed the ingredients. "Or was it New York? No, probably L.A. It would make sense that I had quinoa for the first time in L.A. Actually, I think it might've been Cape Cod?"

Isabella would stuff flat-leaf parsley into a plastic bag and try again when they got back to Molly's. She'd be at the counter, chopping vegetables and boiling the quinoa in a pink pot. (Isabella later learned that all of the cooking equipment had been purchased by Molly's interior decorator to make the kitchen "pop.")

"What about salad? Have you always liked salad?" asked Isabella, doing her cherry-tomato trick, where she put a bunch of cherry tomatoes between two soup-container lids so that she could slice them in half all at once—a trick that she planned to offer up as a cookbook sidebar.

"Salad? I don't think so. I mean, I didn't eat a lot of it growing up. But even when I eat it now, it's just okay? It's not like I love it or anything. It's really kind of basic."

Isabella would go home that night and attempt to spin this conversation into an introduction:

QUINOA SALAD WITH DRIED CHERRIES AND PICKLED RED ONIONS

I don't remember the first time that I ate quinoa, and I can't say that I've ever really been a big fan of salads (they're kind of basic), but I saw this one on Instagram and I was immediately hooked. Tart dried cherries and punchy pickled onions—this salad rescues quinoa from the dusty aisle of the health-food store and whisks it to the sweaty bedrooms of the Red Light District in

Amsterdam . . . where hairy male tourists with stiff erections are straddled by buxom blondes, their breasts glistening lasciviously in the moonlight . . .

Isabella would hit backspace on the only colorful part of her paragraph and try again.

You can bring this salad to a picnic. You can bring this salad to a wedding. You can bring this salad to my funeral, because I would rather die than finish writing this inane headnote.

That night, another string of texts appeared:

Have you ever seen a picture of microwave popcorn out of the bag before you pop it?

Isn't it the most disgusting?

It looks like fake throw-up

I'm weirdly craving it right now

Isn't that sick?????

Like I want to lick it like a lollipop

All that congealed butter

It sounds soooo good right now

Lol

The next day, Fiona would answer the door and say, "Molly's DOA," and Isabella would spend the afternoon putzing around the kitchen, riffing on things that Molly had texted to her from Instagram; a silent, solemn Molly would emerge from her room, grab herself a Pamplemousse LaCroix from the fridge, brush past Isabella without saying a word, and then go back to her bedroom, closing the door a bit too loudly.

Molly's erratic behavior seemed to correspond to the little

blips and blurps of gossip sites that still wrote about her love life (Isabella set a Google alert for "Molly Babcock" just to stay informed), which involved her on-again, off-again fling with her former costar and former heartthrob, Xavier Mordechai. Xavier's ratio of hotness to sleaziness had rebalanced itself over the years; now he seemed more leathery than the clothes he wore. They were frequently seen together stumbling out of bars, stumbling out of concerts, stumbling out of restaurants. The paparazzi's photos painted a clearer picture for Isabella of what was really going on, and would accurately predict the kind of mood Molly would be in the next day.

It got to the point where Isabella felt like she could put literally anything into this cookbook—her aunt Rhoda's kasha varnishkes, sushi to be served on a naked model, her mother's potato fluff (God forbid)—and Molly would either hug her with benign indifference or ignore her completely. It was like she was trying to write a song for a singer who didn't care about singing, who would rather not sing, who didn't really like music, who would actually rather not listen to it if she could avoid it.

Isabella didn't want to admit it, but her mother's advice to quit was beginning to seem like the sanest option. Another job might be just as miserable, but at least it wouldn't require her to besmirch the one thing that she loved the most in the world. She would rather sit in a cubicle writing about sports or mutual funds than sit in Molly Babcock's kitchen for another day, writing a cookbook that was doomed to be not only irrelevant, but downright bad.

· · · ·

"There's something she's not telling you. Something she's hiding."

Alice bit into a brown-butter coconut cookie that she'd made at home from a recipe that she found on the internet: a rare departure for someone who cooked almost exclusively from her thousand-tome cookbook collection.

"What could she be hiding?" asked Isabella as she went for her second coconut cookie. "That she doesn't cook or eat anything? Because, if that's her secret, she's really bad at keeping it."

That morning's Molly encounter had started with Isabella trying to trigger some (any!) memory or anecdote or opinion about food from Molly by bringing in the ingredients to make plain, ordinary, everyday brownies: the kind that every kid at some point makes with their parents or grandparents or friends in high school. The kind where you lick the spoon, the bowl, the beater. The kind that makes you fall in love with cooking in the first place. Perhaps Molly would talk about the time she and her mother made brownies for the Girl Scouts, or the time she lost her virginity while baking a batch of brownies with her high-school sweetheart.

"Can you *not* bring sugar into my apartment right now?" snapped Molly as Isabella started unpacking the groceries. "I'm sorry, but I'm starting a new diet this week, and I'm not doing any sugar or carbs. Just looking at that Ghirardelli is giving me a panic attack."

Isabella repacked the bags and returned the flour, the sugar, the butter, and the chocolate to Whole Foods. (She still hadn't been reimbursed for any ingredient.)

"She must have *some* kind of history with food," posited Alice, who sipped her idiosyncratic tea (Onyx Peppermint Yerba Mate) out of her idiosyncratic mug (a vintage *Regis and Kathie Lee* mug that her mother had scored at a taping). "I bet you anything that she grew up loving to eat . . . that someone in her family was an incredible cook. Why else would she be interested in writing a cookbook?"

"Because it's the last vestige of the failed celebrity? Because she wants to resuscitate her career?" Isabella was dubious that Molly was motivated by anything other than narcissism.

"Maybe," said Alice. "But there's something about the way that she's texting you these food questions late at night, and the way that she knew what to order at Lodi, and the way that she has her defenses up when you're in the kitchen with her—either acting like a total bitch or numbing herself with some kind of drug—that makes me think that she actually really cares about all of this but is afraid to reveal how much."

Isabella initially came to Alice's to treat herself to a few vintage cookbooks with her ghostwriting money. Now she was once again soaking up Alice's wisdom like ladyfingers in a tiramisù.

"If that's true, how do I access that part of her? Because, if it exists, it's buried deeper inside of her than yesterday's raw kale smoothie."

Alice poured more tea for herself from her bright-yellow teapot and audibly said "Hmmm" while she pondered.

"What's your favorite cookbook?" she asked at last.

If a normal person asked this question of Isabella, she'd be flustered. The fact that the question was coming from Alice made it feel extremely high-stakes.

"I guess . . . I'd have to say *Zuni*?" Isabella said after some contemplating, referring to the iconic *Zuni Cafe Cookbook* written by the late Judy Rodgers and published in 2002. "It's got everything. Voice, style, incredible recipes. I could take it to a desert island and never be bored."

"So give her your copy of *Zuni* and explain to her why you love it."

If Alice had suggested that Isabella saw off her right arm and hand it to Molly, the suggestion would've been less shocking.

"You mean give her my own personal copy? As a gift?"

Alice shrugged. "It's just a cookbook. I'll give you another one."

"But why would I give her my copy of *Zuni*?"

"Because," Alice said, as if she were explaining the most obvious thing in the world, "you're trying to convey to her how important cookbooks are to you, why she should be taking this seriously. So the gesture of giving her a cookbook that's so personal to you, so meaningful, might have an effect on her. It might unlock something."

Isabella grabbed a third cookie and contemplated giving

away her most precious cookbook to someone who didn't seem to value much of anything, least of all Isabella.

"I'll think about it," she finally concluded.

"It's just a cookbook," said the woman who devoted her entire life and career to procuring and selling them.

. . . .

What Isabella didn't tell Alice, and what made her hesitate at the suggestion, was that her copy of *Zuni* wasn't just precious to her because she loved Judy Rodgers's recipes and writing. It was precious to her because it was the last thing that her father bought for her before he died.

She remembered the trip to San Francisco more vividly than things that had happened to her just a few days ago. Her mother, of course, stayed home, finding the trip "too indulgent," "too unnecessary," "something that we most definitely can't afford." Her dad, on the other hand, found the trip not at all indulgent, highly necessary, and within their means, especially as a way to support his daughter's burgeoning interest in food.

As an antiques dealer, Oliver often encountered old books— whether at estate sales or garage sales or even online—and when Isabella first showed an interest in collecting vintage cookbooks (the *Time Life* series of cookbooks were her gateway drug), he would bring her any random distinguished-looking tome he could find. The fact that her earliest obsession was *The Chez Panisse Menu Cookbook* led him to propose a trip to Berkeley to eat at the storied restaurant in real life.

"When do we ever go anywhere?" he argued at the dinner table. "When do we ever do anything?"

Jeannie couldn't fathom a worse way to spoil their daughter than to fly her three thousand miles just to eat overpriced versions of fruits and vegetables that they could buy on sale at Gristedes.

"What's this going to teach her? That she can just go on a whim to eat at one of the world's great restaurants because that's what she wants to do?" Jeannie was always fighting for her daughter not to become spoiled, like the wealthy children of doctors and lawyers that she herself went to school with, the ones who grew up to be assholes.

"Exactly," said Oliver. "Because being whimsical is actually a good thing."

It was while they were in San Francisco that Oliver had the idea to add a lunch at Zuni to their itinerary, for the café's famous roast chicken with bread salad. Isabella had heard of Zuni—peripherally, through books like *The United States of Arugula* by David Kamp—but once she was there, in the large houselike structure, she instantly fell in love. They sat at the bar and had oysters and chicken-liver mousse and shiny, briny green olives. Her father ordered her a glass of champagne, even though she hadn't yet turned twenty-one. And when the famous roast chicken with bread salad came to the table, Isabella had never seen anything more beautiful in her life.

On the way out the door, they clocked stacks of *The Zuni Cafe Cookbook* on a shelf by the wall, and her father, without asking, bought her a copy to keep as a souvenir.

"Maybe you'll make me that chicken one day," he suggested. Whenever Isabella opened the book, she got emotional, because she knew, now, that she never would.

In bed, she vacillated back and forth between following Alice's advice and ignoring it. On the one hand, Molly was irresponsible, unreliable, mostly unlikable. The idea of giving her something so precious was not only absurd, it was an act of self-harm. On the other hand, Molly was walled up, disengaged, inaccessible. Being emotional and earnest and sharing with her a prized possession was a big risk, but a big risk with a potentially big reward. A career-saving reward.

The next morning, Isabella texted Molly instead of Molly texting Isabella.

I have a little gift for you.

It took three minutes for Molly to respond:

That's sooooo sweet

Running L8 today

Feel free to get started!!!!

Isabella knew what that meant: a morning of mindless cooking and typing nonsense into her laptop in Molly's enormous kitchen. Since the brownie debacle, Isabella had decided to cook exclusively from the healthy/fitness-forward food accounts that Molly followed on Instagram. Today would be a crispy-rice-and-avocado bowl with mushrooms and furikake.

As Isabella arrived for that day's work—Fiona, of course, let her in and then completely ignored her so she could live-tweet Kitty Lambrusco's interview with Ricky Martin—she held the *Zuni* book under her arm, trying not to think too deeply about what it was that she was about to give away. Did she have to give it to Molly? Couldn't she just lend it to her? No, if she lent it to her, it wouldn't have the same impact. Molly would probably put it aside and never look at it.

As the hours ticked by, Isabella kept studying the *Zuni* book cover out of the corner of her eye, having placed it next to the microwave. She studied it while crisping the rice. While slicing the avocado. While sautéing the mushrooms.

When Molly finally entered the kitchen, she was in workout clothes from Pilates and typing something into her phone.

"Hey, that looks good," she said as she glanced up, observing Isabella's handiwork. "I'm going to go lie down for a bit, but you can just leave it on the counter. I'll scarf it down later."

This was Molly's new thing: treating Isabella like her live-in personal chef instead of her collaborator on a cookbook that she herself was supposed to be writing. Just Molly's dismissive, undermining tone made Isabella want to recant the idea of giving her the most precious thing that she owned, but instead she found herself saying: "Wait, I have a gift for you."

Molly, who'd compartmentalized Isabella's text in the same part of her brain where she kept unimportant tidbits, like her cousin's baby's name, turned back around.

"Oh, right," she said. "You got me a gift. I completely forgot."

Isabella lifted the book off the counter, unsure of what she expected to happen and hoping that Alice—who rarely steered her wrong in life—was on to something and not forcing her to do something that she would deeply regret.

"This is my favorite cookbook of all time," said Isabella, her voice cracking a little. "It's from the Zuni Café, in San Francisco. Have you heard of it?"

"Of course I've heard of Zuni," said Molly, who wouldn't admit it if she hadn't. She hated the idea that anyone might think of her as uncultured.

"This is the copy that my dad bought for me on our trip there. It's actually one of the last things that he ever gave me before he died."

At first, Isabella felt like she'd gone too far, that this was less a stab at intimacy and more an acute case of oversharing. But just when she thought Molly would back away, claiming a migraine, Molly, instead, looked up at her intensely.

"Oh my God. When did you lose your dad?"

She put her phone down on the counter and searched Isabella's face with her probing blue eyes.

"About four years ago. He got killed by a truck."

"I'm so sorry," said Molly, those famous eyes turning watery. "My mom died five years ago . . . I still think about her all the time."

"How did she die?"

Molly leaned back against the refrigerator.

"She wasn't exactly the picture of health," said Molly, almost to herself. "She drank, she smoked, she liked to fry everything, she used butter like it was one of the major food groups. She was an amazing cook."

An amazing cook? Why didn't she mention this before?

"Well, I wanted you to have this," said Isabella, digesting this new information and handing the cookbook over. "It's really important to me, and I thought that it might inspire you to think about what your cookbook can be. Not just in terms of the writing or the recipes, but something that's emotionally important to you . . . the way this cookbook is really emotionally important to me."

Molly took the cookbook from Isabella slowly and deliberately, feeling the cover with her hand and then hugging it to her chest.

"I don't know what to say," said Molly. "Are you really sure you want me to have this?"

Isabella nodded, not sure at all.

Molly put the book down and gave Isabella a big hug, not a perfunctory one like the ones she would sometimes give her when she was in a good mood. This was a solemn hug, the kind of hug you give someone who's suffered the same way that you've suffered.

"It's nice to meet someone who knows what it's like to lose a parent," said Molly softly, as she pulled away and wiped her nose on her workout T-shirt. "Thank you for this. This really means a lot. Truly."

And with that, Molly took the cookbook into her room and closed the door.

Isabella returned to the mushroom bowl, feeling triumphant and hopeful that maybe this would be the turning point; that they might end up writing a decent cookbook after all.

· · · ·

"I don't understand. How could you have zero recipes done? You've been doing this for three weeks!"

Owen's ambitions and Isabella's dreams had never intersected before. As long as she'd known him, Isabella had been aware that Owen could be cutthroat in whatever situation he found himself in: the gym, a gay bar, the line for the bathroom at a Broadway show. But unless they were playing Scrabble or talking politics, Owen rarely displayed his aggressiveness around Isabella. If anything, she brought out his gentler side. Until now.

"Okay, here's the deal," he said, leaning over her at the small kitchen table—too small for him to pull up a chair. "This cookbook is the means to an end, it's not the end."

"I don't follow," said Isabella, who was reading that month's *Food & Wine*, a magazine that she'd been subscribing to, along with *Bon Appétit* and *Cook's Illustrated*, since leaving her mother's apartment, where magazine subscriptions were seen as *The Queen of Versailles*–style excess.

"My job is to get Molly back out there, to send her out for auditions, to put her on TV," explained Owen, as if he were explaining Texas Hold'em poker to a six-year-old. "This cookbook is just a way to raise her profile. To help get her on talk shows, on podcasts, on magazine covers. The sooner the cookbook is done, the sooner she'll have some heat behind her, and—kablam—we're off to the races, and you're off to the races, too, because, the more famous she gets, the more copies she'll sell."

He smacked his hand on the table to emphasize his point, startling Isabella away from a recipe for pork vindaloo.

"Can you calm down? I'm working on it."

"Can you show me what you've done already?"

"No, Owen," said Isabella, invoking his name in a way that she rarely did, unless they were in a fight. "When the deadline comes, there'll be a cookbook, and you can parlay that into whatever you want."

"Don't say 'parlay' to me."

"*Parlay.*"

"Touché."

"By the way," said Isabella, lowering the magazine as she recalled a question that had been bothering her for a while, "when do I get to speak to the editor? It'd be nice to have someone else on my side, to help me figure out what kind of book this is supposed to be, to give me some direction."

Owen was waiting for this one. His tone immediately shifted from playful to corporate.

"Mirror Mirror will act as the go-between between you and the publisher. Any editorial concerns will go through us."

It was like he was reciting a cue card written by his father. Apparently, Lionel wasn't just a manager, he was a micromanager. He wanted to filter the manuscript before the publisher had a chance to filter it further.

"So I don't get to talk to the editor?"

"Nope," said Owen, opening a Red Bull, the fizz sound mirroring the static of his words. "You don't need to. Just write the best book that you can, and we'll take it from there. Now, get to it!"

Owen returned to his room, and Isabella returned to the pork vindaloo recipe, making a mental note that the next time Owen asked about her cookbook progress, she should just lie and say that things were coming along swimmingly.

. . . .

The next morning, Isabella walked from the L train stop on First Avenue to Molly's apartment with a kick in her step. She and Molly had genuinely bonded the day before, hadn't they? Handing her that cookbook had unlocked a door in Molly, just like Alice said it would. Alice was right about everything. For the rest of her life, Isabella would defer to Alice about any issue, big or small, food-related or otherwise. Now it was all so clear: the key to this cookbook was Molly's mother, their relationship, what they cooked together, and so on. At last, there was finally going to be some there there. She just had to continue the conversation that they'd started yesterday.

Even Fiona couldn't puncture Isabella's good mood when she answered the door.

"What are you grinning about?" she asked as Isabella beamed at her, a big smiley Big Bird to Fiona's Oscar the Grouch.

"Just excited to work on the book today, that's all."

"Right," said Fiona. "Can you keep your enthusiasm to yourself? I'm moderating an Instagram Live for Kitty, and I can't have any distractions."

When she entered the kitchen, Molly was nowhere to be seen, but that wasn't unusual. There was a pot of coffee, which Isabella had learned was brewed by a maid who came at five in the morning so that Molly didn't have to interact with her while she did her cleaning (it made Molly feel too guilty, apparently). Making a big pot of coffee was the maid's final task before she left at eight, and Isabella, who arrived every day at ten, partook of it, assuming that it was for everyone.

She was pouring a mugful for herself when Molly emerged from her room, and just from the sound of the door opening, Isabella knew that today was going to be a Bad Molly Day. On a Bad Molly Day, she flung her bedroom door open, like the door itself was a nuisance.

"Is it possible for you not to drink my coffee before I do?" asked Molly when she discovered Isabella in the kitchen.

Molly looked like she'd only gone to bed a few hours earlier—her hair was disheveled, her makeup from the previous night was smeared around her face—and her hangover was so profound, even Isabella could feel it.

"Sorry," said Isabella, stepping out of the way.

"Just so you know, I'm not going to be able to cook today," said Molly, sliding past Isabella and sloshing coffee into a mug, most of it getting on the counter. "You can just keep doing whatever it is that you normally do when you're here."

Isabella knew the ropes. She could now, ever so gently, with the finesse required of a brain surgeon, try to glean from Molly a direction for that day's recipe.

"I totally get it," said Isabella, using empathy as a tool. Then it was time for the prod: "Did you, by any chance, get to take a look at the book?"

The book was the segue, the bridge from yesterday's moment of earnestness to today's moment of sourness. Perhaps the earnestness could undo some of the sourness? Like adding honey to a salad dressing to offset the vinegar?

"What book?"

Isabella took a beat and then gave Molly a look that said, "C'mon, we both know what book I'm talking about." Simply by locking eyes with Molly, Isabella hoped that she could soften her a little; that she could reaccess that part of her, that tender part, that had led to such an emotional connection the day before.

"Oh fuck. You mean that heavy cookbook you gave me? I think I left it in an Uber on my way to dinner."

There were many sentences that had affected Isabella over the course of her life. Sentences that would forever change her, sentences that would live inside of her, the words printed into her skull like they were stamped there with hot lava. One of them was "Izzy, Daddy's been in an accident" (Jeannie on the phone, the night of her father's death); another was "I don't feel the feeling you're supposed to feel when someone has feelings for you" (Jake Lipman, her high-school crush, rejecting her while simultaneously coming out). But no sentence that she would ever hear for the rest of her life would ignite the gas inside of her, activate her inner fury, the way that the sentence Molly had just uttered would. *I think I left it in an Uber on my way to dinner.*

"How could you do that?" stammered Isabella, feeling an actual wound forming somewhere inside of her. "I told you how important that book was to me."

"Sorry," said Molly, continuing to stir oat milk into her coffee. "I'm not sure why you gave me such a personal book if you cared about it so much."

Isabella's fuse, famously long, now blew in an instant.

"I gave it to you . . . because I thought that maybe, somewhere, inside of you . . . there was the tiniest semblance of a *soul*."

Isabella's cheeks were bright red, as was her neck, as hot tears filled her eyes.

"What did you say?"

"I thought that maybe . . . maybe beneath all of the . . . all of the hair products and the lip gloss and the eye shadow," said Isabella, her voice shaking, along with her hands, "there was an actual human being inside of you. But . . . there's nothing human about you."

The look on Molly's face was one of both shock and awe at the fury stirred up in Isabella.

"You're just . . . an empty vessel. You're all exterior. And you'll never write a great cookbook or do anything great in your life, because . . . because whatever part of you was human, whatever part of you existed that could connect with other people, is gone and it's all been replaced by . . . by . . . *Botox.*"

Isabella put her mug down and headed for the door. Molly, too stunned to speak, watched her.

As Isabella pulled open the handle, she turned back one last time:

"Good luck with the cookbook. You can delete me from your phone. I'm going to keep you in mine and change your name to an emoji, just like you did with me. Only your emoji is going to be . . . it's going to be a smiling piece of shit!"

With that parting shot, Isabella slammed the door and felt herself go from transparent to opaque, from vapor to solid, from shadow to the person casting the shadow. She was no longer a ghost, she was a writer.

A writer without a job.

9

HOME-COOKED

Moments later, emerging back into the bright October glare of East Thirteenth Street, Isabella felt certain that the high that she was still experiencing—her heart thumping like a Kitchen-Aid kneading bread dough, her cheeks stained red like she'd dipped her face in strawberry syrup—wouldn't last. It would invert itself like an hourglass, and all the sand in the happy upper part of the chamber would flow into the dark, depressing part of the chamber, and it would take her weeks, maybe months, to recover. She could already anticipate endless days and nights holed up in her bedroom, watching old episodes of *Great Chefs* on YouTube, eating Vienna Fingers, drinking Ramona Singer Pinot Grigio, and ignoring Owen's pleas for her to come out of her room while contemplating how she had destroyed her own future by giving away the thing that she loved the most to the person that she liked the least.

Instead, however, she found herself still feeling elated, confident, invigorated. She took the train straight home, marched into her room—thank God, Owen was at work, or he would've made her go back and apologize—took out her laptop, deleted the UNTITLED MOLLY BABCOCK COOKBOOK file (not exactly a meaningful gesture, since the file had almost nothing in it), and opened a new document and titled it PITCH IDEAS. Who needs to ghost-write a celebrity cookbook when you can write articles under your own name for *Saveur, The New York Times, The Guardian, Food & Wine*?

Despite barely drinking any coffee that day (she'd left her half-filled mug on Molly's counter), she felt completely wired. Stories flew up into her consciousness like balls from a batting machine: "Are Tasting Menus Passé?" "Will Frog's Legs Make a Comeback?" "What Exactly Is a Montreal-Style Bagel?"

True, these stories wouldn't pass muster at *Comestibles* (or most other places), but she no longer worked at *Comestibles*, and these were just ideas. She could polish them later. She was just free-associating, blue-skying, shaking the tree. She started several working lists: "Recipe Ideas." "Restaurant Pitches." "Personal Essays." "Interview Subjects."

Around noon, her stomach began rumbling, and she was just starting to contemplate lunch when the doorbell buzzed. At no point in her history of living with Owen had the buzzer ever buzzed without some kind of lead-up, whether it was a package they were expecting, Owen's Grindr hookup, or a green curry being delivered from the spicy Thai place down the street. Here the buzzing wasn't just unexpected, it was aggressive: the person kept on buzzing and buzzing.

Isabella, figuring it must be a local kid messing with the buttons outside, pressed the intercom:

"Yes?"

"It's me," said the oh-too-familiar voice that Isabella thought she was done with forever. "I'm downstairs."

How could the "me" really be the "me" that it so clearly was? Hadn't she just called that "me" a soulless empty vessel? Filled with Botox? A smiling-piece-of-shit emoji?

Now the elation that Isabella felt moments ago morphed into a white-hot panic. If she didn't do anything, Molly would keep buzzing. If she did go downstairs, who knew how ugly their fight would be? What nasty things Molly would say back to her?

What would the neighbors think? The landlord who lived in the basement? Would they get evicted? How did Molly even know where she lived? Owen must've told her. *Owen!*

Seeing no other option, Isabella walked quickly down the three flights of stairs, preparing herself for a second round of battle. *Remember how she treated you. Remember how she lost your father's gift.* When she opened the front door of their building, she was greeted by an unexpected image: Molly at the wheel of a vintage bronze Mercedes convertible. She was wearing big red retro sunglasses and a silk scarf that was blowing in the wind, just like Thelma or Louise—Isabella wasn't sure which.

"Get in," said Molly, a smirk on her face, as she savored Isabella's stunned reaction.

Isabella was too dumbfounded to move.

"I said 'get in,'" Molly repeated. "Or do you want to read me to filth again?"

Molly seemed more bemused than angry about any of the things that Isabella had said just an hour ago. In fact, she seemed slightly impressed.

Unsure of how to get out of this situation, but also relieved that she hadn't made an enemy of Owen's most important client, she did the only thing that she could think to do under the circumstances: she got into the car.

. . . .

"Do you like Taylor Swift?"

This was the first question that Molly asked Isabella as she pulled out of the little street where Isabella lived with Owen and made her way to the BQE.

"Ummm . . . she's okay," said Isabella, not sure if there was a right answer or a wrong answer to this question.

"She's hit or miss," said Molly as she turned up the volume on *Midnights* playing through her iPhone in its bejeweled case. "But I fucking love this album."

Molly sang along to "Anti-Hero" (a little on the nose?) as

they continued on their mysterious journey. Where were they going? Was she being kidnapped? Isabella had flashbacks to *The Sopranos*, which she'd marathoned during the pandemic (it was her dad's favorite show), and all the seemingly innocuous car rides that the characters would go on only to have their brains splattered all over the windshield moments later. Was this what was happening now? Was Molly going to whack her?

"I'm sorry about losing your cookbook," said Molly, keeping her face forward as she merged onto the freeway. "Things have been really shitty lately with Xavier"—she referenced Xavier as if it were impossible for Isabella not to know who he was, even though she'd never before mentioned his name once—"and last night he stood me up, even though he promised to take me out, so I brought the book with me to read at dinner, and then he changed his mind, and I was in such a rush to tell the Uber driver to turn around that by the time we got back to my place, I totally spaced and didn't realize that I left it until I got home at three in the morning."

Molly, a consummate actress, delivered this monologue with such intensity, Isabella couldn't help but feel sorry for her, even though the story made zero sense and was a lousy excuse for doing something so shitty.

"I even had Fiona go meet the Uber driver to search his car this morning, because he said he couldn't find it and I wanted her to double-check, and she couldn't find it there, either, so clearly some asshole ran off with it."

Hope the asshole likes roast chicken with bread salad, thought Isabella.

"Anyway, I'm sorry for being a bitch this morning. This whole Xavier situation is insane, and I'm just taking it out on everyone else."

"It's okay," said Isabella, still gathering her wits after such a traumatic morning. "I guess, at the end of the day, it's just a book."

"It's not just a book," said Molly, turning her head to look at Isabella directly while going seventy miles per hour. "It was the last thing your father gave you before he died, and I lost it, and now I have to live with that. What I did was really fucked up. You need to hold me accountable."

This language sounded like pure shrink-speak. Isabella imagined Molly making an emergency call to her therapist after she told her off and the therapist telling her to "really apologize," to "hold yourself accountable," to "deal with this right away." And even though Molly seemed sincere in her apology, she seemed more concerned about having apologized (and thereby unburdening herself) than she was about making Isabella feel better.

"So where are we going?" asked Isabella, eager to change the subject.

"That's a secret," Molly answered, an impish grin on her face. "But I'll tell you this: it's going to make your job a whole lot easier."

. . . .

Despite growing up in New York and taking various trips with her father to estate sales and auctions all over the city to find antiques for his gallery, Isabella had never once set foot in New Jersey.

Why would she? She didn't have friends from New Jersey, she didn't have family in New Jersey, and the only thing that might've taken her there, gastronomically speaking, was something that she already had plenty of in the city, that something being pizza.

True, she loved Bruce Springsteen, and she did love all six seasons of *The Sopranos*, but never before had she had an excuse to visit New York's famously combative cousin. She didn't even know that's where she was headed until she saw the official sign that said "Welcome to New Jersey: The Garden State."

"Is this an overnight?" she asked, after an hour and a half in the car with no end in sight. (They'd stopped at a gas station, where Isabella wolfed down a Snickers bar, which didn't really satisfy as advertised.)

"Hell, no," said Molly, lighting a Marlboro Light with the vintage cigarette lighter that only worked intermittently. "My plan is to get in and get out."

"Get in and get out of where?"

Molly blew out a cloud of smoke.

"You like to be in control, don't you?"

It was the first question that Molly had asked Isabella that showed any sense of curiosity about who she was as a person.

"Most people who like to cook are control freaks," said Isabella, taking the question seriously. "It's a way to order your own little universe."

Molly nodded as she inhaled.

"Is that why you do it? To order your own little universe?"

Isabella shrugged.

"I don't know. Maybe I just really like food."

"I wish I could just really like food."

This was such a weird thing to say, Isabella couldn't help but press the issue.

"Why can't you?"

Molly turned and searched Isabella's face to see if she was being for real.

"Oh, sweetie, do you think that you can work in Hollywood if you allow yourself to really like food? I can barely allow myself to look at food."

"I don't know. Isn't that changing, with people being more body-positive and stuff?"

Molly laughed a hoarse, embittered laugh.

"Oh, please. Hollywood's been the same since it started. A bunch of money-grubbing, straight, rich white men who think with their dicks more than their brains and whose only criteria for casting a woman in a movie is: 'Are they fuckable?'"

As brutal as this assessment was, Isabella didn't doubt that, at least for Molly Babcock, it was true.

"We're almost there," announced Molly, as she took the exit for New Brunswick.

Isabella had been too wrapped up in the conversation to notice their surroundings. Molly had put the top up on the car before they got on the highway (which made the cigarette smoke a bit harder to ignore), but now she lowered it, and Isabella could soak in the crisp fall New Jersey air—as toxic as New Jersey air might be.

"Is this where you grew up?" Isabella asked, hazarding a guess.

"Nicely done, Sherlock."

At first, New Brunswick seemed lovely enough. They drove past schools where children were playing on the playground, a clean-looking church, a few shopping centers. But then they wound up on a block where things were a bit less idyllic. A few houses looked completely condemned; a few others looked like graveyards for toys and wheelchairs and other detritus that no one wanted to take or throw away. (It reminded Isabella of her mother's living room.)

Eventually, Molly pulled into the driveway of a totally neutral house, with a pale-gray exterior and white-painted trim that was chipping off in big chunks. There was a mailbox stuffed with mail, a hose uncoiled on the front lawn, and an American flag still flying from July Fourth.

"Home sweet home," said Molly; she put the car in Park but didn't unbuckle her seatbelt.

"Are we going in?" Isabella finally asked, after what felt like a minute.

"Give me a sec," said Molly, who lit another cigarette and puffed on it intensely, like a hamster sucking water from a tube. "I'm working up the nerve."

For a moment, they sat in silence, the radio off, the smoke wafting its way toward Isabella's nostrils. Strangely, she was starting to enjoy the secondhand smoke. It gave her a chance to imagine what it might've felt like dining in Paris back in the heyday of bistro culture, with writers and sophisticates puffing on cigarettes while dragging their baguettes through veal-stock-enriched sauces.

"Fuck it, let's go," said Molly. She put her cigarette out abruptly in the vintage ash tray and got out of her seat.

Isabella followed close behind, nervous to see what Molly was so nervous about.

. . . .

When the woman came to the door, seconds after Molly pressed the doorbell, Isabella was expecting some kind of gargoyle of a stepmother. Wouldn't that make the most sense? Her mom died and her father married a nasty ogre. It was a tale as old as "Cinderella."

Instead, the woman who greeted them seemed soft and warm, in a purple-and-red muumuu, large gold-framed glasses, and a slightly worried expression on her face.

"Molly, is that you?" she asked, taking her glasses off and putting them on again. "I don't believe it. Why didn't you call?"

She gave Molly a welcoming hug, a generous one, though Molly remained as stiff as a board.

"If I knew you were coming, I would've cooked you something," she said, turning from Molly to Isabella. "Who's your friend?"

"This is Isabella," said Molly. "Is he home?"

The "he" had weight to it, and that's when Isabella identified the source of the tension. *It's not the stepmother, it's the father.*

"He's in the den," said the kind-seeming woman. She turned to Isabella, sensing that Molly wasn't going to introduce her. "I'm Frances, Molly's stepmom."

"Nice to meet you," said Isabella, putting out her hand, but secretly watching Molly as she cautiously entered the house, a studied, steely expression on her face that couldn't fully mask her apprehension.

"When did you guys redo the living room?" she asked, as Isabella and Frances followed her inside. The living room was clean-looking and plain. Isabella couldn't imagine how it had been redone except that everything with character or individuality had been systematically stripped out of it.

"Three years ago," said Frances.

"What else did you redo?"

There was a bit of an accusation hidden in the question, as if Molly were blaming Frances for her childhood home's being gutted.

"Just a few things here and there. Your father said everything felt 'old' and he wanted to freshen up the place. Personally, I liked it better before."

"What's all that fucking yapping in there?" came a loud, booming voice from the next room. "I can't hear myself think."

The three women shared the kind of look that soldiers might give one another upon hearing an enemy plane.

"Dad, it's me," said Molly, walking straight into the den; Isabella and Frances followed up in the rear. As they walked to the den through the kitchen, Isabella noted a stove's worth of pots and pans all in various states of use: a lentil soup burbling in one, a chicken stock reducing in another, something that looked like chocolate pudding in another, and a cast-iron skillet in which something clearly had just been fried. On the counter was a Jell-O mold that had just been filled with neon-orange liquid; pieces of fruit bobbed inside like drowning passengers from a capsized boat.

"Well, holy fucking shit," said a large, bespectacled man sitting at a card table in a plastic folding chair, working a crossword puzzle with a Sharpie. Next to him was a half-eaten fried-chicken sandwich and coleslaw that looked like it was made in the hippest Brooklyn café, not in a ramshackle house in New Jersey. "Her Royal Highness has come to grace us with her presence! And to what do we owe the honor?"

Molly's father spoke with the crispness and the clarity of a college professor, but a resentful one, the kind who'd meant to write the great American novel but ended up writing a pamphlet about sexually transmitted diseases.

"Donnie, let's not escalate unnecessarily," proffered Frances, seemingly an expert in her husband's moods.

"Butt out," he snapped, and then turned back to Molly. "So

what brings you back to your old stomping grounds? Researching a part about real blue-collar Americans? The kind who pay their taxes and work actual jobs?"

"I have a few things that I need to go through," she answered, using a crisp and clear tone that mirrored her father's. Her voice was solid, but Isabella could sense the cracks shining through. "Things of Mom's."

At this, Don stood up. He was in his late sixties—maybe early seventies?—but he cut a commanding figure, despite the cane that he used to hoist himself. He was wearing a flannel shirt that struggled to contain his enormous belly and dirty gray sweatpants, and with his left hand he was holding a Diet Peach Snapple outfitted with a plastic straw.

"Let me get this straight," he said, walking closer to Molly and taking a loud sip. There was no sense of affection at all between father and daughter; the idea that he might hug her or even put a loving hand on her shoulder seemed out of the question. "We practically begged you to come here and go through your mother's things for months and months after she died. And then, for years, we texted you, called you, wrote you letters, reached out to your sister. And you didn't so much as answer the phone. And now, all these years later, you just show up out of the blue and expect us to lay out the red carpet and deliver your mother's things to you on a silver platter? Well, that ain't happening, sweetheart. Especially since we gave most of your mom's things away."

As he spoke the last part, Don lowered himself back into the folding chair, a weirdly temporary chair for such a permanent-looking space. The walls were dark brown, with faded articles framed on them. At first Isabella thought they might be articles about Molly, but the more Isabella squinted, the more it was clear that the articles were about Don and his fishing exploits.

"I don't believe you would do that," said Molly. "You don't throw anything away."

She turned to Frances. "Is he telling the truth? Did you throw my mother's things away?"

Frances, who was mostly light and friendly in the doorway, now seemed rigid.

"He's mostly telling the truth. There are a few boxes in the basement."

"What boxes?" snapped Molly's father. "And who's this other person standing here in my house? Is anyone going to tell me who the hell this is?"

Even though he directed the question at Frances, Isabella felt it incumbent on her to answer.

"Hi," she stammered. "I'm Isabella? I'm helping Molly write her cookbook."

At the word "cookbook," Molly inhaled anxiously, and Don burst out laughing.

"Her *what*? Her *cookbook*?" He swiveled his attention back to Molly. "Are you for real? You're writing a fucking cookbook?"

Once again, he got out of his seat, lifting himself up with his cane.

"You . . . you who drove your mother fucking crazy because you refused to eat her food? After she slaved away all day making dishes that you personally requested? Now you're writing a motherfucking *cookbook*?"

Molly, clearly not going to take the bait, turned to Frances. "Where in the basement?"

"I'll show you," she answered.

"You're not showing her a goddamned thing," commanded Don, hoisting his cane as a pointer. "She is not going down into my basement to root around my personal things, taking whatever she goddamned pleases, after years of shutting us out of her ever-so-important life."

"I have no interest in going through your personal things. I just want to look through some of Mom's stuff for the book."

Molly's tone was less one of aggression and more one of exasperation, like she was acting a part in a play that she'd been in for decades, but eager to move on to a more forgiving role.

"And what is this book? Some kind of new narrative you're spinning? The devoted daughter paying tribute to her mother, the cook whose food you never ate? The mother you barely visited or called when you got famous, even though she wanted nothing more than to see you? The mother who you let rot away on her deathbed in this very house without so much as a call or flowers or a card, while you were off partying and doing God knows what else in L.A.?"

"Come on," Molly said to Isabella, grabbing her by the hand. "We don't need his permission. This is my house, too."

Molly led Isabella through to a doorway near the kitchen.

"You've got twenty minutes," yelled Molly's dad. "And if I see you taking anything out of here, I'm calling the goddamned cops!"

Isabella knew that she wasn't in danger—Molly's dad seemed more feeble than ferocious—and yet she felt the threat of violence percolating through the whole house. By the time they'd walked down the stairs into the basement, she felt like Jodie Foster in *The Silence of the Lambs*. She expected Buffalo Bill to come out of the shadows to stab her in the back while moths fluttered all around.

"Help me look," said Molly, as she pulled a chain on the ceiling to turn on the single bulb that lit up the damp, dismal space.

"What am I looking for?"

"Any box that says 'candy.'"

"Candy?" Isabella was confused, and not at all craving sugar at the moment, especially after her Snickers-bar lunch. "Why are we looking for candy?"

"Because," Molly answered as she lifted up a box, "that was my mother's name."

. . . .

Sixteen minutes later, with four minutes left before Don's countdown clock ran out—a rapping of the cane and a loud "Move it!" echoed periodically from above—Isabella stumbled upon a damp and warped cardboard box in a corner with faint red marker on it that said: CANDY'S THINGS.

When she summoned Molly over, Molly quickly tore into it.

"This is it," she said, digging her hands deep inside and lifting out a heavy, large rectangular object. "It's just how I remember it. Thank God, he didn't throw it away."

When Isabella looked closer at what Molly had removed from the box, it was a fat red binder overflowing with papers and Post-it notes and articles cut out of newspapers.

"Look," she said, placing it down on top of a box that was more directly under the swinging lightbulb. "It's like five hundred pages, at least."

The cover of the binder had the words CANDY BABCOCK'S BOOK OF RECIPES AND MAGICAL POTIONS, and as Molly opened it up, a lifetime's worth of dishes, handwritten and typed, flashed before their eyes. There was no method to Candy's madness: buttermilk-waffle recipes were jammed up against green-gumbo recipes stuck to recipes for Christmas ham and "Jewish latkes" (Candy's words). There were letters from friends with handwritten versions of *their* family recipes (apple pie, Planter's Punch) still in the envelopes in which they were sent. Some of the recipes were unreadable because of sauce stains, sloshes of gravy, smudges from damp fingers. Some of the pages were irreversibly stuck together. But, regardless of the readability of what was inside the binder, the binder itself was a living document, an overflowing celebration of one woman's enthusiasm for cooking and feeding others.

"This is . . . beautiful," said Isabella, feeling an immediate connection to this woman she'd never met.

"I'm guessing this will help us write the cookbook?" asked Molly as she loaded it back into the box.

"You guess correctly."

"The only question is: how do we get it out of here?"

Isabella had forgotten about Don's warning not to remove anything from the basement. Would he be at the top of the stairs, waiting for them with his cane? Did he have dogs in cages that he starved and tortured, to deploy at moments like these? Would Frances throw a pan of hot oil at them?

"Why don't I distract them while you go put it in the car?"

Isabella was surprised by her own offer: she had a hard enough time talking to people that she knew, let alone the verbally abusive parent of her cookbook collaborator.

"Are you sure you can pull that off?"

Molly wasn't trying to be mean: she just questioned Isabella's ability to stand up to someone as intimidating as her father.

"Only one way to find out."

Before she could think too much about it, Isabella marched straight up the stairs from the basement, back into the kitchen, where Frances was chopping up more fruit for her Jell-O mold, and into the den, where Don still sat at his card table.

Don regarded Isabella the way a wolf might regard a stuffed panda.

"Is she done down there?"

Isabella was trying to find words to distract him when the sound of Molly bounding up the stairs resonated throughout the house, her loud breathing betraying the exertion.

"What's she carrying?" he yelled to his wife.

"She's got a box," Frances replied dutifully.

As Molly made her way from the kitchen toward the front door, Don rose to his feet and, using his cane, maneuvered his way into the kitchen, while Isabella trailed behind.

"Wait," she murmured. "I wanted to ask you about crossword puzzles. Do you always do them in magic marker?"

Her words were so feeble, and his movements so threatening—he motored through the house like a three-legged machine built for destruction—that, as Molly went out the front door and down the driveway toward the car, Isabella did the only thing that she could think to do. She grabbed the Jell-O mold off the kitchen table—still sloshy with gelatin, water, and fruit—and as he began descending the front steps, she hovered momentarily over him and then dumped the lumpy mixture all over his head.

The orange liquid cascaded down Don's mostly hairless skull, globs of fruit stuck to his glasses, and he was so immobilized by the shock that Isabella could do nothing but push right past him, almost knocking him over, as she herself slipped through the goo.

"Where the hell do you think you're going, you Jell-O-slinging son of a bitch!"

Don reached out and tried to grab Isabella, but she flew down the driveway as Molly, who'd already loaded the box into the trunk, watched from outside the driver's door, cheering Isabella on.

"Slay queen!" she yelled as Isabella, both laughing and shaking with fear, her hands sticky and orange, ran toward the passenger seat and got in.

As a neon-orange Donald Babcock stood screaming on the stoop, with a slightly pleased Frances standing behind him, Molly and Isabella sped off; now they actually did look like a true *Thelma and Louise.* Except, instead of driving them off a cliff, Molly announced that she was driving them to a local bar for celebratory drinks. Isabella wondered if driving off a cliff was a more attractive option.

. . . .

The bar, just a few minutes away, was way too bright for the kind of bar it was supposed to be, that being a dive. Mike and Ike's—named after the twin brothers who had opened it—was where Molly had spent most of her time in high school, flirting with men twice her age and sipping from bottles under the counter while pretending to look for a perpetually lost earring.

"You probably think I'm an alcoholic by now," said Molly as she carried over a tray of four tequila shots and two gin and tonics that had been gifted to her by the gruff bartender, whom she kissed on the cheek, apparently a friend from high school. "I don't normally drink this much. I've just been under a lot of stress lately."

Isabella, who was too rattled to be judgmental, had built up her own tolerance for drinking: especially during the pandemic, when she and Owen were trapped at home and the only thing that they could do together was eat Isabella's food, make complicated cocktails, and binge bad TV.

"No judgment," said Isabella, wondering how they would get home, with Molly inebriated and Isabella not having driven since she got her license, and never on a highway.

"Drink up!" said Molly; she knocked back the two shots, one after the other, then took a sip of her gin and tonic. It was an odd combination—chasing tequila with gin—but Isabella did as she was told, and she had to admit that the alcohol felt good going down, that it was medicine for her unexpectedly stressful morning and afternoon.

"Is your dad always like that?" asked Isabella.

Molly closed her eyes tightly, as if the very thing that she was trying to escape had just shown up in the doorway.

"Let's not talk about my dad or work or anything not-fun. Tell me something about you that I don't already know," said Molly, settling into her seat in the only dark booth in the room. "Something that doesn't have to do with food. Something surprising."

Isabella fished around in her memory for a tidbit that might amuse a difficult-to-amuse minor celebrity.

"Ummm . . . Well, this sort of has to do with food, but not totally. I once gave a blow job to a famous French baker while he was stuffing éclairs?"

Molly almost did a spit take.

"Wow. I did not expect you to say that."

Isabella omitted the part about the baker's being a married lech with bad BO, or her only going through with it because her sexual track record was so unimpressive it bordered on nonexistent.

"Your turn," said Isabella, feeling the alcohol shoot to her brain in record time.

"My last boyfriend used to piss on me in the bathtub and wouldn't let me clean myself until he was done showering."

Isabella nodded, as if that were a reasonable follow-up, the next step in a normal sexual progression.

"Cool," she said, wondering how she would handle such a

situation, and pretty sure she would rather never have sex again than ever go through that.

"Do you give blow jobs a lot?" asked Molly, stirring her gin and tonic with a straw, and looking at Isabella like a powerful sorority sister talking to a meek new pledge.

"I mean, I don't make a regular habit out of it or anything. But . . . I've sucked some D in my day."

Molly burst out laughing, and Isabella laughed, too. She never talked like that; why was she talking like that now?

"You know, you have really good bone structure," said Molly, suddenly taking great interest in Isabella's face. "If you put in a little effort, you could be a real knockout."

Ugh. Isabella already had one Owen in her life; she didn't need two.

"Thanks," she said, eager to change the subject. "So . . . tell me about your mother's recipes. Which one is your favorite? Maybe we can start with that."

"Don't change the subject. Why do you dress like you work at a nursery school for kids with special needs?"

Had Owen written that line for her?

"I don't know," Isabella said, sighing, now feeling a little bit drunk. "If I'm being honest, I always find it a bit insulting when people are, like, 'You have good bone structure' or 'If you just put in a little effort, you could be pretty.' As if me being me isn't enough."

"You being you *isn't* enough," said Molly matter-of-factly, slurping down the rest of her drink and signaling the smitten bartender for another round. "Me being me isn't enough. Most people being them isn't enough. We all have to make some kind of effort to be more attractive, even if it just means brushing your teeth in the morning or wiping your ass. I'm guessing you at least do that?"

Isabella nodded. She did, at least, do that.

"I can tell you a few places to buy clothes where they'll know exactly what to do with you. You'll see: it'll make a big difference."

Isabella nodded as the bartender placed the tray of drinks—another four shots and two gin and tonics—down between them.

"Oh my God, I can't drink another sip," said Isabella, frowning at the little glasses of clear liquid.

"I can help you with that," said Molly, pulling the glassware toward herself.

"Who's going to drive us back?"

Molly rolled her eyes.

"Are you always such a stick in the mud?"

"Are you always such a chaotic mess?"

Molly, who wasn't used to such sass (even from her sister), showed a quick flash of shock, then burst out with a genuine guffaw before downing the four shots one after another.

"Sooo," said Molly, who was surprisingly non-slurry for someone who had imbibed so much booze, "tell me more about all of those D's you've sucked."

"It's not that many, actually," confessed Isabella. "To be honest: it's only three."

As they compared their sexual histories—Isabella's like that of a new country, Molly's like that of ancient Rome—the two of them relaxed into an easy patter that surprised them both, considering their rocky history. By the time five o'clock rolled around, Isabella was so at ease that she actually trusted Molly when she said she was "totally fine" to drive—especially after she chugged back a mug of black coffee like it was the easy antidote to an afternoon of recreational poison.

And though Isabella wasn't religious, she found herself—an hour later—praying to God, Jesus, Dionysus, and any other gods she could conjure up as Molly swerved them in and out of traffic on 95, sometimes going eighty miles per hour, sometimes texting with one hand while holding a cigarette with the other.

Facing the specter of death, Isabella wasn't sure which would be the greater tragedy: that she died without finishing the cookbook, or that she died without having dinner.

10

THE FRIENDLY GHOST

"Where are my pages?"

This was the voice that greeted Isabella the next morning at eight as she woke up to the sound of her phone buzzing and an unfamiliar number on the screen. The voice, once she heard it, was unmistakable.

"Hi, Lionel," she said, not remembering how she'd gotten into bed or put on her pajamas, and if or what she'd eaten for dinner. All she knew was that she felt too hungover and too underdressed to be talking to a person who was probably showered, groomed, and wearing a watch that cost more than she would make all year. "There aren't pages yet, per se . . . but we're starting to make some real progress."

"It's been three weeks. What's the holdup?"

Your client is an immature, irresponsible, unreliable freak?

"Molly's just been really busy . . ."

"Molly? What's Molly got to do with it?"

Isabella was too stunned by the question to answer. Why was Lionel calling her directly? Had Owen sicced him on her? *Of course, Owen sicced him on her.*

"Let me spell it out for you, Isabella. You don't need Molly to write this cookbook. You can write the whole thing from home, make up a bunch of bullshit. As long as there are seventy-five recipes with headnotes and sidebars that sound like Molly wrote them, the publisher will be happy. We'll send a photographer to Molly's place, stage a bunch of pictures with bowls of lemons, and we'll be ready to move on to the next totally unnecessary celebrity cookbook. Speaking of which: how familiar are you with Travis Krenshaw?"

Travis Krenshaw was the host of *Good Morning Live!*, one of the most highly watched morning shows in America.

"I know who he is?"

"Good, because we rep him, and he wants to write a cookbook featuring all of the recipes he's done on air with famous chefs. It's bound to be a bestseller."

A cookbook for Travis Krenshaw? Famous chefs? Bound to be a bestseller? For someone whose greatest food-writing accomplishment in the past year was a listicle about roasted broccoli recipes, this was an enticing offer.

"That would be really cool."

"It is cool. But I can't recommend you until you bang this one out. So—my advice: stop treating this cookbook like it's beef bourguignon and start treating it like the McDonald's cheeseburger that it is. Capeesh?"

"Capeesh," echoed Isabella, but she hadn't finished the word before Lionel ended the call.

She put her head back down on the pillow and contemplated Lionel's advice.

Was she treating Molly's cookbook like boeuf bourguignon? If so, maybe Lionel was right. She was trying to make a four-star dish out of one-star ingredients. She had to stop channeling her inner Gordon Ramsay and start channeling her inner Betty Crocker.

And what *did* she need Molly for? Now she had a red binder full of family recipes curated by someone who really cooked. With that, plus her own ingenuity, she could fashion a Molly Babcock cookbook without Molly Babcock in just a few weeks. The only collaborator she really needed was Candy Babcock's ghost.

At first, Isabella was worried about having the red binder in her possession: not because it wasn't useful, but because she was scared that she'd be tempted, perhaps unconsciously, to lose it on the subway.

"Oh no, I think I left it on the G train," she'd tell Molly. *I see your Zuni and I raise you a red binder.*

But Isabella knew, deep down, that she wasn't capable of such treachery. And she wouldn't really be punishing Molly, who'd left her mother's recipes to rot in the basement of her father's house for half a decade, but Candy herself. This red binder was Candy Babcock's legacy: an enormous, overflowing testament to a life well lived, at least in the kitchen. She deserved to have her recipes commemorated in some way.

When Isabella sat down with the binder the next morning, she felt the urge to light a candle, like she was performing a culinary séance. Opening the binder, she found in the front flap various letters, still in their envelopes, and what looked like journal entries written on yellow legal paper in blue ballpoint pen. She pulled one out and examined it:

> *The secret to a good Chick Parm is saucing it right before it hits the ov. Any sooner, and all of your work getting a crispy crust will have been a big, fat waste of time.*

Beneath it was a handwritten recipe for chicken Parmesan without any source listed (was it her own?). The more Isabella inspected these handwritten documents—one for New England clam chowder ("Use real clams or don't bother!"), one for icebox cake ("Oreos instead of chocolate wafers: TRUST ME")— the more Isabella felt that Candy, way before her daughter saw it as a last-ditch effort to save her own career, wanted to write a cookbook of her own.

The letters in the envelopes furthered Isabella's suspicions. They were rejection letters from various outlets, like *Gourmet* (back when it still existed) and *Parade* (back when it still existed), thanking Candy for her submissions but informing her that they weren't printing articles from outside contributors at that time. She saved them, Isabella figured, to keep a record of where she'd already submitted and how long it had been. Isabella did the same thing herself, back when she was trying to pitch similar outlets, except she used a spreadsheet on her computer.

That was just the stuff in the front pocket.

Once Isabella got into the actual substance of the binder—pages and pages of recipes and notes and articles clipped from magazines—she felt even more connected to this woman, who so clearly relished her time at the stove, trying out new ideas and documenting what she learned. There wasn't a recipe in the book without Candy's handwriting in the margins, written in small block letters with the same blue ballpoint pen. Below a recipe for roast chicken with root vegetables: "Next time, more rutabaga." Atop a recipe for eggs Benedict: "Total disaster . . . hollandaise can kiss my ass!" In the back were her attempts at original recipes—scallop burgers with mustard sauce, black-bean "hummus" with purple tortilla chips, a pimento-cheese soufflé—all written out by hand, with "first attempt" and "second attempt" and "third attempt" illuminating her process.

Just as she was closing the binder, a loose picture fell out and fluttered to the floor. Isabella picked it up, and there, in a little white dress with a tiara on her head, was young Molly, age six (according to the writing on the back of the picture), at her birthday party, with Candy holding a coconut cake with turquoise-blue frosting that looked like a snow-dappled Tiffany box. This was the first time that Isabella had laid eyes on Candy, and, in a way, she could see herself reflected in this woman she'd never met. There was that oh-too-familiar eagerness to please in the sparkle of her eyes; there was that combination of pride and humility in the way she was holding the cake; there was the discomfort in a social situation, with the other adults gathered on the other side of the picture—including Don, who was drinking a beer and ogling a young woman holding a baby. Isabella and Candy were both curvy with moonlike faces, but that's where the similarities ended: Candy was blond and blue-eyed, just like Molly. The look on Molly's face in this picture was one that Isabella had never seen on the grown-up Molly: bright, deliriously happy, proud of the cake that her mother was presenting to her in front of all of her friends.

I can't fake this, Isabella realized as she looked at the picture. *This link between Molly and her mother is specific, it's important. There are real stories here, things that need to be said.* Lionel's advice to do it all on her own wouldn't just be an injustice to Candy; it would be unfair to Molly. Whether she knew it or not, Molly needed to commune with her mother through the process of writing this cookbook. Isabella's job, she now understood, was to facilitate that process, even if it meant losing the chance to write another unnecessary celebrity cookbook for beloved morning-talk-show host Travis Krenshaw.

. . . .

Molly, for the first time in their so-called collaboration, seemed game—and not at all hungover—the moment Isabella walked through the door with the heavy red binder.

Isabella's plan for their first day of real work, post-binder, was to sit with Molly at the kitchen table and go through her mother's recipes, to see which ones she responded to the most and, more important, which ones had the best stories associated with them. Molly, for her part, didn't put up a fight: she came to the table in her pink bathrobe, holding a mug of coffee for herself and one for Isabella, as willing and open as Isabella had ever seen her—as if they were picking up where they'd left off the day before.

"I tried to switch from coffee to green tea," she said as she sat down, more jittery than normal. "But tea doesn't get the job done like coffee does. And by 'the job,' I mean coffee makes me shit."

Isabella pulled the binder from her backpack and placed it on the table. "Same."

Molly looked at the binder for the first time since the great escape from her childhood home, and it was like she was looking into the casket at her mother's funeral. She reached out her hand and touched the cover.

"She always had this with her in the kitchen," she said. "It was like Linus with his blanket. You'd never see her at the stove without it."

"How long did she have it for?"

"Forever."

Isabella had her laptop open across from Molly at the table. Moments earlier, she'd pulled the UNTITLED MOLLY BABCOCK COOKBOOK doc from the trash, even though it would've been just as easy to start a new file. She figured that the file, like Molly herself, deserved a resurrection.

"Her food was so unhealthy," said Molly as she turned to a recipe for chicken in sour cream. "But it was soooo good."

"Unhealthy is relative, anyway. Chicken in sour cream can be healthy if you eat a small portion of it with a salad?"

"You'd have to eat a lot of salad for this to be healthy." Molly pointed to the ingredients. "One stick of butter, one cup of sour cream. No wonder she had diabetes and heart disease."

"Is that how she died?"

"More or less," said Molly, flipping the page. "She was a compulsive eater. And drinker, too, eventually. Chardonnay from a box. She would drink it down with a straw like it was medicine . . . which it probably was. Oh my God, I remember this soup!"

Molly was looking at a page for butternut-squash soup with cayenne pepper and maple cream.

"She made it every Thanksgiving. A big batch, so we'd eat it all winter. She always kept some in the freezer."

Isabella took furious notes as Molly continued talking.

"She always had the perfect amount of cayenne in there, so

it warmed you up when your tits were frozen, but not so much that you would, like, choke to death. And the maple cream balanced everything out."

As Molly continued flipping through the book, Isabella made a point not to interrupt with questions. She figured it was best if Molly stayed in her reverie.

"Awww . . . I loved her coq au vin so much," she said, pointing to a recipe that was stained all over with red wine and chicken splatter. "She took a cooking class when she was in college, and this is the only thing that she remembered from it. She used pancetta instead of bacon . . . maybe because she was half Italian? Or was it a quarter Italian? Either way, she'd always make this on Christmas Eve, and I looked forward to it even more than getting presents."

This is what I was waiting for, thought Isabella. *This is the stuff that'll make the cookbook great.*

"Holy shit . . . bananas Foster!" said Molly, laughing, as she turned the page. "I remember, when she made this, my dad almost killed her, because she set the kitchen hood on fire. But she didn't care—she still served it, and then she made it again every year on her birthday, just to piss him off."

"She made her own birthday dinner?"

"Yeah, she did, because my dad was such a fucking asshole on her birthday. He wouldn't take her out to dinner, he wouldn't buy her anything, he barely even acknowledged her. So she would go to the Stop and Shop and grab whatever she could to make herself something special, and pretend to be happy to be stuck at home with her eight-year-old daughter on her birthday instead of at some four-star restaurant, like she deserved."

There was a ruefulness and intensity to Molly's speech that told Isabella to stop transcribing, that maybe this was too much too fast.

"Sorry," said Molly. "Maybe that's all I can handle for one day. Do you have enough to get started?"

"More than enough," said Isabella, eager to get home to start putting these recipes to work.

"Good," she said, standing up. "If I knew this would be like therapy, I would've doubled my Lexapro."

That afternoon, Isabella went to Whole Foods, stocked up on the ingredients for chicken in sour cream, and banged out the first full recipe for Molly's cookbook, which she gave the temporary title *Just Like Mom Made*.

. . . .

The next day, Isabella returned to Molly's apartment, eager for more of the same.

If Molly could keep pointing out recipes that she remembered and riffing on them, Isabella could run with that: doing all of the cooking back in Greenpoint—despite the smallness of the kitchen, she preferred that to the risk of Molly's throwing out the food for being too smelly—and then, after tweaking the recipe, spending a nice amount of time noodling on the headnote. She felt like she was finally in the zone: she was Jane Goodall with the apes, she was Tom Wolfe with the Merry Pranksters, she was a writer immersed in her subject, and she was loving it.

That was until she entered Molly's kitchen and saw Fiona setting up an iPhone on a tripod, and Molly made up as if she were about to be on camera, which, apparently, she was.

"Hiiii," she said, as Isabella placed the red binder down on the counter. It was the sort of "hiiii" that you say to someone before breaking really bad news.

"What's all this?" asked Isabella, noticing shopping bags on the counter, a cutting board, and a ring light.

"I was talking to Owen last night, and he made a really good point, which is that I sold this book because of all of the cooking that I did on social media during the pandemic, so I should be cooking those kinds of recipes on camera again, and Fiona can cut them into TikToks and Reels, and you can type them up into recipes for the cookbook. It makes so much sense, because the videos will get people more excited for the book, and then the book will have the recipes people want from the videos."

"Okay?" responded Isabella, not sure how to navigate this turn of events. "So, you mean . . . you don't want to include your mother's recipes anymore?"

"They're just so *heavy*," said Molly as she started to unpack groceries from Eataly. "I think the book should feature things that I actually eat!"

Isabella watched as Molly unloaded two big bunches of Tuscan kale and a lemon. "Like this kale salad that I make all the time for lunch? It's so simple and so amazing."

She lifted the wooden cutting board and positioned it in front of the tripod where Fiona was standing. Fiona seemed both catatonic and annoyed, like she'd been lifted up from the couch by the scruff of her neck and plopped into this situation because her sister was having a manic episode.

"Can we speed this along?" asked Fiona. "Kitty's doing cryotherapy with Bethenny Frankel in twenty minutes, and I have to live-tweet it and do the same thing on Threads."

Isabella was too focused on Molly to hear anything that Fiona had just said.

"I get that you want to make videos," said Isabella, still processing this brand-new agenda. "But it seems strange to just abandon all of your mother's recipes after we worked so hard to get them?"

Molly, who'd been moving nonstop since Isabella entered the kitchen, pulled a chef's knife from the knife block.

"We're not abandoning them! I just want to make sure that the cookbook is, like, about *me* and the food that I make, and not some dead woman who cooked fattening recipes that clogged her arteries and gave her diabetes."

The casual cruelty of that statement felt as unnerving to Isabella as biting into a sandy clam.

"Are you ready?" Molly asked Fiona, who was frantically

typing on her phone. "Once I start cutting the kale, that's it, so make sure you have me in the shot."

Stepping back, Isabella had to admit that Molly looked the part of modern-day culinary influencer. Her outfit—a tweed cardigan over a white button-down shirt and blue jeans—was both sophisticated and autumnal. Her makeup wasn't overdone: it was just enough to make her skin look healthy, like it had been slathered in umbilical-cord cream or whatever it was that influencers used to make their skin glow.

"Maybe take notes on your laptop, so you can put this in the book?" she said to Isabella, who was still standing next to the binder. "Just don't type too loudly."

She hoisted the knife and gave Fiona an impatient look.

"I'm recording," said Fiona, defensively, as if that were already an obvious fact, when there was no way to know that she'd hit the Record button.

"Hey, guys," said Molly, her voice shifting from her everyday clipped tone to the bright and shiny one that she used when she was in front of an audience. "I know it's been *forever* since you saw me in the kitchen cooking, because, let's be honest, who after the pandemic was over actually lifted a knife? But I actually miss cooking for you all, so I'm going to show you how to make my favorite kale salad. I literally eat this every day."

What happened next was more traumatizing for Isabella than the time when she watched a whole cow being butchered on YouTube. Molly's way of handling a knife was so haphazard, it looked like a trailer for a Blumhouse movie. She didn't wash the clearly still-dirty kale. She didn't pull the leaves from the stems. She just started hacking the whole thing apart like a serial killer, pieces of kale flying all over; one even landed on Fiona's shoulder.

"It doesn't matter how you cut it," she said, as she hacked away. "It's more about what you do after."

She scraped all of the kale into a large bowl, and then proceeded to scrunch it with her hands, like she was making a mud pie or squeezing an edible stress ball. Isabella had massaged kale before but never attacked it with such vigor.

"You want to massage it, but I'm not talking about the kind of massage with a happy ending," she said, winking. "I'm talking a rough kind of massage. The kind that leaves you black and blue. The kind that makes you beg for mercy."

She said this last part lasciviously, with her signature Molly Babcock blend of competitive prep-school student and unhinged wild child.

By the time she was done, she had what looked like a bowl full of mulch, which she then dressed by slicing a lemon in half and squeezing it over the kale, with so many seeds slipping into it that she could've started a lemon grove. Isabella waited for salt and olive oil, but they never came.

"Mmmm," she said when she finally stabbed a fork in to taste her handiwork. "This salad is so, so good, and so, so simple. And it's so, so good for you!"

Emphasis on the "so-so," thought Isabella.

"Did you get all of that?" Molly asked her sister when she finally finished her presentation.

"Unfortunately," Fiona replied.

. . . .

Isabella was shook-eth, but she at least took comfort in the fact that this video, when it arrived on social media, would either go viral in a bad way—with Molly becoming a meme ("Kale! Kale! Kale!" with the flailing knife)—or, much more likely, be ignored completely.

Instead, the video became an instant sensation.

"Did you see these numbers?" asked Owen when he came home from work that afternoon, finding Isabella at the table with the red binder, writing a headnote for an asparagus frittata with Gruyère that she had just made from Candy's Easter menu, even though asparagus was out of season. "She's already hit half a million, and it's only been up for six hours!"

Owen held out his phone and Isabella took it, seeing Molly's Instagram page for the first time. Most of the pictures were posed shots of Molly: at the beach with friends, laughing in a way that says, "I'm having such a good time," while not seeming to have a good time at all; on the red carpet at the New York Film Festival, looking wasted as she draped herself over Xavier Mordechai's shoulder; and then the Reel of the kale-salad episode that Isabella had witnessed earlier.

"The timing is amazing," said Owen, cutting himself a piece of frittata without asking. "A staff writer from *Malicious Angels* named Bobby Carreno just sold a show to Netflix called *Misery Loves Company*. It's about a woman who got bullied in middle school who takes a job as a seventh-grade teacher to take revenge on the daughter of the woman who bullied her. It's so fucked up, and so perfect for Molly. Mmm . . . is there goat cheese in here? It's giving barnyard."

Isabella was still in denial that this video, which featured a former TV star massacring an innocent bunch of kale, was not only popular, but well received. She scrolled through the comments: "Miss you so much, Molly!" "Sexy as ever. *drool*" "Come back to TV!" "Looking HOT HOT HOT." Was no one paying attention to the lack of expertise, the irresponsible use of a kitchen tool, the violence against an unarmed vegetable?

"Gruyère," said Isabella, handing the phone back to Owen.

"I likey," he said, hovering over the table, still in his sharp suit from his day at Mirror Mirror. "I have a teensy-weensy favor to ask."

"Besides the free piece of frittata?"

Isabella was grateful that Owen didn't reply that the frittata covered half of her rent.

"This guy Bobby is obsessed with Molly. He didn't think that she was still acting, but then he randomly saw her video this morning—it popped up on his feed—and he called Mirror Mirror and told us about this part that he wrote with her in mind!"

"Mm-hmm," said Isabella, wondering if the Gruyère over-whelmed the asparagus.

"So it's a total bird-in-the-hand situation," continued Owen. "But Molly refuses to audition. Something about 'hating rejection' and her 'skin not being thick enough' and 'being burned too many times' or whatever. But this show is a *huge* opportunity for her, and I don't think another will come along like this for a long time. So the favor is: can you nudge her along?"

"She won't listen to me," said Isabella, who was already plotting a way to steer their cookbook back toward Candy's recipes and away from Molly's . . . whatever you would call that atrocity of a salad.

"Don't be so sure," said Owen, cutting himself another frittata slice, probably calculating how many more burpees he'd need to do at the gym to burn it off. "She likes you. I asked her how things were going, and she said that she thought you were really cool."

Molly Babcock thinks I'm cool? Isabella hated to admit how good that made her feel.

"I'll do what I can," said Isabella, closing her laptop. She got up from the table. "Now I have to churn out more pages, in case your dad calls again tomorrow at eight in the morning."

Owen put up his hands to feign innocence, and Isabella went into her room, eager to dive back into the red binder for recipes that didn't involve hacking apart kale like a human lawn mower.

. . . .

For the next two weeks, Isabella played diplomat as Molly waged war on their cookbook.

"It doesn't have to be *all* of your mom's recipes," said Isabella, watching as Molly prepped for a video in which she would cook a boneless, skinless chicken breast on a vintage George Foreman grill, sapping it of all possible flavor and texture. "But it feels like it's a waste to ignore them completely?"

"We don't have to ignore them completely," said Molly as

she plugged the vintage George Foreman into the wall. "I just don't want every recipe to have, like, six sticks of butter and a gallon of heavy cream."

"Yo," said Fiona, standing up behind the tripod. "Since she's just standing here yapping, can Isabella work the camera instead of me? I've got an actual job to do."

Molly looked to Isabella to see if she'd be open to this, and Isabella, to her credit, shook her head no. "That's not my job."

Fiona's scowl turned scowlier, and Isabella was pretty sure she even heard a hiss.

Later, after the George Foreman video was shot—the finished piece of chicken looked more like the sole of a shoe than something you would eat—Molly invited Isabella to Abraço, her favorite coffee shop, for an iced vanilla oat latte.

"Did Owen tell you about the audition for Netflix?" she asked as they waited in the surprisingly long line. "He's *begging* me to do it, and I so don't want to."

Here it was: Isabella's opportunity to do Owen a solid. As she did the calculus in her head, she realized that if she urged Molly on—if Molly did audition and scored the part—it would be good not just for her, but for both of them. As her profile went up, so would the book sales, and so would Isabella's stock as a ghostwriter.

"He did tell me," she answered, as the line inched forward. "I think you should do it. Why not?"

Molly sighed heavily and crossed her arms.

"You don't know what it's like. You've never had to go into one of those rooms, seeing those people, with their coffee cups and their legal pads, looking at you like . . . like you're a bug under a microscope that they're either going to squash under their foot or tap with their magic wand and turn into a butterfly. Writing down mysterious things and whispering to each other. And then you have to thank them and leave and call your agent, and then you wait and there's the not knowing and the more waiting, and then you actually get it and you feel amazing—it's the best feeling ever—but then there's the haggling and the phone calls and the offers, and even when you think everything is said and done, even when you've signed on the dotted line, even when you go out celebrating, you go shoot the pilot and the network can still decide that they 'want to take things in a different direction,' and all of that hoping and dreaming and happiness and sense of accomplishment washes off of you like cheap mascara."

This litany, delivered directly to Isabella, attracted the attention of several other people in line, some of whom probably knew Molly from TV. One of them actually started clapping.

"The point is, I don't think I have the stomach for it anymore," said Molly, whose stomach didn't seem to have room for much of anything.

"You're stronger than you think you are," Isabella replied, not just puffing Molly up to please Owen, but actually believing her own words. "Of course you can handle it. Think of all you've been through in this life. All that you had to overcome. And what is this, a couple of minutes in some office, reading from a piece of paper? What's the big deal? Plus, this guy specifically asked for you. I think you have a real shot at it."

"You think so?"

"Of course I think so. Look at all of those comments in your cooking videos! There's a real demand to have you back out there."

Molly softened the way a child who throws a tantrum softens when someone hands them their favorite teddy bear.

"I don't know. I've been burned so many times before."

"If you can't stand the heat, get out of the kitchen."

Isabella said that sincerely, but for some reason the two of them burst out laughing at the inanity of the statement.

"You're an idiot," said Molly.

"Takes one to know one."

Finally, it was their turn, and Molly treated them both to iced lattes and a piece of Abraço's famous olive-oil cake; Molly tore the corner off it and handed the rest to Isabella, who had no problem polishing it off herself.

· · · ·

The next day, after much hemming and hawing and hesitating and hyperventilating, Molly went to the audition.

Isabella worked from home and had the whole place to herself, since Owen saw it as his duty to accompany Molly, whether she wanted him there or not. (Isabella suspected that Owen went less to provide comfort and more to make sure that she actually showed up.)

Despite Molly's insistence that the cookbook not be filled with heavy recipes with six sticks of butter and two gallons of cream, Isabella continued her campaign to resurrect Candy Babcock from the red binder that haunted her kitchen table.

She was working her way through one of Candy's signature salads: a lettuce wedge with bacon and a blue-cheese dressing made from mayonnaise and sour cream. Isabella had the idea to switch the iceberg with Little Gems, and to add some radishes and cucumbers to freshen it up. She was just writing out her shopping list when the phone rang.

"Do you know what tonight is?" came the oh-too-familiar voice on the other end of the phone.

"Thursday?" said Isabella, who had the sudden idea to add poppy seeds to the list: sprinkling them over the salad might add a great visual pop.

"It's onion-soup-a-palooza!" said Jeannie, who was out of breath, probably from carrying many bags of onions out of the elevator into her apartment.

"I beg your pardon?"

"I told you all about this when you were over a few weeks ago. Don't you remember? I've got all of those bruised onions from Gristedes and you promised you'd help me make a big vat of onion soup to bring to the soup kitchen and we put it in our calendars? Well, tonight's the night."

"Mom, this is the first I'm hearing of this since you mentioned it like a month ago. I have a lot of work to do on the book."

If there was one thing that Isabella was grateful for regarding the Molly Babcock cookbook, it was a legit opportunity to avoid cooking with her mother.

"Don't give me that 'I have to work on the book' crap. I've kept my mouth shut about you writing this farkakteh cookbook with this meshuggeneh movie star. That's your business. But this is a chance to do good for other people for one day of your life. And it's something that you love doing anyway. You can be like Meryl Streep in that movie with the big pile of onions."

"*Julie and Julia*."

"Exactly. You'll be just like Julie Julia." She said that as if the movie were about a woman named Julie Julia.

As Isabella was strategizing her response, Call Waiting started beeping through. She looked at the phone and saw Molly's name.

"Mom, I have to call you back. It's Molly."

"You don't have to call me back. Just come tonight at eight!"

Isabella clicked through to Molly and was immediately greeted with: "Bitch, I got it!"

It took Isabella a second to grasp what she meant by that and then she remembered the audition.

"Holy shit!" said Isabella, genuinely shocked and amazed that it had all happened so fast.

"Yeah, it's so insane. I walked in there, and it was like a lovefest from the get-go. I didn't remember this staff writer Bobby, but he totally remembered me, and apparently I was really nice to him when he was a lower-level and everyone else was giving him shit, and he loved the way that I read the part and . . . I can't believe it, but he just cast me right there in the room!"

"I'm so happy for you," said Isabella, who wondered how this would impact Molly's commitment to finishing the book.

"Where should we go to celebrate? I want to go somewhere new and chic but with really good food."

Isabella, who normally would freeze in a situation like this, had the answer on the tip of her tongue.

"Snakebite," she said, recalling the afternoon—an afternoon that felt like a lifetime ago—when she'd deposited the twenty-thousand-dollar check into her bank account and attempted to go there by herself, though she'd chickened out at the last minute.

"Oh yeah, I've heard of that," said Molly, who very likely hadn't. "I'll have Fiona make the reservation. You should get dressed up so we can celebrate! I'll text you some of those stores I was telling you about."

"Ha," said Isabella, who hoped Molly would've forgotten about this aspect of their conversation at Mike and Ike's.

"I'm serious, Izzy." *Izzy? When had Molly started calling her Izzy?* "It's time you started plating yourself up like the food you're always making."

"I'll think it over."

"So we'll see you at Snakebite? Let's say nine o'clock? Oh my God, I'm so excited I'm going to shit myself! Ahhh!"

Molly hung up, and Isabella remained at the table, feeling a bit giddy herself.

Moments later, a text came from Molly containing a list of stores, with little asterisks and commentary, most of them in SoHo, and Isabella looked at her watch and realized that she did indeed have a few hours to transform her whole look before dinner. She might've had an easier time completing the entire cookbook than performing this mandatory Cinderella job on herself, but for the first time in her life, she decided to turn her back on what her words looked like on the page and focus on how she herself looked in the mirror.

11

SNAKEBITTEN

When it came to ingredients, Isabella always sought out the freshest, most colorful, most eye-catching produce in the store. When it came to outfits, Isabella looked for the complete opposite: the less notable an outfit was, the better. Her style could best be described as Frumpcore. Her outfits, if you could call them that, looked like building materials: brick-colored sweatshirts, slate-colored sweatpants, a concrete-gray winter coat. The only comments that she would draw for her looks would be jabs from Owen:

"Who gave you those overalls? A Minion?"

"That's not an outfit, it's a hate crime."

"You know how some things are so bad they're good? Well, that outfit is so bad . . . it's just really, really bad."

Ninety percent of the time, Isabella found these gibes fairly funny: mostly because she couldn't care less about how she looked or, more specifically, what she wore. She saw her relationship to getting dressed the same way that Owen saw his relationship to making dinner. As in: Why go to the trouble? Why spend so much money? Why not just take the cheap way out and make your life easier?

Tonight, however, things were different.

Tonight she was going with a soon-to-be-famous-again TV star to one of New York's most celebrated restaurants (since she'd chickened out at lunch, Snakebite had been named "The Restaurant of the Year" by *Esquire*, "New York's Hardest-to-Get Reservation" by *New York* magazine, and awarded three stars by *The New York Times*). She had to look the part. For all Isabella knew, there could be celebrities at the table, or TV executives or, at the very least, very sexually attractive people.

With a few hours to pull herself together, she put the book that she was reading into a bag (*Provence, 1970*, into her *Food52* tote) and took the G to the L to the N, until she was in SoHo, the part of New York where people who cared about clothing gravitated to shop the way that people who cared about produce gravitated to the Union Square Farmers Market.

Her food brain tried to steer her to Balthazar for a baguette, or to Dominique Ansel for a Cronut, but she fought these instincts and instead navigated her way to Honey Dijon, one of the stores Molly had put on her list ("Go here first!" she'd demanded). She hovered outside the boutique once she arrived and, peeking through the window, saw rows of clothes in a pristine white space that looked more like an art gallery than a clothing store. In any other context, she would've run away screaming, but she felt the spirit of Molly hovering over her, nudging her along, as she turned the golden handle and walked into the immaculate space.

A salesman in a tight-fitting blue sweater and Jeffrey Dahmer–style glasses waltzed over to her.

"You must be Molly's friend," he said, sensing immediately that this was the Isabella he had been warned about, the one who desperately needed his help.

"I am," she said, feeling like she was about to go under the knife without anesthesia.

"I'm Ricardo," he said, putting out his hand. "Don't worry: I promise I can make this as painless as possible."

Ricardo pulled out several outfits and laid them on the shiny white marble counter.

"Molly wanted you to try this one first."

Had Molly actually looked for outfits for Isabella online? That was actually kind of nice, Isabella had to admit, until she saw the outfit that Ricardo held up: it looked more like a bathing suit than a dress to wear out to dinner. It was a fuchsia two-piece: a top that would clearly show off her belly, and a dress that split down the middle to reveal more of Isabella than Isabella was willing to reveal of herself, even in the shower.

"I'd rather cut off my left pinkie toe than ever wear that out in public," said Isabella, who wasn't used to insulting salespeople but, in this particular case, made an exception.

"I agree, it's a lot," said Ricardo. "And it's not you. We just need something slightly more demure but still stylish that'll make you pop!"

After several false starts, including a top that was so ill-fitting they had to get another sales associate to help zip her out of it, they landed on a dress that made her look, in Ricardo's words, "positively diaphanous." A silk maxi-dress, it had a low V-neck, a fitted waist, a row of covered buttons up the back, and a print featuring a subtle array of pink, red, and white flowers. Ricardo even found her a cozy beige cardigan to throw over everything, since it was getting nippy outside. It was impressive enough to show that Isabella was making an effort but not so ostentatious that it seemed like she was trying too hard.

"You look like you, but better," concluded Ricardo, who also helped her pick out a pair of black loafers to complete the ensemble. ("Heels," Isabella declared, "are out of the question.") Despite her initial misgivings, Isabella was so happy with her new look—she did look like herself, but better!—that she wore the dress and the shoes out of the store and gave Ricardo her ten-year-old ratty jeans and moth-bitten sweater and holey sneakers to throw out into the trash (he took them outside, not wanting to contaminate the trash in the store).

With just two hours left to spare, Isabella decided to build on her new foundation by getting her hair done. She wandered into a salon close to Honey Dijon, where, luckily enough, they'd just had a cancellation. The woman who tackled the "rat's nest" on Isabella's head (Owen's words) had multiple tattoos and piercings, which Isabella took to be a good sign.

"What's the vibe?" she asked as she took a brush to the situation on Isabella's head.

"I just want my hair to look really good without it seeming like I got it done?"

The pierced, painted stylist nodded.

"That's very doable."

An hour later, Isabella emerged from the salon with her hair washed and conditioned and trimmed in a way that made her look like she'd just come from a refreshing spa, but not in a way that said red carpet, Bat Mitzvah, or Glamour Shots circa 1995. She just looked like the freshest, healthiest version of herself: not someone who'd make you stop in your tracks as she passed you by, but someone you might smile at if she met your gaze.

Makeup was a big no-no for her, but with thirty minutes left to go, she walked into a Sephora and played around with the most basic blush and even more basic lipstick, which matched the color of her own lips. She stopped when she, to use her new favorite catchphrase, looked more like herself, but better.

At eight-thirty, she did the math and realized that if she walked to Snakebite she would get there ten minutes early and she'd have to do the same thing that she did the first time she met Molly: walk around the block until it was socially acceptable to enter.

This time, she decided to sit on a park bench and read her book until eight-fifty, at which point she slowly strolled to the restaurant and arrived there at ten after nine. She'd never been so fashionably late in her life, but now that she was so fashionable, she figured: What the hell?

· · · ·

Growing up in the Pasternak household, Isabella had rarely, if ever, gone out to eat: her mother's frugality and her father's work schedule didn't allow for it.

When Isabella started reading *The New York Times'* Dining section at fourteen—Jeannie would yell at her for not reading the Opinion section first—she would print out reviews of restaurants that she wanted to try when she got older and put them into a folder, knowing that someday she might have the wherewithal to go to these places herself.

When she moved back to New York after college and finally *did* have the wherewithal from birthday money or an extra writing gig, she never went. Owen was always working out, drinking protein shakes, never interested in joining her for some lavish four-course dinner made with butter or goose fat. Her other college friends were either too busy or too poor to indulge her. And going by herself to a three-star restaurant, or any restaurant, made her feel too self-conscious, too insecure, too lonely. So, for all of the time that she spent in New York, she rarely, if ever, visited the restaurants that she most wanted to try.

Which is why this moment was so thrilling for her. Not only was she all dressed up, she finally had somewhere to go. Here she was, once again, facing the entryway of Snakebite. What had been a fairly calm atmosphere during the day was now a bustling mass of humanity: diners, servers, busboys, bartenders, and chefs all navigating the space like Cirque du Soleil contortionists.

Through the window, Isabella studied the Dionysian platters of food being served: Giant towers of perfectly crisped shoestring potatoes had been fried with garlic and herbs (Isabella had read about them in the *Times* review; Pete Wells called them "a love letter to potatoes, hot oil, and a mandoline slicer"). Platters of whole branzino stuffed with fennel fronds and lemon had been roasted in a wood-burning oven and looked like something Sophia Loren might be holding on the cover of one of her cookbooks. She watched a waiter present the famous baked Alaska to a table of thirtysomethings all holding their phones aloft as he set it ablaze with a long match.

Isabella took a deep breath, walked through the front door, and pushed through the mass of people gathered there, who were huddled like vultures, scanning vigilantly for a seat at the bar. Like the red shoes in the famous fable, her new outfit and haircut seemed to carry her along, making her feel more capable of announcing herself at the host stand. The fact that she was meeting Molly Babcock for dinner made her feel even more worthy of her place, giving her a confidence that she needed to be heard above the din.

"Hi," she said, when she finally came face-to-face with the too-handsome-not-to-be-a-male-model twentysomething with long blond hair who was standing there.

"Name on the reservation?" he asked.

"It's actually not under my name," she said, her voice a pitch too loud. "I mean . . . it's under another person's name . . . Molly Babcock?"

She felt like she should maybe explain her connection, in case they didn't believe that she was really there to meet her, that she was some crazed fan or unabashed paparazzo dropping a celebrity's name. Instead, she watched as the host scanned the list.

"It should be for nine o'clock?" she added, hoping to clear up any confusion, since he seemed to be confused.

The male model looked back at Isabella with concern.

"Molly Babcock's here," he said. "But her reservation was for seven? She's just finishing up downstairs, in the private dining room. I can show you down?"

Isabella felt the words go into her ears like quarters into a slot machine, but instead of three cherries popping up after pulling the handle, three broken hearts appeared, one by one, as lumps of coal came clanking out the bottom.

How could she be so stupid? How could she put so much energy into this? How could she trust someone so inherently untrustworthy?

"Follow me," said the host, who started walking away before Isabella had a chance to respond. If Isabella hadn't been such a people pleaser, she might've spun around on the heel of her brand-new black loafer and raced out of there before he noticed. Instead, like a failed Persephone being escorted back to the underworld, she lowered her head and trailed behind.

The same outfit that had made her feel so powerful moments earlier now made her feel self-conscious. Who did she think she was, wearing such a conspicuous dress with such a conspicuous V-neck? Such an unnecessarily fitted waist? Such a delicate row of buttons? The pink, red, and white flowers no longer seemed subtle but extremely loud, like the wallpaper in her grandmother's bathroom. And her freshly conditioned hair made her feel like a weird, unwanted Barbie doll, every follicle announcing itself in a way that made Isabella want to scream: "Shut up!"

When they finally hit the basement, where dishwashers and busboys were spraying down whole vats of dishes (Isabella wanted desperately to join them), the host pushed open a secret door hidden in the wall, and there, in a dark lair lined with vintage hardcover books and illuminated with dripping wax candles, was a tight table of seven people all surrounding Molly Babcock, like an *Interview* magazine version of the Last Supper.

"Here you go," said the host, watching Isabella walk in, to make sure that she was, indeed, an invited member of the party.

Isabella felt that horrible feeling that she used to feel in the middle-school cafeteria, wandering around with her tray, searching for a place to sit. Only now it was like the cheerleaders asked her to join them for lunch, and when she showed up, not only did they not have a seat for her, they pretended like they didn't know her.

"Hey," said Isabella, trying to catch Molly's eye.

Molly, whom Isabella had seen just a day earlier, whom Isabella had encouraged to audition for the very part that she was now celebrating, looked like a deflated parade-float version of herself. She was wearing a cream-colored blazer dress that showed off her body, a body that was slumped over: three martini glasses were emptied in front of her, with olives still at the bottom.

She was draped over her on-again, off-again paramour, Xavier Mordechai, whom Isabella only knew from his character on *Malicious Angels*. On TV, Xavier was suave and dangerous, another generation's answer to James Dean. In real life, he seemed slightly damaged; the six years since the show had ended hadn't been kind to him. His eyes were red and puffy and panicked-looking; he constantly pinched his nose and sniffed; his cheek had a noticeable scar on it that looked like a slash mark, like someone had attacked him—or defended themselves from him—with a kitchen knife.

Xavier inhaled from a vape pen as Molly batted her eyelids until Isabella came into focus.

Once she realized who Isabella was, Molly attempted to pull herself up: "Izzy-bella! Where w-e-e-ere you? Did you get Fiona's text? They could only get us in at seven."

Isabella now studied the other faces at the table. Of the seven people, she only recognized four of them: Molly, Xavier, Owen—who was looking down at his phone and didn't seem to register that Isabella had entered the room at all—and Fiona, who had a look on her face of smug satisfaction.

"Oh no," she said, reacting to what Molly had just said, and facing Isabella with a look of fake apology. "I totally fucked up. My bad."

The other three faces belonged to Molly's friends, and they were like funhouse versions of Molly's: one had the same innocent quality, though the white powder under her nose told a different story; one had the same lusty glare, though without the bone structure to match it; and one had the same look of being extremely annoyed, a look that she was directing at Isabella right now, as if Isabella were an unwanted creature that she spotted crawling up the wall.

"OMG, you look soooo cute," called Molly again, noticing Isabella's outfit. "Did you go to Honey Dijon? Didn't you love Ricardo? I love makeovers. They're so inspiring."

Owen, looking up from his phone, finally clocked Isabella.

"Hey!" he said, standing up. "Were you coming to this dinner? I didn't realize, or I would've texted."

He then noticed her outfit.

"Look at you," he said approvingly. "It's giving Selena Gomez, it's giving Mindy Kaling, it's giving Kelly Clarkson."

"It's giving me a headache," said the annoyed Molly clone, eager to be done with this conversation.

As Isabella tried to deflect all of this unwanted attention, she couldn't help but notice all of the half-eaten platters on the table. There were the famous shoestring potatoes with the garlic and herbs, barely touched; there was the branzino, its body mostly intact, the lemon wedge next to it barely squeezed. Before Isabella could find a chair to pull up to the table to try a nibble, busboys swooped in and began carrying the platters away.

At the same time, a voice came booming from the doorway: "I hope we all saved room for de-zert!"

A tall, severe, thirtysomething-year-old man with impeccable hair and chef's whites—a man Isabella immediately identified as the chef, Casper Dusolier—entered the dining room, holding the famous baked Alaska. Behind him came a crew of about three other chefs, presenting the rest of the dessert menu: chocolate mousse with pink peppercorns, a trio of tropical sorbets (mango, papaya, and kiwi) in a bird's nest made of coconut, and a banana cake with rum dolloped with a swoop of pineapple-infused whipped cream.

After Chef Dusolier presented each dessert—lighting the baked Alaska on fire with a blowtorch cigar lighter, which Molly tried to capture on her iPhone, though she forgot to hit Record—he wished the diners "Bon appétit" and left.

Two of the chefs followed him out, but one chef stayed behind. He was lingering, and directing all of his energy toward Isabella.

"Hey," he said. "You finally made it inside."

Isabella, who was lusting after the desserts, which the loons at the table were too busy taking pictures of to eat, looked at him. There he was again: Gabe Kohl, with his boyish face, chipmunk cheeks, little red freckles, and all.

"Hi," she said. "Yeah, I guess I did."

"How was your doctor's appointment? Everything okay in there?"

Isabella looked puzzled for a second, then remembered the lie she'd told the last time she ran away from Gabe.

"Oh yeah . . . fit as a fiddle," she said, feeling more like a sad trombone.

"Oooh, look, Izzy's flirting," said Molly, suddenly getting a second wind. "He's really cute, Izz. You go, girl!"

The other Mollys laughed as Isabella flushed red.

"So what did you think of dinner?" Gabe asked her, ignoring the attention.

"I actually didn't get a chance to try it," she said, an unmistakable sadness in her voice. "They gave me the wrong time. I just got here."

The look on Gabe's face would've been the same if she'd told him that her entire family had just been massacred on the street outside.

"That's just not acceptable," he said, looking aghast. "This needs to be remedied right away."

He took Isabella by the hand and started leading her out of the room.

"Where are we going?" she asked, unsure of what was happening but extremely grateful to be led out of this insidious den of Mollys.

"Fuck his brains out, Izz!" Molly called as he escorted her out of the room. "Go suck some more D!"

He led her back up the stairs and through the dining room.

"How do you know those people?" he asked, emphasizing the final two words in a way that suggested that he wasn't such a fan.

"I'm ghostwriting one of their cookbooks," she answered, figuring that, since he didn't know who they were, it was safe to tell the truth.

"No way," he said, as he pulled her toward the packed bar. "I got ghosted by a ghostwriter."

Despite the people hovering behind every stool, waiting for

a chance to sit, there was one seat at the end of the bar, right by the wall, with a little placard in front of it that said "reserved" and a round purple pillow on the stool saving its place.

"This seat is for VIPs only," he said, removing the placard and lifting the pillow. "That would be you."

Isabella felt like a piece of mozzarella cheese that'd been stretched and dunked and stretched again as it arrived at its final destination. A night that was supposed to be celebratory had become royally embarrassing, and now it was taking a turn toward the romantic?

"This is so nice," she said, finally looking at Gabe as he escorted her to her stool. His face was open and eager and focused entirely on Isabella. Was it because of her hair? Her dress? Her makeup? Well, no: when he'd first met her, she was wearing overalls and a tie-dyed Ben & Jerry's T-shirt and hadn't showered in two days and was about to get fired, and he'd still seemed smitten.

"Will you let me cook for you? Put yourself into my hands?"

If Isabella had a kink, this would be it.

"Ummm . . . a hundred percent yes?" she answered.

"BRB," he said, dashing away, as a cluster of eager patrons lined up behind Isabella's stool, trying to discern who this person was who was getting such VIP treatment.

Gabe returned moments later holding a champagne glass and a frosty bottle.

"This is what they're drinking downstairs," he said. "They won't notice if I send a little your way. Actually, they won't notice much of anything."

Isabella didn't know anything about wine or champagne, though she wished she knew more. The label seemed fancy and French, and as Gabe filled her glass, she watched the bubbles fizz up to the top and then dissipate.

He produced a second champagne glass from his apron and poured just a little in.

"Quick," he said. "Before my boss sees."

He lifted his champagne glass up.

"To not getting ghosted the third time around," he said.

"Cheers," said Isabella, feeling like that finished ball of mozzarella, now bathing in expensive olive oil on a gilded plate.

. . . .

The first thing that Gabe brought her looked like a tiny teacup on a tiny saucer.

"Celeriac soup with balsamic-glazed pear," he announced as he placed it in front of her. She looked down at the white liquid canvas with a burgundy sliver of pear floating in it. The teacup itself looked like a prop from *Alice in Wonderland*, and the little spoon that it came with was so adorable, she wanted to sneak it into her pocket and take it home.

"And to pair with that," continued Gabe, pulling a wineglass out of his apron and brandishing another bottle of wine, "a Riesling from Austria that's just a teensy bit sweet . . . It'll play off the celery root and the pear beautifully."

"Do you talk to all of your guests this way?" asked Isabella, who was already feeling the effects of the bubbly.

"Only the pretty ones," he replied.

The next hour became, for Isabella, one of the most romantic and culinarily dazzling of her life. When else does an ardent suitor have the means and the wherewithal to cook you a personalized meal using the finest ingredients in the world? How Gabe Kohl managed to do this without arousing the suspicions of his boss—Isabella could see Chef Dusolier yelling from behind the pass—on the busiest night of the week was too much of a marvel to question.

After the soup came a piece of toasted house-made brioche topped with creamed morel mushrooms foraged that morning, paired with a Beaujolais ("I like to shake it up with the red and the white . . . I'm wild that way"), then a single seared scallop in a sauce made from rehydrated seaweed and the liquid from oysters, paired with a chilled Albariño.

While she was slowly savoring the scallop and the briny

sauce, chasing it with the crisp, nutty wine, Isabella caught out of the corner of her eye the Group of Seven emerging from their secret underground lair.

Owen seemed to be shielding Molly from the crowd of onlookers. She was slumped between him and Xavier, with Fiona and the other Mollys forming a phalanx around them.

Isabella looked down at her plate and prayed that Molly wouldn't spot her there, sitting at the VIP seat at the bar, being wined and dined. Fortunately, Molly couldn't see much of anything: at one point, she fell to the floor, and Owen and Xavier had to scoop her back up before the iPhones came out and the gossip rags had a giant picture of her splashed on them the next day. The only person who seemed to notice Isabella was Fiona, who gave Isabella a quick "I see you" bit of eye contact before heading out the door.

Gabe returned with a plate that was the plate of Isabella's dreams. It was like he'd read her mind when she was outside pining through the window. There on the glossy white surface, in an individual portion, was a fillet of branzino, and next to it a big tower of matchstick fries with a scattering of garlic and herbs.

"These are some of our signature bites," said Gabe before producing another wineglass.

"Oh, I know!" said Isabella, definitely a bit tipsy. "I was hoping that you'd bring me exactly what you just brought me."

As Gabe poured her a Pinot Noir from the Russian River Valley, a forceful voice startled them out of their reverie.

"What is happening here?"

Chef Dusolier was standing behind Gabe, nostrils flared, catching Gabe red-wine-handed.

"Since when do we serve an individual portion of branzino? Where is the other half?"

Gabe, flustered, didn't respond.

"And since when do we open expensive bottles of wine to serve one glass to nonpaying customers?"

Casper Dusolier took the bottle from Gabe's hands and studied it.

"This is coming out of your paycheck."

"Oui, chef."

Disgusted, Casper reentered the kitchen, and an embarrassed Gabe put his hand on Isabella's shoulder.

"Don't worry. He'll forget all of this by tomorrow. Plus, he's shorthanded anyway, he can't fire me. I'm too good."

Gabe followed the chef back into the kitchen, and Isabella studied the food in front of her. It wasn't as elevated as the previous dishes: it seemed like it would be more at home at a gastropub or a French bistro. But that's what she loved about it: it was just homey enough to be reproducible in her own kitchen, but not so homey that she would actually take the time to do it. Who would buy a whole branzino just for themselves? And who would go to the trouble of making their own shoestring fries?

Isabella gently guided her fork to the fish and lifted a piece of the pristine white flesh, lightly drizzled with Italian olive oil and dusted with fennel pollen, to her mouth. She closed her eyes as she tasted.

It was simple, but not simple in the pejorative sense. It tasted clean, like the fish had emerged from crystal-blue water already on a plate, just waiting to be enjoyed. The olive oil added depth, and the fennel pollen a floral whiff.

The fries were another story. They crackled under her teeth, and every bite was a salty surprise. There was a sprig of rosemary. There was a whole piece of lemon peel. Was that a caper she detected? There was also some kind of chili dusted on top, giving everything a capricious heat that kept making her go back for more.

The Pinot Noir was like drinking a plum that'd been reclining on a leather chair, and the trifecta of the fish, the fries, and the wine became for Isabella a lodestar, a benchmark against which she would measure all other meals.

As she processed all of these sensations, she saw Gabe watching her from the kitchen, an eager puppy-dog look on his face. She couldn't help but beam her enjoyment back at him.

For the first time in a very long time, she felt completely

happy. It was as if this night, which had seemed so awful at first, was designed in such a way that the lowest lows could build to the highest highs.

At the peak of her gastronomic orgy, and at the height of her surge of happiness, she felt a vibration in her pocket.

She was in such a state of bliss that no text from Molly could disrupt it. No call from Lionel begging for pages would upset her. Even if it was Dana calling to remind her that she had zero personality, her good mood couldn't be punctured.

Instead, it was an unfamiliar number that kept ringing and ringing.

Isabella, more curious than anxious about who could be calling her at ten-thirty on a Friday night, decided to answer. She struggled to hear above the noise, but what she made out involved "hospital" and "your mother."

"I'm sorry," she said, standing up from the stool and plugging her other ear with her finger to hear better. "Can you say that again?"

". . . New York Presbyterian. Your mom's had a fall . . . hit her head . . . We want to keep her overnight for observation."

Her mother.

Her mother, who was expecting her to come to make onion soup tonight.

Her mother, whom she had completely abandoned, was now in the hospital.

"I'll be there right away," she said, and scrambled to find her tote bag with the book in it.

She tried to catch Gabe's eye in the kitchen, but he was nowhere to be seen.

So she grabbed a cocktail napkin and a pen from behind the bar and wrote in big block letters: "SO SORRY. MOM IN HOSPITAL. FOOD AMAZING. PLEASE CALL ME!" with her number circled underneath.

She then did something that made her feel extremely guilty when she thought about it later, but in the moment seemed like the right thing to do.

As quickly as she could, she returned to the plate for one more sublime bite of fish and one final handful of potatoes. She washed it down with the last splash of the Pinot Noir, and then navigated her way back to the door.

For the third time in two months, the ghostwriter ghosted the chef.

12

NOBLE ROT

Some are born guilty, some have guilt thrust upon them, and some, like Isabella, have both: a predisposition for guilt *and* a parent who fuels the guilty fire.

As Isabella exited Snakebite to wait for her Uber to the hospital, rain poured down, and she felt her own voice mingling with her mother's voice inside of her.

How could you forget you were supposed to help your mom tonight? Did you forget, or did you skip it on purpose? You promised you'd help her make soup . . . not just soup, but soup for actual unhoused people who could be eating it right now, drenched from the rain. And what did you do instead? Spent three hundred dollars on a dress for yourself at some bullshit store named after a dressing? Not to mention getting your hair done at a fancy salon, and putting on makeup at Sephora? Oh, and to rub sea salt into the wound, you ate a lavish meal all by yourself, sampling the rarest mushrooms, sipping the finest wines, flirting with the chef, while eight hundred thousand people go to bed hungry every night!

The wine that Isabella had imbibed over the course of the meal—adding up to about three full glasses—did nothing to quell her inner prosecutor. Instead, the voices grew louder: she had abandoned her mother, her widowed mother, who spent all of her time alone and had no one looking after her. Isabella was her only connection to the world, her only protector, and how often did she check in on her? Once a week? Since starting the book, even less than that.

When her dad was alive, she never had to worry about her mom. With Oliver, Jeannie had a constant companion. They were high-school sweethearts, borderline codependent, with Jeannie monitoring every move that Oliver made, and Oliver relishing all of the attention. They rarely ever left the apartment: at home, Jeannie would make her signature Frankensoups, and Oliver would sit at the kitchen table with a magnifying visor and tiny tools, repairing vintage dollhouses, birdhouses, and typewriters that he'd often gift to Isabella.

Isabella didn't understand it growing up, but her parents' affection for one another was highly unusual. They made each other laugh in ways that often made her feel like the third wheel. Why was it so funny that a *Jeopardy!* contestant mispronounced "misshapen" as "Miss Happen"? Why did Isabella slipping on an actual banana peel induce such a fit of giggles in her parents that her dad almost called 911 because her mom couldn't breathe?

These things mystified Isabella as a child, but once she was in her twenties, she began to understand that the two of them were inseparable because they were meant to be together, the way turkey and cranberry sauce were meant to be together, the way pastrami and grainy mustard were meant to be together. Of course, it all ended when that Boston Market truck plowed through their spiritual union and Jeannie was left to fend for herself. That's when the real guilt began. Her mother, who had never been alone since she got married at twenty-two, was now in a big, empty, rent-controlled apartment by herself.

Isabella visited as often as she could, but as a twentysomething just starting out in the job market and living in Greenpoint, she couldn't afford the time (or the energy) to go to the Upper West Side every day after work. And that's when her mother's hoarding started. The hoarding and the charity work. Isabella would try to keep her mother company, but Jeannie wouldn't keep still. It was like she was staving off loneliness by constantly staying in motion. All of her activities—from lifting dinner rolls from bread baskets left on outdoor restaurant tables, to convincing kids in the school yard to donate half their lunches to the hungry—always included passive-aggressive invitations for Isabella to participate.

"You're going to make me do charity work all alone?"

For Isabella, "charity work" was a euphemism for "busywork." If her mother had truly wanted to spend time with her, she could've met her at least halfway. She could've come to Brooklyn to hang out with her and Owen. Or they could've gone to an interesting restaurant in Union Square instead of dumpster diving for dented soup cans that would be mixed together in stomach-churning combinations.

Still: her mother's loneliness weighed on Isabella. Especially on Friday nights, when Isabella would come home exhausted, eager to cook a gourmet meal for herself, the kind where she would spend money on superior ingredients, the kind of meal that people who stopped by to visit Owen would be desperate to try. But there'd always be this awareness in the back of her mind that her mother was alone, not by choice, but by truck. Instead of her sitting on the couch with Oliver, watching *Jeopardy!* like usual, Jeannie was likely sitting on the filthy, unvacuumed floor of her apartment, going through garbage bags of whatever strange items she had brought home that day.

It was this flavor of guilt—the guilt of leaving her already isolated mother even more isolated on a night when she'd promised to cook with her—that pervaded Isabella's consciousness the most at this particular moment. When the Uber finally arrived, Isabella's dress and cardigan were soaked, and her newly styled hair was matted to her head, as if the weather itself were condemning her for her selfish actions before she'd even had a chance to defend herself.

. . . .

The upside to being drunk and guilty is that, when you have to come face-to-face with the source of your guilt, you're a bit numb to the realities surrounding you. So, as Isabella entered the fluorescent waiting room of New York Presbyterian's Emergency Room at eleven-thirty, she saw everything through a haze: an old man moaning in pain as he held an ice pack to his head; a young woman, about her own age, sitting in a wheelchair, breathing intently as she waited to give birth, no discernible companion in sight.

She would've called her mother to find out which room she was in, but her mother was against having a cellphone because . . . of course she was. Instead, Isabella waltzed past the front desk and wended her way from room to room until she heard an unmistakable voice call out to her:

"I'm in here."

Even with an injury that would leave her hospitalized overnight, Jeannie could sniff out her daughter from a mile away. Isabella, her dress still wet, her hair still damp, entered her mother's hospital room and found Jeannie sitting up in bed, knitting a scarf with yarn and needles that Isabella had never seen before. She didn't even know that her mother knew how to knit.

"Why are you soaked? Get some paper towels and pat yourself dry before you get sick."

"Mom," said Isabella, ignoring her mother's instruction (at least for the time being). "What happened? They scared me half to death when they called me from the hospital. They said you fell and hit your head?"

"I'll tell you what happened," said Jeannie, as if she relished this opportunity to relate her sorrowful tale. "I was making that big pot of onion soup that you promised to help me with—"

"I know, I'm sorry, I—"

"And at some point I said to myself: Jeannie, how are you going to get all of this soup to the shelter? I didn't have a Tupperware big enough. But I remembered that I had freezer bags at the top of the pantry, only I couldn't reach, so I grabbed a kitchen chair, and I was on my tippy-toes, trying to get to the bags in the very back, and the next thing I knew, I was on the floor with blood trickling down my head."

Isabella approached the bed to get a better look at her mother. Indeed, there were stitches on her head, from the top of her forehead into her scalp. "What did the doctors say?"

"The doctors," said Jeannie with contempt, returning to her knitting work. "They said: 'You hit your head and you have a concussion, and we're going to make you stay the night to make sure you don't drop dead in your sleep.'"

Jeannie's gallows humor may have been funny to outsiders, but for Isabella it was distressing. When Oliver died, Jeannie used humor to deflect from her real feelings of devastation. The night when they went to view his body at the morgue, she said: "He couldn't get hard for fifteen years, and now he's a human Popsicle."

"I'm glad to see you're in good spirits despite everything," said Isabella, finally taking her mother's advice and patting herself down with paper towels next to the sink. There was a curtain dividing the room in half, and on the other side, Isabella could hear loud beeping and pumping noises but couldn't see or hear the person connected to all of the machines.

"And what was so important that you got all dressed up and ditched your mother?"

This was delivered as a half-joke, half-attack, and Isabella took it as such.

"Molly got a job on a new Netflix show. So we all went out to dinner to celebrate."

"Who's Molly?" asked Jeannie, and this time Isabella couldn't tell if she was kidding or being serious.

"Molly Babcock, the TV star whose cookbook I'm ghostwriting?"

Jeannie made a tutting noise that sounded like musical disapproval.

"You're still working on that farkakteh cookbook? I thought you were done with that?"

"No, I'm not done with that," said Isabella, though, after tonight, she wished she could be done with that. The way Molly and her friends had laughed at her when she went off with Gabe was enough to make her want never to go back to work again, it was so humiliating.

"I'd understand it more if you were supplementing it with something meaningful, something respectable, something noble," said Jeannie, looking up at her daughter over her knitting. "But to put all of your energy into something so meaningless and shallow . . ."

"Let's not fight about this now."

"Fight about what? I'm just worried about your spiritual life."

A loud sigh was suddenly emitted from behind the curtain, and Isabella and Jeannie gave each other a look.

"Is there anything I can do for you now?" asked Isabella, glad for the diversion from their conversation about her career. It was easy for her mother to judge: Her mother grew up wealthy. Her mother inherited a sizable sum from her parents, and then more from the judgment against Boston Market. She could afford to be noble; Isabella, who wasn't granted access to that money, couldn't.

"I'll tell you what you can do," said Jeannie, sitting up even higher in the hospital bed. "You can go to the apartment and ladle the soup into freezer bags—they fell down along with your mother—and take the soup to the shelter. They were waiting for it earlier, and this nice man named Rob is up at all hours. He'll take it from you."

Isabella started doing the math in her head. It was almost midnight. By the time she got to her mother's apartment from the hospital, it would most likely be twelve-thirty. And by the time she ladled a pot of onion soup into freezer bags and brought them to the shelter on Eighty-sixth Street, it would be close to one in the morning.

"Can't we do this tomorrow? Wouldn't it be better if I stayed here with you?"

"No, we can't do this tomorrow. I promised them the soup tonight, and they were counting on it to feed the hungry tomorrow."

This seemed highly suspicious to Isabella. A soup kitchen that relied solely on her mother to feed the hungry the next day? Didn't they have soup that they made themselves? Shouldn't a soup kitchen actually be a soup kitchen?

"If that's what you want me to do, I'll do it," said Isabella; it might not be a rational thing, but at least it would appease her unappeasable mother.

"I don't want you to do it for me. I want you to do it because it's the right thing to do."

"If you say so," said Isabella as she stood up from her mother's bed.

"Go back to my apartment when you're done, and sleep in my bed. You can come get me tomorrow."

And the guilty, guilted Isabella left to do just that.

. . . .

Every time Isabella had been in her mother's apartment since her father's death, Jeannie had been there to mitigate the incremental, but increasingly odd, changes that she was making to the space. Very discreetly, she'd removed all of the pictures from the walls: pictures from her wedding, from Isabella's Bat Mitzvah, from Isabella's graduation. Nothing went up in their place. Instead, the apartment began to fill with bric-a-brac. Folding tables took the place of chairs. On them were stacked papers, none of which Isabella had ever bothered to look through, but she figured they were somehow related to her mother's enterprises.

The carpets were no longer visible on the floor. In their place there were cardboard boxes piled on cardboard boxes, each one filled with an assortment of doodads and thingamajigs that Jeannie had come upon in her lonely escapades around the city. One was filled with battered-looking dog toys. Another was filled with an assortment of takeout menus, some of them from the eighties. One was filled with something wet, and Isabella didn't dare peek inside: she just saw the splotches of moisture on the outside of the box.

As disturbing as this all was, it felt somewhat rational in Jeannie's presence. She assured Isabella that there was a method to her madness, and Isabella believed her. But when she entered her mother's apartment on her own on this particular night, these things took on a different hue.

For starters, there was the smell. Whenever Isabella was there, Jeannie would be cooking up something so foul in and of itself that it would mask whatever deeper scent had taken over the space where Isabella had spent her childhood. Now, walking in, she felt like she'd been smacked in the face with a dead fish.

What was that smell? There was the scent of the onions and the beef broth, which Isabella traced directly to the stove, where she saw a giant stockpot filled to the brim with whatever brown muck her mother had conjured up. The soup smell was slightly stale, almost like the scent of a nursing home, the pungency of onions mixing with the unmistakable scent of urine.

But where was the urine smell coming from? Isabella traced that to a garbage bag on the couch. When she opened it up, it was filled with what appeared to be soiled bedsheets. Where she'd found them, God only knows, but the fact that she'd brought them into the apartment was worrisome to Isabella. Was her mother cracking up? Was she a hoarder? Or was this still part of her charity work?

As Isabella pondered the question, she felt her phone buzz in her pocket. She glanced down and saw a text from an unfamiliar number:

How's your mom? This is Gabe by the way. The chef who just cooked you dinner?

If Isabella felt nauseous from the smell—like she was on a rocky boat—this text from Gabe felt like Dramamine.

Gabe! she immediately texted back. *Mom's okay. She got stitches on her head. Dinner was amazing. Thank you again.*

What are you doing now? he texted back.

It was a bit forward, but Isabella liked that. It made her feel sexy.

Ummm . . . ladling onion soup into freezer bags to bring to a soup kitchen?

She knew it was weird, but it was the truth.

That's what I figured. JK. WTF? Dinner next week?

Isabella felt like a human blush emoji when she read Gabe's invite. When was the last time she'd been asked on a date? And asked by a person she'd met in the real world, not some loser from Jdate?

I'd love that, she wrote.

Great, he immediately replied. *Now where to take you that'll impress you? More soon . . .*

She hearted that message, as her own heart beat twice as fast, and then returned to the work at hand. It was almost one, and she hadn't even started ladling.

She stepped into the kitchen and located the freezer bags on the floor. The chair that her mother had used was still tipped over, and she saw a smear of blood on the floor, which she wiped up with paper towels before righting the chair. Finally, she began ladling the yellow-brown liquid into freezer bags. When she was finished—and it took her a good twenty minutes to ladle out the whole pot—Isabella placed the freezer bags into the wheeling cart that her mother kept in her entryway. It was the kind of cart Isabella would see senior citizens pushing around the Upper West Side whenever she visited her mother. Jeannie seemed too young to have one of her own, but now Isabella was glad to make use of it. She piled up the soup bags and pushed the cart out into the hallway.

As soon as she left the apartment, she felt the relief that you feel when you've held your breath underwater a little too long and come exploding to the surface, gasping for air.

When Jeannie said that Isabella should stay in her bed that night, it made good sense, since it was only four blocks from the hospital. But now that she'd been in there alone, now that she'd smelled that rancid smell in isolation, Isabella would rather take the hourlong subway journey back to Greenpoint than to re-enter that cursed, stifling space.

But first she had to deliver the soup.

. . . .

The address that her mother gave her required a twenty-block walk with the soup cart, in her ruined dress, through the rain. This was its own cruel version of a walk of shame for abandoning her mother: she felt like a Jewish Cersei Lannister being paraded through King's Landing on *Game of Thrones*. Instead of a shame nun, she imagined a female rabbi with a bell behind her, calling out: "It's a shanda! A shanda! A shanda!"

When she finally arrived at the shelter, it took her a moment to remember the name her mother had given her. Was it Richard? Ricardo? No, Ricardo was the salesperson at Honey Dijon. Did all of that happen on this same night? It seemed impossible. At last, Isabella remembered the name—Rob—as she rang the bell outside the doorway to the industrial-looking building.

She looked at her watch: it was one-thirty. That someone was going to answer the door at one-thirty in the morning seemed highly unlikely, but after all of the trouble that she'd gone to— after getting soaked, inside and out—she would stand there for an hour if it meant finally being able to deliver this goddamned soup.

To her infinite surprise, a man actually did show up at the

door. He looked like a PE teacher: Bald, with a beard, he had a gold chain around his neck and a gold hoop earring, and he was wearing athletic clothes. Despite his apparel, he had a warm, welcoming face.

"Hey," he said, opening the door, as if this were a regular occurrence. "We're at full capacity, but I know it's raining. Do you need a place to stay tonight? We can probably find some room on the floor."

He scanned Isabella up and down to make sense of what he was looking at. Was she a drug addict? An emancipated sex worker? A college student having a nervous breakdown?

"No, I'm not here to stay or anything," she stammered. "I'm delivering soup for my mother . . . Jeannie Pasternak? Are you Rob?"

The look on Rob's face—for he was, indeed, Rob, as he quickly acknowledged—told many stories at once. As soon as Isabella invoked her mother's name, Rob's eyebrows went up, his nostrils flared, he took a deep breath. His eyes went from projecting concern to projecting what seemed to Isabella to be a combination of pity and contempt.

"You're Jeannie's daughter?"

"Yes," she said, eager to get out of the rain. "I'm Isabella. Should I bring these inside?"

"No," he said firmly, finally noticing the bags of soup piled up in the cart. "Do not bring those inside. You can come inside. Those stay out here."

There was something about his tone that made Isabella feel like she was being summoned to the principal's office. *What now?* she thought to herself as she followed him down a long corridor.

Cots lined the hallway, with various sleeping occupants, as Isabella followed Rob toward an office in the back. She saw a room also filled with cots, with children asleep with their mothers, and some people on the floor.

"Right in here," he said, holding the door to his office open.

There was a steaming cup of Dunkin' Donuts coffee on the table, and an open carton with several doughnuts inside.

"Would you like one?" he asked, catching Isabella peeking at the flavors.

"No, thanks," she said even though a doughnut sounded good at this moment, especially given the hangover that was sure to arrive tomorrow morning.

She sat down in the chair across from Rob, who sat behind his desk, crossed his arms, and looked Isabella over again.

"So . . . Jeannie is your mother," he said, as if he wanted to confirm that she, this normal-seeming person, was related to that odd specimen known as Jeannie.

"Yes, she is," Isabella replied, as if they'd already been over this, which they had.

"Well, let me cut to the chase," said Rob. "Your mother is a bit of a notorious figure around here."

Notorious. That wasn't a good word.

"How so?"

Rob stood up from his chair and leaned against the wall, still facing Isabella.

"She's made a lot of people very sick. All around the city. She's even sent some people to the hospital."

He pulled open a drawer and removed a flyer. On it was a picture of Jeannie and in bold block type above it: DO NOT ACCEPT FOOD FROM THIS WOMAN.

"This is hanging in soup kitchens all over Manhattan right now," he said, handing Isabella the flyer.

She looked down at the image of her mother—a grainy image taken from a security camera—and almost had to laugh. Her mother a criminal? Her nebbish mother, who still watched *Jeopardy!* every night, who read *The New Yorker* cover to cover every week, who did the Sunday *Times* crossword puzzle in pen? Now she looked like a Jewish Jesse James on a wanted poster in the Old West.

"This is actually really serious," said Rob, noticing Isabella's smile.

"I'm sure it is," she replied. "Sorry. I'm just exhausted."

"Your mom is relentless."

You're telling me? Isabella wanted to reply.

"We told her to stop making food and bringing it here, but she does everything in her power to defy our requests. She uses ingredients . . ." He made a whistling noise. "I don't know where she finds them. But she's brought us rancid chicken. Expired milk. Chili that smelled like dog food . . . that may have actually been dog food. And before we knew better, before we knew who we were dealing with, we actually gave this to people to eat. And a lot of them spent several nights throwing up or sitting on the toilet. One had to have her stomach pumped."

Now Isabella's amusement transformed into genuine shame.

"I knew that she used . . . questionable ingredients," said Isabella. "But I didn't know that they were so dangerous."

"Very dangerous," said Rob, sitting back down. "Especially to people who are already vulnerable, people who are just trying to survive on the streets. Can you imagine how destabilizing this can be for someone who's already hit rock bottom?"

The way Rob talked about this made Jeannie seem like some kind of culinary predator who targeted the unhoused. Which maybe she was, in her own innocent way?

"I'll tell her she has to stop," said Isabella, unsure of how she'd ever broach this with her mother.

"Good," said Rob. "Because if she keeps this up, we're going to get the police involved. After a certain point, you can't claim naïveté. After a certain point, she has to be aware of what she's doing."

Isabella nodded, eager to get out of the chair, eager to get away from this night, with its ups and downs and sudden twists and turns.

"I guess this means you don't want her onion soup?" joked Isabella.

Rob didn't smile.

"Sorry," she said. "Not funny."

"Throw all of it away," he said. "Every last drop."

"Okay," she replied, standing up. "Actually, I think I will have a doughnut."

She took a strawberry glazed and bit into it—stale as it was, it tasted so good, so necessary—as she followed Rob back out of the building. He wished her a good night and she returned to the cart, the soup still in there, the freezer bags all wet with rain. She threw all the bags, one by one, into the trash on the corner, convinced that it would be highly unlikely that any person going through the trash would open up a bag of this dank brown liquid to drink it.

More tired than she'd ever been, Isabella decided to end the night by treating herself one last time: she ordered herself an Uber back to Greenpoint, and even though it was a dented 2002 Camry that picked her up, it might as well have been a limousine. She'd never been happier to go home—her *own* home—in her entire life.

13

EXPEDITING

An industrial-strength pencil sharpener—or something that sounded like one—startled Isabella out of such a profound sleep, it took a few seconds for her to realize that she was no longer in an Uber, that it was the next morning, and that she was in her own bed. Once again, she didn't remember getting under the covers. She didn't know what time she'd gotten home. When she finally opened her eyes, she saw that she was still wearing the dress from the night before, a dress that had been through so much over the past fifteen hours, it looked the way she felt: ragged, beat up, unsalvageable.

Another burst of the grinding noise led Isabella out of bed and into the kitchen, where she discovered a sharply dressed Owen grinding espresso beans in a gleaming red tractor-like Marzocco espresso machine: the same one that they used in all of the fanciest coffee shops in Brooklyn. It was set on the kitchen table, taking up the only space Isabella had to chop vegetables, roll out pie dough, and season chicken thighs.

"Espresso? Cappuccino? Latte?" asked a chipper Owen, grinning at Isabella as he latched the portafilter onto the machine. "You look like death warmed over. I'll make you a Red Eye."

"What is this? It's big enough to be a car." Isabella wondered how she would ever be able to cook in this kitchen again.

"It's a gift from my dad, for getting Molly the Netflix gig! He said the only network that would've hired her before I came on the scene was OnlyFans."

Owen was in such a good mood, Isabella didn't want to puncture it by bringing up the fiasco the previous night at Snakebite.

"Did you see TMZ this morning?" he asked, as the machine began pushing out espresso with the force of a hundred baristas. "Molly's plastered all over it."

The fact that Owen thought that Isabella would look at TMZ first thing in the morning, on this morning or any morning, revealed something about how little he understood her.

"I must've missed it," she said, as she leaned against the doorway, watching Owen begin to steam the milk. From the way he held the wand, she was certain he was going to splatter oat milk all over his thousand-dollar jacket. Instead, he dipped the wand in too deep, saving the suit but ruining the froth.

"The headline is 'Good Golly Miss Molly!' It shows her falling on her drunk ass on her way out of Snakebite, with every single person recording her on their iPhone. It's like you can't even sneeze in public anymore without it showing up all over the internet. But I actually think this is a really good sign," he said as he recklessly poured the half-steamed oat milk into the double shot of espresso at the bottom of his Inked Giuiette Jonathan Adler mug. "It means people care about her again. I guess after *Deadline* ran the announcement about the show, people started remembering who she was."

Isabella nodded as if she found this fascinating, when, in fact, the only thing that she cared about was making sure that Owen wouldn't be grinding espresso beans again as she crawled back into bed.

"And now that she's having a mo'," said Owen, as he took a sip of his handiwork, a self-satisfied look on his face, "the publisher is horny to get the book out sooner. They want to time the book release to coincide with the show's premiere."

"O-kay?" Isabella knew nothing about TV timelines or book

release timelines, so she stood there dumbly, thinking she would need six espresso shots to get her brain working again.

"How soon can you get everything done? Like the fastest you think you can possibly do it?"

Isabella pondered this question the way that someone might ponder an equally impossible feat, like "How long would it take you to build a life-sized replica of Grand Central Station with marshmallows?"

What made it feel so impossible was Molly's renewed lack of interest and participation. How could she force a cookbook out of someone who didn't care about cookbooks or cooking, especially now that she was going to be famous again? How could she gather enough material to write the introduction and the rest of the front matter, plus all of the headnotes, not to mention the interstitial material: the little boxes with tips and advice and anecdotes about Molly's life? Plus the recipes themselves?

As Isabella stood there questioning all of this, she remembered what Lionel had told her a week ago: "You don't need Molly to write this cookbook."

When Lionel said it, Isabella thought that was the most absurd thing that she'd ever heard. It would be like saying, "You don't need Chilean sea bass to make Chilean sea bass." But the more that Isabella contemplated it, the more that she realized Lionel was right. Molly was never going to help her write this book. Not only that: if she did let Molly help, it'd all be hacked-apart kale salads and God knows what else. It was time to go rogue. It was time to lean into her secret weapon, Candy Babcock's binder.

She could pull recipes from that and write everything as Molly Babcock, only with a little more refinement. The same way that the Honey Dijon dress made Isabella look like Isabella, but better, Isabella's ghostwriting would make Molly sound like Molly, but better. Without Molly, she could bang out this cookbook in a few weeks, and then—at long last—work on building up her own career as Isabella Pasternak: she could start her own

Substack, pitch stories to *Eater* and *Grub Street*, grow a following on TikTok . . . if she could get over her fear of being on camera.

These were the things that she'd been pondering the previous night as she slipped in and out of consciousness in the back of the Uber. Something important had shifted inside of her when Rob revealed that her mother had made so many people sick with her "charity" work. Jeannie, whose high horse was practically a member of the family, had made Isabella feel so shallow and selfish for wanting to pursue a career as a food writer. But who was Jeannie to judge? Had Jeannie really been doing good for the world, or only doing good for Jeannie? How could Isabella have let her mother hold her back for so long? She felt like she'd been living in a cult with strange soup rituals, and only now, after Rob opened her eyes, did she realize that her life with her mother was spooky and disturbing enough to be a miniseries. It was like she was in a car with a crazy person behind the wheel, and only after the car was almost driven off a cliff did she have the sense to wrest control for herself.

"Three weeks," said Isabella, after Owen watched her perform the calculations in her head.

Owen, who expected her to say three months at the least, looked startled.

"You can finish the *whole cookbook* in three weeks?"

"Yup," said Isabella, more confident than she'd ever sounded in her life. "But you're going to have to drive that espresso truck into your room. I'm going to need all of the space I can get."

. . . .

Organization was never Isabella's strong suit. Her bedroom had three piles of clothes on the floor: the "mostly wearable," the "slightly wearable," and the "totally unwearable." Her cookbooks, despite some loose organizing principles, were in constant disarray. Her birth certificate was buried somewhere near her diploma, which was ensconced in a menu that she'd kept from Gramercy Tavern that one time she got to write about it for *Comestibles*. No, organization was not Isabella's strong suit . . . *except* when it came to writing.

With a writing project in front of her, she became like a TV detective who spends hours constructing a bulletin board with pictures of all of the possible suspects, pieces of string connecting everything together. Isabella did the same, only now she would do it with recipes.

As she made her way to Office Depot to pick up index cards and multicolored Sharpies to begin shaping the book, her phone rang (it was 9:00 a.m.), and she knew immediately who it would be, just from the intensity of the buzz in her pocket.

"How did it go?" came her mom's unmistakable voice. "Did you meet Rob? I'm checking out of the hospital, if you want to walk over."

"I'm back in Greenpoint," said Isabella, huffing as she faced the cold, windy day. "I brought the soup to Rob. He didn't want it."

There was a pause. In that pause, Isabella wondered so many things: Did her mother send her to the soup kitchen so that Rob would expose her? Did she want to be found out? Why else would she pick a person who so clearly had her number? Who obviously had turned her away many times before?

"I can't stand that Rob," said Jeannie. "Imagine rejecting perfectly good soup that hungry people could be eating."

"He had good reasons. In fact, he told me a lot; he told me that—"

Jeannie immediately cut her off.

"So am I supposed to walk home by myself *with a concussion?*"

"You'll be okay, Mom," said Isabella, not at all worried about her mother's making it home, and much more worried about getting her to talk about the wanted poster with her face on it in soup kitchens around the city. It was a confrontation that she wanted to put off for as long as possible, but also, for the sake of the next round of soup victims, one that she needed to have ASAP.

"Well, let's just hope that I don't drop dead on the street," said Jeannie, only half kidding. "I'll text when I get home."

When Isabella got back from Office Depot, she made her bed—something that she rarely did—so that she could lay columns of index cards on it. Each column was a different section of the book: Appetizers she renamed "Appe-Teasers" because it sounded like a Mollyism. Salads became "Something Crunchy," soups became "Liquid Yum," entrées became "Kind of a Big Deal," desserts became "Little Sweeties."

Then she pulled out the red binder and began pulling recipes at random.

In the Appe-Teaser column, she put Candy's "Epic Cheeseball," which Isabella translated to "That's Soooo Cheesy" in Mollyspeak. In the "Liquid Yum" column, she put Candy's Minestrone with Summer Vegetables, which she changed to "Vegging Out." In "Kind of a Big Deal," she put Candy's Pot Roast with Mashed Potatoes, titling it "I Like It Wet and Meaty." (Pretty gross, she knew, so she'd go back to that one.) And in "Little Sweeties," she added Candy's Ricotta Cheesecake, which was the first thing Isabella wanted to make when it came time to start testing the recipes. She changed that to "Cream Your Shorts Cheesecake."

The more she worked, the more this methodology of writing Molly's cookbook without Molly made complete sense to her, with one exception: testing the recipes would undeniably be easier in Molly's kitchen. With that giant island in the middle and the two ovens, not to mention the aesthetically pleasing, top-of-the-line cooking gear that Molly never used, Isabella could bang out five recipes a day, easily. In her own kitchen, just doing one recipe might take her all afternoon, given all of the negotiations that she had to make with the space: constantly cleaning cutting boards and knives instead of pushing them aside.

As she continued to write, she realized that it probably wouldn't hurt to have Molly in *some* proximity to the content going into the cookbook with her name on it. Isabella didn't want to run anything past her—God only knew what Molly's moods would do to Isabella's work flow—but if she went in there assuredly and just told her this was what they were doing that day, she was pretty sure that Molly, who was probably totally consumed with her show coming up, would be okay with it.

Thus, Isabella made and started to execute her plan: her first week, she would write as much as she could possibly write without cooking; her second week, she would go to Molly's and start recipe testing, adding tips and tricks and little sidebars to the recipes as she worked her way through them, maybe even asking Molly for a comment or two. And the third week she would use to polish everything before submitting it to Owen, Lionel, and the publisher, and wiping her hands of this project once and for all.

First up? The introduction. Since the book was ostensibly titled *Just Like Mom Made*, Isabella took a swing at writing about Molly's mother, based on the very little that she knew about Molly's mother:

My mother, Candy Babcock, collected recipes the way some people collect baseball cards. She kept everything in an enormous red binder, where everything from her Thanksgiving Turkey (see page 00) to the cake that she made for me every year on my birthday (see page 00) was tucked in along with random recipes for Spanish Paella (page 00), Russian Borscht (page 00), and Jewish Penicillin (aka her famous chicken soup, page 00), which she made even though she was Presbyterian [fact check?]. When she died, this binder became like a living relic of everything that I loved about her as a person.

Isabella chose to ignore the part about Molly's leaving the binder buried in her father's basement for half a decade, only to retrieve it when the opportunity arose to write a cookbook. She also left out the part about Molly's having abandoned her mother toward the end of her life. Wasn't that what her father was yelling about when they made their great escape? Was that why Molly was so cagey about making her mother's recipes? The less Isabella knew about it, the better.

Over the next week, she wrote headnotes for pierogis with pork and sauerkraut ("Dumplings for Days"), buttermilk pancakes with real maple syrup ("Cake for Breakfast!"), and strawberry shortcake ("Bury Me in Berries"). She wrote headnotes that sounded like Molly, but better. Like her headnote for Candy's BLTs:

> *A good BLT happens like a three-way. The bacon seduces the lettuce, which pulls in the tomato, and before you know it, there's an orgy on a mayonnaise-lubricated piece of toast.*

Did that sound like Molly? Well, it had sex in it, so Isabella figured it at least checked one of the boxes.

By day three, a Wednesday, she had cranked out thirty headnotes with thirty loosely formed recipes that she would test later, plus the introduction and a section on equipment and ingredients that was pretty standard for most cookbooks. (Isabella wrote it using her own expertise, since she didn't think Molly was even aware of what was in her refrigerator *or* her kitchen drawers.) At one-thirty, after a quick lunch of her signature not-too-soft, not-too-hard scrambled eggs on toasted brioche—Isabella still took the time to cook for herself—she got a message from Gabe, who'd been texting her on and off throughout the week:

I hear you have a hot date
on Friday.

                        Oh yeah? With who?

With me, dummy.

                        Where are you taking me?

Wouldn't you like to know.

                        I would. How else will I know where
to go?

Meet me in front of the
Brooklyn Bowl at 6:30.

We're going bowling? Gross!

Bowling alley hot dogs are
the best! But that's not where
we're going.

I'm intrigued.

Good! Come hungry.

I always do.

Now Isabella had something to push toward: if she could hit sixty recipes by Thursday night, she could swing by Molly's on Friday and start testing them. Then she could be relaxed and carefree on her date with Gabe, a date she'd been looking forward to ever since she scribbled her number on a cocktail napkin.

Owen's espresso machine, which he never took off the table, became an energy IV for Isabella as she plowed through writing the recipes. On Thursday, she had so much espresso she literally felt her hands vibrating as she typed headnotes for lentil soup ("Totally Mental Lentil Soup"), spaghetti and meatballs ("On Top of Pascetti"), lemon semifreddo ("Pucker Up Lemon Cream"), and vinegary coleslaw ("Mayo Is Gross Coleslaw").

To come up with stuff to say about all of this without any frame of reference was a task built for Isabella. She'd read enough recipes in enough cookbooks over the years to know the basic format by heart. A personal anecdote, a little quip, a little advice about the ingredients, and on to the next one. She couldn't make up the personal anecdotes, but sometimes a stain on the side of Candy's recipe would be enough of a prompt:

Fried chicken is meant to be messy. If you don't have oil stains on your shirt by the time you're done, you're not doing it right.

Or an ancient restaurant menu with a recipe scribbled on it allowed Isabella to take some liberties, especially with the help of Google images:

Gino's Wharf in Wellfleet, Massachusetts, is the place all oysters want to go to die. If the building looks like a shack, that's because it is. There's not much to it besides the bar, the oyster counter, and a few rickety tables. But their clam chowder is the best you'll ever have.

Occasionally, Isabella would question whether a particular recipe was Mollyesque or not. The clam chowder, for example, had two cups of cream in it. If Molly were to see the calorie count on that, plus the potatoes, not to mention the butter, she'd probably lose her breakfast and lunch at the same time, assuming she'd had breakfast or lunch that day. On the other hand, Candy was her mother, and this cookbook was going to be a tribute to her mother's recipes (whether Molly wanted that or not . . . Isabella just needed to get this done!), and clearly this was one that Candy attached to some happy memory in Wellfleet, so it was going in.

By the time Friday rolled around, Isabella had accomplished the impossible: she'd made it to seventy rough headnotes, with only five left to go. She figured that she could leave those final five recipe ideas to Molly. Maybe squeeze in a hacked-apart kale salad with lemon juice, like the one she so violently made on TikTok. Let Molly feel a part of things. If that's what Molly wanted. (She hoped that wasn't what Molly wanted.)

. . . .

As soon as she entered Molly's apartment that afternoon, Isabella felt a sense of unease.

It had been more than a week since she'd been there, testing recipes before the infamous Snakebite dinner. Now the place looked like a combination of Christmas morning and backstage at a school play: There were scripts laid out on various surfaces, red markers, a tripod set up with a ring light. Outfits were draped over couches, some still in their garment bags. Boxes of shoes from expensive-seeming places (Isabella only knew the names from *Sex and the City*), makeup kits, a hair dryer next to a giant hairbrush next to a giant curling iron that was still plugged into the wall.

"What did they say *exactly*?" Isabella heard Molly ask from the kitchen.

The front door was unlocked, so Isabella had let herself in, but as she entered, she felt like she was intruding on something unusually private and important. Then she heard Owen's voice.

"They're not saying anything definitive," he said, a telling quiver in his own voice, too. "They're just saying that some of these articles coming out about . . . your antics are giving a few of the executives pause."

"Which executives? That douche-y one with the blond hair? Or that uptight one with the reading glasses?"

Isabella announced her presence by coughing as she made her way into the kitchen, but, as when she arrived at Snakebite, she felt like the human manifestation of an afterthought.

"It doesn't matter which ones," said Owen, who was sitting at the kitchen counter and eating a salad from a plastic container. "The point is, they're nervous that Molly two-point-o is acting a lot like the original model. Maybe you should stop hanging around with Xavier for a bit? Just until the show starts up?"

Xavier, Isabella knew, was riding Molly's coattails as far as he could out of his own obscurity. Despite not reading TMZ in the morning (or at any other time of day), Isabella had seen a picture of them together on Google News; Molly, once again, was draped over Xavier, who was smirking as if he were pulling a fast one that everyone was aware of except its victim.

"Xavier's fine," said Molly, who was busy eating a salad of her own, moving the parts around and only occasionally taking a bite. "He's letting me use his cottage upstate this weekend to decompress."

"He can afford a cottage upstate?" Owen let the question

pop out before he realized that it would be an insult to Molly's taste in men.

"Yes, he can afford a cottage upstate. Xavier's done very well for himself with Bitcoin, FYI," she said, lobbing those last three letters like darts.

Annoyed with Owen, Molly let her gaze settle on Isabella.

"Hiiii," she said, as if she were finally done with an onerous task that was keeping her from her friend. "I feel like I haven't seen you in forever. What happened the other night at dinner? Did you fuck that chef?"

"No," said Isabella with a laugh, as if Molly catcalling after her and Gabe was the funniest thing ever instead of mortifying. "But we're going on a date tonight."

"Ooooh . . . where's he taking you?"

Owen was frantically typing into his phone, though he lifted his head at the question. Isabella gave him a look to see if he was at all intrigued that the person he'd been forever urging to get on Hinge, Tinder, Scruff—anything to meet another human being in a romantic context—was finally taking a leap into the dating pool. Instead, he lowered his head back to the phone and continued his frantic typing.

"I'm not sure yet. He said I should meet him by the Brooklyn Bowl, but that we're not going bowling?"

"Ew, he is *not* taking you bowling. Tell him to take you somewhere fancy!"

"Maybe he will."

"Oh, honey, you have to make it clear from the get-go. You know my motto? Two cocktails and a meal, or no big reveal."

Isabella forced a laugh at Molly's rhyme, even though she thought it was dated, idiotic advice.

"So," said Isabella, attempting to pivot, "I've been working at home on the cookbook, because I know you're so busy with the show and everything."

"You have?" Molly jabbed a piece of iceberg on to her fork, studied it, and put it back down. "That's good. TBQH, the cookbook has been the last thing on my mind. It's been so insane with the show. The first table read is, like, three weeks away!"

"Wow," said Isabella, grateful that Molly was distracted enough to let her take the reins. "So I was wondering, while you're working on the show and everything, if I could use your kitchen to test recipes? Mine is super-small; otherwise, I'd just test them at home."

Molly eyed Isabella as she finally chewed a piece of cucumber, seeming to work out some calculus with every chew.

"Why don't you come with me to Xavier's cabin this weekend, and we can cook some of the recipes together? I'm going to be bored out of my mind anyway, and it'll help me take my mind off things."

This invitation was as surprising and undesirable to Isabella as cracking into an egg and finding a dead chicken embryo. Why in the world would Molly want to spend the weekend alone with Isabella? Didn't she have real friends she could go away with? Who were those other Mollys at the table? Why couldn't she go with them? Or with Owen? Or Xavier? Or Fiona? Why did it have to be her?

"Sure," said Isabella, wishing for her appendix to burst or her lung to collapse to give her any excuse not to go.

"Great," said Molly. She stood up and threw most of the salad away. "I'll pick you up tomorrow, and we'll drive there together. It'll be a good distraction from this Hollywood bullshit."

She directed that last line to Owen, who was still typing on his phone, looking more and more concerned with every text.

"Cool . . . it'll be fun," said Isabella, knowing that a weekend alone with Molly would be many things but that fun wouldn't be one of them.

14

SECOND FIDDLES

The last time that Isabella went on a date, her suitor—a young NYU dental-school student named Mike Slivovitz—took her to a greasy sports bar, where he ate chicken wings like a feral animal, placing the bones in front of him in a cryptic semi-circle, and insisted that they split the check at the end, even though she'd only had an undrinkable glass of red wine. When he invited her back to his apartment, she faked an asthma attack to escape the clutches of the sauce-spattered close-talker with hot-sauce chicken breath.

And that was a fairly decent date compared with some of the duds that she'd met up with from Jdate. Her pursuit of "a nice Jewish boy," part of her mother-pleasing agenda, had led her to a fortysomething-year-old accountant who was apparently still married ("I'm not giving her the satisfaction of a divorce!"), a twentysomething reality-show producer who said he was "bi" but read as so gay that Isabella wanted to throw him his own personal Pride parade; and a thirtysomething social-media manager who claimed to be "on the spectrum" and used that as an excuse to scroll on his phone throughout their whole, merci-fully short dinner.

All of this made her date with Gabe—the only activity that she was looking forward to now that a weekend with Molly was looming over her—one that she didn't want to screw up. From the little time that she'd spent with him, she had a really good feeling. It was the kind of feeling that people tell you about ("When you know, you'll know," her grandmother used to say, even though her grandmother was thrice divorced) but that you don't believe exists until it happens. Gabe had been her knight in shining armor that night at Snakebite; he took care of her in a way that nobody else in her life—not her mother, not her best friend, not even herself—did. And that was only their third meeting.

When she arrived outside the bowling alley, Gabe was already there, scanning the distance for her as she approached and lighting up when their eyes connected. He was wearing a red-and-navy flannel shirt, a tan corduroy jacket, and tight dark-blue jeans that showed off his strong legs. Isabella had pulled out her only other decent outfit from the "mostly wearable" pile: a button-down white shirt with a green argyle cardigan that she wore with her "slightly wearable" everyday jeans.

"You showed up!" he said, opening his arms and pulling her into a bear hug. He was giving big-brother energy, like your best friend's big brother whom you secretly have a crush on.

"Did you think I'd ghost you again?"

"I wasn't sure . . . I'm clearly very ghostable," he said as he released her and gripped her shoulders. "Are you ready for a culinary experience unlike any other culinary experience you've experienced before?"

"If you're talking about bowling alley nachos, I've already had them."

"Oh, dear, sweet, innocent Isabella," he said, taking her hand. "Where we're going, you won't see a nacho for miles. In fact, you won't see much of anything."

. . . .

Dining in the Dark was a concept first pioneered by Michel Reilhac in Paris back in 1997. The idea was simple: Diners are blindfolded and placed in a pitch-black dining room where visually impaired waiters serve dishes that you can't prejudge with your eyes. Your only experience of the food comes from your senses of touch, smell, sound, and, most important, taste.

"Usually, my dates blindfold me *after* dinner," joked Isabella as Gabe tied a blindfold around her head in the lobby of the New York outpost.

"I have a leather mask with a ball gag for later," Gabe retorted, while blindfolding himself.

A manager told Gabe to put his hands on a waiter's shoulders and Isabella to put her hands on Gabe's shoulders, and they were led into what Isabella sensed to be some kind of large warehouse. There was no music playing, no art to look at on the walls (and possibly no walls), a faint scent of bread baking in the air.

The manager led them to a table, guiding them each into their chairs, before leaving the two of them literally in the dark.

"Am I that bad-looking that you had to take me here?" asked Isabella, putting what she assumed was a napkin on her lap.

"No, the opposite," said Gabe. "You're so good-looking, I needed to be blindfolded so I could carry on a decent conversation."

Gabe was so sweet, so earnest, and so clearly smitten with Isabella that this whole date felt like an elaborate prank that Molly was somehow pulling on her. Had she hired an actor that she knew from acting school to play this part? Was Gabe a trained thespian, hiding his Yale-drama-school-cultivated mid-Atlantic accent, playing this lovable chef just to string Isabella along so that he could crush her? *No*, Isabella figured. *That's most likely not the case.*

The first course arrived on a tray of chipped ice. Isabella put her fingers directly into the cold smashed cubes and then found her way to what felt vaguely sluglike and vaginal.

"Oooh," said Gabe, making a slurping noise. "Oysters. I think these are Blue Point."

An arancino, a round ball of fried risotto, felt like a crusty, hot tennis ball when she first touched it. The lamb ribs, which came shellacked in a tamarind sauce, felt like the most delectable, sticky dinosaur bones.

"Our faces must be covered in sauce right now," said Isabella as she gnawed a second rib.

"Only one way to tell."

Isabella could sense Gabe getting out of his seat and leaning across the table to kiss her; only, in the process, he knocked down what sounded like two wineglasses and a small carafe of water. Still, he followed through, his lips landing near her left eye—she burst out laughing—before kissing their way down the path of sauce on her cheek to her lips, which opened up to help them finally connect with their target.

"All clean," said Gabe, after kissing her for a good twenty seconds and returning to his seat.

"You're better than a Wet-Nap," responded Isabella, who was blushing several shades of red and glad that nobody—especially Gabe—could see.

. . . .

When the meal was over, Isabella had to blink several times as the light hit her face in the lobby, squinting to bring Gabe back into focus.

The Gabe that she'd imagined in front of her throughout the meal was less attractive than the actual Gabe who was standing before her in the light. It was almost as if her unconscious didn't want her to believe how handsome Gabe was, so that she wouldn't be disappointed when she saw him illuminated.

"Shall we take a stroll?" Gabe offered, looping his arm through Isabella's.

Isabella hadn't been linked in public with a romantic partner since that time in theater camp when she agreed to "go steady" with Joshua Levin, who ended up going home early with a rare case of encephalitis.

"So," said Isabella, as they walked past the Wythe Hotel,

home to one of the city's buzziest restaurants, Laser Wolf. "How much longer do you plan on being a sous-chef?"

If, in one moment, it's possible to puncture a wonderful mood like a dart thrown at a hot-air balloon, Isabella had just achieved that. Gabe's stance immediately shifted.

"Ummm . . . forever? I love being a sous-chef."

Isabella sensed his agitation but still pushed ahead.

"Don't you want to open up your own restaurant someday?"

Gabe flinched.

"Absolutely not. Do you know what a nightmare it is to open up your own restaurant? What it's like having to deal with all of the overhead, all of the employees, being responsible for so many people and customers, dealing with all of those Yelp reviews and health inspectors and liquor licenses and reservation systems, not to mention meat purveyors and launderers, the electric company, the gas company—"

"Okay, okay, I get it."

Isabella sensed that this line of questioning was nothing new to him; it was probably something girlfriends and his parents had hounded him about before.

"I guess you don't care about being a big name in the food world," she said, using her tone to spin that in the most positive way.

"Not at all. I want to stay as obscure as humanly possible. The more obscure the better."

Isabella felt a combination of disappointment and admiration for Gabe's words. He seemed completely at ease with his level of accomplishment, even if that level was halfway up the mountain, a rest stop for the more serious climbers.

"What about you?" he asked, turning the tables on his sudden interrogator. "How much longer do you plan on being a ghostwriter for celebrity cookbooks?"

Isabella didn't have to take any time to answer that one.

"The sooner I can be done with it, the better. It's so embarrassing."

"Why is it embarrassing?"

"Because!" Isabella looked at him like it was obvious. "Writing a cookbook for a celebrity is like . . . taking a crap on everything that I know and love."

"Vivid," said Gabe, a bit surprised by Isabella's vitriol.

"It's true. Molly Babcock cares more about . . . eyelash extensions than she does about roasting a chicken."

"What if you put eyelash extensions on a chicken before you roasted it? Would she care then?"

"Probably not."

They walked past a nurse helping an elderly woman down the street, one small step at a time.

"I mean, I see what you're saying," said Gabe as he paused behind the woman, not wanting to embarrass her by walking around her. "But I also think it can be really fulfilling to help somebody achieve their vision."

"That works if they have a vision," said Isabella, trying to steer Gabe around the old woman but trying not to be too forceful. "I'm afraid Molly doesn't have one."

Gabe considered this.

"Well, she has a vision for her image, right? Her career? Her 'brand'?"

"She played an evil sexpot on TV ten years ago. Not sure that's what I would call 'a vision'?"

"Let's not evil-sexpot-shame," said Gabe, finally taking Isabella's cue and crossing the street to the other side to bypass the slowpokes. "Molly Babcock's cultivated an image in the public eye for almost a decade, and I bet that takes a lot of work and discipline. The fact that thousands of people want to read about her in the gossip columns every day says something about her ability to remain relevant."

Now Isabella was getting annoyed. Was Gabe being serious? Molly "cultivated" her image? Her image of what: being a totally unlikable, semi-abusive, slightly alcoholic muddle of a human being?

"I really don't think it's that hard to be famous," said Isabella, eager to move on. "You just have to want to be famous to be famous."

"I don't think it's that easy to be . . . If it were, we'd lose most of our waitstaff."

They were both tickled and annoyed by their first little spat.

"Anyway," said Gabe, "I think there's something cool about being a ghostwriter and helping her translate her concept of herself as a celebrity into a cookbook. It's like how I help Chef Dusolier translate his ideas into actual dishes. It's about putting your ego aside and serving somebody else's vision. It's all about the work, it's not about you."

They were almost at the water at this point, and the wind-chill factor was picking up.

"That's the problem," said Isabella, pausing to look at the skyline of Manhattan, all twinkly and clear on this cool night. "Maybe I don't want to put my ego aside. Maybe I want my picture on the cover of the cookbook, not hers."

Gabe gave her an incredulous look.

"That's surprising," he said. "You don't seem like someone who enjoys being the center of attention. Actually, from the little I've seen of you, it seems like you might actively avoid it?"

Isabella felt seen but not entirely understood.

"There's more to me than meets the eye."

"I'm a fan of your eye," he said. "I kissed it at dinner."

"Are you going to kiss it again?"

"You don't have pink eye, do you?"

"No. But I'm crawling with STDs."

"Good, so am I."

As he bent down to kiss her on the eye again, Isabella felt a vibration in her pocket. The Pavlovian effect of having a phone vibrate against your body is such that, even if you don't want to, you can find yourself reaching your hand in to pull it out. So, as Gabe's lips once again grazed her eyelashes, she removed the phone from her pocket and saw the name on the screen over Gabe's shoulder:

MOM.

Shit, thought Isabella. *Of all the times, of all the moments for her to call.* Isabella had been avoiding her mother since the Soup Kitchen Incident, and though they'd played phone tag, she'd yet to confront her about what had happened that night.

"Sorry," she said, "my mom was just in the hospital, and I probably need to take this."

"Go ahead," he said, leaning back. "I'll practice on my own eye in the meantime."

Isabella swiped to answer, and immediately she heard her mother's voice: "Izzy, are you there?"

"Is everything okay?"

It was a dangerous question. Was anything ever okay with Jeannie Pasternak?

"No, things aren't okay. I need you to come here right away. It's an emergency."

Isabella already felt her guard going up. What could this emergency be? Had she twisted her ankle trying to find aluminum foil? Had the neighbors finally complained about the smell, and was she being evicted? Had she eaten her own food and made *herself* sick?

"Mom, I'm in the middle of something—"

She watched as Gabe stuck out his tongue and pointed it toward his left eye.

"Isabella," said Jeannie in a stern tone she only pulled out once every few years. "You left me at the hospital with a concussion and I didn't say anything, and you've been avoiding my calls all week. But now I'm in over my head . . . I'm scared I'm going to set the kitchen on fire or fall off another chair, I'm so overwhelmed. Just come, and you'll understand. I'll see you soon."

Jeannie hung up before Isabella could protest—a winning strategy by a master guilter.

"I can't believe this," said Isabella as Gabe leaned against a fence, watching her with an amused look on his face. "But my mom's having an emergency."

"You're ghosting me again?!"

"Is it ghosting if I'm telling you what's happening and making a plan to see you again ASAP?"

"I guess it's not full-on ghosting. But it's certainly ghoulish behavior."

Isabella laughed and then did something unexpected. She took Gabe by the collar and leaned in and kissed him, this time a long one where they could actually see each other's faces, as much as you can see your partner's face when you kiss.

"Thanks for dinner," said Isabella, as she reoriented herself toward the subway. "Next time, maybe take me somewhere with lights?"

"Maybe just a candlestick," said Gabe. "I like to take things slow."

"Bye for now!" she said, turning away, then turning back to catch one last glimpse.

He blew her a kiss and she caught it and brought it to her eye, a gesture that had a very good chance of becoming their thing, assuming they ever had a thing, which Isabella was pretty sure they would.

· · · ·

When she walked into her mother's building an hour later, Isabella sensed an eeriness to things that she'd never noticed before. Growing up here on West Seventy-second Street, she'd always found her building to be storybook charming, like she was a grittier version of Eloise at the Plaza.

Now everything seemed to have a synthetic yellow glow, as if the lobby were a haunted science lab or a creepy motel. She heard a faint buzzing sound as she walked in—was that buzzing always there before?—and she saw a few flies sitting on an ashtray on top of the garbage by the elevators.

The ride up in the elevator felt more like a descent, like she was sinking down into the bowels of the building, where all of the secrets were kept. Was all of this because of the revelations

Rob had given her about her mother? Was she actually scared to see Jeannie face-to-face after what had happened?

The answer came to Isabella when the elevator doors opened and she hesitated getting out. She hadn't actually told her mother that she would come. She could still return to the lobby, zip out the door, and head back to Greenpoint, where she could hide in bed and text Gabe all night until Molly came to pick her up the next morning.

But no: what had to be done had to be done. She needed to confront this woman who had raised her, who was now taking things too far. And who knew? Maybe there really was an emergency.

When she got to the door, she rang the bell, even though she had a key. She wasn't sure why she did it; maybe she wanted Jeannie to have a chance to compose herself, in case something disturbing was happening inside. What if her mother had moved on to roadkill or subway rats or Central Park pigeons? Anything seemed possible.

Almost instantly, the door opened, and Jeannie, looking even more frazzled than usual, eyed Isabella up and down.

"There you are. Why didn't you use your key? Come in, come in, wait until you see what I'm dealing with here."

Isabella followed her mother into the apartment and was startled to discover, on almost every surface, cartons of eggs. There were egg cartons on the couch, egg cartons on the table, egg cartons on the kitchen counter, egg cartons stacked on the floor.

"Can you believe it?" said Jeannie, her voice filled with wonder. "Costco called: they were going to throw all of these expired eggs away, and I said, 'Over my dead body!' So they brought them over this afternoon, and I'm overwhelmed, to say the least."

There was a smell in the air that Isabella hadn't fully processed yet, but now that she was inside and near the kitchen, she realized that it was the smell of sulfurous eggs being cooked.

"I'm making frittatas," said Jeannie, answering Isabella's question before she could ask it. "I figured frittatas were the way to go: I can wrap them up easily and they'll taste good at room temperature. What do you think?"

If Jeannie were a weather event, she would be a tornado rather than a hurricane. A hurricane moves through a place, leaving a path of destruction, but then moves on. A tornado sucks everything in its path into itself, the way Jeannie was trying to suck Isabella into her crazy egg-orbit.

"Mom," said Isabella, not even sure where to begin, but certain that she had to begin somewhere. "We need to talk."

"Talk!" said Jeannie, grabbing a spatula. "There's no time to talk. We'll talk once we start cooking. Here, I have an apron for you."

"We're not cooking," Isabella answered, refusing to get pulled into the chaos. "We're sitting down and having a conversation."

Isabella had never spoken to her mother in this particular way. For the twenty-five years they'd known each other, which is to say the entire duration of Isabella's life, Jeannie was every kind of authority: the moral authority ("Writing a thank-you card costs you nothing"), the financial authority ("Don't buy anything that you can get for free"), the college authority ("Tufts makes more sense than NYU . . . It'll be a real college experience"), the fashion authority ("Horizontal stripes do you no favors"), even the dental authority ("You need to floss after every meal, you get all of that lettuce caught in your teeth").

For Isabella to take any kind of authoritative tone toward her mother was new for both of them.

"What's this about? Are you still angry that I wouldn't help you out with money? Izzy, I just want you to be able to stand on your own two feet. Trust me, you'll thank me when you're older."

"Mom, sit down."

Isabella lifted several egg cartons off the couch and made room for them to sit. Jeannie went to the kitchen and turned off the stove, then finally sat down next to her daughter in the living room, still holding her spatula.

"You're throwing my whole production out of whack."

"Mom, you can't serve these eggs to anyone," said Isabella as calmly as she could, considering the force that she was going up against. "You've been making people very sick."

"That's what you wanted to talk about?" Jeannie said, and laughed. "So Rob filled your head with that garbage about people getting sick from my food? Let me tell you right now: it's a load of baloney. I'll tell you why he said that: because those people prefer my food to that slop that they serve at the soup kitchen! Honest to God. They practically kiss my feet when I walk through the door with my Tupperware."

Isabella had had no experience of dealing with the mentally unwell, unless you counted Molly, and up until recently she never would've put her mother in the same category. But suddenly she was trying to recall everything that she'd learned from listening to Esther Perel's and Brené Brown's podcasts, so that she could navigate this conversation correctly.

"This isn't an argument. You've been this way since Daddy died, and I didn't notice it because I thought you knew what you were doing, but—"

"So I'm crazy? Is that what you're trying to tell me?"

"I'm not saying you're crazy, but I'm saying that you're doing things that aren't good for you and, more important, they're not good for other people."

"Who are you to tell me what's good for anyone else? You . . . who only thinks of herself? You, who always puts herself first!"

Isabella didn't know everything that there was to know about herself, but one thing that she did know—especially now—was that she rarely, if ever, put herself first.

"You've been telling me that my whole life," said Isabella, softly, almost to herself. "And it's such a lie. Your definition of me putting myself first is my not going along with whatever it is that you want me to do."

Jeannie had never heard her daughter talk like this, and she was beginning to vibrate with anger.

"So now I'm a terrible mother? That's what you're trying to say? That I made you feel bad your whole life, and that I make unhoused people sick, and that I may as well lock myself up in my room, crawl into a ball, and die?"

Jeannie had a flair for the dramatic, a flair that usually had an effect on Isabella. But not this time.

"You can do whatever you want, but I can't let you cook poisoned food for people anymore. And if you want me to be in your life, you're going to have to start respecting my boundaries."

There it was: the million-dollar word, the preeminent concept in all therapy podcasts and self-help books, and the one that Isabella heard about all the time and had never applied to herself. Only now, in this moment, did she finally understand it.

"Boundaries! What does that even mean?"

"It means no more calling me out of the blue claiming it's an emergency because you want to make frittatas with questionable eggs not good enough for Costco. And no more commentating on my career choices or my fashion choices or who I date or where I live or who I'm friends with, unless you have something productive to say. You've been negging me my whole life—"

"Negging you? What do you mean, 'negging'?"

"Being negative toward me. I've taken it the whole time, because I thought you were trying to help me, but now I see, with all of this"—she indicated the whole room, piled high with even more junk than the last time she'd been here—"it's not mothering, it's . . . delusions of grandeur! You think you're saving the world when you can't even find time to go to your daughter's apartment and have lunch with her."

This last bit came as a surprise to Isabella as she said it. Was that what was beneath all of this sudden burst of sadness and rage? That she wanted her mother to mother her for once, instead of strangers whom she was actively harming?

Jeannie looked shell-shocked: she was red in the face, fuming, but also her eyes were darting all around while she processed what her daughter said.

"I don't know where all of this is coming from," she finally said, "but I have frittatas to make for people who need them. So, if you don't want to help me, if you want to be selfish, that's fine, but that's what I'm going to do."

"Mom, they have flyers at soup kitchens all over the city with your face on them," Isabella finally revealed; she'd saved this harshest bit for last. "They warn people not to take food from you. That you make people sick."

Jeannie stood up.

"Then let them throw it all away. That's up to them. What I'm doing is good . . . You can't convince me that it's not!"

Isabella was not a violent person. Never in her life had she ever hit anyone, pushed anyone, pulled another girl's hair. When she was taunted in middle school, she absorbed it like a mushroom dunked in water. But something about her mother's resistance here, something about her mother's unwillingness to accept the real damage that she was causing, drove Isabella out of her seat and toward a ratty old broom that she saw in the corner.

"I can't let you do this anymore, Mom," said Isabella. "It's over."

She took the broom, hoisted it in the air, and just when Jeannie thought her own daughter was going to beat her to death, Isabella brought it down on a stack of egg cartons right near the door, yolks shooting out in all directions.

"Have you completely lost your mind?" screamed Jeannie.

"You always wanted me to be more charitable," said Isabella. "This is my way of giving back!"

It was like a giant game of Whac-A-Mole, only Isabella was smashing egg cartons left and right: the ones on the couch, their eggy goo seeping into the ancient, musty fabric; the eggs on the kitchen counter, the dining room table, the ones near the bathroom. By the time she was done, Isabella had smashed close to three hundred questionable, expired, foul-smelling eggs.

She was out of breath, panting. Mother and daughter studied each other, trying to figure out which of the two of them was crazier.

Jeannie crossed her arms.

"So how does it feel? How does it feel, having destroyed hundreds of perfectly good eggs, stealing meals from countless unhoused New Yorkers and their children? Tell me: how does it feel?"

"Honestly," said Isabella, setting down the broom and catching her breath, "it feels wonderful."

15

PACK YOUR KNIVES
AND GO

If only they made on-off switches for your brain, Isabella might've been able to fall asleep that night. The emotions coursing through her were so complex, so conflicting, she felt like a human traffic jam. There was the giddiness that she felt about her date with Gabe (that kiss!) pressed up against the exhilaration that she felt about standing up to her mother (those eggs!) pressed up against the dread that she felt about going away alone with Molly (ugh, Molly!). Her life had been so quiet and staid before: she'd bake cookies, take them to work, sit in her little cubicle, write about muffins, go home, watch *Barefoot Contessa* reruns, rinse, and repeat. Now her life felt as full and chaotic as a Las Vegas seafood buffet.

Of all these emotions, the one that she'd dealt with the least was her dread about Molly. She was so distracted by Gabe and her mother, she hadn't really thought about what she was about to undertake: a weekend alone with a person who acted like her best friend one day and her mortal enemy the next. When she traced their journey together, there was that first meeting at Lodi, where Molly was friendly and engaging. Then there was the Molly who threw her fish away and kicked her out of the apartment. The Molly who was so touched to receive Isabella's most prized cookbook, her last gift from her father, and then the Molly who cruelly left it in the back of an Uber, shrugging it off as if it were nothing. That brought out vulnerable Molly, who took Isabella to her childhood home, exposed her to her semi-abusive father, revealed her mother's sacred recipe binder, took her out for drinks, and finally committed to their writing the cookbook together—only to morph back into selfish Molly, hacking apart kale on Instagram, landing a gig on a Netflix show, and inviting Isabella out to celebrate at a restaurant Isabella suggested, only to change the start time and to mock her when she showed up late.

What did all of this add up to? A bad person? A damaged person? Her own personal antagonist? No, Isabella realized. An antagonist is someone who cares enough about you to make you their target. Molly had never cared about Isabella; she only ever did what was best for Molly. Now Isabella just had to do what was best for Isabella: test the recipes that she needed to test, collect whatever tidbits she could from the cookbook's official "author," and survive the weekend the best that she could, so she could finally get Molly Babcock off her plate and make room for better things.

· · · ·

The next morning, before Molly arrived to pick her up (*Running late as per uzh*, she texted, twenty minutes after the initial pickup time), Owen—again in a slick suit, making an oat-milk latte with the design of a heart that unintentionally looked like a penis—revealed that he didn't approve of the two of them going away together.

"I want her to keep her head in the game," he said, while finishing that day's scrotum. "The first table read is three weeks away."

Owen was nervous, because the studio execs were still cagey about hiring someone as unpredictable and untamable as Molly. Especially with the recent Page Six stories coming out about her antics—apparently, she'd stood on a table at Cipriani and kicked over a thousand-dollar bottle of Dom Pérignon—Molly was walking a tightrope, where the notoriety that made her a sexy casting choice was the same notoriety that could lose her the gig.

"We're just cooking together," said Isabella, as she shoved a few items from the "mostly wearable" pile into her backpack, next to Candy Babcock's binder. "I doubt that she's going to wild-out over salmon."

"I've seen her freak out over a crouton," said Owen. "You need to keep watch over her. Think of her like a rare truffle that you're saving to shave over a cheese soufflé."

"You wouldn't shave a truffle over a cheese soufflé. The cheese would smother the flavor of the truffle."

"And I'm going to smother you if anything happens to her. This might be the last chance Molly has for a while."

It was only then that Isabella realized what a close eye Owen had been keeping on Molly since she became his client. He was the one trying to shield her from the cameras when she fell at Snakebite; he was the one who was monitoring the situation with the studios. He was as protective of her as he'd ever been about anything, even Isabella. It was like Molly herself was his golden ticket, and he wasn't going to let her flutter through the slats of life's sewer.

"Don't worry," said Isabella when she heard Molly beep her horn outside. "You can only get so drunk on vanilla extract."

. . . .

The conversation that Isabella planned to have with Molly on their drive up to the Catskills was going to involve gentle inquiries into the various subjects that she'd been riffing on for a week in her headnotes. It was one thing to write as Molly talking about clam chowder, it was another thing to hear the real Molly talk about clam chowder, and to weave those specifics back into the work, if possible.

None of this came to fruition, however, because, the entire drive up, Molly was hard at work in what was clearly becoming her mobile office: the Bluetooth speaker blasting calls from PR teams, entertainment reporters, fashion designers, and, currently, the showrunner of *Misery Loves Company*.

"Babe, how are you holding up?" he asked, probably on a Bluetooth speaker in a Mercedes convertible of his own.

"I'm rattled, Bobby," said Molly, as she rolled the window down and lit a cigarette. It was forty degrees outside and they were on the highway, but that didn't stop her. "I feel like they're going to yank the rug right out from under me."

"Honey, I went to bat for you," Bobby assured her. "I said, 'I'm not doing this show without Molly Babcock. I wrote this part for Molly Babcock, I sold this show because of Molly Babcock, Molly Babcock is the only person who can play Vivian Colby. If she goes, I go, too.'"

"I love you so much, I don't even have the words," said Molly, making kissy sounds loud enough to travel the three thousand miles to California.

"I love you so much, too," said Bobby in a baby voice that made Isabella want to seal her ears shut forever. "Now, take good care of yourself—no more drunken escapades! Get lots of rest, eat lots of fruit, use your meditation apps. We want you nice and fresh when we start shooting in three weeks."

The call ended, and Isabella was about to start a conversation about onion dip when another call came through: this one from a podcaster who was scheduled to interview Molly about returning to TV after half a decade.

"It's so weird," said Molly, seamlessly merging onto the highway as the podcaster hit Record. "I honestly feel like I'm so much more capable now than I was back when I was doing *Malicious Angels*. I was just an idiot kid then . . . I didn't know what the hell I was doing."

As Isabella listened to Molly navigate this interview as well as the highway, she couldn't help but recall Gabe's words about the hard work that Molly put into cultivating her image. Right here, right now was proof of what Gabe had been saying: she was witnessing the Molly Babcock Industrial Complex in action. If Molly didn't field these calls from the showrunners and the journalists and the podcasters, Isabella wouldn't have a book to ghostwrite.

"How did you keep busy for all of those years while you were unemployed?" asked the faceless podcaster, who sounded like she didn't care a fig about Molly's answer but knew other people might.

"Oh my God, I did so many things," answered Molly. "I studied yoga. I traveled to Bali. I watched every season of every spin-off of *Below Deck*."

She went on and on, and Isabella was amused, if not slightly disturbed, that the one thing she didn't mention was cooking.

· · · ·

As the car finally exited the highway and began to make its way through the winding roads of the Catskills, Isabella felt a certain sense of peace about the weekend ahead. The late-October trees were beginning to bald, with yellow and red leaves still clinging on for dear life. The roads were empty, the summer visitors gone back to the city for their jobs and their kids' schooling and all the other things that draw normal people back to their normal day-to-day lives.

When Molly finally finished her interview, it was as if she'd just noticed Isabella in the car with her for the first time.

"Heyyyy," she said. "Sorry for all the yapping. Things have been so insane."

"You're pretty popular."

"It's fucking crazy how the same people who piled on me when I left *Malicious Angels* are all revved up now that I'm doing *Misery Loves Company*. It's like, when they're done tearing you down and kicking you on the ground, they wait for you to rise back up so they can do it all over again."

It had to be strange, Isabella thought, to be at the mercy of public opinion—to have your entire livelihood and self-esteem wrapped up in how people perceived you.

"Well, this weekend should be a nice break," said Isabella. "I have a bunch of recipes set aside for us to test."

Before Molly could respond, another call came in, this one from Owen.

"Did you make it yet?"

"Oh my God, Owen, will you stop worrying about me? We're going to a cabin in the Catskills, we're not going to an all-night rave on Ibiza."

"Just text me when you get there. And no drinking! And no drugs!"

Molly let out a guffaw.

"Why don't you go pester your other clients?"

He doesn't have any other clients, Isabella wanted to say.

"Be good," he said, before hanging up.

"Your roommate needs a hobby," said Molly.

"He's been practicing latte art."

But Molly didn't hear her. By the time Isabella finished her sentence, Molly was on the phone again, this time with her financial adviser, who wanted to know if it was okay to invest in AI, even though it might ultimately infringe on her livelihood.

"I'm barely hanging on by a thread," she said. "Let the robot overlords take all the parts. Just make me rich while they do it."

. . . .

When they finally pulled into the driveway of Xavier's cottage in the Catskills, Isabella—who was expecting something masculine and unkempt—was surprised at how charming it was. Xavier looked like someone who'd be more comfortable living in a garage than a storybook house with a little garden out front, but that's precisely what this cottage was: it looked like something right out of *Grimms' Fairy Tales* or *Downton Abbey*.

"Thank God we're here," said Molly, putting the car into Park. "I need to take a major nap."

It was almost noon, and Isabella was wondering about lunch: a good thing to wonder about, since there was a decent chance that Molly would be skipping it. As Isabella pondered her options (Could she borrow the car? Order something on Postmates?), she was startled to see the front door open, seemingly of its own accord, and then Xavier himself stepping out, in just shorts, to greet them.

"Surprise!" he said as Molly got out of the driver's seat.

"What the fuck, Xavier?!" she replied. "What happened to apple picking in Vermont? We're supposed to be working!"

She ran to him and kissed him so hard it looked like she was eating his face.

"I like the apples better here," he said, eyeing her chest.

Isabella, meanwhile, felt her stomach churn. It was one thing to be trapped alone in a cabin with Molly Babcock; it was another thing entirely to be the third wheel to Molly and Xavier's debauched and frequently disgusting union. No wonder Owen was so worried. Trouble seemed to follow Molly everywhere she went.

After kissing for what felt to Isabella like an eternity, Molly finally pulled away and walked back to the car to get her things.

"You remember Isabella? She's my ghostwriter or whatever?"

Molly's tone was obligatory. Xavier's response was complete indifference, to the point where he didn't even look in Isabella's direction.

"Babe, I turned on the hot tub."

"It's forty degrees," said Molly. "And I didn't bring a bathing suit."

"Forty degrees is perfect hot-tub weather. And you don't need a bathing suit. I've seen those titties plenty of times."

Isabella wondered how much it would cost to stay in a hotel or a motel or an Airbnb where somebody had gotten murdered: anything as long as it wasn't this.

"You want a Bloody Mary? I have a pitcher inside. I didn't have enough V8, so it's more like a pitcher of slightly red vodka."

Xavier held the front door open as Molly walked inside and Isabella trailed behind.

To Isabella's surprise, the interior of the cabin was even more charming than the exterior. Everything was tastefully done: the furniture was mid-century modern, the art was eclectic, and yet the room wasn't overly designed. There were hardcover books scattered throughout, little mementos from trips, dolls, even a vintage globe. She noted framed original posters for *A Streetcar Named Desire* and *Who's Afraid of Virginia Woolf?*

The best part, though, was the kitchen. Right next to the entryway, the kitchen was everything that Isabella could want in a country cabin. Square windows looked out onto the front garden, with red checkerboard curtains, just above the vintage-looking stove. There was so much attention to detail: the dishes, which were stacked in open cabinets, all seemed one of a kind, like they had been scavenged at a French flea market. On the counter were old-style ceramic mixing bowls, an ornate cake stand, even a mid-century citrus press. The fact that all of this was Xavier's boggled the mind.

"How long have you had this place?" she asked him, finally attempting to break the ice.

"It's not technically mine," he responded, as he walked to the pitcher of vodka with V8 on the long wooden dining room table. "It's officially my acting teacher's. She said I could use it whenever I wanted to, and I never took her up on the offer, and now, sad to say, she's in the hospital with a bad case of pneumonia and they don't think she's going to make it, and I realized that if I was ever going to take her up on the offer, now was the time, you know . . . before her kids inherit it or something."

So we're squatting in your acting teacher's cabin without her permission? Isabella wanted to ask, but she kept her mouth shut as she watched Xavier pour two very full glasses for himself and Molly.

"You want one?" he asked Isabella, after he handed Molly her glass.

"I'm good," said Isabella. "Can you show me my room?"

Xavier led her down a hallway and opened the door to a welcoming, airy bedroom with a sliding door to the outside and a four-poster bed festooned with decorative pillows. It looked like a child's bedroom: maybe where the acting teacher's son or daughter grew up?

"Thanks," said Isabella as she put her backpack on the bed.

"Enjoy," said Xavier, and he closed the door behind him, less to give Isabella privacy and more to keep her away from him and Molly.

I'm trapped in Hell.

> Already? Didn't you just get there?

Yes but we're not alone.
Xavier Mordechai is here too.

> I don't know who that is.

Her fucked-up celebrity boyfriend!

> Is he hitting on you? I'll come there with my boning knife.

Worse: they're ignoring me.

> Isn't that good? Can't you just cook and stay out of their way?

I guess I could. I suppose Molly wouldn't be a big help anyway.

> Pretend you're the caterer or their personal chef. Test the recipes you need to test, then get out of their way, and go to bed.

Sounds like you've done this before.

> That's the thing about being back of the house. You don't have to deal with the assholes in the front.

Bolstered by Gabe's counsel, Isabella emerged from her room an hour after settling in and found Molly and Xavier sprawled on the couch, both on their phones, both giggling, many Bloody Marys in their systems.

Isabella was holding Molly's mother's book of recipes, the enormous volume that took up 90 percent of her backpack space, and the basis for her endless nights of labor writing the rough draft of Molly's cookbook.

"Hey," said Isabella, hoping to ease into the Molly-Xavier wavelength without being too disruptive.

"What up?" said Molly, not looking up from her phone.

"I was thinking that maybe I'd go do some food shopping? Get some ingredients for tonight's dinner? Maybe I could borrow the car?"

Isabella was also starving and needed to find herself lunch.

"The keys are on the front table," said Molly, relieving Isabella of her fears that Molly would want to drive her.

"Cool," said Isabella. She put Candy's recipe book down on the larger dining room table, far from the wet rings left behind by the Bloody Marys.

"So I was thinking I'd do some of the recipes that you were most enthusiastic about?" She opened to the first of several pages with Post-it notes she'd placed on them. "The butternut-squash soup, the coq au vin, and the bananas Foster?"

Isabella knew that these were the dishes that Molly had been the most passionate about when they first went through the book together. She was hoping they would trigger an onslaught of memory and stories. Plus, it would be a crisp fall night, and this sounded like a perfectly cozy meal.

"That sounds heavy," said Molly, as if she were at a resort, lounging poolside, while the waiter read off the menu.

"It is heavy," agreed Isabella. "But I feel like these are the recipes that you might have the most to say about if I make them?"

"I don't want heavy recipes in my cookbook," said Molly, still lounging, still scrolling through her phone. "My mom's recipes are super-heavy and super-unhealthy. I want things that I actually eat: salads, acai bowls, plain chicken. I don't know why you're so obsessed with my mom's binder. For all I care, you can throw that shit away."

The casual way Molly dismissed the hours and hours of work that Isabella had poured into adapting her mother's recipes into a cookbook was almost as jarring as the casual way she dismissed her actual mother. *For all I care, you can throw that shit away.* Did she really just say that?

"But why did you take me to your parents' house?" asked Isabella, her voice cracking slightly. "What was the point of finding your mom's book?"

Molly shrugged.

"I thought it might give you a few recipe ideas. But not, like, all of the recipe ideas. I sold this book because of me, not my mother."

Molly had been so disengaged for so much of this process, and now, as they were finally nearing the end, and the book itself, despite Isabella's misgivings, was actually shaping up to be *good*, Molly wanted to torpedo it.

"So what should I make for dinner, then?" snapped Isabella, her voice barely able to mask the rage simmering inside of her.

"Babe, what do you want for dinner?" Molly asked Xavier. Isabella tried to remember Gabe's advice to just act like their personal chef and what a relief it would be to hide out in "the back of the house," which, in this particular case, was the charming kitchen in the front of the house. Isabella would put her emotions into the food and then deal with the book fallout later.

"Kale could be good," said Xavier.

"Let's do a kale salad, something with tofu, and some kind of grain . . . maybe quinoa."

Whether these were suggestions for cookbook recipes or just what Molly wanted for dinner, Isabella didn't know and didn't care. All she knew was that she wanted to get the hell away from these two semiconscious Hollywood monsters.

"Kale salad, something with tofu, some kind of grain, maybe quinoa," repeated Isabella, walking toward the keys. "Got it."

"Oh, and get some rosé," Molly called after her.

"And some beer," Xavier added.

Anything to shut you guys up.

"No problem," she said, before aggressively closing the door behind her. She didn't slam the door, but she didn't not slam the door. She closed it with emotion.

· · · ·

The closest grocery store that Isabella could locate on Google Maps, the Catskill Food Emporium, looked to be generic and lifeless: perfect for the food that she was being asked to make.

Molly's change of tune about the book was galling on many levels, but worst of all was that Molly wasn't wrong about the cookbook. In fact, everything that she said was 100 percent correct: people wanted to buy the Molly Babcock cookbook because they wanted to eat like Molly Babcock. More specifically: they wanted to *look* like Molly Babcock. They wanted to know her fitness tips, her exercise regimen, what she ate for breakfast, how she dressed her salads, how she dealt with dessert cravings.

This would've been completely obvious to most ghost-writers, and yet Isabella had completely circumvented it in order to write something more "meaningful." When she looked at it from a distance, she saw how absurd her plan was: a meaningful cookbook from Molly Babcock? It was like trying to make potatoes dauphine from a Mr. Potato Head.

And Isabella would've arrived at this conclusion, would've understood this point eventually, if it hadn't been for the trip to New Jersey and the discovery of Molly's mother. Candy Babcock, with her collection of recipes and little notes to herself and articles that she clipped, had all of the depth, the culinary point of view, the hard-won kitchen knowledge that Molly lacked. Candy had something real to say about food, something important: it came from a lifetime of making it, thanklessly, for a husband and daughter who clearly took it all for granted.

And that triggered something in Isabella. The farther she drove through the mountains, the more she realized that the ghost of Candy Babcock had inhabited her that day in the basement of Molly's childhood home. After that, Isabella's job was no longer to facilitate Molly's vision, of which there was very little; her job was to vindicate the life of a woman who had lived in the shadows, whose passions went uncelebrated, whose contributions went unrecognized. A woman, it turned out, who was a lot like Isabella.

Was that why all of this felt so personal to her? Was that why, when she finally arrived at the grocery store, she found herself loading up her cart with onions and a whole chicken and smoky bacon and red wine and butternut squash and brown sugar and bananas and a pint of vanilla ice cream? She totally bypassed the kale, gray and brittle-looking; she didn't bother to dig out the quinoa from the musty, dusty health-food aisle. It was as if her arms were acting of their own accord, as if the shopping cart were pushing itself.

Was she possessed by Candy Babcock? Was Candy acting from beyond, leading Isabella to the checkout aisle without anything that resembled tofu in the cart? Or was Isabella acting of her own accord, willfully defying her employer, who was probably three sheets to the wind at this point and unlikely to eat anything for dinner, much more likely to be snorting coke naked with Xavier in the hot tub?

Isabella wasn't sure, but one thing that she *was* sure about was that the menu she was planning—butternut-squash soup, coq au vin, and bananas Foster—was a hell of a lot more interesting than the menu that she'd been asked—no, *commanded*—to make.

As she filled the trunk of Molly's Mercedes with the heavy shopping bags, she felt the giddiness that you feel when you break the rules combined with the giddiness that you feel when you're about to cook a really fabulous dinner. It was a mixture of dread and excitement, hunger and enthusiasm, self-recrimination and self-satisfaction.

She was going to battle with Molly Babcock once and for all, and she was doing it on her own turf, the place where she felt the safest, the place where she had the most power. That place, of course, being the kitchen.

16

NOW WE'RE COOKING WITH GAS!

Coq au vin is a deceptively simple dish. The steps themselves are fairly straightforward: render the bacon, brown the chicken in the bacon fat, sauté the mirepoix (carrots, onions, celery), add the flour, stew with red wine. What separates the good from the great is the execution: How well do you brown the bird? How vigorously do you simmer the meat? Do you cheat with frozen pearl onions, or do you peel fresh pearl onions yourself—boiling them first, shocking them in ice water so the skins come loose—or do you skip the pearl onions altogether?

Isabella approached her coq au vin the way that she approached all of her cooking: gently, carefully, with thoughtfulness and a light touch. Instead of normal bacon, she used pancetta, just like Candy did in her recipe. She didn't crank the burners up too high during the most important step, the browning. She caramelized the chicken a few pieces at a time, careful not to crowd the pan, careful not to flip them until the skin detached naturally, a sure sign that she had done her job well.

She seasoned the meat with the fluidity of a conductor, raining the salt and pepper down onto the cutting board as her arm swooped back and forth rhythmically. She applied the butter and olive oil to the pan with the generosity of a proud father pouring champagne for his guests at his daughter's engagement. She played with the heat knobs like a pipe organist in a grand church, centered in her task and keenly aware of the spiritual stakes.

When she first arrived back at the cottage with her numerous grocery bags, she was fully prepared for some kind of confrontation with Molly as she unpacked the not-kale, not-tofu, not-quinoa ingredients that she'd brought home. Instead, she came back to what seemed like a completely empty space, but for the empty glasses, empty pitcher, and what seemed like a baggie of coke, with a few lines of white powder on the coffee table.

She figured that they were in the hot tub as she cooked—a blessing from beyond: to cook in silence!—until she started hearing loud slamming against the wall, the bed in the primary bedroom clearly pressed up against the back of the kitchen, with Molly calling out in ecstasy and Xavier yelling out: "Oh fuck, oh fuck!"

Isabella paid it no mind. The more distracted they were, the better off she was. Let them make love to each other while she made love to a butternut squash, using a sharp knife (she'd brought her chef's knife from home) to peel off the skin before cutting it into cubes for the soup with a vegetable stock that she was making herself from fennel fronds, onion skins, and the top parts of leeks. She was wary of serving a butternut-squash soup before the coq au vin: it violated one of her precepts, which was not to serve something soft and mushy before something else soft and mushy. She'd learned that from a chef she'd interviewed for *Comestibles:* each course should offer a different texture. A better choice might've been a frisée salad, with lots of bitterness and crunch, or gougères, with their crispy exterior and fluffy interior, but, as it was, she wasn't preparing a classic French bistro meal, she was channeling the ghost of Candy Babcock. And if she did her job correctly, these dishes would hit their intended target.

That, more than anything, was what was driving her to put

her heart and soul into this three-course meal. She was a ghost advocating for a ghost; she was channeling Candy to reach her daughter from beyond. Molly had told her to throw away her mother's book, but what she really meant was: *I don't want to deal with the feelings that you're conjuring up in me right now.* So, like a good culinary therapist, Isabella was forcing Molly to confront those emotions with butter and garlic and chicken and salt. It wasn't an accident that the picture that fluttered out of the red binder when Isabella first rifled through it—the picture of Candy presenting a turquoise-blue coconut cake to a beaming Molly at her sixth birthday party—was now resting, ever so subtly, on top of the binder, ready and waiting to spring its emotional trap.

The smells emitting from Isabella's kitchen—it really did feel like her own kitchen as she moved through it, the light growing dimmer in the windows as four o'clock turned to five o'clock and five o'clock turned to six—were intoxicating. If Pepé le Pew were there instead of a vain TV star, he would've followed the scent Looney Tunes–style, floating through the air, eyes whirling in ecstasy, until he reached their source.

Unfortunately, Isabella could now hear les skunks in the other room, snoring loudly, as they slept off their drinking and drugging and fucking. Isabella didn't judge them for it: everyone had their chosen pleasures, their particular ways of dealing with life. She just wanted them to give hers a chance.

As the coq finished coquing, and the soup was properly blended and strained—the small, ancient blender that Isabella found required her to work in several batches—Isabella set the long wooden table with three place settings (she would eat with them, whether they wanted her to or not), using the antique forks and knives that she found among the eclectic silverware.

The sequence would go as follows: the butternut-squash soup would be served with white wine (she'd bought a Sancerre at a decent-enough liquor store next to the grocery market). The coq au vin, which she would serve over buttered egg noodles, would go with the Pinot Noir that she'd also brought home. Then, finally, she would flambé the bananas Foster with them looking on—igniting it dramatically with a tablespoon of the rum that she'd found in the liquor cabinet (no sense in buying a whole bottle for one tablespoon)—and serve it all over vanilla ice cream.

Who could resist a meal like this? Who, after eating it, wouldn't want these recipes going into their cookbook? Who wouldn't want *this* to be their legacy?

As she waited for her targets to emerge, she cleaned the kitchen of all the debris from her chopping and stewing and blending and sweating: the onion skins, the squash seeds, the banana peels. There wasn't a dishwasher, so she had to wash each cooking tool by hand in the tiny sink.

As the water poured over the pans, pans that had done their service, she thought about her own service, the job that she was doing and the jobs that she would eventually do. Gabe's whole attitude about the ego—setting it aside, serving a larger vision—was noble indeed, but not as appealing to Isabella as it was to him. Her heroes all had prominent names that everyone in the food world knew: Ruth Reichl, Edna Lewis, Gabrielle Hamilton, Nigel Slater. All of these heroes had set their egos aside at some point in their careers to serve a larger vision—*Gourmet* magazine, Gage & Tollner, Prune, *The Christmas Chronicles*—but their names wouldn't be names if they hadn't served their own personal ambitions as well. Was she willing to give up her own dream for herself in order to serve the likes of celebrities, such as the one who was snoring so loudly that the entire kitchen wall was vibrating?

When the dishes were finally done, Isabella set her station for that evening's service. She had soup bowls ready for soup, plus the cayenne pepper and maple cream (just heavy cream sweetened with maple syrup) that would garnish the top. She had the water boiling and salted and awaiting the egg noodles. She had the parsley chopped for the coq au vin, which was keeping warm on the back burner. And, finally, she had the large skillet and the bananas set aside next to the bottle of rum for the bananas Foster. Like building a new roller-coaster ride at a theme park, she'd fully set the tracks for the dinner: all that was left to do was put the car on the track, fill it with passengers, press the button, and pray that everyone made it out alive.

. . . .

Just as Isabella decided to treat herself to a glass of the Sancerre, Molly came bursting out of her room. She was freshly showered, in jeans and a T-shirt, and she had an almost inhuman smile on her face as she held her iPhone out in front of her with Owen on Speaker.

"You're not fucking with me, Owen? Tell me you're not fucking with me."

"I'm not fucking with you," he said. "The studio sent over the contract. It's one hundred percent *official* official. You have the part, the project is greenlit! You'll be in L.A. next week for fittings and to meet the other actors."

Molly was jumping up and down with excitement.

"You had me so nervous," she said. "I honestly thought I was a goner. That they were going to kick my ass to the curb."

"To tell you the truth, I thought they were, too," confessed Owen. "The way that they were talking, I was practicing all week how I was going to break the news to you."

Xavier emerged from the bedroom in jeans and a black tank top.

"What's going on?" he asked, running his hand through his bed-headed hair.

"I got it," she said, with her hand on his shoulder. "Like really got it. Like they-sent-over-the-contract got it."

"No fucking way," he said, his voice a mixture of excitement and a barely discernible twinge of jealousy.

"So what happens next?" asked Molly, twirling away from Xavier. "Do I need to come back to the city? Should we come back right now?"

"No, no, no. . . ." said Owen. "Stay there, take it easy, relax, and then, when you're back, we'll go over the logistics. But congratulations! You are officially Vivian Colby on *Misery Loves Company* on Netflix. Go celebrate!"

Isabella was watching all of this from the kitchen, and if ever the stage were set for an easy transition into a lavish celebratory dinner—the dinner that Molly had explicitly said she didn't want—this good news was it.

"Congrats," said Isabella, stepping out of the kitchen with a glass of white in each hand for Xavier and Molly.

"I'm just so relieved," said Molly, still processing, as she took the glass from Isabella. "It's like I didn't want to let myself acknowledge how badly I wanted the part and how scared I was, but I was basically shitting myself every day. What smells so good?"

Molly, just as Isabella hoped she would, followed her nose into the kitchen. She sniffed the air and began glancing down at the pots and the pans, lifting the lid on the coq au vin, stirring the soup with a wooden spoon. As Molly poked and prodded, Isabella watched a small movie play out on Molly's face; a face that, to its credit, had no trouble conveying emotion. The movie began with Molly's sense of recognition, the smells comforting and consoling her, the menu cozy and familiar. Everything shifted, however, when Molly glanced over at the red binder and saw, resting on top of it, the picture of her mother holding the turquoise-blue coconut cake, her six-year-old self beaming up at this woman who had spent so much time on something just for her. Suddenly the shadows emerged on Molly's visage, a storm gathered in her eyes.

"What is all this?" she asked, a hint of menace in her voice. It was like she had made a choice to be disgusted rather than delighted, and Isabella knew it the second she asked the question.

"I know that you said you wanted a kale salad and tofu, but I just figured . . . if I cooked these dishes, maybe—"

"Maybe what? That I'd change my mind? That I wouldn't want to eat something good for me instead of six sticks of butter before I have to appear naked on national television?"

"Looks good to me," said Xavier. "I'm starving."

Xavier was ready to go into the kitchen to start loading up his plate, but Molly barred the way, holding out her hand.

"What is wrong with you?" Molly asked Isabella, visibly perturbed by Isabella's defiance. "No, seriously: why are you so obsessed with cooking my mother's recipes? It's like you want this book to be something that you would write instead of something that I would write, which makes no sense, because you're literally my ghostwriter."

Isabella leaned against the dining room table, feeling Molly's words like large rubber balls pelted at her head in a game of dodgeball, her hands tied behind her back.

"That's really not it," Isabella tried. "It's more like you have this amazing food legacy and I just don't want it to go to waste."

"No one gives a shit about my food legacy!" Molly was clutching the kitchen counter, her hands turning red. "No one gives a shit about my family! They just want to see pictures of me in slutty outfits, holding trays of vegetables, and gossiping about being on TV. This isn't one of your fancy cookbooks."

No shit, Isabella wanted to say. Instead, she said, "I know that."

"I really don't think you do," said Molly, walking toward Isabella. "I think that you wish that you were me, that you had a platform of your own, that you had a built-in audience, that people would want to read about your recipes and your stories and your cooking tips . . . but since no one has any idea who you are, and probably never will, you're using my mom as a stand-in for yourself. You're trying to take over this book by saying it's about her, but it's really about *you*. You: a person who nobody gives a shit about. You: a person with zero talent. You: a nobody destined to become even more of a nobody by the time you're thirty."

Isabella had been riled up by Molly once before, that day when Molly told her that she'd left her father's cookbook in the back of an Uber. But this felt different. This felt like getting struck over and over again with a hot poker, the pain relentless and aggravating to the point where there was no choice but to lash out in the other direction.

"At least I can cook," said Isabella, the words bursting out of her like a spray of bullets.

"What?"

"You heard me," said Isabella. "Do you honestly think people aren't laughing at you when you make food on your Instagram? Do you know how ridiculous you look, chopping kale, hacking it like a blind executioner, and making a salad that wouldn't be good enough for a hamster cage?"

"She's just jealous," said Molly, turning to Xavier, who was watching all of this while vaping against the wall. "She can't handle the fact that I'm pretty and thin and famous and that I can do what she does just as well as she can, only I look better doing it."

"Ha!" said Isabella. "That's such a fucking laugh. Do you think you could *ever* make this meal?" She indicated the food in the kitchen. "Do you think, in a million years, with a million lessons and a million cookbooks and a million helpers, you could ever make a coq au vin or butternut-squash soup? I bet you don't even know how to turn on the heat."

"Oh, please," said Molly. "I could do all of this in my sleep."

She marched into the kitchen and saw the laptop open on the kitchen counter. She glanced at what was on the screen.

"Bananas Foster," read Molly. "Oooh, this is so hard," she said, studying the recipe. "Cook butter and sugar and bananas. How will I ever figure that one out?"

She tottered over to the stove, and it was only then that Isabella realized that, despite being showered and freshly groomed, Molly was still somewhat inebriated. The three Bloody Marys plus the cocaine and now the wine and who knows what else—Xanax? Lexapro? Adderall?—were also circulating through her system.

"Why are you making dessert before we eat dinner?" asked Xavier.

"Shut up," said Molly, as she turned on the burner with the empty skillet on it, and added the butter and brown sugar that Isabella had already prepped and set aside for it. "Oooh, look at me, I'm cooking. What a challenge! I wish I were as smart as Isabella, with her bad clothes and her bad skin and her sense that she's better than everyone else because she takes food oh so seriously while the rest of us just aren't clever enough to understand it."

Isabella felt hot tears forming in her eyes. It was a mixture of shame and anger and annoyance and hatred and just straightforward hurt. She'd put so much love and care into this meal, she'd thought that she could reach Molly, and Molly was making such a mockery of it all, making such a mockery of *her*, that she felt like she was sitting on top of an enormous dunk tank and Molly was dropping her into it again and again.

"Now we add the bananas," said Molly, like she was hosting a cooking show. "Will I be able to do this right? It's so hard to put sliced bananas into a pan."

She put the bananas in and shook everything around. She did it in a way that showed that she was confident at the stove, that, despite her lack of experience or finesse with a knife, she had the one quality required of any great chef: a belief that you know what you're doing, even when you don't.

"So we are doing dessert first?" asked Xavier. "Because I really want some of that chicken."

Isabella thought about storming out of the room, racing out the front door, and Ubering to a train station. Maybe she would lose this job, after weeks of soul-crushing work; maybe it didn't matter, since Molly was going to make her rewrite the whole cookbook anyway—if Molly didn't just fire her outright. Maybe Molly was right: maybe she did need to build a platform of her own so she didn't have to deal with shitty celebrities like this for the rest of her career. Maybe she just wanted to go home and curl up into a ball and never do anything again. That seemed like a career path worth exploring.

As Isabella was on the precipice of walking away from Molly forever, Molly hoisted the bottle of rum.

"And now we flambé," said Molly, addressing an invisible camera. "Xav, make a video on your phone. I'll put it on my Insta."

Xavier, annoyed, pulled his phone out of his pocket and hit Record as Molly unscrewed the cap of the rum bottle.

Isabella, who seconds earlier had been halfway out the door, now looked on with alarm. For years to come, she would wonder if she could've stopped it in time. There was certainly a beat while Molly waited for Xavier to hit Record, a beat during which Isabella could've told Molly that pouring alcohol directly from the bottle over a live flame was dangerous, that she should pour the rum into a little bowl or a ramekin first and pour it in from there. But would Molly have listened? Would it have made a difference? Could she have stopped what later seemed inevitable?

Isabella would never know.

What she also didn't know, and would only learn later, was that the bottle of rum that she'd pulled from the liquor cabinet wasn't just everyday, ordinary rum. It was Bacardi 151. While most liquor has 40 percent alcohol, Bacardi 151 has 75 percent. Why Xavier's drama-school teacher had this in her liquor cabinet instead of the regular stuff, Isabella would never find out. What she did know was that the flame ball that came exploding out of the pan as soon as the liquor hit the heat was so blinding, so bright, so hot, it felt like the actual sun had materialized in the kitchen and scorched everything that it touched.

It was hard to remember when the screams started, when the curtains caught fire, when it was clear that the hot, sticky caramel in the pan had splashed up onto Molly's face and stuck there, burning her even more than the flames would. Isabella remembered Xavier grabbing the flaming pan—a pan filled with hot flaming rum—and trying to run it out the back, only in the process he splashed the hot, burning liquid onto the carpet, which in turn caught fire, as well as the couch and the dining room table and the front door.

Isabella remembered running toward Molly to beat the flames out of her hair and to help her splash cold water on her face to stop the burning. For a moment, Molly's entire head looked like an image straight out of Greek mythology: as if all of the beauty that Molly worked so hard to maintain, to highlight, to exaggerate, was sucked away by the fire, so that all that remained was a primal scream, a scream so piercing and endless that when the fire trucks and ambulances finally came, the transition in noises was seamless; it was hard to distinguish one from the other.

The last thing that Isabella remembered seeing as she led Molly out the front door, away from the smoke, was the red binder on the kitchen counter, its pages turning charcoal black, its red cover—CANDY BABCOCK'S BOOK OF RECIPES AND MAGICAL POTIONS in her own handwriting—melting away forever along with the picture: a lifetime of work and meals and memories gone in a flash.

. . . .

Isabella was drinking coffee. It was ten at night, and Isabella never drank coffee past noon or she wouldn't sleep, but now it was just an hour before she normally went to bed and she was sitting on the curb in front of the cabin, drinking a Dunkin' Donuts coffee that a policeman had brought her, and the hot liquid was strangely soothing, despite its stimulating qualities. It tasted slightly rancid, but in a good way: as if the emotions that she was feeling were distilled into a drink that she could physically put into her body.

The night air was crisp, and the sky was black, and the only light was the swirling red and blue coming from the emergency vehicles all parked outside the smoldering remains of Xavier's drama-school teacher's house. Xavier was nowhere to be seen. As soon as Isabella was calm enough to talk to the detectives, she explained that they were guests of Xavier's, and when they asked who Xavier was, she wanted to point and say "that guy over there." But there was no guy over there. There was no one anywhere except for Isabella.

Molly had been loaded onto a stretcher the moment the EMTs found them collapsed outside. Isabella was conscious but delirious: she remembered watching them apply compresses to

Molly's face—her neck and cheek were flecked with blisters, her hair was charred like a burnt broomstick—put an oxygen mask on her as they cut open her clothing with scissors, and carry her into the back of the ambulance. She might've gone with Molly, but because she had no visible injuries, unless you counted being in a complete state of shock as an injury, the officers thought it would be better to keep her around to answer questions.

Her answers were all fast and, for a writer, not particularly colorful.

Her ghostwriter.

Xavier's her boyfriend.

Bananas Foster.

A bottle of rum.

The story that the detectives put together about the fire required very little finessing: this was a cooking accident, a tragic one, but an accident nonetheless. What they were much more interested in was how it came to be that a former acting student of Linda Williams—for that was the acting teacher's name—came to be in possession of her summer home when Linda Williams herself had been living with dementia in a senior facility in Vermont, near her children, for more than a decade, children who had no idea that anyone named Xavier had been staying there and were devastated to learn that the cabin itself had burned to the ground. Xavier could be charged with breaking and entering, not to mention sued for the damages to the property.

As the emergency vehicles started pulling away, Isabella wondered if she should go to the hospital or back home. If she went to the hospital, Isabella might be the last person that Molly would want to see when she came to: she might blame her for triggering her to the point that she set herself on fire. On the other hand, who else did Molly have to be there at her bedside, to counsel and console her? Not her father and stepmother, that was for sure.

As she pondered the question, a red Jeep came screeching down the street and up the driveway.

At first Isabella thought it was Xavier. She hadn't noticed

his car in the driveway, but maybe he'd parked his Jeep on the street, and he was finally coming back to fess up to his part in everything that had happened.

But the person who got out of the car wasn't Xavier: it was Fiona.

Fiona looked puffy-eyed and inflamed, like she herself was burning, only from the inside. A few hours had passed since Molly was taken to the hospital. Had the hospital found Fiona as her emergency contact? Who else would've notified her?

As Isabella watched Fiona search the crowd, she wondered who Fiona was trying to find. Was there a head detective that she wanted to ask for more information? An EMT who might have more details about Molly's injuries? Maybe she, too, was trying to find Xavier?

But as soon as Fiona locked eyes with her, Isabella knew. Fiona was there for her and her alone.

She came bounding toward her.

"How did this happen? How could you let this happen?"

Fiona was sobbing, wiping tears and snot from her face with the back of her hand. She was wearing her green Jets jersey with a puffy gray jacket over it.

"My sister. My beautiful sister—you let her set herself on fire!"

For the entire time Isabella had known her, Fiona had been dispassionate, disengaged, as lifeless as a rock. And now it was as if the rock had come to life and become a flesh-and-blood human with one purpose and one purpose only: to seek vengeance for her closest living relative.

"Your sister was out of control," said Isabella, as gently as she could. "She had a lot to drink and was doing a lot of drugs, and I really didn't want her in the kitchen, but she was trying to make a point and I couldn't stop her."

"Her face might be ruined . . . Do you know that? Her face is so red and burned and covered in blisters. She could end up looking like the Elephant Man!"

Fiona was heaving with sobs. Her whole body was lifting up and down with each breath.

"I'm so sorry, Fiona," said Isabella, meaning it more as an expression of empathy than an acknowledgment of guilt. "Can I help in any way? Drive you to the hospital? Get you some coffee?"

With that final question, Fiona stopped her sobbing. She glared at Isabella with all of the fury she could muster, as if she were finally confronting the tumor that had infected their family from the moment she arrived.

"I'll tell you what you can do," said Fiona. "You can get your ass out of here and leave my sister alone forever. Never call us again, never come over, never mention her name . . . especially at restaurants. You think I didn't see you at the bar that night, acting like the Queen of Sheba, when you never would've gotten so much as a takeout order from that restaurant without my sister's help?"

Isabella flashed back to that night at Snakebite, to Fiona clocking her at the bar from across the room.

"Well, now it's all over—the gravy train has come to an end. You're done with her, you're done with me, and you're done with the cookbook. If it's not clear enough, let me spell it out for you in words that you can understand. You're fired."

And for the second time in her life, and also that year, Isabella was dismissed from her job.

"Got it," she said, before turning away from Fiona and walking down the driveway in silence. At her last job, she'd left behind a jacket, a few framed pictures, a box of Milk Duds, three pink furry-topped pens, and a Tupperware full of Key Largo oatmeal cookies. Now she was leaving behind a house in ruins, a permanently scarred actress, and the ashes of an irreplaceable cookbook, not to mention two courses of a three-course dinner that she'd put more heart and soul into than any meal she'd ever made.

As she summoned an Uber with her flimsy signal, a thought occurred to her that was so dark she could never say it out loud. *At least I don't have to do the dishes.*

17

SCORCHED EARTH

Every friendship has a breaking point, though not every friendship reaches it. Owen and Isabella had survived a few brushes with their breaking point over their seven-year union. There was the time when Isabella bailed on a trip that Owen had planned to Provincetown, realizing—a bit too late—that she wouldn't just be the fifth wheel, she'd be the spoke: the only female in a house filled with a revolving door of gay men. Owen made her pay for her room anyway, which seemed fair—but not really, since Owen was obnoxiously rich. There was also the time when Owen threw out Isabella's Valrhona chocolate because it was "too tempting to keep in the house." And the time when Isabella tripped the circuit breaker with her waffle iron and Owen's alarm clock didn't go off, making him late to a meeting with Lance Bass (the fact that Lance Bass himself never showed did nothing to mitigate his anger).

All of these events, major or minor, caused rifts between them but were never enough to end their friendship. They carried on with their regular Punch and Judy show: Owen ribbing her about her clothes, Owen ribbing her about her love life, Owen ribbing her about her skin-care routine (of which she had none). He had fortunately never ribbed her about her weight, but that was just because it was taboo, these days, to do so. (He did glance in her direction whenever she ate something particularly indulgent, like a fried-chicken sandwich slathered in mayonnaise, giving her a look of "Are you really eating that?," which she returned with a "Yes, I really am eating that, so leave me the hell alone" expression of her own.)

As abusive as this relationship seemed on the surface, Isabella held significant power over Owen. She was the only one who had known him before he was a polished gay. She'd seen him at his lowest (what he called his "Banana Republic era"), she'd seen him through his coming out, his parents' divorce; she even knew about his secret plastic surgery to get his ears pinned, to stop them from sticking out so far from his head. At the base of his teasing was the fact that she was the most important person in his life: she was his family, even more so than his actual family.

Which is why, the next morning, Owen sat at the kitchen table in a tortured silence when Isabella came out of her room at ten. He was too bereaved to make himself a cappuccino with his fancy La Marzocco, which normally gave him such joy. Now it seemed like a relic from another era.

Isabella, for her part, was still slightly shell-shocked and delirious. The Uber home had cost an obscene amount of money, money that she didn't have—especially since Fiona had texted her at 3:00 a.m.:

We want that twenty thousand dollars back. Hope you didn't deposit it.

She was pretty sure that they couldn't actually ask for the first half back—she'd started work on the book; in fact, she'd nearly completed it—but this made her nervous nonetheless.

When she saw Owen at the table, her first thought was one of relief. Finally, here was a person she could talk to about everything that had happened, the horror that she'd witnessed—lived through!—and the trauma from which it would take her years to recover. These were the thoughts going through her head until she saw the look on Owen's face. The look was not a warm one.

"Hi," he said, his voice cracking and sounding much more like the insecure Owen whom she first met back at Tufts in the basement of their dorm.

"How is she?" Isabella asked, knowing that the source of his consternation could only be one person.

Owen looked up. His eyes were rimmed with red, and it was clear, just from his look, that he'd been up all night, and only then did she realize that the clothes he was wearing—a suit, a loosened tie, a white shirt with the top buttons undone—were the same that he'd been wearing yesterday morning, when she left.

"They transferred her to a burn center on the Upper West Side," he said, his tone so flat and emotionless it sounded like an Amazon device. "She has burns all over her face. They don't know yet how bad the scarring will be . . . if any of it's going to be permanent. Her hair looks like a Sia wig that fell into a volcano."

Isabella smiled, but Owen wasn't consciously trying to be funny.

"She lost the Netflix gig, by the way," added Owen, as if this were just a casual fact and not the most devastating blow so far in his career. "Bobby called this morning, when he heard the news, and he said there's no way they'd have time to wait for her to heal. Everything's in motion; it's too late to put anything on pause. I think the execs were relieved to have an excuse to get rid of her."

He paused here for Isabella to respond. She ventured a "That sucks."

Owen's face grew tense. "You know what sucks more? My dad's so furious, he's demoting me back down to assistant. He says he'll reconsider in a year . . . a year of me fetching coffee again, taking lunch orders, remembering who gets the vegan chicken salad and who gets the half-caf, extra-hot, soy almond mocha."

Isabella couldn't believe how much had transpired just overnight. She wondered how Owen had found out about the fire in the first place, but it didn't seem an appropriate moment to ask him.

"I'm sorry, Owen," she said, once again apologizing for something that she wasn't entirely sure was her fault. *Was* it her fault? When she played back the scenario in her head, she recalled the devastating way Molly had dismissed all of her hard work, telling her that she'd have to start again with the cookbook and throw away all of the headnotes that she'd spent so much time writing. So was Isabella wrong to push back by making three of her mother's recipes in order to win her back? How could she have known that Molly would have the reaction that she did? The way Molly got so triggered—that was based on her own issues with her mother, issues that were clearly unresolved, issues that Molly should've worked out with a therapist long ago. If Isabella did one thing wrong, it was to tell Molly that she couldn't cook—this was only after Molly called her a cypher, a nobody, and relentlessly mocked her—and if that was what led Molly into the kitchen, it still wasn't Isabella's fault that Molly decided to pour rum directly from the bottle into a fiery pan. Though it was Isabella's fault, possibly, not to have examined the rum that she took from the liquor cabinet in the first place. But anyone could've made that mistake. Couldn't they?

"I feel like things have been building up to this for a long time," said Owen.

"Building up to what?"

"I need you to move out," said Owen, as if this were a foregone conclusion—as if she were a troubled employee he'd given several chances to, but now she'd crossed a line that she would never be able to uncross.

Owen's words were words that Isabella had never expected him to say: not now, not ever. For the past four years, they'd lived together in relative peace. He was a flibbertigibbet, always flitting about, going to parties and bars and events, and she was his anchor: she kept a cozy home for them with her cooking and tidying and knickknacks and cookbooks. They balanced each other out in ways that they'd each have a hard time trying to find in somebody else, even a life partner.

"Don't you think you're overreacting?" she said.

"I'm not overreacting," he said as if he'd given this deep thought and she was only now catching up. "We're completely codependent, and it's not healthy. We're at a point in our lives where we're holding each other back and not helping each other. You need to move out and find a new situation. It'll be good for the both of us, I promise. Think of it like a friendship enema."

Had Owen, Molly-style, emergency-called his therapist from the hospital? Or was this something that he'd been talking to his therapist about all along, Isabella being such a burden?

"Where is this coming from?" she asked, fairly certain that this was just his way of lashing out because of what had happened with Molly.

"I spend too much time taking care of you," he said, as if that were the issue, instead of his client setting herself on fire and ruining her own career. "Sometimes it's so bad that I forget to take care of myself."

Isabella understood, on some level, what Owen was saying. He was always worrying over her, fretting when she stayed home on a Friday night, pestering her about her career aspirations (he was the one who'd pushed her to take the job with Molly in the first place). But Isabella, over time, had begun to think of Owen's monitoring less as altruism and more as a form of narcissism: constantly showing her how much more tasteful, put-together, and cultured he was than his book-obsessed, badly groomed, seemingly unlovable roommate. If she'd ever stopped to do the math, she would've realized that Owen's input made her feel seriously worse about herself than no input at all.

"I think you take pretty good care of yourself, Owen," she said, hoping to return him to some sense of reality.

"You don't have that much stuff," he replied, pivoting back to the subject at hand. "So I figured that you could just put what you can into a suitcase today, and any random pickles or mar-malades that you forget I can messenger over to you later in the week."

Wait: he wanted her to move out . . . today? This was starting to feel less like a fight and more like a breakup. Not just a breakup: a formal divorce with a definitive separation. She wondered, only half-jokingly, if she needed to hire a lawyer.

"I couldn't have done anything to stop her," said Isabella. "You know what she's like when she gets out of control . . . espe-cially when Xavier's around. It's not like I could've prevented this. She's lucky nobody else got hurt!"

"I'd rather be forced to watch *Dr. Pimple Popper: Biggest Pops* than hear another thing about what happened in the fire," he said.

He put his face in his hands. Isabella had never seen Owen so defeated. Only at this moment did she realize how much he lost when Molly set herself ablaze: not only did he lose the victory of landing Molly a job at Netflix, he lost Molly altogether. If she was permanently scarred—and, based on the damage Isabella saw in that flicker of a moment outside on the stretcher, Molly's face looking like the surface of Mars, it seemed like she might well be—how would she ever get another gig? She hadn't just lost the Netflix job; she'd lost the possibility of ever working again, and Owen, therefore, had permanently lost a star client. His only client. Isabella felt awful for both of them, especially since it was all instigated by her.

"I know things seem really bleak now," said Isabella, just above a whisper. "But if there's one thing I know, it's that you're going to land on your feet . . . with or without Molly."

"It'll be a lot harder without Molly," he replied.

"Maybe it'll be easier! Maybe you'll find a new client who doesn't require you to hold her up on the way out of a restau-rant, who doesn't date smarmy drug dealers, who isn't as unpre-dictable as a pot of hot polenta when it just comes to a boil."

"Maybe," said Owen, not getting the reference. "But as for

right now, I really need some time to myself. I can help you lift down your suitcase if you want. That'll be my workout for the day."

Isabella might've argued about having a right to stay because of the rent that she paid, but then she remembered that she only paid a fraction of it. She'd been a charity case this whole time and refused to see it that way, even though, deep down, she knew that it was true.

"Can I at least cook you eggs one last time?" she asked before venturing into her bedroom to pack up her life, or what remained of it. "For old times' sake?"

Owen shook his head slowly.

"No, thanks," he said. "I've never been less hungry."

. . . .

Moving out of Owen's had always been an inevitability, but this particular inevitability arrived at the most inconvenient time: a time when she had nowhere else to go.

Ever since she smashed her mother's questionable eggs, she hadn't heard a peep from the peepiest person in her phone. For her mother not to call her, not to check in on her at least twice a day, was an aberration that at first felt freeing but now felt like a major absence. Especially since the only place that she could conceivably go with her suitcase at this moment was the apartment where she grew up.

Isabella packed as slowly as she could in order to figure out not just her situation, but her destination. She still had money in the bank: she'd barely touched that twenty thousand dollars, though she had spent money on groceries that she hadn't been compensated for and now probably never would.

If Fiona hadn't sent that text, she might've used some of the money to rent an Airbnb for herself until she found a better option. Maybe a studio in Bed-Stuy or Queens. But on the off chance that she would have to give the money back, she didn't want to gamble on something so indulgent.

She surveyed her three piles of clothes—the mostly wearable, the slightly wearable, the totally unwearable—and shoved them willy-nilly into the battered green suitcase that she had inherited from her father. The clothes she didn't care about: they could be furled or unfurled in any which way, and it didn't matter to her.

The books, on the other hand, were a cause of great concern. These cookbooks that she kept under her bed were too precious to leave with Owen to messenger over, and yet too plentiful to carry around with her: especially since she'd be wandering the streets for the next few hours, figuring out where to go. She ultimately made the decision to put into her suitcase the tomes that she cared about the most: *The Breakfast Book* by Marion Cunningham, *The Taste of Country Cooking* by Edna Lewis, and *Comfort Me with Apples* by Ruth Reichl, not necessarily her favorite Reichl book (that would be *Garlic and Sapphires*), but the one that felt the most nourishing for this particular moment.

The rest she put into a cardboard box that she found in the back of her closet, and she wrote a note to Owen telling him to keep her cookbooks until she had a place to send them. (She heard the front door close, so she knew that he was no longer in the apartment.)

As for the kitchen, the cookware was mostly Owen's: generic pots and pans from Bed Bath & Beyond (RIP) that would've horrified a Gwyneth or an Ina. Mixed in there were a few doodads and keepsakes that she'd brought home from *Comestibles:* an egg timer, a Microplane grater, a tea infuser. These she threw loosely into her suitcase, along with a wooden spoon that wasn't hers (it was technically Owen's) but that she'd used so often she felt like its adoptive parent. She'd earned the right to assume custody.

When she was done with her suitcase, she zipped it up slowly to buy herself more time. It turned out that despite living here for four years she'd accumulated very little. The only thing that she really cared about in this apartment, besides her cookbooks, was the person whose apartment it was. But after their exchange in the kitchen, Isabella questioned whether Owen was really her friend anymore—whether he'd actually been her friend for a long time. He'd changed so much since she first knew him, and not for the better. He used to have a sweet, playful side, but he'd grown increasingly sour. He used to resent his father's career and his father's wealth; now he wanted nothing more than to attain it all for himself. Isabella had gone from an essential person in his life to collateral damage. Why, she wondered, had she put up with Owen for this long?

Cheap rent was the best answer she could reach. A pretty good answer in New York.

As she hoisted the suitcase off the bed, an idea occurred to her that was so absurd, so asinine, that all the relationship gurus in the country would've thrown themselves in front of her to stop her from making such a catastrophic move. This idea involved propositioning a person whom she'd ghosted not once, not twice, but three times (four, if you count leaving their date); a person whom she'd been texting with all night and all morning (he'd offered to come pick her up, but she hadn't wanted to put him out; plus, by the time he'd borrowed his friend's car and driven to the Catskills, it would have been the next day). They'd barely kissed, and he'd talked several times about taking things slow because of relationships that he'd rushed along too quickly, only to have them blow up in his face. They had a date planned for the next week: he was going to cook for her, and she was going to bring something for dessert. It would be best—no, smart—to put him out of her mind and make some kind of peace with her mother, so she could at least hover on neutral ground until she made her next move.

Instead, she lifted her phone and dialed his number, telling the relationship guru in her head to take a hike.

. . . .

"See, normally, you date for a few weeks, then you have sex for a while, then you eventually meet each other's parents, and then, maybe after a year, sometimes two, even three . . . you move in together," said Gabe as he helped Isabella carry her suitcase up the three flights of stairs to the Williamsburg loft that he shared with three roommates, most of them sous-chefs at the city's top restaurants.

"You know how some people eat their steak from the inside out?" she answered, carrying her ultralight backpack, and enjoying Gabe's chivalry. "That's what we're doing: eating the best part first."

"This is the best part? I thought sex was the best part?"

"The two things aren't mutually exclusive," she answered, wondering if that was too forward.

"Well, that's a horse of a different color!" he said, and suddenly bounded up the stairs.

The call that Isabella had placed to Gabe an hour earlier was full of humor and self-deprecation and apology and hilarity at the situation. Gabe wasn't put off by any of it. In fact, he was so amused and touched by Isabella's orphaning, it made him even more smitten.

"Our couch is pretty gross," he said as he opened the front door of the all-white space, where badly assembled IKEA furniture and a few dying houseplants were illuminated by several shafts of light coming from skylights in the ceiling. Isabella saw jars of kimchi fermenting on the windowsill, a countertop flour mill, and a coffee setup with so many beakers and burners it looked like Dr. Bunsen Honeydew's lab on *The Muppet Show*.

"This is Vikash," said Gabe, pointing to a young Indian guy in a white T-shirt with an egg on it, who was frying sausage patties and eggs in a large cast-iron skillet in a tiny, closet-sized kitchen. "He works at Jean-Georges."

"What up?" he said by way of greeting, flipping the eggs in the air with just a shake of the pan.

"And this is Louie," Gabe said, pointing to a redheaded guy on a La-Z-Boy, sipping a purple smoothie with a giant straw, playing *The Legend of Zelda: Tears of the Kingdom*. "He works at Misi."

"Yo," he said, frantically tapping the controls, helping Link cook some mushrooms to restore his hearts.

"Hey," said Isabella, no stranger to the game. The last guy that she'd hooked up with had canceled their second date because he was deep inside a shrine.

"And that's Moses," said Gabe, pointing to a guy asleep at the kitchen table with a giant copy of the *Larousse Gastronomique* open in front of him. "He works at Shake Shack but he's applying for a job at Le Bernardin."

Moses grunted a hi from his sleep.

"And here, madame, are your accommodations," said Gabe, indicating the couch.

The couch was so beaten up, so sunken and stained, that if you had told an army of children to dishevel, disembowel, and discolor a couch as much as they could over the course of a day, it couldn't have looked worse than the one that Gabe was presenting.

"Did you do this to the couch so I'd have to share a bed with you?" asked Isabella, only half joking.

"I wish I'd thought of that," he said. "But if you want to see my room, I can show you alternative accommodations."

Isabella wasn't a prude, or, if she was, she wasn't one voluntarily. Life had just made her a prude because of her lack of access to nonprudish things. She hated bars, she hated dating, she hated the apps. Sex, for her, was the stuff of fantasy, and, frankly, it took up less fantasy space in her mind than the fantasies she had about eating at the city's great restaurants.

But somehow, at this particular moment in her life, when she'd lost her job, her best friend, her apartment, and (at least for the time being) her mother, she found herself following Gabe into his room and falling immediately into his arms.

This kiss, unlike their first, didn't involve broken wineglasses or a misplaced tongue. In fact, this kiss would be, for Isabella, the one that she'd compare all others to for the rest of her life. It was a kiss that she desperately needed, a kiss that she savored, a kiss that told her that she was safe, that she was protected, that she was—even at this early stage—loved.

It was during this kiss that Isabella started processing the trauma of the previous night. What had happened right there in front of her was an act of violence. The screaming, the scarring, the sirens—she'd repressed them all until this very moment. Images of Molly's hair on fire, of smoke filling the cabin, of Candy's cookbook melting all came flooding back to her, and she fell on top of Gabe and began taking off his clothes in an act of passion that was as much about her need to distract herself, her need to soothe herself, as it was about both of their pleasure.

"One second," said Gabe, sliding out from under her.

Gabe closed the door to his room—Vikash, Moses, and Louie looking on in admiration—and Isabella didn't sleep on the couch that night, or any night thereafter.

18

MAKING A MEAL OF IT

The sounds of Molly's screams woke Isabella from a deep sleep. At first she thought that she was still dreaming. Of course, it would make sense to have a nightmare about what had happened in the Catskills: it would be weird *not* to have a nightmare about what had happened in the Catskills. And when, fully conscious, she kept hearing Molly's screams, she thought that the dreamy part of her brain was just in overdrive. *Hey, team,* went the voice in her head. *Time to shut things down.*

But then Gabe opened his eyes and asked, "Do you hear screaming?"

The two of them got out of bed, threw on the clothes that still remained on the floor from the night before, and opened the door to the living room. It was 10:00 a.m.—Isabella was so exhausted, she could've slept for another ten hours—and Louie, Vikash, and Moses were all crowded around a laptop, watching what seemed to be Isabella's dream on the screen.

"Holy shit," said Vikash, turning toward Isabella. "Is that you?"

Stepping over to where they were sitting, Isabella saw in illuminated pixels the very images that had been haunting her unconscious mind moments before. There was the explosion of fire when the rum hit the pan. There was Molly's hair bursting into flames. There was Isabella rushing her to the sink. Then it all went dark. How was this possible? What was happening? Was she on drugs?

And then she remembered what had happened in those final moments, right before Molly poured the rum into the pan: she'd asked Xavier to record her on his phone to put on her Insta.

"Where are you seeing this?" asked Isabella, leaning over Vikash's shoulder and watching as the clip played on a loop: Molly once again at the stove, once again holding the bottle aloft, once again setting the kitchen ablaze. "How did you find this?"

"Are you kidding?" asked Louie. "It's everywhere. It's on Google News, CNN, *Deadline Hollywood*. On TikTok it's been viewed almost two million times."

Isabella looked at the numbers next to the screen. Vikash had TikTok loaded up on his laptop, and the numbers didn't lie: this incident, which had happened only two nights ago, now had a higher viewership than anything Molly had ever done on TV. She read some of the comments underneath the video: "She's never looked hotter!"; "What an idiot—you're supposed to use brandy for bananas Foster"; "Ouch, there goes her acting career"; "What acting career?"

Isabella could see herself in the video as it played over and over again on a loop. It was surreal to have a trauma from your life that you hadn't fully processed there for you to study at your leisure. If it were only images, she might've been able to do just that; but the sounds were so upsetting—those piercing, inhuman screams—that Isabella had to ask Vikash to put the computer on mute.

"How did this get out there? Were there security cameras?" asked Gabe, who put his hands on Isabella's shoulders, sensing her unease.

"Molly's boyfriend . . . Xavier," she said. "Molly asked him to film her cooking, and then he ran off when the fire happened. I bet he sold that video for a lot of money. You can do that, right? Sell videos of celebrities to the press?"

The four current and aspiring sous-chefs didn't know anything about that. Vikash closed his laptop and said that he had to get ready for work, as did the others, including Gabe, who hopped in the shower (Isabella politely declined to join him) before he left for Snakebite to oversee that day's prep. Just as she was trying to figure out what to do with her Monday—not to mention her life—her phone rang. She looked down and saw MOM written on the screen. She didn't want to admit it, but she was relieved to see that name.

"Hello?" she answered, her voice half tentative, half solicitous.

"Izzy, oh my God, I have people calling me right and left," said Jeannie, her voice already at a fever pitch. "Are you okay? Why didn't you tell me what happened? I just saw the video online, and I'm shaking. I can't believe you were in a fire and you didn't call me!"

It's one thing to have a mother worrying over you; it's an entirely different thing to have Jeannie Pasternak worrying over you. For the first time in Isabella's life, Jeannie's concern was more than welcome: it was needed. She craved those unhealthy levels of nurture and attention, extreme care that only her mother could provide.

"I'm fine," said Isabella. "Rattled, but okay."

"When can I see you? Where are you?"

Isabella told her that she was staying with a friend in Williamsburg but that she could come up to the Upper West Side to meet her for dinner later. Jeannie took her by surprise and said, "No, I'll come to you."

If Jeannie had said she was becoming a shark on *Shark Tank*, Isabella would've believed it more readily.

"Really? It's kind of far."

"What else am I doing? Text me the restaurant, anywhere you want to go, and I'll see you there at seven."

. . . .

Once the apartment was emptied out, Isabella made Gabe's bed—with its boyish blue sheets and its red flannel comforter—and unpacked her suitcase into the highly organized closet. Of course it was highly organized: Gabe was a sous-chef at a Michelin-starred restaurant. How long would it take him to figure out that, despite any appearances to the contrary, Isabella was a total slob?

Louie had left behind a little coffee in the chemistry set, and after having some, Isabella sat down and contemplated her trajectory. She scrolled on her phone for a bit—she had countless Instagram messages and Facebook messages and DMs from people that she hadn't heard from since high school, all of whom had seen the viral video—and, overwhelmed, she plopped it onto the table, took a shower, got dressed, grabbed her backpack, and forced herself to go outside.

Despite its being nearly November, the day was a comfortable fifty degrees. Unconscious of where she was headed, Isabella found her feet carrying her in the same direction that they'd carried her the last time that she lost a job, which was not even a few months ago. The walk from Williamsburg to Greenpoint wasn't a long one—she passed pork stores and parks and playgrounds—and before she knew it, she was on her favorite block in the city, the block that was home to Alice's Cookbook Emporium.

Only, when she arrived at Alice's, the store was no longer inside the store: it was on the street. OUR GOOSE IS COOKED! THANKS FOR TEN DELICIOUS YEARS was written in red magic marker on a piece of paper taped to the glass door of the now empty space. In front of it was a large table covered with vintage cookbooks of every stripe: books by Maida Heatter, Paula Wolfert, Richard Olney, Edna Lewis, Craig Claiborne. Behind the table was Alice, sitting in a chair, wearing a winter coat, a hat, a scarf, mittens, and sunglasses that disguised her so much it took Isabella a moment to realize that Alice was actually Alice, not an Alice mannequin.

"Alice!" she said, her voice a mixture of shock and heartbreak. "What's going on? When did this happen?"

"Babe, it's always been happening," she answered. "Turns out selling used cookbooks isn't the gold mine that I thought it would be."

"But this store is your *baby*," said Isabella. Already she'd started to examine the precious cookbooks on the table, knowing that she couldn't in good conscience buy any with her limited budget and zero storage space, but tempted. "What are you going to do now?"

Alice shrugged. "Back to the coal mines with me," she said. "And by coal mines I mean taking care of my mother in Jersey City. She's a monster with emphysema, but she'll be dead soon, and then I'll get the house."

Alice's glib manner flew directly in the face of Isabella's emotions about the store closing. For Isabella, Alice's store wasn't just a resource, it was a refuge. What other home could she truly call hers? Uptown, her mother had transformed her former childhood bedroom into a storage facility. And here in Brooklyn, she'd been ejected from the tiny shoebox that she called a bedroom, only to move in with a person that she liked but barely knew. Alice's was her constant, her permanent safe space, her fortress of solitude. For it to no longer exist made her feel like a turtle ripped from its shell.

"What about you?" asked Alice, sensing Isabella's unease. "How's the ghostwriting gig? At least tell me that you're thriving."

When Isabella told her a quick version of everything that had happened, Alice shook her head.

"Well, look at us," she said. "Isn't it ironic? The food world chewed us up and spat us out."

"At least you still have your cookbook collection," said Isabella, eyeing the piles of books on the table. "I have nothing to show for almost two months of work. I may as well flush the last six weeks down the toilet."

Alice was quiet for a minute. She poured tea from a red checkered thermos into an *Alvin and the Chipmunks* Christmas mug and took a sip.

"You do have *something*," she said, almost offhandedly.

"And what's that?"

"The story," said Alice. "It's got to be worth something, right? A first-person account of being Molly Babcock's ghost-writer, all leading up to that big fiery scene in the kitchen? I bet someone would pay a lot of money for that . . . especially if what you say is true and the video's all over the internet."

Why this hadn't occurred to Isabella before, she wasn't sure. But now that Alice had presented the idea, it seemed like the most obvious thing in the world.

"That's smart," said Isabella, playing it all out in her head. "Only . . . there's a small problem."

"What small problem?"

"I signed an NDA."

Of course, the one silver lining to this entire miserable experience—the ability to tell the story of what happened—would be buffed out by Molly and her lawyers.

"Bummer," said Alice.

Just as Isabella was going to sink back into the sadness of her situation, combined with the sadness of Alice's situation—which was a lot of sadness all around—she had a sudden epiphany. *Is it possible? It can't be possible.* She took her backpack off and slowly unzipped the zipper. She reached in and pulled out a bunch of papers: the same papers that Fiona had handed her the very first day she'd shown up at Molly's apartment.

"Holy shit," she said, looking down at them, flipping through them to confirm her suspicions.

"What?"

"I never signed it!" she said, showing Alice the paperwork. "She never asked for it back."

"Jackpot!" said Alice, and she laughed a hearty laugh, her first suggestion of joy since Isabella's arrival. "At least one of us is having some good luck."

Isabella smiled, too, though the morality of this new course of action began to worry her. Would she really be able to write a tell-all about everything that had happened with Molly? Would that be fair to Molly? Did she have to be fair to Molly, after how unfair Molly had been to her?

"Isn't it a little sketchy to use Molly's tragedy for my own benefit, though?" Isabella asked, trying to walk back her enthusiasm a little.

Alice rolled her eyes.

"Sweetie, it's your tragedy, too!" she said, once again showing Isabella the big picture that she refused to see. "And if you can't write about your own experiences, what can you write about? Plus: it's the perfect way to launch yourself as a singular voice in the food world. Isn't that what you've always wanted? To get your name out there?"

It was true, this was what she'd always wanted. This was her Le Cirque moment. When Ruth Reichl was the food critic at *The New York Times*, back in the early nineties, she famously went to Le Cirque—then the city's buzziest restaurant—twice: first disguised as a dowdy old woman, when she was treated terribly, then again as herself, the *Times* critic, to whom Sirio Maccioni, the famous owner, said: "The King of Spain is waiting in the bar, but your table is ready."

Isabella's table was ready.

She finally had the material to spin into a noteworthy piece of food writing. This could be her James Beard award winner, her contribution to the annual volume of *The Best American Food Writing* edited by Sohla El-Waylly or Gabrielle Hamilton or that year's food world superstar. Maybe she would edit the following year's!

"Do you know anyone who'd want to buy such a juicy, salacious piece of food writing?" Alice asked.

Isabella paused and sighed.

"In fact, I do."

. . . .

The gray, imposing TriBeCa building that had been such an integral part of Isabella's life for two whole years and loomed so large in her imagination didn't seem as daunting to her now as she made her way, once again, through the enormous revolving door. No Tupperware shield was necessary this time: she didn't need to hide behind baked goods anymore.

As if picking up on her new confident energy, the security guard, who'd barely lifted his head every morning that Isabella had walked through the turnstile, looked up at her this time as she approached the desk.

"Afternoon," he said.

"I have an appointment with Dana Scanlan," she said, before telling the guard her name.

He found it on the computer and buzzed her through the gate—a strange sensation, when she'd slipped through that gate so many times unnoticed.

On the elevator up, a few of the riders eyed her with a sense of familiarity. Had they seen the video, too? Did they recognize her hands as the ones that had batted the flames out of Molly Babcock's hair? If they did, none of them said anything.

When the elevator doors opened onto the *Comestibles* offices, Samantha was waiting at the front desk with open arms.

"Isabella!" she said, coming up to her and giving her a huge, totally unexpected hug. "I can't believe it. You're famous!"

Word of her arrival had traveled through the offices. Yellow Cap (still wearing it), Teenage Grandma, and Lollipop emerged from their cubicles and joined the party, asking Isabella how she was, whether she'd been hurt in the fire, whether she was still in touch with Molly Babcock.

"Are her scars permanent?" asked Yellow Cap.

"How soon will her hair grow back?" asked Teenage Grandma.

"Will she ever work again?" asked Lollipop, sucking on a purple one that made her breath smell like synthetic Concord grapes.

Before Isabella could answer, Dana Scanlan herself—still looking tall and intimidating and impeccably dressed, in a gray woolen pantsuit—emerged from her office.

"Isabella," she said, walking right up to her and giving her a kiss on both cheeks, like they were old French colleagues meeting up in a Paris café. "Come, come," she said, taking Isabella by the arm. "Don't let the hungry mob peck at you. Shoo, you vultures!"

As Dana led Isabella into her office, Isabella felt the ridiculousness of her situation: how, in a matter of weeks, the tables had turned and somehow, through an unlikely series of events, she—not Dana, but she, Isabella Pasternak—had the upper hand.

"Sit down, sit down," said Dana, opening a mini-fridge under her desk that Isabella didn't even know existed and handing Isabella spring water in an ornate glass bottle from a company so exclusive it didn't even advertise its name.

"Thanks," said Isabella, recalling how, the last time that she'd sat in this very seat, Dana had told her that she had zero personality and her voice wasn't "notable."

"Tell me about this story," said Dana, referring to the email that Isabella had sent from a park bench outside of Alice's two hours ago; she'd gotten an instantaneous response, inviting her into the *Comestibles* offices right away. "How do you envision it? Do you see it as a love letter or a hit job or a combination of both?"

Isabella wasn't sure either of those approaches captured how she wanted to write about her experiences as Molly Babcock's ghostwriter.

"It's fine if you want to soft-pedal it," added Dana, sensing Isabella's discomfort. "But if you really dish the dirt—and really write about all the filthy details?—this story will go so viral, there'll be a second pandemic."

Dana laughed at her own joke, and Isabella smiled a fake smile.

"I guess I just want to tell the truth about what happened?" offered Isabella.

"The truth," echoed Dana, curious about the concept. "Okay. How many words?"

"Five thousand?"

"Let's do ten—it'll up the prestige factor," said Dana, also thinking of the awards this might garner.

"Okay, ten." Were they really haggling over the length of a personal essay about one of the most gutting experiences of Isabella's life? She felt like she was putting her personal traumas on the auction block at Sotheby's. What next? The story of her dad's untimely death? The time she broke her wrist in two places attempting to play beach volleyball?

"When can we have it? Because the sooner the better. In a week, nobody will even remember this happened."

"I mean . . . I think I'll need at least a week to get it together."

Dana lifted a pencil and stuck the eraser end in her mouth, chewing on the metal bit as she contemplated.

"Fine, I'll give you a week. But you've got to make that week count."

Isabella hadn't asked about money, and the old Isabella definitely wouldn't have asked about money, but this new Isabella wanted to know how much she would get paid to betray a person who, at one point, she'd thought of (very loosely) as a friend.

"How much do you pay for a ten-thousand-word essay?"

Dana took the pencil out of her mouth and squinted her eyes.

"Fifty cents a word," she answered, as if that were the most generous offer she could muster. That, Isabella quickly calculated, would add up to five thousand dollars.

"I'm going to need a dollar a word," she countered, sensing that she had something valuable and that taking the first offer would be selling herself short. "I'm giving you an exclusive about something literally everybody in the world is talking about right now. The video alone has over two million views."

Dana gave Isabella a look of recognition: shark recognizing shark.

"You drive a hard bargain," she said, before sticking out her carefully manicured hand. "What can I say? You've got a deal."

· · · ·

Because Isabella was in Manhattan already, and already on the West Side, she decided not to make her mother come all the way to Brooklyn. She called her and told her to meet her halfway: at Buvette in the Village.

When dinnertime rolled around—Isabella had killed the rest of the afternoon wandering the Village, contemplating her article—she half expected her mother to cancel at the last minute, telling her that she wasn't feeling up to it, that Isabella should just come to her the way that she always did, that it would be cheaper and more satisfying to eat canned soup.

Instead, Isabella arrived at Buvette and found her mother sitting at the bar, sipping a glass of white wine and studying the menu.

Her mother, at least since her father's death, hadn't put any effort into her appearance. Her frizzy hair, her drugstore reading glasses, her schmattas (what she called her blouses) made her look like a Roz Chast cartoon. When Isabella was growing up, Jeannie always seemed younger than her age; but after Oliver's death, she started looking older. She was only in her mid-fifties, but her wild graying hair and the purple bags under her eyes made her look like she was in her sixties.

Tonight, for the first time in a long time, Jeannie had clearly put in some kind of effort. Isabella couldn't tell exactly what it was: Had her mother dyed her roots? Put on makeup? Purchased a new outfit? The room was so dark, it was hard to tell, but the change was a good one: her mother looked more like her old self, which is to say her younger self; more exuberant, more alive.

"Oh, honey," she said when Isabella entered her field of vision. Jeannie got up and clenched her daughter in her arms before Isabella could even say hi back.

Isabella let her mother hug her, and then gradually pulled away. She took her jacket off and hung it on the hook under the bar, and sat on the stool next to her mother as Jeannie sat down, too.

"I can't believe you actually came," said Isabella, still in shock to see Jeannie out at a restaurant, drinking a glass of wine that cost more than she'd spend on food in a typical week.

"I know you can't believe it," said Jeannie. "That's why I did it. I was becoming too predictable."

"Predictable" wasn't the word that Isabella would've chosen to describe her mother: she never knew what brand of chaos she'd be walking into when she went over to visit. But she understood what her mother was trying to say.

"So what's good here?" asked Jeannie, lifting the menu. "Oooh, they have coq au vin. I love coq au vin. I haven't had that in years."

"Actually, that's the one thing I'd rather not get," said Isabella. Off her mother's confused look, she added: "It's what I made the night of the fire."

"Oh," said her mother, finally comprehending.

The two of them sat quietly for a moment. Isabella didn't know where to begin. *Sorry for smashing all your eggs? Sorry for saying you were killing unhoused people with your cooking? Sorry for making you feel like a terrible mother?*

"Izzy, before we order, I need to get something off my chest," said Jeannie, putting her hand on Isabella's.

Buvette was a tiny restaurant. It was both extraordinarily intimate—you felt like sardines while eating imported French sardines—and strangely open: the way that it was lit, the giant mirror on the wall, made it feel like a little theater. New York was like that sometimes: both private and public all at once. When Jeannie took her hand, Isabella felt like she was onstage, acting out a scene for everyone's consumption about a mother and daughter reconciling.

"Okay?" she said nervously.

"I know I've been a little . . . manic these past few years," Jeannie began, and before she could get to the next sentence, she scrunched up her face like something rancid was in the air and started to cry. She immediately opened her purse, dug through random brochures and receipts and key chains to pull out a wad of tissues, and dabbed herself on the eyes as the tears kept flowing.

"Mom," said Isabella, suddenly shifting from super-self-consciousness to genuine concern for her mother. "It's okay, Mom. Really. You didn't do anything wrong."

She rubbed her mother's back, the first time she'd done that since her father's funeral.

"For you to be that angry at me . . . ," said Jeannie. "I've never seen you like that before. You had so much rage pent up inside of you . . . so much resentment about how I'd been spending my time."

A distracted bartender walked over to ask for Isabella's drink order, but when he saw Jeannie crying, he discreetly spun away.

"I was so convinced that I was doing some good in the world," she said, between small breathy sobs. "And, meanwhile, I was hurting the one person who matters more to me than anyone."

Jeannie looked up at Isabella with puppy-dog eyes: they were swimming in tears and they were pleading and fearful all at once.

"I felt so powerless after Daddy died. He was such a good man and worked so hard, and for what? And when that money came . . . it was like a curse. I didn't want anything to do with it, but it all just snowballed out of control: the lawyers and the lawsuit and the settlement, and before I knew it, I had all that money in the bank, and I was never more miserable in my life."

Isabella had never heard her mother talk about any of this. She completely disengaged after the funeral: the lawsuit was something that her mother took care of on her own. And even though she knew on some level that her mother was uncomfortable with the money, she also thought, on another level, that her mother was glad to have it.

"And then there was Daddy's store and all of the stuff in it, and it was all so overwhelming, and it felt wrong to go in there to push mid-century crystal chandeliers onto Wall Street tycoons when I already had this money that I didn't need, and selling the store felt wrong because of how much work he put into it . . . so I just locked the doors and walked away. And that was when, on my way home, I found an entire crate of basmati rice outside a Gristedes, and when I asked about it, they said it was past its sell-by date and going to the dump."

At this point, Isabella didn't need to hear any more. She understood how a snowball would start rolling down the hill, building its own momentum, not able to redirect itself no matter what (or who) got in the way. That didn't excuse the years of her mother's undermining her about her career choices, but this new leaf that her mother was turning over felt like a promising start.

"I can't stand the idea of you hating me," said Jeannie, finishing her prepared speech.

"I don't hate you," said Isabella, finally inserting her voice into the conversation. "I just feel like you don't get me. Like you don't want to get me."

Jeannie's wet, searching eyes grew wider.

"I do want to get you!" said Jeannie a bit too loudly, gripping Isabella's hands with both of hers. "I'm sorry if I made you feel like I didn't. That's all I want. More than anything."

Isabella wasn't a crier. Besides crying when she sliced onions, she only cried at her father's funeral or when she listened to *West Side Story*. But now, swept up in her mother's emotions, she felt hot tears coming to her eyes.

"Good," said Isabella. "I want that, too."

The two of them hugged from their wobbly stools, tears streaming down their faces.

"And I want to put the apartment back the way it was," said Jeannie, pulling back and grabbing Isabella by the shoulders. "I want you to like coming there. I want it to feel like a home for you again."

These were words that Isabella wanted to hear more than anything else.

"I can help with that," Isabella replied, the first time she'd voluntarily offered up her services to her mother since the manic charity work began.

"Okay, good. We can start tomorrow."

Of course her mother would push it.

"I'm actually working on an article . . ."

Her mother's needy look led her to add, "But I guess I can write it from there."

The bartender, looking both annoyed and apologetic, returned.

"Sorry to interrupt," he said. "But we do have people waiting for these seats."

Indeed, a small crowd was gathered in the entryway; it was seven o'clock, prime dinnertime, and the West Villagers were glaring at the newly reconciled mother and daughter. Isabella, feeling bad, grabbed the menu and quickly improvised.

"We'll have the escargots, the dauphinois, the carrots, and . . . we'll try the coq au vin."

Jeannie raised an eyebrow.

"I thought you said you didn't want the coq au vin?"

Isabella turned to her mother.

"I'm giving you a second chance . . . I can do the same for a dead chicken."

Jeannie burst out laughing, and Isabella laughed, too, as the waiter took the menus away and sighed heavily.

This was going to be a long night.

19

CHARITY BEGINS AT HOME

Molly Babcock is on fire.

Molly Babcock is on fire and I'm halfway out the door.

Molly Babcock is on fire, I'm halfway out the door, and for a second I think about letting her burn.

Isabella deleted that last one, even though it was punchy, because it wasn't true. Or was it true? No, it wasn't true: she hadn't wanted Molly Babcock to burn. She was just really angry at Molly Babcock when Molly Babcock set herself on fire, and maybe, on some level, she wanted Molly to get hurt on the outside the way Isabella felt hurt on the inside, but not to the degree—or degrees—that Molly ultimately did.

These were the conversations that Isabella was having inside her head as she sat with her laptop in her mother's cramped living room, working on her *Comestibles* tell-all, while Gabe and Jeannie, who'd met that morning—"Look at that handsome punim!" declared Jeannie—filled black garbage bags with assorted rubbish from several years' worth of collecting. Isabella had seen the show *Hoarders*, and she knew the difference between her mother, who kept her mess mostly organized and whose living room was, for the most part, penetrable, and the kinds of people who found dead cat skeletons buried among their books. That said, there was more than a slight whiff of *Hoarders* in the air once the pleasantries were over, and Gabe, who had the day off and was eager to help (and to impress Isabella's mom), began picking through the items one by one.

"So . . . this busted Monopoly board . . . this is trash, right?"

He gave her his signature fresh-faced smile as he held up a Monopoly board that looked like it had been put through a shredder. Jeannie shook her head.

"It's still playable," she said as Isabella, who was trying not to pay attention so she could focus on her writing, looked up.

"Even Edward Scissorhands couldn't play with that, Mom."

"I'm afraid I agree with Isabella," ventured Gabe, who was still trying to make a good impression. "This board is game over."

"Fine, put it in the recycling," said Jeannie, obviously girding herself for more important battles.

Isabella was an hour into working on her essay and monitoring her mother and boyfriend—Was he really her boyfriend? They were living together, so he was probably her boyfriend? Or just a really handsy roommate?—when her phone rang. When she looked at the screen, her stomach lurched:

FIONA.

She had Fiona's number in her phone from those early days when she'd be running out to get groceries and Fiona had to let her back through the door. Fiona had never called her, not once, but now her name was popping up on her screen, and Isabella knew that could only mean one thing: she really was coming after the twenty thousand dollars.

She sent the call to voicemail and waited a few minutes to see if there was a message. Eventually, one appeared, and when Isabella pressed Play, she heard Fiona, gruff as usual, say: "Hey. Call me back. It's important."

Didn't Fiona have more vital things to worry about? Like her sister's recovery? Like her own attachment to and dependence on someone so obviously unstable? Why was she harassing a poor, unemployed food writer for money that her sister clearly didn't need and that Isabella clearly deserved after weeks (months!) of trying to coax a cookbook out of someone who barely knew the difference between salt and pepper?

The rest of the day went by fitfully, as Gabe and Jeannie dug through the random rubble—knockoff *Frozen* Elsa dolls, Tootsie Rolls from the early aughts, snapped-in-half candlesticks—and Isabella rewrote her first sentence over and over again:

Molly Babcock is on fire and I'm on fire, too: only Molly's fire is literal and mine is metaphorical.

Bad. Delete.

Molly Babcock is on fire and part of me wonders if she's doing it for the camera.

Not bad, but unkind. Delete.

Molly Babcock is on fire and the bananas Foster isn't.

You can't end on "isn't."

As she continued her writing and deleting, her phone would ring periodically, and she'd look down to see Fiona's name, only to send it to voicemail each and every time. Occasionally, Jeannie would freak out about Gabe's going through things too quickly—"I barely know you and you're throwing away half a decade's worth of work!"—and Gabe would patiently talk her down from the ledge, reminding her that it wasn't worth filling the already crowded apartment with unusable items if they were alienating the people she loved the most (he'd seen a few episodes of *Hoarders*, too), particularly her daughter. Jeannie couldn't fight with that.

By five o'clock, the three of them were starving—they'd been snacking on granola bars and potato chips all day (Isabella insisted that they bring their own food, a wise decision)—and instead of subjecting themselves to one of Jeannie's soupstrocities for dinner ("I still have some Campbell's?"), Gabe offered to cook.

The idea of a chef of Gabe's caliber cooking in a kitchen that had produced some of the most repulsive meals of Isabella's life was both amusing and horrifying to her.

"You really don't have to," she said. "We can order in."

"I want to," he said, and before they could stop him, he skipped off to Fairway with a whole meal already mapped out in his head.

"He's tough, but fair," said Jeannie as she sat down at the table with Isabella to sip her fourth tea from the same expired teabag. "Are you two shtupping yet?"

"Mom! Boundaries," said Isabella, and before Jeannie could react, the doorbell rang.

Isabella figured that it had to be Gabe, who'd maybe left his wallet or his jacket (he could be a little absentminded that way). Instead, she opened the door, and standing there was Fiona wearing a heavy gray winter coat, with a dark-green knapsack and yellow rain boots even though it wasn't raining.

"Hi," she said. "You weren't answering your phone."

The fact that Fiona had come all this way to collect money was so astounding to Isabella, so unnerving, that she was rendered truly speechless. Was this what it's like to owe money to the mob? Was Fiona going to break her legs?

"How did you know I was here?"

"Owen gave me your mom's address. He said it was the most likely place you'd be."

Owen. Of course he'd rat her out.

Fiona glanced over Isabella's shoulder at the apartment.

"Can I come in, or what?"

Isabella stepped aside, and Jeannie, figuring this person for a friend of Isabella's, stood up.

"Hi," she said, walking over with her hand out. "I'm Jeannie, Isabella's mother."

"Mom, this is Molly's sister," she said, meaningfully, as in: *This isn't a friendly visit.*

"Oh, I'm sorry, I . . ." Jeannie stammered, awkwardly pulling her hand away. She wasn't sure how to finish that sentence, especially since Isabella had walked her through the whole situation the night before at Buvette, including their wanting the money back. "Why don't I let the two of you talk."

Jeannie slunk off into her bedroom, which was packed, floor

to ceiling, with boxes, as Fiona entered the apartment and took in all of the garbage bags and still-unsorted items on the floor.

"Are you guys moving?" she asked, trying to make sense of it all.

"Something like that," said Isabella, not sure how she would deal with this in-person confrontation. Didn't Fiona understand the post-Covid protocol of doing everything online, including forcing someone to cough up twenty thousand dollars that they desperately needed to live on for the coming year?

Fiona sat down on the only clear part of the couch (the rest was covered with assorted used medical-school textbooks), and Isabella, not wanting to hover over her, pulled up a chair, making sure to keep some distance.

"Listen, Fiona," Isabella said preemptively, as she sat down. "I know you want the money back, but here's the thing . . ."

"We don't want the money back," said Fiona. "That isn't why I'm here."

Isabella stopped herself. If it wasn't for the money, why else on earth would Fiona come all the way from the East Village to the Upper West Side to see someone she loathed?

"I know you and I haven't always seen eye to eye," said Fiona, her gaze glancing over Isabella's head, unintentionally illustrating her very point. "But I'm worried about my sister. She's not doing so hot."

An unfortunate turn of phrase, considering the fire, but Isabella suddenly felt a wave of self-recrimination wash over her. Why, during all of this aftermath, hadn't she once considered Molly's well-being? Was it because she was fairly certain that half the world was worrying over Molly, that Molly had the best doctors and plastic surgeons, that Molly had agents and managers like Owen who'd tend to her every need?

"Are the burns really bad?" asked Isabella, not sure what to say.

"She was lucky. She'll have some scarring on her left cheek, but she's already home from the hospital. They're mostly first- and second-degree burns, whatever that means."

Isabella was relieved to hear that. In her effort to spin the situation into a story, she hadn't stopped to think about what it would mean to write a tell-all about her ghostwriting experiences as Molly underwent major, possibly painful plastic surgery to keep her from looking like an open wound for the rest of her life.

"That's good, isn't it?" tried Isabella.

Fiona scooted closer to Isabella and finally made eye contact, her eyes glassy with emotion.

"You'd think, but no. Ever since she found out that she lost the Netflix show, she's been inconsolable. She won't talk to me, she won't eat, she won't go for walks. She just scrolls on her phone all day and takes really long naps and won't let anyone visit. Not even Owen."

Isabella willed herself not to feel too sorry for Molly, or she wouldn't be able to write the article.

"I'm not sure how I can help?" said Isabella. "I'm probably the last person she wants to see, considering everything that happened."

This was so clear to Isabella, she couldn't believe that it wasn't clear to Fiona.

"That's actually not true. She's embarrassed about what happened that night. I think finishing the cookbook with you is the only thing that might get her motivated again."

Ah, so there it was. The real reason for the visit. She wanted Isabella to return to the thankless, arduous task of ghostwriting Molly's cookbook: after everything that had happened! After a fight so intense there were permanent scars.

"I really don't think I can do that," said Isabella. "If you want the money back, I'll understand."

"This isn't about the money!" snapped Fiona. "It's about getting my sister out of the deepest depression of her life. It's about giving her something to look forward to. It's about giving her a taste of human contact . . . even if that human contact has to be with *you*."

Isabella was at a loss. When Fiona fired her, just a few days prior, she thought she was done with the Babcock family for good. Now she was being enlisted to be some kind of emotional healer? And wouldn't that be the height of hypocrisy, considering the article that she was about to write? And how much she'd triggered Molly in the first place?

"Plus, if you come, I have a really cool gift for you," said Fiona. "Something you'll really want."

The idea that Fiona could have anything that Isabella wanted was almost laughable. What: a T-shirt from *The Kitty Lambrusco Show*? A tumbler full of room-temperature beer? A soggy, half-eaten pretzel?

"I really don't know," said Isabella.

"My sister needs you," said Fiona, leaning forward in her seat like a football coach on the brink of victory. "After all she's been through, you at least owe her a visit."

As Isabella pondered her reaction, the front door swung open and Gabe came bounding in with three very full bags of groceries.

"Hope you guys are hungry," he said. "I went a little overboard."

When he saw Isabella talking to a scowling person on the couch, Gabe took a step back.

"Sorry . . . didn't realize you had company," he said.

"It's okay, I'm leaving," said Fiona, hoisting herself off the filthy couch. She turned to Isabella. "Come see my sister or you might regret it for the rest of your life."

With those words, Fiona slung her knapsack over her shoulder, zipped up the winter coat that she'd been wearing the whole time, and made her way out the door without saying goodbye.

"She seemed nice," joked Gabe as he carried the groceries into the kitchen, ready to start his work.

"Right," said Isabella. "She's a real mensch, that one."

. . . .

Chef food isn't like normal-people food. You can have the same ingredients, the same resources, the same environment, and a chef will generate something geometric or architectural or deconstructed, whereas the best you can do if you're not a chef is to create something homey.

Isabella liked homey more than cheffy.

The reason that she loved cookbooks so much was that the people who wrote them were experts at food who *weren't* chefs. They could tell you how to make the coziest roast chicken with root vegetables, how to bake up a lasagna that might reunite even the most fractured family. If a chef baked a lasagna, they'd probably roll all the pasta sheets from scratch, using 00 flour imported from Italy; they'd add some rare and unexpected cheese, char the sides of each individual piece in a skillet to give it a restaurant sheen, add microgreens, and swirl some unneeded sauce around the plate before making the waiter give a speech on how to eat it properly. Why go through all of that trouble when a basic, familiar lasagna is the kind of comforting, rib-sticking goodness that most people want?

When Gabe started unpacking his groceries, Isabella saw all kinds of vegetables—carrots, onions, celery (classic mirepoix), plus Japanese turnips, radishes, and fennel, not to mention garlic—in addition to white beans, big bunches of thyme and rosemary, and a giant jug of olive oil.

"You know this is an old Jewish lady's apartment," said Isabella. "Not The French Laundry."

"Even the The French Laundry was once a French laundry," Gabe responded.

From the table, Isabella watched as Gabe finely diced the mirepoix and began sautéing it in a large, chipped navy-blue Dutch oven, one that Jeannie had inherited from her own mother (and one of the only things in her mother's apartment that Isabella loved). He sprinkled everything with salt and monitored the heat before he started chopping the rest of the ingredients.

Isabella could only imagine what odd concoction he was

cooking up: Would it be some kind of vegetarian pâté? A vegetable mousse? Something he'd shoot out from a canister? Or turn into a gel?

The smells, as Gabe coaxed the ingredients along, adding the garlic and the rosemary and the thyme, were undeniably alluring. So much so that Jeannie, who'd fallen asleep on her half-covered bed, was lured out of her bedroom to ask, "Why does it smell like heaven in here?"

"While you're waiting . . . ," said Gabe. He produced a bottle of chilled Mâcon-Village and poured some into her mother's souvenir McDonald's cups from the 1970s (Isabella got Grimace, Jeannie the Hamburglar; Gabe took Ronald). He also set out a platter of cheeses—Mimolette, Comté, Laura Chenel goat—with crackers, dried figs, Marcona almonds, and Medjool dates.

"Cheers," he said, toasting Isabella and her mother.

"I don't know how you found this person," said Jeannie before clinking, "but never lose him."

Isabella couldn't believe her luck. Who would've thought that here, in her mother's gloomy apartment, she was about to eat a meal cooked by her chef boyfriend, who liked her so much he let her move in with him after only one official date?

On top of that, she'd sold an article to *Comestibles* that was destined to put her on both the culinary and the literary map. She was still stuck on her first sentence—"Molly Babcock is on fire . . ."—but once she got over that hump and really got into the nitty-gritty, it was destined to be great. How could it not be? With the story she had to tell, and the general interest in Molly right now—Isabella's phone kept pinging with messages from old acquaintances who had seen the video, which was up to eight million views—the story would basically write itself.

She was sitting pretty, in the catbird seat, if not for that unexpected, unshakable visit from Fiona.

Isabella knew a thing or two about guilt—she was the daughter of one of its master mongers—and she tried not to let

Fiona's appearance cloud her judgment about what made the most sense for her and her own future. There was the question of making up with Molly, but there was also the larger issue of finishing the cookbook. Even though Candy's binder was gone forever—a tragedy in its own right—she still had all of the recipes on her laptop, which had somehow survived the fire along with Isabella's backpack.

If she weren't writing this article, wouldn't she want to finish what she started? If not for Molly, then at least for Candy?

And even if she did write this article, wasn't it possible to do both—to finish the cookbook and to write about what had happened with Molly? True, Molly would feel betrayed when the article came out. And, true, Molly would probably kick her out and never want to speak to her again. But if they submitted the cookbook before all of that happened, wouldn't she get the best of both worlds?

When Gabe finished cooking, they all sat down at the table—Jeannie had a surplus of ancient silverware too damaged for the thrift shop, with which they set the table—and he presented each of them not with a gelée or a foam but a humble and hearty vegetable soup: an Italian minestrone without the pasta.

"This smells like a hug," said Jeannie.

"It's so pretty," said Isabella, genuinely awestruck. The soup was humble, but that didn't mean it wasn't beautiful to look at: the radishes and Japanese turnips looked like little planets, the fennel cut into pieces that spread out like little fans, the herbs so finely minced with the garlic that they perfumed the soup without overwhelming it.

They all dipped their spoons in, and in that moment—even before they tasted it—Isabella finally understood what Molly so desperately needed right now. Despite the small population of nurses and acolytes surrounding her, despite her agents and managers and lawyers and even her sister, she didn't have anyone to really take care of her. To worry over her. Her sister was worried over her, but her sister couldn't nurture Molly with any real feeling or talent.

"Oh, Gabe," said Jeannie—that desecrator of soup who thought Swanson's was the height of luxury. "This is next-level."

Isabella took her first bite and closed her eyes.

"Well?" asked Gabe, watching intently for her reaction.

"It tastes like home."

. . . .

The next morning, waking up with Gabe (she'd found the perfect nook between his armpit and his elbow in which to sleep), she made the mistake of telling him about the article.

Up until this point, all he knew about Molly was what had happened in the cabin and that Isabella had been fired from writing the cookbook. But now that she'd been reenlisted by Fiona, Gabe saw the ethics of the situation laid out like a philosophical mise en place.

"You have to call off the article," he said as Isabella wrapped her arm around him. "You can't co-write a cookbook with her and stab her in the back at the same time!"

"It's not that simple."

"What's not that simple about it?"

"This article's a huge opportunity for me," explained Isabella, now pulling back her arm and lifting her head off his chest. "It's my Gay Talese on Frank Sinatra, my Taffy Brodesser-Akner on Gwyneth Paltrow, my Barbra Streisand on Barbra Streisand."

"I don't get those references."

"If I just do Molly's book, it'll go uncredited. No one will know that I worked on it. It'll do nothing for me or my career. I may as well have not written anything at all."

"But is that what this is all about for you? You and your career? Is that why you became a writer, so that people would know who you are? Or was it to do work that matters?"

This was spilling over into the same debate that they'd had on their first date. Gabe was comfortable in the shadows, setting his ego aside and staying out of the limelight. But was Gabe doing the honorable thing or the cowardly thing? What kind of career could you have—as either a chef or a writer—if nobody knew who you were? Isabella wasn't sure that she wanted to give up her shot at the limelight just yet.

"You can be a well-known writer who does good, meaningful work . . . They're not mutually exclusive," countered Isabella.

"Is it good, meaningful work when you're betraying someone who trusts you? To expose all of their secrets and stories from their private life?"

That one stung.

"It's not a betrayal when you're telling the truth," argued Isabella, repositioning herself to face Gabe.

"If someone lets you into their world," said Gabe, rolling to face her, "isn't there a presumption of privacy? I can't imagine writing a tell-all about any of the chefs that I've worked for, even when the chef was shitty. Nobody in my industry would ever do that."

"Of course they would! Haven't you ever seen *The Bear*?"

"*The Bear*'s a TV show."

"But it started as a book."

"I'm pretty sure it didn't."

"The point is," said a flustered Isabella, getting out of bed, "the right choice will be obvious to me when it's time."

She said it with such conviction she almost believed it herself.

"The right choice is obvious to me now."

"Well, aren't you a saint, Gabriel?" she said, as she grabbed a towel and headed for the bathroom. Gabe was the perfect boyfriend, but Isabella didn't always want or crave perfection. Sometimes a greasy hamburger was preferable to perfectly poached halibut. She was craving the company of someone who was flawed the way that she was flawed.

Which is how she decided, then and there, to go and visit Molly.

. . . .

What do you bring to the home of your former employer whose injuries were sustained in an argument involving you? Whom you provoked for not being able to cook, only to have her set herself on fire in trying to prove that she could? Roses? Chocolates? A Hallmark card? Did they make one for that?

Isabella, thinking it over, brought the next-best thing that she could: leftovers from Gabe's incredible soup.

Though she had a key, when she arrived at the familiar front door she rang the bell, like she did the very first day she came there.

Fiona answered more promptly than ever before. It was as if she knew not only that Isabella would come, but exactly when she would come: as if she were hovering just inside the door, ready to open it.

"She's awake, but groggy," said Fiona by way of greeting, taking the soup from Isabella. "Did you make this?"

"My boyfriend did," Isabella replied, feeling obnoxious but also self-satisfied at being able to say "my boyfriend."

Fiona closed the front door and led her through the apartment, which was weirdly clean and lifeless. Had Fiona actually gotten off her butt and mopped and dusted and put things away? Was that a result of her anxious energy, not knowing what to do with herself since Molly was out of commission?

"Does she know I'm coming?" asked Isabella, trying to slow down their pace as they made their way through the kitchen toward Molly's room.

"No. It's a surprise."

Isabella nodded as she watched Fiona put the container in the fridge. She was nervous to reunite with Molly—she wasn't sure what she was going to say yet, their last encounter had been so harrowing—so she decided to stall.

"Did you say you had some kind of gift for me?"

Fiona froze and then slowly turned around. "Yeah . . . I do."

She opened a drawer and put her hand on something that Isabella couldn't see.

"I've had this for a long time. I meant to give it to you sooner, but, to be honest, I really hated your guts at the beginning."

She reached into a drawer and pulled out Isabella's *Zuni Cafe Cookbook*: the very copy that Isabella's father had bought for her on their trip to San Francisco, the last gift that he'd ever bought her; the same book that Molly had left in the back of the Uber, and the very same one that Fiona claimed not to have found when she went looking for it.

"You had this? The whole time?"

Isabella took the book from Fiona and hugged it to herself like a beloved stuffed animal or a favorite article of clothing.

"As I mentioned, I hated you," said Fiona.

"Yes, you mentioned that."

"So, when I found this in the back of the Uber, I brought it back here and put it into this drawer. I was still pissed that Molly asked you to ghostwrite her cookbook instead of me. I figured I would give it back eventually. So here it is."

Isabella wasn't sure whether to be grateful or to press charges. Instead, she just said, "I'm glad you did."

Armed with her good-luck charm, Isabella turned back around and walked to Molly's door. She hesitated before knocking. Fiona looked on, amused.

"She won't bite," she assured her. "You have too many calories."

Isabella smirked at the slightly insulting joke and knocked softly.

There was no answer.

Isabella knocked again.

She looked at Fiona, who gave her a nod, telling her it was okay to just go in.

Isabella carefully turned the knob and entered the pitch-black space—pitch-black except for the glow of Molly's phone, which she held under her face, while propped up by three pillows in bed.

"What time is it?" asked Molly, whose face—just from the phone light—looked like a painting by Rothko.

"I think it's eleven?" said Isabella, announcing herself.

Molly put the phone down, rendering the room completely black.

"You can open the shade," she said after a pause. "Though I should warn you: my face is giving Freddy Krueger."

Isabella took out her own phone and used its glow to navigate to the window. She pulled the shade open in one large gesture, and the blast of sunlight that came through was such a shock to the system, it was like plunging into a pool of ice water. Isabella's eyes had just adjusted to the darkness, and now they were struggling to stay open. Molly put her hand over her eyes, too, both to protect her from the sun and to hide her face.

"Wow, the daylight is being so extra right now," said Molly.

"Do you want me to close them back up?"

"No," said Molly, slowly lowering her hand. Isabella looked on, and what she saw on Molly's face was a road map of pain: deep-red patches intersecting bright-pink ones all over the formerly impeccable face of one of "TV's Hottest Stars" (*People*, 2015). Her hair was cut awkwardly to hide the singes; her eyebrows were completely gone. On her cheek, Isabella could see a constellation of pink dots that, funnily enough, looked like an upside-down ladle: a ladle that might be hanging there permanently.

Isabella sat on the edge of the bed—both of them, in their silence, acknowledging the damage that had been done.

"Does it hurt?" asked Isabella as she studied the topography of Molly's face.

"Like the worst sunburn of my life. I could take pain pills, but, knowing how much I like drinking, I don't want to get hooked. Once you do, you never stop."

This was the first indication that Molly—who previously would have snorted and drunk her way out of any situation—had grown more self-aware. Had the fire made her question her reliance on chemical substances?

"So . . ." said Molly, sitting up farther, attempting to change the subject. "What's new?"

She asked the question both sarcastically and sincerely, mocking the idea that anything that was going on with Isabella could be as dramatic as what was going on with her, but also genuinely curious.

"Not much?" Isabella proffered, not sure what she should and shouldn't reveal: specifically about her new writing gig.

"C'mon, I've been in doctors' offices nonstop for days . . . I'm sure there's more going on with you."

"Ummm . . . I think I have a boyfriend now?"

"The chef from that restaurant? The cute one with the dimples?"

Isabella nodded, flattered that Molly called her boyfriend "cute" and that she remembered his dimples. Fiona quietly entered the room and, to Isabella's complete surprise, brought her coffee and a Danish from some local bakery, which she put on the nightstand, so as not to interrupt the conversation before discreetly exiting.

"Well, that's cool, that you have a boyfriend," said Molly. "I don't think I'll be dating anyone again for a long time. Especially after that piece of shit Xavier ran off and stranded me at the hospital and sold that tape of me setting myself on fire to the press. I've never been so embarrassed in my life."

Isabella nodded, trying not to think about how her own article would embarrass Molly even further.

"God, that night was so fucked," added Molly, lowering herself back into the bed. "I can't even remember what we were fighting about."

"We were fighting about the cookbook," Isabella answered, not wanting to open an old wound, but knowing it was necessary if they were actually going to work together again. "I was really confused about why you brought me to your dad's house to find that book of your mother's recipes if you didn't want to use them in the first place? Why did we go through all of that? What was it all for?"

Molly was now the one who looked uncomfortable.

"I don't know," she admitted, and then she crossed her arms, hugging herself. "I guess . . . part of me wanted to share the recipes that I grew up with, but another part of me found the whole thing too hard to confront."

"Why was it so hard?"

"You met my dad," she said, pulling the blanket up closer to her chin. "Imagine him the way that you saw him, only ten times worse. That's how he was to my mother."

That was a lot to imagine.

"She waited on him hand and foot and he treated her like shit. I grew up with that, and I vowed I'd never be that way, that no one would ever talk to me the way my father talked to her. And when I got famous, I finally had the chance to get my mother out of there. I begged her to come live with me in L.A., or to let me buy her an apartment in the city, or . . ."

She trailed off.

"But she stayed?"

"Not only did she stay. She got sick. And even though I had the means to, I just couldn't go back there to see her, because I couldn't be around *him*. Did you know that he started dating Frances while my mother was still at home, dying in her hospital bed? She was my mom's nurse. The whole thing was so twisted."

For the first time, Isabella was getting a clearer picture of why these recipes were so triggering. It wasn't that Molly hated her mother; it was that she loved her mother so much and felt endlessly guilty about abandoning her.

"Don't you think that writing about your mother's recipes is a way to honor the parts of her that you loved the most? It doesn't all have to be about what happened at the end of her life."

Molly considered this.

"I just feel like it's a lie to write a cookbook and have it be all about how much I loved my mother and her food when I let her die alone in the living room of a house where her husband was fucking her nurse on the other side of the wall. It just feels wrong."

Molly's resistance suddenly made sense to Isabella. She understood the delicate membrane between truth and fiction that all nonfiction writers, including cookbook writers, have to navigate. The "tribute to my beloved mother" aspect of Isabella's take on the book just felt false to Molly. And Isabella had to respect that.

"I get it now," said Isabella.

"Do you?" Molly's eyes searched Isabella's, looking for a safe landing.

"I do. It wouldn't be fair to put her recipes in your cookbook when you feel like things between you and your mother didn't end well."

Molly nodded.

"That's exactly it."

Isabella sat still for a moment. Then she had a thought.

"What if it's not a cookbook? I mean, not a traditional cookbook. What if it's more of a memoir? With recipes? That way, you can put everything into context."

Isabella wasn't a fan of the celebrity memoir, especially a celebrity memoir by someone barely in their thirties. But Molly had a story to tell, especially now: a story about her childhood, a story about her mother, a story about escaping it all, starting her career, refusing to go back, the recipes that she'd rediscovered, and then the fire that swallowed those recipes whole, although they still lived, miraculously, on Isabella's computer.

"It's not a bad idea," said Molly. "I always felt like a bit of a fraud writing a cookbook anyway."

"I wouldn't say 'fraud,'" replied Isabella. "More like an impostor."

Molly laughed. "So you'll help me write that? A memoir with recipes?"

"Of course," said Isabella. "What's a ghostwriter for?"

For the first time since she took on this project, Isabella felt genuinely optimistic about the book that they were going to write together. Despite all of her previous fears and misgivings, she realized that this book—this personal memoir with recipes—could actually be good. She wouldn't be perpetuating a fraud; she'd be helping write something real. Something worthy. This might even become a book that Isabella herself would actually buy.

She was giddy about it the whole way home, smiling on the subway, riffing on chapter titles, until she remembered her other writing assignment, the one that stood in direct opposition. How could she write an emotional culinary memoir for Molly Babcock when she was writing her own emotional culinary essay about working *for* Molly Babcock, due in less than a week?

Suddenly writing a listicle about broccoli didn't seem so bad after all.

20

STIFF PEAKS

WE'RE CHOMPING AT THE BIT! HOW'S IT COMING?

It was eight the next day, and Dana's text (of course it was in all caps) blasted Isabella awake. She texted back a short and sweet message:

It's coming!

She added a brunette female shrug emoji, which, in her bleary morning brain, she meant to convey that she didn't know how much longer it would take, though it unintentionally conveyed a certain ambivalence about the article itself. Which, oddly enough, was actually how she was starting to feel.

KEEP AT IT! Dana texted back with a boxing-glove emoji—conveying both that Isabella should show strength and that she might get punched if she didn't do a good job?

Gabe was already gone: he'd left for a jog, although it was drizzly and cold (was he trying to get away from her after their fight?). Isabella was left alone with her thoughts, and her thoughts were all a jumble. What was it that she wanted, ultimately? To be a literary sous-chef like Gabe, ghostwriting cookbooks for the rest of her life? Or to be a famous literary chef-chef like

Gabrielle Hamilton, having her name on the cover of her own books, books that people bought because of her?

Obviously, it didn't all hinge on this one decision, but it sure felt like it did. If she wrote about her experiences working for Molly, who else in their right mind would ever hire her again as a ghostwriter? She would have betrayed the fundamental tenet of the job. Namely: to stay invisible.

On the flip side, if she dropped the article and worked with Molly on the book, how quickly would she regret her choice when Molly revealed her ugly side again? Despite how meek and humbled Molly had seemed the day before, Isabella knew that somewhere lurking in there was a viper waiting to strike. She flashed back to the things that Molly had said to her right before the fire: "You: a person who nobody gives a shit about. You: A person with zero talent. You: a nobody destined to become even more of a nobody by the time you're thirty."

This was who she was worried about wounding? This was who was going to shatter upon reading the article? Puh-lease. Molly wasn't going to feel betrayed . . . She was going to be impressed! Finally: the talentless nobody stepped up and became a somebody.

As she opened her laptop to start another stab at "*Molly Babcock is on fire*," her phone rang and this time she got another shock.

OWEN.

"Hey, can you meet up?" he asked, once she answered (she let it go for a few rings). "Are you at your mom's?"

Leave it to Owen to act like nothing had happened between them, like he hadn't kicked her out of their shared apartment at the lowest moment of her life, like he hadn't formally ended their friendship.

"I'm in Williamsburg . . . at my boyfriend's."

That'll give him a shock, she figured, just slipping in that she had a boyfriend who had an apartment.

"Cool," he said, not taking the bait. "Can you meet at Hungry Ghost in twenty?"

Isabella did the math in her head: she could throw on clothes, brush her teeth, and splash water on her face and make it in time. Who was she trying to impress? Definitely not Owen.

"See you there," she said, and hung up, beating him to the punch.

· · · ·

Hungry Ghost, despite being a chain, was Owen's favorite place to grab coffee before his father bought him the La Marzocco. Isabella had spent many a morning here with a beat-up-looking Owen, regretting his choices from the night before, nursing a hangover with a decent-enough scone and a Red Eye (coffee with espresso), his go-to morning-after drink, which he swigged like water.

When Isabella walked in on this particular morning, she saw Owen sitting at their usual table: a tall cup of coffee in front of him, and Isabella's usual cortado waiting for her.

"Hey," he said, standing up. "You still take it with whole milk?"

This was a touchy subject, since Owen was always trying to get her to switch to soy or oat or at least skim.

"I do," she said, unapologetically. "Thank you."

The two of them sat down. Owen was wearing his original Mirror Mirror uniform, from before he became a manager: AG jeans, a Rag & Bone cashmere sweater, a Paul Smith tan corduroy jacket. He must've arranged to meet her before going into the office to make copies.

"So . . . who's this new boyfriend?" asked Owen as an ice breaker. He seemed uncharacteristically sheepish, like he'd pulled a chair out from someone before they sat down and now he was visiting them while they were in the hospital with a broken coccyx.

"His name's Gabe," said Isabella. "He was that chef that I met the night you guys had dinner without me at Snakebite?"

This line was lobbed at Owen like a test grenade. She wanted to see how it would explode in his brain, to see if it conjured up any sense of self-recrimination for the way that he'd behaved over the past few weeks.

"I felt bad that night," he said. "I didn't realize you were invited. Honestly. I was so wrapped up in making Molly happy, I could barely register anything else. I wasn't sleeping, I wasn't eating, I wasn't watching Bravo. I'm sorry for all of that, Izz. I really am."

Was he also sorry for kicking her out of their apartment on the morning after the worst night of her life? For telling her that she was a drain? A charity case that he could no longer afford?

"Listen," he said. "There's a lot I feel bad about. Everything that happened. I didn't want things to end the way that they did between us. I was hoping for a Gwyneth-style 'Conscious Uncoupling,' and what I served was more of a *Kramer vs. Kramer*."

Isabella softened.

"I suppose I played my own part in things," she admitted. "Our arrangement wasn't exactly fair . . . especially since you don't eat."

"I eat," protested Owen.

"Snorting protein powder doesn't count."

Owen laughed. "I inject it now."

They both grinned.

"So is this why you wanted to meet for coffee?" she asked. "To apologize?"

"Yes," he said.

"Okay," said Isabella. "Apology accepted."

Owen nodded, and Isabella felt good that they'd reached some sort of rapprochement.

"There's another reason I wanted to meet you, too," he added.

She looked up. Of course there was another reason. It wasn't in Owen's nature to ask someone out for coffee just to apologize, even Isabella.

"Molly told me about the memoir idea."

So here it was. Just when she and Molly finally agreed on a

concept that they could both be happy about, he was here to shoot it down.

"And I love it. I do. A memoir makes so much more sense than Molly writing a cookbook."

The way he said that last part almost made Isabella burst out laughing. After all of the pushing that Owen did to get her to ghostwrite for Molly, here he was, finally admitting the essential truth that she'd known all along: Molly's cookbook was bogus! Molly couldn't cook! And he thought so, too, only he wouldn't admit it until now.

"Here's the problem," he said, leaning in as he took a big sip of his Red Eye. "The publisher has cold feet about Molly. They like that the video went viral, but they think it makes her look like an idiot in the kitchen. Which, to be fair, it kind of does. Who pours a hundred-and-fifty-proof rum from a bottle over an open flame? They're not sure anyone's going to want to buy her cookbook or her 'memoir with recipes' now."

So the publisher had caught wise, too. What kind of universe was this, where the most obvious thing in the world—that a celebrity who can't cook shouldn't write a cookbook—takes a catastrophic fire for people to figure out?

"So they're calling off the book?"

"They said they'd reconsider if we can rehabilitate her image as a cook," he said, sipping the last drops of his battery acid and exhaling a cloud of espresso-coffee breath.

Okayyyy, thought Isabella. *So they're calling off the book.*

"Luckily, Molly's good friends with Kitty Lambrusco, and Kitty's willing to have her on the show right away—she says it'll be great for the ratings, especially with that video still setting the internet on fire . . . No pun intended."

That's not a pun, thought Isabella.

"But what about her burns?" Isabella remembered the pink-and-red road map that was Molly's face from the day before. "Do you really think she should go on TV with her face looking like it does?"

"We think it'll generate lots of sympathy. There's already a

campaign online for Netflix to rehire her, protesting discrimination. We really want her to tell her personal story—the same one
she's going to write with you—about her mother being a cook,
her abusive father, her mother's untimely death, using drugs and
alcohol to hide the pain, and how it all literally blew up in her
face. That'll set up a memoir announcement perfectly."

Isabella realized that this apology meeting was really a Hollywood pitch meeting, and she was the one being pitched.

"Where does the cooking come in?"

"The second segment," explained Owen. "And that's why she
needs your help. We want her to do something really impressive.
She can't fuck it up: it's all about resuscitating her image, not just
for the book, but for the rest of her career. Right now, people
think she's a joke. We need to show that she has her shit together
and that she knows what she's doing in the kitchen."

"But she doesn't have her shit together and she doesn't know
what she's doing in the kitchen."

Owen shrugged.

"So be her Mr. Miyagi and teach her."

"I'd have to be Jesus, because it'll take a miracle to get her to
cook anything decent."

"Then be Jesus."

Isabella pulled her hair back as she furrowed her brow, actually enjoying this banter with Owen, even after he'd exiled her
from his life.

"I don't even know what I could teach her that would be
impressive in just a week."

"Oh, she already knows what she wants to make," said Owen,
cracking his knuckles, as if this were a done deal.

"And what's that?"

Isabella could only imagine what Molly would consider
impressive in the kitchen: a Goopy bone broth? A homemade
avocado mask? Some kind of turmeric tincture?

Owen smiled a wicked smile.

"She wants to make a soufflé."

. . . .

That afternoon, Isabella pushed her tell-all essay aside and started riffing on Molly's new cookbook/memoir instead.

Still at Hungry Ghost, she took her laptop out once Owen left, having agreed to help Molly practice the soufflé, even though she couldn't imagine that it would go well, and started a new document.

Out of the gate, she found that shedding the constraints of a traditional cookbook—with the mandatory headnotes and recipe tips, none of which felt authentic for Molly—was extremely liberating. In this new format, she could channel Molly's voice and really sound like Molly; she even had a strong first sentence:

> *For the first half of my life, food was my biggest source of comfort; for the second half, it was my biggest source of pain.*

She wrote about Molly's mother, using things that Molly herself had told her:

> *Mom would butter her grilled cheese twice. First she'd butter half of the bread and toast it in a skillet. Then she'd take it out, flip it over, put the cheese on the golden, toasty part, butter the outside, and fry it again. It was the best grilled cheese I'd ever had, and I've never had one that tasted better, even when I make it exactly the same way.*

She even attempted to write about the fire, a strange experience since she was also trying to write about it from her own point of view in her essay for *Comestibles*:

> *The urge to prove that I knew what I was doing in the kitchen, that I hadn't completely abandoned my mother and her legacy, was so overwhelming, so all-consuming, that I literally and figuratively burst into flames.*

If she hadn't had anywhere else to be, she could've kept going—she'd already banged out three thousand words—but it was one o'clock, and she'd promised Molly via text that she'd come that afternoon to begin "soufflé training." She dragged the document into a folder labeled NEW MOLLY and then dragged herself onto the subway, unsure if today's Molly would still be New Molly, or if New Molly had reverted back to the old file.

. . . .

The sight that greeted Isabella when she walked into Molly's living room was so startling, so unfamiliar, that she had to blink twice to make sure that it was real.

Molly, dressed and out of bed, was eating. No, she wasn't just eating: she was devouring. On a table in front of her was an enormous spread from Russ & Daughters: a dozen assorted bagels, smoked mackerel, smoked salmon, three tubs of cream cheese (plain, scallion, horseradish-dill), sliced tomatoes and onions, capers, and an entire chocolate babka, plus black-and-white cookies and hamantaschen.

"Can you believe all this?" asked Molly, as she chewed a giant bite of pumpernickel bagel schmeared so heavily with cream cheese it was almost an even ratio of dairy to carb. "Netflix sent this! They're worried about the campaign to get me reinstated and that I'll call them on discrimination online, which I might still do. You have to try some of this!"

Their roles must've genuinely reversed, because Isabella, for the first time in her life, had forgotten to eat lunch, and she *never* forgot to eat lunch. This Russ & Daughters arrived at the perfect moment.

"The only thing Netflix sends me is a bill," said Isabella, expertly loading up her bagel with horseradish-dill cream cheese, a few slices of smoked salmon and raw red onion, sprinkling on some capers at the end. Her father had taught her how to eat a proper bagel at Barney Greengrass, and she firmly believed that the worse it made your breath the better.

"I haven't had bagels in so long," said Molly, staggering her bites of bagel with bites of babka. "That's the nice thing about getting scars all over your face. You can get fat and no one will care."

Isabella nodded. That *was* the nice thing about getting severely burned, she had to agree.

"The last time that I ordered a bagel, I made them scoop it, and even then I only ate half."

Isabella couldn't really relate to any of this. Her relationship with carbs was so pleasure-focused, so unapologetically visceral, that she felt like she was talking to a virgin who'd finally agreed to sleep with her supermodel boyfriend after three years.

"How do you do it?" Molly asked Isabella, watching her enjoy her second bite.

"Do what?"

"Eat like that and not care about what it does to your body?"

Isabella couldn't tell if she was being insulted (Old Molly?) or complimented (New Molly?) or both (merged documents), so she answered truthfully:

"We're all going to die, so why not eat what you want? It's not worth it to deny yourself really good spaghetti carbonara, or a rib eye with creamed spinach, or a big fat slice of cheesecake, just so you can look good at the beach in a bikini."

"I don't know," said Molly, not completely convinced. "Looking good in a bikini feels pretty good, too."

"That's why you're you and I'm me."

"Thank God for that," said Molly, clinking her bagel bite against Isabella's.

Eventually, they migrated to the kitchen, where Isabella expected to see the ingredients for a chocolate soufflé, the same ingredients that she'd encountered months ago in the *Comestibles* kitchen. Instead, she saw a jar of mayonnaise, a block of cheddar cheese, a carton of eggs, and a jar of pimentos.

"I thought we were making a soufflé?" asked Isabella, only then noticing the soufflé mold next to everything on the counter.

"We are . . . my mother's pimento-cheese soufflé!"

The recipe, one of the few that Isabella hadn't included from the red binder, was one that she vaguely remembered. Molly, meanwhile, pulled out a folder, inside of which was a printed-out email from Candy dated September 14, 2018.

"My mom worked on this recipe forever," explained Molly. "She tried to get it published in so many newspapers and magazines, and they all rejected her. She sent the recipe for me to test once, and I never did, but I remembered it when Owen told me I was going on TV. I thought I could talk about it and her and tie it into the book."

The fact that Molly was now at last interested in making one of her mother's recipes was such an unexpected development, Isabella completely ignored the fact that this untested, unproven recipe was probably the last thing Molly should make to prove her expertise on national television.

"Wow," said Isabella, taking the email from Molly and studying the steps.

"Is making a soufflé hard?" asked Molly.

"Have you ever separated an egg?"

"I had my eggs frozen, if that's what you mean."

"That's not what I mean."

Isabella took the carton of eggs, grabbed two bowls from the cabinet, and began demonstrating to Molly the process of separating an egg: she cracked an egg on a flat surface, pried it in half, caught the yolk in one half-shell as the white fell into the first bowl, and then passed the yolk back and forth until all of the white was out.

"That seems easy enough," said Molly.

"Give it a shot."

Molly took an egg out of the container, tapped it gently on the counter and didn't get a crack right away, so she tried it again, only the second tap was more of a smash, and the entire egg oozed out over the marble.

"Oops."

"A little too aggressive," said Isabella.

"So I've been told."

For the next five days, Isabella lived two separate lives.

In one life, she was Molly's cooking coach, supervising her as she folded together the mayo and cheddar and pimentos (actually tasting the food herself), as she lined a soufflé mold with parchment (several forests were destroyed in the process), and attempted to whip egg whites long enough by hand so that she got to stiff peaks and could hold the bowl over her head without the whites falling into her hair (which happened more than once; Molly said it reminded her of a bad date).

In her other life, Isabella felt like a one-woman Woodward and Bernstein, banging away on her typewriter/laptop, eager to meet her deadline, as her Katharine Graham (that would be Dana) periodically texted: *CAN I SEE WHAT YOU HAVE? DYING TO READ.*

I'll have everything to you on Wednesday! Isabella texted back.

The cruel twist was that Isabella was thriving in both endeavors. She and Molly had never gotten along better, despite their soufflé travails, and her writing had never been livelier. It was like she was on a runaway train but didn't know which track it was ultimately going to take. Where was she headed with all of this? What was her endgame?

If she turned the article in on Wednesday, like she promised, it would most likely go online within the next forty-eight hours: that's how eager Dana was to publish it.

But Wednesday was also the day of the Kitty Lambrusco taping, and if that went well—and Isabella was fairly sure it'd go well, because Molly's face alone would elicit major sympathy—they'd have a memoir to write together.

But when the article came out the next day, Isabella would no longer be working on the memoir, because Molly would kick her out of her life and never want to speak to her again.

If she dropped the article, Isabella would be working exclusively on the memoir, but with a person who might go back to treating her like shit, making her regret not seizing the opportunity to launch herself when she had the chance.

That night, Gabe was cooler to her than normal.

"I think I'll retire early," he said when he came home from that night's service and found her in the living room watching *Chopped* with Vikash, Louie, and Moses.

"Everything okay?" she asked, munching on seaweed popcorn that Vikash had whipped up.

"I'm just really tired," he said as he went into his room.

Isabella followed him there and closed the door as he quietly took off his work clothes.

"Are you mad at me?" she asked.

"Are you still writing that article?" he replied. The retort came so fast, he'd clearly had his verbal gun cocked and loaded.

"Maybe."

"Then maybe I'm still mad at you."

Isabella was getting tired of this routine.

"You know . . . I don't go to where you work and judge you for under-seasoning the ravioli."

"That's because I don't under-season the ravioli."

"Or short-shrifting a customer on meatballs when you normally put four meatballs on the plate but only have three meatballs left so you pretend that's the normal amount."

Isabella had no idea what she was talking about anymore, and Gabe could tell.

"How am I supposed to trust you in our relationship if you're so willing to stab someone in the back who thinks of you as a friend?"

"Because she's not my friend. She's my boss."

"She's not your boss currently," Gabe reminded her. "Right now she thinks you're helping her cook on TV out of the goodness of your heart. After everything that happened, do you really believe that she thinks of you as an employee? Fiona said that you were the only person Molly wanted to see when she was depressed. Don't you think that makes you betraying her much, much worse?"

It did, but there was one thing that Gabe didn't know about writing that Isabella did. It was right there in the title of the documentary about Nora Ephron: *Everything Is Copy*. Her writing heroes were unafraid to capture everything and everyone that entered their lives. Did Ruth Reichl worry that she'd hurt her mother's feelings when she called her "taste-blind" in *Tender at the Bone*? Did Anthony Bourdain vacillate about pulling the curtain back on the kitchens he exposed in *Kitchen Confidential*? Did Norah try to protect Carl Bernstein from her ire when she literally shoved a pie into his face at the end of *Heartburn*? As Anne Lamott wrote: "If people wanted you to write warmly about them, they should have behaved better."

"Can't we just agree to disagree?" she asked.

"It's a little bigger than that," said Gabe as he got into bed.

"Meaning?"

"Meaning, it's making me question your character."

Isabella didn't have a smart comeback for that one. Instead, she watched as Gabe turned out the light. She shuffled back to the living room to rejoin the others at the TV, wondering if and when she herself was going to get chopped.

. . . .

The day before the taping, Isabella was pumped. Her article was basically done. She'd even mastered the first sentence:

Molly Babcock is on fire and I'm the one who lit the match.

That was the breakthrough that she needed: to bring herself into the story, to own up to her part in what happened, to be as hard on herself as she was on Molly. In writing the piece, she arrived at many realizations, including the harsh truths embedded in the words that Molly had flung at her that awful night: *Why are you so obsessed with cooking my mother's recipes? It's like you want this book to be something that you would write instead of something that I would write, which makes no sense, because you're literally my ghostwriter.*

Candy Babcock, Isabella realized through her writing, was more of a symbol than a subject:

I realized that, in fighting for Candy's legacy, I was fighting for my own. We—the Candys of the world—rarely get our moment in the sun. The Mollys of the world are the ones who stake their claim before we even have a chance to enter the room. In cooking those recipes that night in the cabin, I must've known they would trigger Molly; I wanted them to trigger Molly. I wanted to wake her up to how callous she was being, to the shallow disregard she was showing for the woman who had spent so much time loving and nurturing her. And wasn't that my job, too? To nurture her cookbook, to make it grow, a thankless task for zero credit? Wasn't I picking up where Candy left off?

When Isabella finished the essay, she read it back to herself several times—tweaking and adjusting as she went—and then she opened the email to send it to Dana a day early. What difference did it make if the article went up during the Kitty taping or not? It was like ripping off a Band-Aid. The sooner Molly found out, the better.

Only, Isabella realized, she herself might feel funny coaching Molly from the sidelines, knowing that the *Comestibles* Art Department would already be illustrating Isabella's text, highlighting the moments of Molly's most egregious acts (losing *Zuni,* changing the start time at Snakebite, etc.). So she saved the document to send the next day, then went to Molly's for one last soufflé session before the big day.

When she arrived, this time using the keys that she still had, the place was completely silent.

As she walked into the eerily quiet apartment, gray light glowing in the windows, she found Fiona sitting on a chair in the kitchen staring into space.

"Hey," said Isabella.

Fiona looked up, startled, her face red, tears streaming down her cheeks.

"Oh, hi," she said, wiping the tears away.

"What's wrong?"

"Nothing," said Fiona. "I'm just upset about Molly. She's back in bed. She thinks she's going to make a fool of herself tomorrow. That people are going to laugh at her when she tries to cook."

Isabella, who was already overwhelmed with both the essay and the training, hadn't seen this particular turn coming. Molly was in such great spirits . . . she even ate a bagel!

"I guess I should go talk to her?" Isabella asked the question with a sigh, like a tired parent or an exhausted employee dealing with an eccentric boss.

"You know that you're her best friend, right?"

This question—or statement—landed with such a thud, Isabella almost laughed.

"I sincerely doubt that," said Isabella. "She has so many closer friends than me in her life. What about all of those friends at Snakebite?" She remembered the table full of Mollys.

"A bunch of phonies," said Fiona, taking a swig of beer that she'd been hiding under the counter. "She's only friends with them because she's too scared not to be friends with them. You're the one she can be vulnerable around. She took you to our dad's house. She would never take any of her other friends there in a million years."

Isabella processed this little bit of information. She tried to imagine Molly bringing one of the other Mollys to New Jersey, exposing them to her father and stepmother, their disgust when they saw the decrepitude of where Molly grew up.

"You know," said Fiona, trying to open up, but struggling, "before you knew me . . . I used to be something of a . . . a challenging person."

Used to be?

"I had a really hard time making friends. I didn't do well in school. I fell in with a bad crowd."

What was this: Fiona's pitch for a memoir that she wanted Isabella to ghostwrite?

"Okay?" said Isabella, unsure of where this was headed.

"Molly and I have the same father but different mothers. My mom committed suicide when I was twelve. No one was looking after me, and by the time I was nineteen, I was a mess. Shoplifting, all kinds of drugs, getting into fights. Molly and I weren't close, especially when she became famous . . . In fact, she barely acknowledged my existence."

That tracks, thought Isabella.

"At some point I got arrested for assault—it was a dumb fight I got into with a woman basketball player who stole my iPhone at a bar—and I beat her up bad, and I was going to be in jail for a while. Molly heard about it from our dad, and she flew to New Jersey from L.A. and bailed me out."

Isabella nodded as Fiona wiped more tears away.

"That's when she gave me an intervention and asked me what I was doing with my life, and she said that I could come live with her, get myself back on my feet, help her around the house. She gave me a sense of purpose. She gave me a sense of family. She even helped me get a job, doing social for Kitty Lambrusco, because they knew each other from TV. If it weren't for her, I'd probably be talking to you from a ditch right now, because I'd be dead in one."

Isabella paused and processed what Fiona was saying. From what she'd seen, she'd always assumed that Fiona was a leech and that Molly liked having someone to abuse. But now she understood that their dynamic was much more complicated than that: Molly had no reason, beyond altruism, to let Fiona come live with her. If she needed a personal assistant, she could've hired a much better one. Fiona's lazing around the house was actually a result of Molly's being generous rather than taking advantage. She was keeping her half-sister out of trouble, keeping her safe, keeping her connected to her only family.

"I had no idea," said Isabella.

"Molly's not a bad person," Fiona said, as if she knew what was really going on in Isabella's mind about her sister. "She just plays one on TV."

Isabella laughed, and Fiona laughed, too. Then Isabella wandered over to Molly's door and knocked on it.

Without waiting for an answer, she opened it and found Molly under the covers, in the pitch-black room, eyes open and staring at the ceiling.

"I can't do this," she said in such a soft, scared voice, Isabella almost thought it was a different person. "I can't go on TV looking like this."

Isabella had been so wrapped up in her own inner conflict, she'd dismissed whatever conflict Molly might be feeling: how jolting it would be to go from being a dazzling beauty on a primetime soap, inducing lust and jealousy in male and female viewers alike, to becoming an object of pity—a victim of her own carelessness, even if the story was more complex than that.

Instead of saying, "You'll do great" or "Hang in there," Isabella said: "I get it."

Molly reached over and turned on the lamp, illuminating her still deeply scarred face.

"Do you think I'm a joke?" she asked, her eyes brimming with tears. "Am I going on TV to make a fool of myself? Everyone who's seen that video thinks I'm a fucking idiot . . . and that I deserved it, too."

Isabella hadn't considered what Molly might've been looking at all that time she was in the dark, scrolling on her phone, but now she realized that Molly had been reading the comments under the video (which had hit thirty million views just the day before).

"I don't think you're a joke," said Isabella, thinking back to her own article, which explored Molly's complex psychology and behavior. "I think you were going through something. And that everybody fucks up. You just happened to fuck up in front of thirty million people."

Molly let out a small laugh.

"Am I going to fuck up the soufflé tomorrow? Maybe I should've made a salad instead."

"I've seen you make a salad," said Isabella. "That you'd *definitely* fuck up."

Molly laughed again. "You'll be there?"

"Of course I'll be there," said Isabella, patting Molly's leg. Somewhere in the room, she felt the presence of Gabe shaking his head in disapproval. *Nicely done, Judas,* she heard him say.

"You know that night in the cabin, the night of the fire . . . I said some things to you that I really regret."

Molly had never apologized for those things, even though Isabella had Molly's speech memorized, hearing it quite often in her head.

"I don't think you're talentless or a nobody. I actually think you're the opposite of those things."

"It's okay," said Isabella, already feeling too torn up inside to add a new layer of emotion.

"I'm being serious. I said you were jealous of me, but the truth is that I was jealous of you," said Molly.

"C'mon," said Isabella, knowing a lie when she heard one. "That can't be true. You were not jealous of me."

"I was too!" said Molly, gaining volume and energy as she spoke. "You may act insecure, but when it comes to what's important?—what really matters?—you're extremely confident. You know who you are. You have integrity."

Oh, do I? thought Isabella.

"Everything that I do, everything that I've ever done," continued Molly, tears starting to stream down her cheeks, "it's on the surface. And everything that you do comes from inside. It comes from somewhere deep inside you, a place that I don't have inside of me. All that I have inside of me is . . . chewed-up bubble gum and used-condom wrappers."

Isabella shook her head. "You have a deep place inside of you, too," she said, now feeling tears forming in her own eyes. "You've just been trying to avoid it for most of your life."

Both of them were quiet for a moment.

"Don't worry about tomorrow," said Isabella. "I'll be right

there with you. You're not going to screw it up. And even if you do, people will still love you, because you're showing them that deep place inside of you. It's a Molly they've never seen before. A Molly they can relate to, a Molly that reminds them that none of us are perfect, that we're all human."

"Do you promise?"

"I promise," said Isabella.

Molly leaned over and gave Isabella a hug, a real hug, the kind of hug that expresses need and connection at the same time, the kind of hug that revealed to Isabella that, despite all appearances to the contrary, Molly really was one of her closest friends and that she really was one of Molly's closest friends and that, after all of her hemming and hawing and inner turmoil, Gabe was right: it was wrong to write this article about Molly. Her friendship with Molly mattered more than launching her career. Molly's feelings mattered more than making a name for herself. There would be other things to write about, other opportunities. She didn't need to betray someone who thought of her as her best friend to become a notable writer.

She was ready to call off the article.

She just wasn't ready to call Dana.

. . . .

The greenroom of *The Kitty Lambrusco Show* was like a Who's Who of the last two months of Isabella's life.

In front of the mirror in a tall chair was a nervous-looking Molly, getting pampered by Hair and Makeup. "We want them to see the scars," said Owen to the makeup person. "Don't cover up too much." Behind Owen was Fiona, who was loading up her backpack with *Kitty Lambrusco* swag: hats, fanny packs, books from the storage shelves. (Apparently, she'd only ever done her job remotely; this was her first time in the studio.)

Also there, because he had the day off and he'd never been to a TV taping, was Gabe. He came there with Isabella, quiet the whole subway ride over (she still hadn't told him that she'd changed her mind about the article, in case she changed it back), and now he was standing out of the way, sipping free coffee from a Styrofoam cup, and watching the show on a monitor. Jeannie was next to him, mirroring Fiona in that she, too, was pilfering goods, only hers were pastries, which she was wrapping in paper napkins and depositing into her pocketbook.

Isabella, meanwhile, stood alongside Molly, walking her through the soufflé process for the sixteenth time that morning. She held out her phone as Molly studied the steps once again:

"Six egg whites," she read off the screen. "Cream of tartar. I always forget the cream of tartar."

"They'll have it all laid out for you," Isabella reminded her. "You really don't have to remember anything."

When a producer came in to grab her for the first segment (the interview), Molly took a deep breath and looked at Isabella.

"You'll do great," Isabella assured her. "Talking about yourself is your specialty."

That brought a smile to Molly's face as a producer led her into the hallway. Isabella wasn't worried at all: this part, she knew, would be a breeze. Chatting came naturally to Molly; and telling the story of the fire and all that led up to it would take very little effort on her part.

Sure enough, as they all watched her on the monitor, Molly sailed through the first segment.

"By now, almost everyone's seen the video," said Kitty, with her bright-red lipstick and bright-yellow dress, as the clip played behind them.

"Thirty million people," said Molly. "I've never been more on fire."

The audience laughed.

"How did all of this happen?" asked Kitty, indicating Molly on the monitor, her hair in flames. "I mean . . . Were you high? Were you drunk? What was going on, girlfriend?"

Molly walked her through that day: how she was on the chopping block for this Netflix show, how her then boyfriend ("Xavier Mordechai," Kitty informed the audience) was an enabler and a bad influence, and how she was using drugs and alcohol to protect herself from feeling rejected.

"Been there, done that," said Kitty as the audience nodded in recognition, even though most of them hadn't been there or done that.

When the segment was over, Molly had done a superb job of owning her mistake and showing that she'd grown from it. The audience was completely on her side.

"When we come back," announced Kitty, "Molly's going to show us that she actually knows a thing or two about what she's doing in the kitchen. She's going to show us how to make her mother's famous pimento cheese soufflé."

The audience oohed, the director yelled "Cut," and Molly slinked off the set and found Isabella standing in the wings with Gabe.

"You did amazing," said Isabella, truly impressed by Molly's ease in front of the camera.

"Let me see the recipe one more time," said Molly, taking Isabella's phone from her hands.

This, Isabella knew, was completely unnecessary. Not only were the ingredients already measured out; there were little index cards next to them that said "half a cup butter," "two cups grated cheddar," so that Molly could just read that and be okay. And even if she completely screwed up, there were already swap-outs prepped by the on-staff food supervisors.

As Isabella glanced over Molly's shoulder, studying the recipe along with her—*whip the egg whites to stiff peaks*—a message appeared in the center of the screen:

IZZ—WHERE'S YOUR MOLLY BABCOCK TAKEDOWN? WE WANT TO RUN IT ASAP! ART DEPARTMENT HAS AMAZING ILLOS OF HER BURSTING INTO FLAMES . . . EVEN HAVE HEADLINE IDEA: BURN MOLLY BURN! (THOUGHTS?) PLS SEND!

The block of words felt like a jack-in-the-box, bouncing out of the screen and knocking Molly in her already wounded face.

"What is this?" Molly asked, reading the words, and looking to Isabella with genuine confusion and hurt.

Isabella, who felt her heart do a somersault down into her stomach, couldn't come up with a speedy enough lie.

"Just . . . something that I was working on . . ."

"About me?" Molly's voice sounded like a delicate sculpture cracking.

"About both of us," she said, as if that would solve the problem.

Gabe, who'd been hovering nearby, gave Isabella a look. It wasn't an "I told you so" look as much as it was an "I was scared this was going to happen" look.

A producer grabbed Molly: "We're ready for you!"

Molly returned the phone to Isabella as the producer guided her back onto the stage, this time to the kitchen set, where Kitty was already standing in an apron.

"Ready?" she asked Molly, who looked up startled.

"And we're back in three . . ." said the director. "Two . . . one . . ."

Kitty seamlessly picked up where they left off.

"And now my old friend Molly Babcock, who's currently working on a memoir with recipes, is going to show us that she actually knows her way around the stove. . . . She's going to show us how to make something that sounds completely wild: a pimento cheese soufflé."

Molly, who was standing next to the oven, which was heated to four hundred degrees, had sweat dripping down her forehead.

"So . . . Molly, where do we start?"

On the table in front of her, just like when they practiced at home, were the mayo, the cheddar, the pimentos, the flour, and the soufflé dish. Next to this, a dozen eggs and two bowls.

Molly, head spinning, opened the carton of eggs.

"We . . . ummm," she said. "We have to . . ."

She took an egg out and in trying to crack it, she once again smashed it on the counter.

"Whoa," said Kitty, as the yolk slid onto the floor. "Man overboard."

The audience laughed as Isabella, watching from the sidelines, had flashbacks of her own meltdown in front of the camera. She remembered that sense of helplessness, that sense of the room spinning, that sense of having zero idea of what to say, what to do, where to go.

Watching Molly go through the same ordeal, the same emotions, Isabella suddenly felt possessed by a wave of unfamiliar energy; her body began to take hold of her, her brain completely out of the picture, her legs carrying her forward and her fingers typing by themselves onto the phone.

"Hey, you can't—" said a stagehand, putting his hand on Isabella's shoulder, but Isabella shook it off.

When she finished typing, she glanced up and saw that she was inches away from Molly and Kitty. Walking any closer would put her on camera, the last place Isabella ever wanted to be. That was, in and of itself, a revelation. She *didn't* want to be on camera: Molly did. That's who Molly was, but Isabella wasn't that. But for this one moment, she would become that.

She stepped out onto the stage as Kitty, good at improvising, said: "Oh, hello, and who is this?"

Before Isabella could answer, she held her phone up in front of Molly so Molly could see what she had written:

FUCK YOU DANA AND FUCK YOUR ARTICLE. MOLLY BABCOCK
IS MY FRIEND. I'M NOT SENDING YOU SHIT.

She hit Send so that Molly could watch it go through.

Molly turned to Isabella, eyes watery, her face filled with gratitude and relief.

"Is this your sister? Your bestie? Your agent? What's happening here?"

Molly pulled away and, shifting back into TV mode, she put her arm around Isabella's shoulder and said, "This is Isabella Pasternak. She's my ghostwriter."

Isabella, barely dressed for the day, not to mention TV,

blushed bright red as she saw Gabe eagerly watching from the sidelines.

"Your ghostwriter?" asked Kitty. "Aren't ghostwriters supposed to be anonymous?"

Molly, who was already in the process of separating an egg, this time the correct way, shrugged.

"She's not anonymous anymore."

"WITH" FULFILLMENT

After five years of sitting unoccupied, Pasternak Antiques had become something of an antique itself. Situated on East Forty-sixth Street, the store had been out of use for so long that it almost seemed not to exist. Passersby wouldn't clock it: with the shades pulled and the lettering on the storefront peeling off, it looked more like an abandoned aquarium than what used to be a flourishing mid-century-furniture dealership.

When Isabella first had the idea for how to repurpose it, Jeannie was thrown.

"Books? What do I know about selling books?"

But then Isabella and Gabe hosted a dinner to introduce Jeannie to Alice—Gabe's roommates, Vikash, Louie, and Moses, each contributed a course—and the two women, both maternal figures in Isabella's life (one of them actually being her mother), immediately hit it off.

"She can be so pigheaded sometimes," Jeannie said about her daughter, as Alice listened.

"I'm exactly the same way," Alice confessed. "They say you are what you eat, and I eat a lot of pork."

The collaboration, as Isabella called it, would involve a hunter-gatherer-type relationship. Jeannie, who was used to scouring the streets for donatable items, would now be scouring the streets (plus estate sales and flea markets) for books. Specifically, cookbooks.

"Think of all the paper you'll be saving," Isabella assured her. "And think about all of the writers and chefs whose work you'll be helping to endure."

Jeannie didn't care about any of that. What she did care about was that her daughter, who so rarely wanted to be at home, would eagerly want to spend time at a store filled with cookbooks that Jeannie and Alice would oversee. And though Jeannie didn't have an interest in literature of any kind, she did have an interest in revitalizing other people's trash. So, in addition to seeking out books, she would also seek out discarded cooking implements—vintage eggbeaters and oven mitts that she would salvage from thrift shops and garage sales—a perfect complement to Alice's cookbook collection.

The space was cozy and elegant: both Alice and Jeannie agreed to keep some of the mid-century furniture (including the illuminated chandeliers) to give the space more character. Not only was it a delightful place to spend an afternoon, it was the perfect venue for a party. Especially the party for the release of Molly's memoir.

It had been one year exactly since the episode of *The Kitty Lambrusco Show* in which Isabella and Molly made the pimento-cheese soufflé. The publishers were so pleased with Molly's poise and the sympathy points she garnered that they immediately gave the green light to the memoir with recipes, wanting to get it out as soon as possible. Meanwhile, the campaign to get Molly reinstated on *Misery Loves Company* on Netflix gained so much traction, and generated so much prepublicity for the show, the executives reversed course and let the showrunner—who thought Molly's scars would only deepen her character—dump the actress who was taking her place and put Molly back in the part. (Molly had Fiona send the actress a care package from Russ & Daughters—her way of paying it forward.)

By the time Molly arrived at her book-release party, she hadn't just resuscitated her old career, she'd surpassed it. Paparazzi were waiting outside to get pictures of her as she arrived with her new boyfriend, Zeke Templeton, the actor who was playing her former best friend's son. (Xavier Mordechai had since been arrested on drug charges, in addition to the breaking-and-entering and other charges associated with the fire.)

Molly was wearing a gold sequined dress and Christian Louboutin shoes that cost more than Isabella used to make in a week at *Comestibles*. Isabella, for her part, was wearing the same Honey Dijon maxidress that she never really got to show off at Snakebite (a new one, since the first one had been destroyed). It was what was on her finger, though, that attracted the most attention.

"Is that what I think it is?" Molly asked after the two of them hugged in the entryway to the store, where a table was piled high with *If You Can't Stand the Heat: A Memoir with Recipes* by Molly Babcock with Isabella Pasternak. The cover featured Molly in a red dress in a bright-red kitchen, with several pans on fire, while she held a fire extinguisher and was about to pull the pin.

"It's not a big deal," Isabella assured her, showing off the ring, as Gabe came from behind and put his arm around his fiancée.

"Not a big deal?" he said. "Gee, thanks a lot."

The party featured a dais with two chairs on it, for Molly to be interviewed by Alison Roman, part of the lure to get people to come to the book party.

"Hey," said Alice, coming over to Isabella, half a pig-in-a-blanket in a napkin in her hand (Vikash, Louie, and Moses had done the catering). "We only have two chairs up there. Should I put up another one for the Q and A? Do you both want to answer questions together?"

"Yes!" said Molly, happy to include Isabella and eager not to be up there alone.

"No, no, no," said Isabella. "It's her book."

"Your name's on the cover, too!"

Isabella was grateful for that. In the past few months, she'd gotten two other cookbook ghostwriting gigs because of the credited work that she did on *If You Can't Stand the Heat*. (The early reviews were all positive, calling the book "a delicious excavation of the self," "surprisingly candid," "sympathy- and hunger-inducing.") Now she was ghostwriting a cookbook for Travis Krenshaw, a gig that Lionel had offered up as soon as Isabella turned in Molly's manuscript. She was also ghostwriting a book for Casper Dusolier, the celebrated chef at Snakebite, whose sous-chef had highly recommended her, saying he knew her work "intimately."

Ghosting, it turned out, suited Isabella: she could be transparent when she wanted to be (useful during kitchen tirades and marital spats) and opaque when the moment required (asking questions, fine-tuning recipes). She thought of what she did as a kind of possession: she would enter the mind and body of a chef or cookbook author, spend the day in it, then exorcise herself and cook dinner for Gabe and his roommates, enjoying the tastes and sensations of reentering her own corporeal form.

"Seriously, I'm fine," said Isabella, in transparent mode. "I'm happier over here. Honestly."

As Molly took the stage and started fielding questions from Alison Roman about her childhood, her mother, and the famous fire that reignited ("no pun intended") her career, Isabella and Gabe slunk off to the used French cookbook section, holding hands.

"Are you sad not to be up there?" he asked.

"Not at all," she said, speaking the truth.

She looked around, not just at the people—she spied Lionel and Owen (dressed again in his manager suit, once again promoted), both scrolling in sync on their separate phones; she spied Fiona sneaking copies of Molly's book into her backpack; she spied her mother and Alice both putting canapés into their purses—but also at the names and faces on the French cookbooks surrounding her: Jacques Pépin, André Soltner, Anne

Willan, Julia Child. Now her name was on a book, too. True, it was a celebrity's book, a book that probably wouldn't be talked about in a hundred years (let alone ten), but it was a real book that she had helped write, and now it was here among all these others.

And isn't that what she wanted, more than anything? To be here, in this very place, both in print and in person? With the love of her life—Gabe took her hand—at a party for a book that wouldn't exist without her? What did it matter if she wasn't the one holding the fire extinguisher on the cover? What did it matter if her name came second on the inside back flap, with a one-sentence bio, below Molly's massive, puffed-up résumé?

When the Q and A was over, Isabella watched as Molly signed book after book and posed for selfie after selfie with her adoring, aggressive fans. Up onstage was where Molly belonged—smiling her hard-won smile over and over again—while Isabella watched from the sidelines, glad to have made this moment possible, even more glad that it wasn't her.

ACKNOWLEDGMENTS

To my agent, Jenni Ferrari-Adler, who believed in this book right from the beginning and who had the smarts to change the title from *Ghost Bitten* because it sounded like a YA vampire book. Also a big thanks to everyone at Verve.

To my incredible editor, Jenny Jackson, whose brilliance and know-how are overshadowed by her humility and disarming nature. It's a dream beyond dreams to have you edit my first novel.

To everyone at Knopf: Jordan Pavlin, for bringing me into the fold; Kathleen Fridella, for helping me keep my chronology straight; Casey Hampton, for making the text look so good; and Janet Hansen for your incredible jacket. Sara Eagle, Elka Roderick, and Emily Reardon . . . thank you for your passion and creativity. Also: a shout-out to my good friend Chris Dufault, my early champion both in life and in work.

To my first readers: Diana Fithian, Ryan O'Connell, and Jonathan Parks-Ramage, thank you for your insight and your encouragement.

To Ryan Bergsman: for not only talking to me about fire, but also touring us around your firehouse in Seattle. Next time, I'll make the chili.

To Casey Elsass: for sharing your stories about being a cookbook ghostwriter and for introducing me to the bacon, egg, and cheese on a scallion pancake at Win Son.

To my parents for believing in my writing early on and, more important, for turning me into a food person.

I based Alice's Cookbook Emporium on a few of my favorite cookbook stores: Bonnie Slotnick's in the East Village, Archestratus in Greenpoint, Kitchen Arts & Letters on the Upper East Side, and Omnivore Books in SF. If you haven't patronized these fantastic stores, please do.

In the fall of 2022 I told my husband, Craig, that I wanted to move back to New York from L.A. (we'd been there for twelve years) and that we'd be okay financially because I was writing a novel. This came across like a sick joke, but somehow he took me seriously enough to pack up our entire lives and our beloved dog, Winston, and relocate three thousand miles away, to the city where we first met as grad students at NYU.

This leap of faith, and Craig's unflinching support (financial, emotional, psychological), is the only thing that made this book possible. Now we live in Brooklyn, Winston is in street smell heaven, and I'm officially a novelist. Thank you for believing in me and for making my dream life possible.

A NOTE ABOUT THE AUTHOR

Adam Roberts is the author of *The Amateur Gourmet*, *Secrets of the Best Chefs*, and coauthor of *Give My Swiss Chards to Broadway*. He started his food blog, *The Amateur Gourmet*, in 2004, and currently writes *The Amateur Gourmet Newsletter* on Substack. Roberts has also written for the *Washington Post* and the *Los Angeles Times*, and for film and television. He lives in Brooklyn with his husband and their dog, Winston. *Food Person* is his first novel.

@amateurgourmet